# ABANDONED

Cody McFadyen

# ABANDONED

A THRILLER

BANTAM BOOKS | NEW YORK

Copyright © 2009 by Cody McFadyen

Published in the United States by Bantam Books,
an imprint of The Random House Publishing Group,
a division of Random House, Inc., New York.

BANTAM BOOKS and the rooster colophon are
registered trademarks of Random House, Inc.

Library of Congress Cataloging-in-Publication Data
McFadyen, Cody.
Abandoned : a thriller / Cody McFadyen.
p.  cm.
ISBN 978-0-553-80695-3
eBook ISBN 978-0-553-90706-3
1. Murder for hire—Fiction.   2. Spouses—Crimes against—Fiction.
3. Serial murders—Fiction.   4. United States Federal Bureau of Investigation—
Fiction.   I. Title.
PS3613.C438A63 2009
813'.6—dc22          2009028588

Printed in the United States of America on acid-free paper

www.bantamdell.com

2 4 6 8 9 7 5 3 1

First Edition

*Book design by Laurie Jewell*

This book is for David, my father.
The one who raised me and taught me to
be a man. Without him, I'd never have
found my way back to shore.

# ACKNOWLEDGMENTS

Thanks go to my agent, Liza Dawson, as always. She's my constant cheerleader and therapist combined. To my able editors, Danielle Perez and Nick Sayers, as well as all of those I've yet to meet who are doing such a great job with my books in various parts of the world. To Chandler Crawford—I want her frequent-flier miles, but I don't want her job. To the readers now and the writers past.

A shout-out to a particular author, Mr. John Connolly. I was nearing the last third of this book and feeling less than inspired. I'd lost my way, or at least I thought I had, and any writer can tell you that your mental outlook is a lot more than half the battle. I was flying to San Francisco, and I happened to start reading one of his novels, *The Unquiet,* on the plane. I continued reading it while I was there on my business, over room service and bleak morning coffee. By the time I finished it, I had been jump-started, and I proceeded to write like a madman in that San Francisco hotel. It never stopped.

We're constantly inspired and influenced by our peers, but sometimes it deserves a special note. John's a writer's writer, and this book owes him a debt.

PART ONE

# THE SUN

# CHAPTER ONE

## PRESENT DAY

Everyone is alone. That is what I have learned, in time.

Don't get me wrong. I love a man. And when I wake up in the night, and he is there next to me, and I can touch him and maybe wake him and smell him and fuck him, feel him in me as he sweats and his hands wander over me like a badland, I appreciate it. I share the private knowledge that few share (not none, but few) of what his flesh feels like against my flesh. The velvet steel of it. I know our unique sounds, our sharing and wanting and crying out, me and only me, and I feel a certain selfish pride about it all. I am, in those moments, a possessor of secret knowledge. A holder of hidden things.

But in the end, nothing changes the truth: He doesn't know, in that dark, what I am thinking in my heart of hearts, and I don't know the same of him. This is the truth. We are all separate islands.

I am okay with that now. There was a time when I fought against the idea, as I guess everyone does. We want to know everything about our partner, share every last detail. We want to read minds and have our mind read. We want to erase all distance between us, become one person.

But we're not one person. However close we get, some distance will always remain. Love, I've come to realize, lies not only in sharing each other but in being at peace with those parts that will never be shared.

I turn on my side, my cheek against my hand, and look at my man. He's beautiful, I think. Not beautiful in a feminine way, but beautiful in the "man" of him. In his quiet ruggedness. He is sleeping deeply, and he sleeps with his mouth closed. I'm afraid to stare at him for too long. He might feel my gaze and wake up. He's alert that way, because he, like me, knows that death is a real thing. An ever-possible moment. You learn to sleep lightly when you do what we've done, see what we've seen.

I turn onto my back and look out the open balcony door to the night sky beyond. We'd left the door open so we could hear the ocean. The temperature here allows it. We're in Hawaii, on a five-day vacation, my first in more than a decade.

We're staying on the Big Island, the land of fire and ice. When we drove away from Hilo Airport, Tommy and I looked at each other, wondering if maybe we'd made a terrible mistake in our choice of islands. All that had been visible, as far as the eye could see, was black volcanic rock. It was as if we'd landed on the surface of a hostile moon.

We'd gotten more hopeful as we approached our resort. Off in the distance we could see Mauna Kea, almost 14,000 feet high and snow-capped. It felt odd to look out the car window and see evidence of snow in Hawaii, but there it was. Trees and sparse grass had begun to clamber out of all that rock, striving for life and giving insight into the changes destined in the geologic future. Someday, the grass would overcome the rock and make it soil and things would change again. Tommy and I and our ancestors would be long gone, but it would happen. Life is always striving. That's what life does.

The reception area of the resort had taken our breath away. It looked out over the endless ocean and the perfect beaches, and a temperate breeze had kissed our cheeks as if to welcome us here. "Aloha," the young man at the reception desk said, white teeth against tan skin, seeming to agree with the breeze.

We've been here for four days now, doing much of nothing. Hawaii took us in gently, ignoring the blood on our hands, telling us with its beauty to rest for a while. Our hotel room is on the third floor, and our balcony is no more than fifty yards from the ocean. We spend our days lying on the beach and making love and our nights walking on the beach and making love and marveling at the overwhelming panoply of stars in the ancient sky. We watch the sunsets until the moon calls the night sky to the sea.

It's a temporary peace. We'll go back to Los Angeles soon, where I head the local branch of the National Center for the Analysis of Violent Crime—or NCAVC. The NCAVC is based in Quantico, Virginia, but someone in every FBI office in every city is assigned as the NCAVC coordinator. In many places, that job is a second hat, worn only occasionally. In Los Angeles, it has been a full-time endeavor, and I've been in charge for more than twelve years now, running a four-person team including me.

We're called in for the worst there is. Men and women who murder men and women and (far too often) children. Serial rapists. The people we hunt rarely do what they do in the heat of the moment. Their actions are not a momentary anomaly but a solution to a need. They do what they do for the joy of it, because emptying out others fills them up like nothing else there is.

I spend my life peering into the darkness these people radiate. It's a cold blackness, filled with mewls and skittering things, high-pitched screeching laughter, unmentionable moans. I have killed bad men and been hunted by them too. It is my choice and my life, and I wake up to it, I come home from it, I sleep with my man and wake up to it again.

So it's rare that I lift my head and really see the stars. We all live and die under them, but I tend to be most concerned with the dying part. I've had dreams of victims, on their backs, hitching final breaths as they gaze up at those ruthless, forever points of light.

Here in Hawaii, I've taken time to see the stars. I've turned my face to the sky every night and let the stars remind me that something beautiful has already burned far longer than any of man's ugliness ever will.

I close my eyes for a moment and listen. The ocean beats against the shore outside like an unending exhalation of someone greater than us. If I was certain where I stood on God, I'd think of that sound as His heartbeat. But God and I are on shaky ground, and though we're closer now than we were years before, we rarely speak.

Something is out there, though. Something undeniable and endless rides those waves into the sand, again and again, in rhythm with the world's metronome. There is a vastness to the ocean in this place, a purity of sound and color and sweetness too unbearably wonderful to be an accident. I'm not sure it cares about us, whatever it is, but perhaps it keeps the world turning while we make our own choices, and perhaps that's the best we can ask for.

I open my eyes again and move away from Tommy, slow and quiet as I can. I want to go out onto the balcony, but I don't want to wake him. The sheets silk across my skin and then I'm free of them. My feet find the carpet floor. The moon lights up the room, so locating the bathrobe (which I plan to steal when we leave) is no problem. I shrug it on but don't belt it, glance one final time at Tommy, and step out onto the balcony.

The moon, always a disinterested witness, shines over everything tonight, covering the world with its soft silvers and gently glowing ambers. It hangs above the ocean like a ragged pearl, and I study it with muted wonder. It's just a ball of rock that throws off a cold light, but it has such power when the sky dims. I reach up and pretend that I am brushing my fingers through its illuminations. I almost feel them for a moment. Murky rivers of velvet light.

Because of what I do, the moon has lit my way almost as often as the sun, but it lights a path for the monsters as well. They love the moon, the way it fails to really banish the darkness. I love it too, but it's as much of an adversary as a friend.

The temperature outside is perfect, and I let my eyes roam across the sky. In Los Angeles, stars are small scatterings of brightness on an ocean of blackness. Here, the brightness gives the blackness a run for its money. I'm able to pick out Orion's belt just above me, and I track across the sky to find the Big Dipper and, from there, the North Star.

"Polaris," I whisper, and smile, remembering my father.

Dad was one of those men who get enthusiastic about too many things to ever become really expert in any of them. He played guitar, passably. He wrote short stories that I loved but that were never published. And he loved the night sky and the stories of the stars.

*The North Star,* I remember him telling me one night, pointing it out. *It's called Polaris or sometimes the Lodestar. Not the brightest star, like many people think. Sirius is the brightest. But Polaris is one of the most important.*

I was nine at the time and hadn't really cared about the stars, but I'd loved my dad, so I had listened and made sure my eyes were wide with wonder. I'm glad I did that now. It made him happy. He was dead before I was twenty-one, and I cherish every memory.

"What you thinking?" the voice murmurs from behind me, thick with sleep.

"My dad. He was into astronomy."

Tommy comes up and encircles me with his arms. He's naked and warm. The back of my head finds a place against his chest. I'm only four-ten, so he towers over me in a way that I like.

"Couldn't sleep?" he asks me.

"Not *couldn't,*" I murmur. "Not the right word. Just comfortable being awake."

It's as if I can hear him smile, and this tells me, like so many other things, how we're getting closer. We're picking up each other's cues, reading the signs beneath the surface. Tommy and I have been together for almost three years now, and it's been careful and wonderful. In many ways, this unexpected love has saved me.

A little more than three-and-a-half years ago, a man I was hunting, a serial killer by the name of Joseph Sands, broke into my home. He tortured my husband, Matt, in front of me, and then he killed him. He raped and disfigured me, and he also caused the death of Alexa, my ten-year-old daughter.

I spent six months after that wrapped in an agony I can't truly remember now. I can see it intellectually, but I think we have a protective mechanism that prevents us from actual sense memory of that kind of pain. What I remember is that I wished myself dead and came close to making it happen.

Tommy and I had come together in the aftermath. He was ex–Secret Service, and he owed me a favor. I called in the favor during a case I was on, and somehow we ended up in bed together. It was the last thing I expected. Not just because I was still mourning Matt, not just because Tommy was a drop-dead handsome Latin man, but because of what had been done to me.

Joseph Sands had cut my face with a big old knife, and he'd cut it with a mix of concentration, rage, and glee. He left permanent evidence of himself on me, a branding of blood and steel.

The scar is continuous. It begins in the middle of my forehead, right at the hairline. It goes straight down, hovering above the space between my eyebrows, and then it shoots off to the left at an almost perfect ninety-degree angle. I have no left eyebrow. Sands carved it off as he meandered across my face. The scar travels along my temple and then turns in a lazy loop-de-loop down my cheek. It rips over toward my nose, crossing the bridge of it just barely, then changes its mind, cutting diagonally across my left nostril and zooming in one final, triumphant line past my jaw, down my neck, ending at my collarbone.

I remember, when he'd finished cutting, how he paused. I was screaming, and he looked down at me, his face inches above my own. He nodded. "Yeah," he said. "That's good. Got it right the first time."

I had never considered myself beautiful but was always comfortable in my own skin. After that night, I feared the mirror, like the Phantom of the Opera. If I didn't kill myself, then at the very least I envisioned a life spent locked away from the eyes of the world.

So when Tommy kissed me—and then later, when he took me to my bed and kissed my scars—well . . . it was not the kisses but the unselfconscious heat of his need that undid me. He was a man, a handsome man, and he wanted me. Not because I'd been hurt, not to comfort me, but because he'd fantasized about having me and now he could.

Time has passed, and those first moments have turned into something much bigger. We live together. We love each other and have said so. Bonnie, my adopted daughter, loves him, and he loves her back. Best of all, it's guiltless, blessed by the ghosts of my past.

"Jesus, this is beautiful," Tommy whispers. "Isn't it beautiful, Smoky?"

"Unreal."

"Pretty good idea on my part. Brilliant, maybe."

I grin. "Watch the ego, buddy. It was a good call, but don't expect it to bail you out in the future."

His hands creep around me, finding their way under the bathrobe. "Guess I'll just have to count on the sex for that."

"That . . . could work," I purr, closing my eyes.

He kisses my neck, and it makes me shiver in the warm air. "So?" he asks.

I turn in to him and angle my head up as an answer. His lips find mine as the moon watches. We kiss, and I feel myself stirring inside as he stirs against me.

"I want it here," I mumble, my hands in his hair.

He comes up for air, one eyebrow raised.

"*Here* here? As in on the balcony?"

I point to the long, reclining lounge chair. "There, actually."

I see him scanning the grass below, and I grab his head and pull him down to me again.

"Stop thinking so much. It's three in the morning. Just us and the moon."

It doesn't take much selling. I end up on top, with the moon and the North Star behind me. The ocean talks in its low rumble, and Tommy gazes up at me with a look less of hunger than of passion. Toward the end, I lean down and whisper the three words that used to be so hard to tell any man besides Matt. I see his answer in his eyes, and we fall asleep together on the balcony, draped in the bathrobe.

I wake up in bed, languid and refreshed. I have a dim memory of Tommy carrying me inside sometime in the latening of the night. It's early now; the sun is rising. For whatever reason, we've been waking up before 6:00 A.M. every morning since we arrived in Hawaii. I'm not complaining. Our balcony faces west, so we get to see the sunsets more directly; thus, they are more spectacular. But watching the first light from the sun hitting the water is nothing to sneeze at.

I throw on the trusty bathrobe and walk out onto the balcony. Tommy's already brewed a pot of coffee and has it sitting on the balcony table. He's wearing a pair of jeans and nothing else, and I stir a little at the sight of him. Tommy is all man, about six feet one, with the trademark Latin dark hair and dark eyes. His gaze is somehow both open and guarded, the result of being an honest man who's killed people. His face is somewhere between rugged and pretty, with a small scar at his left temple.

"You look delicious," I tell him.

"Thanks. Coffee?"

Tommy's laconic. It's not that he's uncommunicative. He just feels that if you can say it with less words, so much the better.

"Yes, please."

He pours me a cup as I sit down on a chair and pull my knees up to my chin. I take the cup when he offers it to me, sip, roll my eyes in appreciation.

"Jesus. They still won't tell you where we can get this stuff?"

"Nope. All they'll say is that it's the house blend."

"Maybe we can take some back with us, get it analyzed by the lab."

He smiles at me, and we fall into a comfortable silence. I watch the ocean, and time passes without the need to mark it. Clocks seem almost ugly here.

"What are you thinking about?" he asks me.

I glance at him, realize he's been watching me. "Truth?"

"Of course."

"I was thinking about Matt and Alexa."

"Tell me."

He reaches a hand across the table, touches one of mine, then retreats back to his coffee cup with it. It's a short gesture, him showing me that he doesn't mind.

I squint at him over the top of my cup. "This really doesn't bother you?"

A single dismissive shake of his head. "I'll never be that guy, Smoky. The guy who gets jealous because you loved the family you had before."

The words bring a lump to my throat. No tears—I'm pretty much past that, these days. "Thanks."

"So? What were you thinking?"

I sip my coffee and look out across the ocean. Sigh. "I was thinking that Matt and I talked about getting out to Hawaii one day, but we never did. We'd even considered having our honeymoon in Maui, but . . ." I shrug. "We were young, just getting off the ground."

"And Alexa?"

I smile faintly. "She loved the ocean. This would have 'boogled her mind,' as she used to say."

He's silent, thinking over what I said. "So remember them," he finally replies. "That's kind of like bringing them here, isn't it?"

The lump again. I reach for his hand and he gives it to me. "Yeah. Kind of."

We watch the ocean, ignore the clock.

I shake my head. "We're pretty sappy these days, aren't we?"

He brings my hand to his lips, which are warm from the coffee he's been drinking. "We're due."

He brings up the question again after breakfast, the one and only thing that's threatened the bliss of our stay while we've been here.

"You given more thought to telling them?" he asks.

"Nothing's changed, Tommy," I say. "I know you don't like it, but it's going to have to be our secret for now. You need to respect me on this. It's a secret I've trusted you with, and I'm trusting you to keep it that way."

His eyes cloud over at my words. I feel irritated and afraid at the same time. I'm still suspicious of our happiness, fearful it's going to fly away. I look deep into his eyes and try to find the truth there. Whoever said the eyes are the windows of the soul was never a cop, that's for sure. Cops know better. Until the masks come off, killers have eyes like the rest of us.

"I don't understand," he says.

"I know. I'm sorry."

He looks away, and I can feel his own irritation rolling off him. Then he sighs.

"Fine," he says. "As long as you promise me it won't always be the case."

"I promise."

It seems to satisfy. The tension dissipates, and the lopsided smile, the one that gives me the good-shivers, appears. He cocks his head at me and my heart skips a beat. God, he's sexy.

"So, how about it?" he asks.

I roll my eyes. "Jeez, Tommy. It'd be nice to see something besides the ceiling while I'm here."

"How about the inside of the shower?"

"Been there, done that." Which was true. Twice.

He shrugs, as if to say, *What can I do?* "It's a small room, Smoky."

I giggle. "Fine, Mr. Horndog, but I want to go into Kona this afternoon to do some shopping."

He holds one hand up, places the other on his heart. "Promise."

We're heading for the bed when I hear the chirp from my cell phone that tells me I've received a text message.

"No way," Tommy groans.

"Hold your horses," I tell him. "I'll be right there."

I pick up the phone and open the message. What I see makes me smile, at first.

It's raining here, and you're there in paradise. I should hate you, but all is forgiven as long as you're engaging in endless rounds of monkey sex.

The smile fades as I read the rest.

On the serious side, we just caught up with the big bad man who was stuffing all those dead children into Porta Potties. He was neither big nor bad, no surprise. His name is Timothy Jakes—Tim Tim to his friends. (So he says. I doubt he has any friends. He's far too creepy.) He blubbered like a baby and wet himself when the cuffs went on. I found that quite satisfying.

Enjoy the sun, honey-love. Be hussified and raise a toast to Tim Tim, who'll surely be introduced to new and exciting things by Bubba or whoever it is that comprises the prison-rape welcome committee these days.

I close my eyes once, as a feeling of relief rolls through me. The case was open when I left, and it had come with us like an extra piece of luggage with a corpse inside. As beautiful as this place is, all those dead children stood on the far periphery, watching me as I gawked at the stars and communed with the moon. I sense them now, turning away, marching into a faded sea.

"What is it?" Tommy asks from the bed behind me. He's sensed something.

I flip the phone closed, take a deep breath, and make sure my smile is just a little bit lascivious as I turn around and let my bathrobe fall to the floor.

"Callie. She wanted to make sure we were having lots of monkey sex."

I'll tell Tommy the details eventually, but I don't need to tell him right now. I'm good at this kind of compartmentalization. It's a skill you learn early on if you want to have a life. I've gone from looking at the body of a raped and mutilated twelve-year-old girl to kissing my daughter on the cheek an hour later.

He grins. "I think we're safe on that account, but let's make extra sure."

"I wish we didn't have to leave tomorrow," I murmur, as I clamber atop him.

"Why don't we stay a little longer, then?"

"I'm the co-maid of honor at Callie's wedding. She'd kill you and then me if I missed it."

"That's true."

I bend at the waist and breathe into his ear. "Now shut up and do that thing I like so much."

And he does, and the sun keeps rising and the ocean beats against the sand, and I cherish the minutiae of every moment. But even as we roam against each other, I know this peace is fleeting. We don't belong here, in this place of too much light. I see other children in my mind, waiting for my return.

Tommy kisses me and I cry out, and the island says good-bye.

# CHAPTER TWO

### 1974

"I'm going to be life."

The man said these words to the Boy. The Boy took the timbre of his tone and got himself ready.

"Yes, Father."

"You'll be you, and I'll be life."

"I understand."

It was a role play.

His father held out a hand, palm up. It was a big hand. It was a hard hand too. The Boy knew that from experience. It had fallen against him many times.

"Give me a dollar."

His father regarded him and the Boy regarded his father, waiting for whatever was to come. It was the head of a brute, the Boy thought, not unlovingly. A head and face to match the hands, skull rough-cut from a block of concrete or a hunk of slag metal. His eyes were ice blue and ice cold, and they were the eyes of a philosopher and a murderer together.

The Boy was growing the same eyes, with his father as their gardener.

"I don't have a dollar."

"Well, now," his father said. He looked down at the tabletop, tapped a single thick finger on it, as though lost in thought. "Well, now. I'll ask you one more time." He returned his gaze to his son's face. "Give me a dollar." He held out his hand again, closing and opening it in a gesture of wanting and demand.

"I already told you, I don't have a dollar. Asking me twice isn't going to make it so."

He was rewarded with a glint of approval. What he'd just done was dangerous, but it was also brave. Brave was good.

"I told you I was going to be life," his father intoned, in a low, patient voice. "When life asks you for a dollar, you either provide it or life punishes you 'til you do."

The table was small and his father's arms were long. The hand came down against the left side of his face, thunderous. He saw blackness almost immediately. He woke up on his stomach, chair overturned, his palms against the floor where he'd caught himself. His ears were ringing, and he could taste his own blood in his mouth. Numb buzzing filled his head.

"Get up, Son."

His head swam. He fought to find the words.

"Yes, Father."

He was grateful.

The Boy was only ten, but he'd already observed some of the workings of the world, and he had a pretty good idea that his father was onto something. Life was going to go on, with you or without you. Probably without if you were weak. His father wanted him to be strong. What other kind of love could a father show a son?

He struggled to his feet. He swayed briefly but caught himself. Weakness was the cardinal sin, cowardice the second.

"Never just take it, boy," his father said. "Always fight back. If you're going to lose a fight, then make them pay for every punch they throw."

"Yes, sir," he agreed. He brought his fists up, marveling at how small they were compared to the massive ones his father had now raised and clenched.

"Life wants a dollar, boy," his father said.

The Boy didn't land a single blow, but he kept his mouth shut as his father beat him into unconsciousness, and he didn't cry.

The Boy came to in his own bed, shivering and hurting. He wanted to moan, but he bit it back. His father was sitting on the edge of the bed next to him, a hulk in the dark, silvered by the moon bleeding through the curtains.

"I'm being life, and life wants a dollar, Son. I'm going to ask for a dollar every week until you give me one. Understand?"

"Yes, sir," he said through cracked lips, making sure his voice was strong and clear.

His father gazed out the window, watching the moon as though the two of them had something to commiserate on. Maybe they did.

"Do you know what joy is, Son?"

"No, sir."

"Joy is anything that comes after survival."

The Boy filed that away, in the deep-down place where he held the great truths, and then he waited, because his father wasn't done. He could tell.

"We only have one purpose in this life, Son, and that's to draw our next breath. Everything else is just a dressed-up lie. You need food, you need shelter, you need a place to sleep and a hole to shit in." The big man turned on the bed to look at him directly.

The Boy had never really been afraid of his father. In all the lessons in all the times, through the brutal and the painful, he'd never doubted that the man who'd given him life would preserve it. Until now. Now was different, and he held his breath and his tongue and he waited, watched by two eyes that were lit up like dying stars.

"Why'd I pick a dollar? Because money is at the base of it all. Life wants a dollar, Son, it wants it each and every day, from now 'til you go under the ground. If you can't pay, you can't eat. If you can't eat, you can't live. There's nothing else to it. You follow me?"

"Yes, sir."

"I'm not sure you do, boy, but we'll find out. This is a test. I'll give you some tries, but eventually, if you don't come up with that dollar, I'm going to have to put you down and start over."

His father turned away after a stretched minute and resumed his communion with the moon.

"There isn't any God, boy. There's no such thing as the soul. There's just blood and flesh and bone. You weren't put here by a higher power. You were put here because I stuck something in your mother and the meat of you grew into something else. That meat needs to be fed, and you need dollars to do that, and that's the sum of all we are and ever will be."

The big man stood up and left without a further word. The boy lay back on his bed and watched the moon and thought about what had been said to him. He didn't question the lessons, and he didn't resent the pain. That ship had sailed, then sunk, long, long ago. There was a time he remembered being angry and sad, but it seemed more like a dream than a memory now. His father's fists had hammered that weakness from him, like a hammer smoothing the dimples from a sheet of metal. His father was his God, and his God was teaching him to survive.

He needed a dollar. If he didn't come up with it, he'd die. That was all that mattered, so he put his mind to it. By the time he'd fallen asleep, he had a plan.

The Boy had just started fifth grade. School was something mandated by his father as a necessity.

"You need knowledge to feed the meat, Son, and school's free. Only an idiot would turn that deal down."

He sat in his class and waited for the closing bell to ring. He had no friends and wanted none. Other people were opponents. Best to keep to yourself, so he always did.

The Boy watched Martin O'Brian, the school bully, gauging him with a critical eye. Martin was big and brutal. He had flat brown eyes and thin brown hair that always looked like it had been cut at home, and badly. He wore sneakers a few years too old, and some of his blue jeans had holes in the knees. Sometimes, Martin would come to school with a black eye, or maybe wincing as he walked, and those were terrible days for the weak. On those days, Martin was a thunderstorm.

He was feared by everyone, even the sixth graders. Martin dispensed his bullying and misery with a wild light in his eyes, as though he were somewhere else entirely. You could never be sure just how far he'd go, and this, in many ways, was the secret to his power. Anyone can be huge. Not everyone can be terrifying.

Martin would pull your arm behind your back and tell you to call your mother a whore. If you refused, his eyebrows would come together and some part of him would go away. Once that happened, it was anything goes. He'd even cracked a kid's arm once.

It was the kind of brutality that parents couldn't believe in a ten-year-old (or chose to ignore, suspecting its origins), so Martin was scolded and grounded or suspended but not much else. He was left free to rampage, an elephant set loose among the pygmies. Adults watched as the village burned but refused to smell the smoke.

The Boy smelled it. Surely. He'd seen the gleam rise in Martin's eyes once, when the bully was deep in his work with another kid. They'd been madman's eyes, set above a feverish smile that seemed more about tears than laughter.

Martin was what he was, and because of this, Martin was the solution to the Boy's problem.

The bell rang and the Boy went to his locker. He put all of his books inside and left them there; he'd done his homework in class so he could keep his hands free. He grabbed the other item he'd put in the locker that morning and walked out of the school door without a second look back.

He walked off the school grounds and sat down on the curb of the residential street, waiting. It was a nice day. The sun warmed his shoulders. An impatient breeze hurried by, ruffling the leaves in nearby trees and giving his cheeks a distracted kiss before moving on to whatever would come to stop it.

Nearly ten minutes passed before the bully walked by. Martin was whistling to himself, smiling at some private thought, his fists clenching and unclenching in unconscious, continuous rage. The Boy watched him go, then stood up and followed from a distance.

Martin stayed on the road for about five minutes, then turned onto a side street. Just two more turns before Martin was home.

Now or never, and never was not an option.

The Boy ran forward, gripping the thing from the locker in his hands. His heartbeat was slow and steady. He reached Martin in ten steps and swung on him.

The Boy had cut the broom handle in half before school. It hit Martin in the left kidney with a hard *thump*. The bully froze for a moment and then he screamed in pain. He reached back a hand, and the Boy hit that too.

The bully turned to face his attacker and was rewarded with a jab in his solar plexus that sent him to his knees, gasping for breath. Another whack broke his nose. The Boy hit Martin with method and patience, taking no joy from the act. He wasn't a sadist. This was a means to an end, no more, no less. He needed Martin to break, and he'd stop when that point had been reached.

Martin fell and curled into himself on the sidewalk, covering his face and head with his hands, trying to present the smallest body area possible to his attacker. The broomstick kept falling. Again and again and again. Arms, legs, back, butt. Not hard enough to break any bones or rupture anything inside, but more than hard enough to bring agony and waves of red mixed with spots of bright and black.

The Boy stopped when Martin began to mewl like a kitten.

"Martin. Look at me."

The bully didn't reply, still curled into a fetal ball, wailing, shaking, farting in little bleats of sheer terror.

"Martin. If you don't look at me and listen to what I'm telling you, I'll start hitting you again."

That got through. The bully uncurled in jerky motions, fits and starts of fear. His eyes were wide and roaming. Snot ran from his nose in a gooey river, mixed with blood and tears. A knot was already rising high on one cheek. His lips would need stitches. His breath hitched as he fought to get a grip on his runaway hysteria.

"Martin." The Boy's voice was as patient as his eyes were empty. He wasn't breathing hard. "You're going to start doing something for me. If you do what I say, you're safe. If you don't, there will be penalties. Do you understand?"

Martin stared up at his attacker, not saying anything. The Boy raised the broomstick.

"Yes! Yes!" Martin screamed. "I understand!"

The Boy lowered the stick. "Good. You're going to get me three dollars a week. I don't think that'll be a problem, right? I've been watching you. I know you rob other kids. Lunch money, allowance, things like that?"

"Y-yeah . . ." Martin whispered. He'd begun to tremble uncontrollably.

"So you just have to keep doing what you're already doing. The only difference is that you have to give me three dollars every week. Understand?"

Martin nodded. He couldn't speak anymore. His teeth were chattering too hard.

"Now, this next part is really important, Martin, so I need you to pay attention. If you ever—ever—tell anyone about what I did to you here, or about the three dollars, or if you don't get me the money, I'm going to show up in your house one night. I'll kill your mom and your dad and then I'll kill you too. And it'll take a long, long time."

Martin heard these words, and time stopped. Everything became both unreal and more distinct. He saw the present and the future and was filled with a vibration that rushed the fear from him.

The sun is out in a cloudless sky. The concrete on the sidewalk is warm but not hot, and he is only five minutes from his house. He'd get home and grab a Coke and one of Mom's brownies and head to his room. He'd kick off his tennis shoes and read the latest Batman comic. Mom would call him to dinner (meat loaf, probably) and they'd enjoy it together because Dad was off on the road, doing his salesman thing. No Dad meant neither he nor Mom would feel THE FISTS (that's how Martin thought of his father's clenched hands—THE FISTS). Maybe later they'd watch *Happy Days* together. His mother might even laugh.

Martin thought these things, and—just for a moment—his attacker's words seemed silly. Murder? Naw. They were ten! The sun was out!

The eyes looked at him, and he looked at the eyes, and Martin understood something in that moment with a clarity he almost never had. Something important.

Martin wasn't smart, but he was smart enough to know that he was a bad kid. He hurt other kids and stole from them and terrorized them. He made them beg and sob and, a few times, had even made them wet their pants. It didn't much matter that he did these things because they provided relief. THE FISTS weren't enough of an explanation for why he sometimes grinned when others were weeping. He was bad. He accepted this as he accepted his inability to change it.

The eyes looking down at him belonged to a whole different level of bad. They were devoid. There was no grief or joy inside them, no unspent tears, no laughs waiting to happen. This wasn't a kid who went home to read Batman, and Martin would bet sure as shit he'd never watched a single God damn episode of *Happy Days*.

The eyes watched Martin, the whole of him, they waited with implacable promise, and he knew in that moment that it didn't matter about the sun and the sidewalk or that they were ten years old; the only thing that mattered was understanding this: Every word had been a promise, and every promise would be kept.

"I understand," he whispered.

The eyes watched him, searching for the truth, and Martin wept as he waited, hoping to be believed. After too long a time, the Boy nodded, straightened, and tossed the half broom handle away.

"First payment is this Friday," the Boy said.

Then he turned and walked off.

The Boy got home satisfied. He didn't whistle like Martin, and he didn't smile a secret smile. Those were unnecessary things, ornaments of humanity. But he was satisfied. He hadn't just solved his problem, he'd solved every facet of it.

What if, for example, his father upped the ante in the future and wanted more than a dollar? It was a thought that had occurred to him last night, as he'd considered and ached in the dark. He'd decided it was very possible. If life could want a dollar, couldn't it want two? Or three?

The shortest distance between two lines was to take from those who had, but that presented another problem: how to keep from getting caught.

All roads had led to Martin. The larger boy would do the work and he'd take the heat when it came. And if Martin did decide to tell on the Boy, who'd believe him?

The rest was just judgment and calculation. How much pain to cause, how much fear to instill, how much certainty would result. Human calculus was the easiest math of all, if you had a knack for it, and that was the day the Boy learned that he did.

Not all evil is an accident. Sometimes it is grown in a dark cellar under a dark sun, tended by a dark gardener with a hoe made of bone.

# CHAPTER THREE

## PRESENT DAY

I long for my gun to be in my hand right now. It is a Glock 9mm, and I am as comfortable with it as I am carrying a purse or wearing a pair of well-fitting shoes.

I am a markswoman with a handgun. It's a skill that seems to have crawled out of some ancestral DNA, because neither my mom nor my dad liked guns. I was introduced to this passion when I was eight by a friend of my father's. He was a gun nut, and so was I after that day. There was something just . . . *right* about having a gun in my hand. It belonged.

I was a natural from the start, and though I've never competed, I suspect I'm in the top hundred in the world. It's a skill that's come in handy far too often, and one I wish I could utilize now.

"This dress is too damn hot," I growl.

It's late February in Los Angeles, and Callie's wedding is just off the beach. The air is cool, but for some cursed reason there's no discernible wind today, and the sun that would be comfortable in normal clothes is turning my maid of honor dress into a miniature sauna.

"My ass is sweating," Marilyn whispers back to me, and giggles.

Marilyn is Callie's daughter. She and Callie reconciled only a few years ago. Callie got pregnant at fifteen and gave Marilyn up for adoption at the urging of her parents, something she always regretted. One of the men we were hunting had ferreted out this information and threatened to use it against Callie. The result was a reunion of necessity that has turned into a real relationship.

"Quiet, Mama-Smoky," Bonnie chastises. "You too," she tells Marilyn.

I glance over at Bonnie, who stands next to me in her sun-yellow bridesmaid dress. She has her hair up and tied with a yellow ribbon, like all the women. She is beautiful, and I smile at her.

Bonnie is thirteen, and she looks like her mother, all blond hair and crisp blue eyes. The same perfect white teeth. It's what's behind her eyes that makes her different. She's a thirteen-year-old physically, but there's a stillness to her gaze that belies that. She's seen and experienced too much.

Her mother, Annie King, was my best friend in high school. She was murdered and mutilated by a man because he'd wanted me to hunt him, and he forced Bonnie to watch it all.

Annie had left Bonnie to me. I still don't know why.

Avenging Annie became the first lifeline in the aftertime of Joseph Sands; Bonnie became the second. Bonnie was driven mute by witnessing the murder of her mother, but over time she's come back to herself. She is thirteen now; she speaks; I love her. She's my child in all the ways that count.

Bonnie smiles back at me, and it burns away that watchful look in her eyes like the sun burning away the fog.

"You're not hot?" I ask her.

She shrugs. "I can take it. It won't be for long."

I glance over at Samuel Brady, the man Callie will be marrying. He's the head of the SWAT team at the Los Angeles FBI office, and he looks the part, even in his black tuxedo. He's tall, about six feet four, and he keeps his dark hair like all the SWAT guys do: short and tight, military style.

"Sam doesn't seem nervous," I whisper to Marilyn.

"I don't think much scares him," she whispers back, "except maybe Callie."

I stifle a snort at this. Callie Thorne is both my friend and a long-term member of my team. She's a tall, skinny, leggy redhead with a master's in forensics and a minor in criminology. She's known for her irreverence, which is generally excused by her competence. She is ruthless in her search for the truth.

The fact that she's getting married is still a surprise to everyone at some level. Before Sam Brady, Callie was what we affectionately called a "serial non-monogamist."

Standing next to Sam is Tommy. He catches my eye and gives me a wink. I stick my tongue out at him, which earns me another nudge and frown from Bonnie.

"When did you become such a little narc?" I whisper to her.

"Since Kirby made me second in command," she answers.

Now it's my turn to frown.

Kirby Mitchell is an assassin. She also happens to have assumed the role as Callie's wedding planner. She's got the look and attitude of a California beach bunny, but her history is much darker than that. There were vague rumors of her using threats, even flashing her gun, to get some of the vendors to cut Callie a break. I'm not sure how I feel about Bonnie getting close to her.

I let it go, as I let so many things go in my life. It's not like I have much choice. I'm surrounded by people like me, people who have both visible and invisible scars, people who have killed others and will kill again. It may not be the best environment in which to raise a child, but it is the one I've chosen and the one I have.

Next to Tommy are the last two members of my team, Alan Washington and James Giron. Alan is the oldest of us all, almost fifty now. He's a linebacker-large African American man. His tuxedo tightens dangerously every time he moves, straining at the seams. Size hides the truth of Alan; he's got a mind for detail and an endless patience that makes him a formidable investigator.

James checks his watch, and a sour expression crosses his face. I roll my eyes. At thirty-one, James is the youngest member of my team. He's also a misanthrope. I can't say that he hates people, but he sure doesn't seem to care for them. He has no use for social graces and generally gets on the wrong side of everyone he meets, present company included. What James lacks in the likability department he makes up for with his mind. James is a genius. He graduated high school at fifteen, burned his way through a PhD in criminology in four years, and joined the FBI.

One hint of James's humanity lies in his reasons for becoming an agent. He had a sister, Rosa, who was murdered when James was twelve. She was twenty. It took her three days to die as she was burned with a blowtorch and raped repeatedly. James decided at her funeral that he wanted to join the FBI.

He also shares my gift: the ability to understand the dark things. Like me, he can sidle up against the hissing and the slithering and the sticky, he can smell the smell and taste the taste, and come away changed but intact. Much as I dislike him sometimes, when I need someone to commiserate with about the mind of a killer, James is my invaluable and constant companion.

I look out at the attendees, seated in their plastic folding chairs. There aren't all that many. Callie's parents aren't here; they weren't invited. She's never forgiven them for forcing her to give up Marilyn. Alan's wife, Elaina, is there. She smiles at me, a crinkling of the eyes. I smile back. Elaina is one of the few truly good people I've ever met.

I view almost everyone with a cynical eye. I'm too familiar with the secrets people keep behind their cloaks of decency and their bright-toothed smiles. Elaina is different. She's not perfect, not Pollyanna. She can get angry and she's had moments of poor judgment, like all of us. But Elaina is the one who came to see me in the hospital after Sands's attack, when I was lying there in my shock and agony, staring at the white ceiling tile and listening to the cold beeps and hisses of the medical machines. She pushed the protesting nurse aside, and she came and gathered me up in her arms and both made and let me cry. I sobbed myself out against her until I literally passed out, and when I awoke, she was still there.

I love her. She's like a mother to me.

AD Jones, my boss, is seated next to her. He seems to be tolerating being here, but no more than that. I guess getting married and divorced two times would do that to you. His smile is more of a scowl, and he keeps sneaking glances at his watch. AD Jones has been my longtime mentor, sort of my professional rabbi. He's too much of a leader to be a real friend, but he's a great boss.

There are others in the audience: Sarah, now nineteen. A man had chased her through her life, killing anyone and everyone she ever loved. Theresa, her foster sister, sits next to her. Both have suffered more than

I have in their short lives, which gives me pause. Perhaps that's why Bonnie feels such a kinship with them.

The chairs are filled with ex-victims and hunters and a mix of the two. People who deal in suffering and death. I glance at Bonnie again and stifle a sigh.

This is my life. It's not perfect, but this is my life. And she is loved.

I recite the words and even believe them. Mostly.

My cell phone chirps, signaling the arrival of a text message.

"Turn that off!" Bonnie whispers, outraged.

"Can't, honey," I murmur, plucking the phone from where I'd stuffed it in the bouquet I'm holding. She grumbles something by way of reply and stares daggers at me.

I open the phone and freeze as I read the message.

I'm sending something to you, Special Agent Barrett.

I look up and around, scanning the crowd and surrounding area. I see a couple walking on the beach who've stopped to take in the wedding. A dedicated surfer is paddling out in what has to be freezing cold water. The hotel nearby has people coming in and out, but I don't see anyone stationary.

Could have rented a room. Could be watching us from a window.

I look up, but the windows are one way, and besides, the hotel has ten stories and four sides. I close the phone and put it back into the bouquet.

Sending me something? What? And now or later?

I'm more afraid than angry. He knows my cell phone number—not an easy trick—and he might be watching us right now. Us, including Bonnie. I look at her and find her staring right at me, assessing my state of mind with those too-old eyes.

"You okay?" she asks me.

Time to compartmentalize. I can stand here and worry about something beyond my control, or I can do what I'm here for.

I free a hand from the bouquet and touch her cheek. "I'm fine, honey. Where the hell is Callie?"

We left her almost ten minutes ago. She had her dress on; her makeup was perfect; all she needed to do was slip on her shoes and cue up the music.

"Maybe something with Kirby?" Marilyn whispers.

It's true, the simultaneous absence of Kirby is disturbing. I look at the priest, Father Yates. He smiles at me, the picture of patience. I met Yates during our last case, and our relationship has continued. I am a long-lapsed Catholic, but he seems to be enjoying the chase. He's another giant, standing almost six-five.

I point this out to Marilyn. "Look at all the guys. They should start a basketball team."

She fights back another giggle, which gets me going again and earns me another stare-down from my adopted daughter. Then the music starts up, forcing us to stifle it. I watch Kirby hurry down the aisle to her spot in the front. She seems angry.

"That's not the song Kirby chose," Bonnie whispers.

What's playing is "Let It Be," by the Beatles, the original version, just Paul and his piano. I think it sounds great.

"What did Kirby want?" I ask.

" 'Here Comes the Bride.' "

Well, no wonder, I think. Conformity isn't exactly Callie's style.

The woman of the hour appears, and my mental chatter dies away. I stop worrying about the mysterious cell phone message and the sweat sliding down the small of my back. Callie is too beautiful.

She's wearing a simple long white satin dress. Her red hair is down and wreathed in flowers. It looks like horses made of fire galloping down her back in the afternoon sunlight. She sees me gawping, gives me a wink. My heart squeezes in my chest.

I was always afraid that Callie would end up alone. I'm forty-one now, and Callie is about the same age. We are at our prime, but I've seen the future, the coming cusp, the place where the dust begins to settle and the lines begin to deepen. A time will arrive when this thing we've devoted our lives to, this chasing of the insane, will reach its end. We'll lay down our rifles, too old for the hunt. Maybe we'll teach the newer, younger hunters. Maybe we'll grow old at home, bouncing grandchildren on our knees, but whatever happens, old age is coming. I can hear the hoofbeats clearer now than when I was a fresh-scrubbed twenty-one.

So I worried about my best friend growing old and alone, and I find myself relieved and happy. She loves a man. He loves her back. They'll be together now, whatever happens.

The joy I feel is tempered by another, sudden vision. I see Matt and me on our wedding day. I wore white satin too. Matt and I were both incredibly young, a youth I can barely remember. Most of that day is a blur, but three things stand out in clear relief: our love, our laughter, our joy. Who knew that it would end the way it did?

Callie arrives next to Samuel, and he grins at her. It's the grin of a boy, beautiful on this normally taciturn man. It strips ten years off his age. Callie's smile in return is shy, which is almost as strange and at least as wonderful. Father Yates begins the ceremony, written by Callie herself. It is a mix of religion and promises, with no trace of humor. This surprises me on some level.

I think about my life now, about the divisions I've placed between myself and aspects of the truth. There is the secret I've sworn Tommy to keep. Then, of course, there's the one big secret, the new and devastating one. Who knows what I'm going to do about that? I hide some of these things not out of fear, some of them out of love. This is my life, for better or worse. I feel the sun on my neck and watch my friend fall into happiness.

"You may kiss the bride," Yates says, smiling, and Samuel does. The breeze finally blows a little, chilly but happy, and the sun shines hard, doing its best to bless the day.

I catch Tommy's eye, and we grin at each other.

"May I present Mr. and Mrs.—"

Father Yates is cut off by the black Mustang with the tinted windows that roars up in the parking lot about fifteen yards away. It stops, engine rumbling. The door opens and a woman is tossed out onto the asphalt. The door slams shut and the car speeds off. The car has no license plates.

The woman stands up. She's shaved bald and is wearing a white nightgown. She stumbles toward us. When she's about five yards away, she puts her hands to her head, turns her face to the sky, and begins to scream.

# CHAPTER FOUR

We're a strange group for the hospital. Callie is still wearing her wedding dress, though she slipped on a pair of tennis shoes. I'm still in my maid of honor gear, and Tommy and Samuel and Alan and James are in their tuxedos.

The woman collapsed after screaming, and we sprang into motion. Callie and I ran over to administer first aid. Tommy and Samuel raced to see who could call 911 first. Kirby went racing after the black Mustang, heels and all, with a gun that had somehow been secreted underneath her bridesmaid's dress.

Until the ambulance arrived, the woman remained essentially unconscious, her eyelids fluttering and the occasional moan escaping from between her lips.

Her appearance had been shocking. She was gaunt, though not emaciated. Her lips were cracked and she appeared to be dehydrated. The skin under her eyes was almost black, but not from physical abuse. They were the eyes of someone who hadn't slept in days, or maybe weeks.

Her skin was the whitest I'd ever seen, pasty, almost paper white. She reminded me of those blind albino rats you hear about sometimes, born in the dark and raised without ever seeing the light.

"Marks on her wrists, ankles, and neck," Callie had noted with a nod of her head.

I'd checked, and she was right. They were scars, though, not just marks. The signs of someone who'd spent years in shackles.

"What happened to you?" I murmured, as the ambulance pulled up. The paramedics jumped out and rushed over, all business. "I'm going with her," I said.

"I'll take Bonnie home," Elaina offered.

Bonnie protested. "I want to go to the hospital."

"No, honey." I guess there was something in my voice that told her not to argue; she wasn't happy about it, but she left with Elaina and no further protest.

"We'll meet you there," Alan said. "Hell of a way to end a wedding."

"I guess we'll see you guys later?" I asked Callie and Sam. "You have a honeymoon in Bora-Bora. You're hitched, so head out."

"Tsk-tsk," Callie said to me, shaking her head. "You should know me better than that."

There was nothing after that, because the paramedics had hustled the woman into the back of the ambulance and were eager to get rolling. They'd already placed an IV by the time the doors closed behind me.

"She's severely dehydrated," one of them said to me, shouting to be heard over the sirens. "Heart rate is way too fast."

He didn't have any other wisdom to impart, and we fell silent. I studied the woman as we barreled down the highway.

I put her in her early forties, about five-five. She had a long face, not unattractive, and a slender frame to go with it. Lips neither full nor thin. There was nothing striking about her—hers could be the face of a hundred middle-aged women—but I could not shake the idea that she was somehow familiar to me.

Her fingernails were a little too long, and they were filthy. So were her toenails and her feet. I'd moved down to examine them more closely and noted that the bottoms of her feet were heavily calloused.

"Almost like she never wears shoes," I muttered to myself.

The scars on her ankles were thicker than I had first noticed, uneven circular bands, as though they'd been cut open and healed again and again. Which they probably had.

We're in the hospital now, and I'm watching as the doctors and nurses attend to the woman. She's started to come awake and is fighting them. She's screaming. Her eyes are wild.

"Put her in restraints," the doctor orders, and the woman goes even more insane.

I rush over and put a hand on the doctor's arm. He glances at me, annoyed at the interruption of his rhythm. I show him my FBI badge and explain to him what I think. Point out the scars on her wrists and ankles.

"Can't you just sedate her?" I ask.

"We don't know what's wrong with her," he says. "Her heartbeat is erratic; we don't know if she's been given any other drug. Restraints are safest."

"If you put her in restraints, you're going to send her over the deep end. You'll be doing more harm than good. Trust me, please. I've seen this before."

I don't know if it's my badge or my scars or the certainty in my voice or all three, but I seem to get through to him. He nods once.

"Four milligrams of Ativan, IM," he barks. "No restraints."

The team changes gears to accommodate this new order without a hiccup, and I back away to let them do their job. The woman howls as they hold her down and jam the needle into her arm. She continues to struggle for a few moments, and then she starts to relax. Gradually, they let her go. Her breathing slows and her eyes close again.

"Doctor," I say, getting his attention again. "Sorry, one other thing. I need her checked for signs of sexual abuse. Full kit, please."

He agrees and turns back to his patient. That's when I notice something on the floor under her gurney. I insert myself and I bend down and pick it up. It's a single sheet of white letter-size paper, folded into a square. I open it. Black typed letters say:

As promised, now delivered. Follow the line of inquiry. In answer to the questions you'll have later: Yes, there are more. Yes, I will kill them if you come after me. Be satisfied with what I've given you.

I scan the woman's gown and see a single side pocket. The note must have fallen from there. I refold it and put it inside my jacket.

Games. So many of them like games.

I watch them work on the woman and I wonder: What is it about some of these predators that they get off on stealing a life from another person? Isn't it enough to rape them? Why is such complete destruction necessary?

It's a silly question, a mix of the rhetorical and wishful thinking. I know all the answers to all the questions. If not intellectually, then in the core of me.

It's a ratio. A mathematical thing. The greater the degradation, the more intense the sexual high. It's really no different, in its own way, than a meth-head or a heroin addict. Many rapists and serial killers talk about their first rape or murder as a pinnacle. The first high is the highest; everything after is an attempt to recreate it.

I'm involved in the Behavioral Analysis Unit's interviews of captured serial murderers. We contact them, try to get them to fill out a questionnaire, and then get them to agree to a taped interview. Some aren't interested, but most are. They're malignant narcissists—how could they refuse?

One of the men I interviewed kept recordings of the screams of his victims. Nothing else. He didn't have photographs, he didn't video the rapes or murders, and he kept no physical trophies. His fulfillment came from the auditory reliving of his victims' screams.

He was a small, squat man named Bill. He wore glasses—old-fashioned horn-rims—and was in his early fifties. I'd seen photographs of him before prison, and he was a family man, as some of them are. There was one photo of him with his somewhat-withdrawn wife. His arm was around her, and he was smiling at the camera. They were in their front yard and it was a sunny California day and he was wearing a chambray shirt, a pair of blue jeans, and tennis shoes. A set of suspenders held up the pants.

Three things struck me about the photograph. One was the date: The photo had been taken while Bill was holding his second-to-last victim. He'd abduct them (middle-aged women, always with dark hair and large breasts) and keep them in a soundproofed trunk inside a soundproofed storage shed on the rear of his property. Bill had bought land in Apple Valley some time ago, and he had nearly an acre.

The second was that smile. It was utterly benign. There was nothing about him (other than perhaps the downcast eyes of his wife) that said you should beware. Bill wasn't the next door neighbor you needed to keep an eye on. He was a balding, middle-aged man, who looked like his worst fault might be some slightly off-color jokes at the wrong times, for which he'd apologize profusely.

The last was his belly. It wasn't huge, but it was fat, and it didn't fit the rest of him. He didn't have a fat face, or thick arms, or heavy legs. It was the belly of a troll from the fairy stories. The belly made my stomach churn a little, because of all the facts I knew.

His last victim, Mary Booth, had survived her ordeal. It was her testimony, more than anything else, that put Bill away. There were certain things in her testimony that I couldn't help remembering when I looked at that photograph. Her interviews had been digitally recorded, and I had listened to them the week prior to my meeting with Bill. I could hear her voice in my head as I looked at Bill's smiling face and fat stomach.

It had been Alan who was called in to interview Mary. We hadn't been the ones to catch Bill, but Alan was the best at interviewing either victims or criminals, and her testimony was too important.

"Mary," he'd said, his voice gentle. "I'm going to take you through slowly. There's no rush here, okay? Anytime you need a break, you tell me, and that's it. We stop, and we stop for as long as you need us to."

Some people would assume Alan's size would work against him in interviewing a rape victim. He had a way of turning it around, though. Instead of being threatening, he became their protector. The hugeness of him became the most comforting thing there was.

"Okay," she'd agreed, her voice faint but strong. Mary Booth turned out to be a tough cookie, all in all. She'd been rocked hard by what Bill did to her, but she hadn't been broken.

"It's important that we're thorough, Mary," Alan had said. "The more specific you can be, the better. It'll be easier for him to attack generalities, you understand?"

"Yes."

"So if there are any tics to the guy, like, phrases he used a lot, if he ever hummed a song, or if he has any distinguishing physical characteristics, such as moles or tattoos, anything at all, it'll help. I realize remembering those kinds of things won't be easy for you, but I also know you want to put him away, so I'm going to push you on the details."

"I don't want to put him away," she'd said.

Alan paused. "You don't?"

"No," she'd replied. Her voice wasn't faint anymore. It was clear and level. "I want him to die."

To his credit, Alan had taken this in stride. I could almost see him, no expression of surprise or widening of the eyes. Just a nod to show he understood. Which he would have. "Fair enough. So then—you ready?"

"How's this for a distinguishing physical characteristic?" she'd asked, continuing as though Alan hadn't spoken. "He has a giant cock."

This time, I'd heard the surprise in the length of Alan's pause.

"Sorry?" he finally managed.

"Bill," she'd said, her voice still strong but with a faraway sound to it that made me certain she was looking off, remembering. "He has the biggest cock I've ever seen. It has to be ten inches long and God knows how thick. I remember clearly how it would stick out past that fat white stomach."

"I see," Alan said, finding his stride again. "He has a large penis. Anything else?"

"He has a scar on the inside of his right thigh."

"Okay. This is good, Mary. What else?"

It had been her turn to pause. Something in the nature of that pause, the feel of it, made me certain what she was going to say next was something horrible.

"He has a tattoo on the bottom of his stomach. He'd lift up the fold of fat when he was making me . . . pleasure him with my mouth. 'Look!' he'd say, and I did. There were two letters."

"What were the letters?"

"An S and an O."

"Did he tell you what they stood for?"

"Yes. He said they stood for *Slave Owner*."

There was more, too much more. Hours of it. Alan took her through every brutal moment, demanding every sordid detail with that same gentle insistence. There were times she wept, but most of the time her voice was strong.

The prosecutors made the jurors listen to every minute, and her testimony did its job, along with the damning physical examination and other evidence.

So number three, when I saw that photo, was the belly that poked at the chambray shirt. I couldn't stop seeing it hovering above her, pendulous and sweaty, with the code tattoo that only his victims would ever understand. That and the smile, the endless false smile.

His hands had been folded and perched on the belly when I came into the interview room. The smile had been there too. Only his eyes betrayed him. They'd roved over the scars on my face like a starving man looking at a thick and juicy steak. He wasn't cuffed, and we were alone. I wasn't afraid of him here. Bill would love to record my screams, but setting was everything to him, as was privacy, and this wasn't the place.

I sat the digital recorder on the table.

"Mr. Keats, as agreed, I'll be recording this."

"Of course," he said.

We went through the usual set of questions, and he was pretty cooperative. His mother had been the abuser. She abused his sister physically and him sexually. She forced him to abuse his sister sexually. He grew to like it, or so he thought. His mother had dark hair and large breasts, of course, just like his victims. It was both predictable and pathetic, and I remember that it made me feel a little tired, though I was careful not to show it.

We arrived at the area that interested us both the most, though for different reasons: the screams.

"Has that always been a source of sexual excitement for you?" I asked.

Everything in these interviews is very formal, including the phrasing. It's always a *source of sexual excitement*, never a *turn-on*. This is deliberate. Keeping things clinical and professional makes you a mirror, neither a judge nor a participant. They love to look at themselves in the mirror.

"Not really," he said, in an even, pleasant voice.

"I see. Was there a point where that became a necessity of fixation?"

He rolled the question around, watching me as he did. I saw the change in his eyes, the calculation. He was looking for feedback. Locked away from the world, from his drug of choice—rape and murder—he was searching for a way to feed his hunger.

He leaned forward, letting those hungry eyes stare at my scars without restraint.

"Did you scream when he cut you, Smoky?" he asked me.

I stifled the sigh. I'd expected this. I wasn't offended or disgusted or angry. I felt nothing. This was a game, and he was playing his part, thinking he was original when in fact he was as expected as they come.

"Yes," I said. "Of course I did."

His eyes widened, almost fluttered. "And did he like it when you screamed?"

"Yes."

"How did you know? That he liked it?"

I wanted to deny him this, but I knew that shame would only be a bigger turn-on for him. I also knew this was the price for his explanation. I could refuse it, of course, but I wanted to know why he loved their screams so much. I met his gaze without flinching.

"His penis grew inside me when I screamed. It got harder. I could feel it."

I said this with the same clinical detachment that a physician might use. *Tumescence,* I heard in my mind.

It didn't matter to Bill Keats. He couldn't hide his reaction. He sucked in a breath and crossed his legs involuntarily. One eye twitched.

"It's your turn, Mr. Keats."

He blinked a few times, reining himself back in from whatever great dark ocean he'd been drifting on. I could almost see him filing away the image of me in his mind for later use. He nodded. He leaned back in his chair again and perched his hands atop his belly. The smile returned.

"The first woman I ever raped," he said. "I went to penetrate her."

I remember thinking his use of *penetrate* was prissy and that this was telling.

"And?" I coaxed.

"I hadn't even entered her yet. But she knew what I was about to do and she screamed. It was the most amazing thing I'd ever heard. She knew what was about to happen and knew she couldn't change it. The misery I heard in that scream was . . . well. It was perfect. I ejaculated then and there, before I even got inside her." His look grew pensive. "She never screamed again like that. Not even when I was strangling her. That was the sound of her breaking." His eyes found mine again, and the smile returned. It seemed more thoughtful to me, somehow. "I've been searching for that same sound ever since. I didn't get that scream on record. I wasn't prepared. It's my greatest regret."

"And did you?" I asked. "Did you ever find that same sound again?"

He shook his head, wistful. "Close," he said. "Very close, sometimes. But never the same."

It took another ten minutes to complete the interview, and I was glad when it was done. I'd gotten what I wanted. Now I'd get to walk out of that place, while Bill—he of the belly and the horn-rims and the big false smile—would not. He'd die in a cage. Not enough by far, but it would have to do.

"Come on," he said to me, as I was turning to leave. "Tell me something about myself."

I frowned. "Sorry?"

He shrugged. "You've read everything about me, heard everything. I've answered all your questions, filled out all your forms. So? You're the expert. What can you tell me about me?"

I saw the real desire in his eyes. I'd seen it before in the eyes of these men. It was one of those injections of humanity, a shade of gray where you'd prefer just black and white. Their own misery was their biggest secret. *Why?* they wanted to know. *Why am I the way I am?*

I wanted to hurt him with my words. To say something so insightful that it would shatter him. The problem was, there was nothing revelatory about Bill Keats.

"You were excited by having sex with your mother but were deeply ashamed of that. Your wife reminds you of your sister, which is why you married her and why you probably never slept with her. Your victims reminded you of your mother, which is why you killed them." I paused, the last thing I was to say sliding in place like a puzzle piece. "You overeat because you disgust yourself and are only comfortable seeing something disgusting in the mirror."

It was the last thing that cut him the deepest. I saw it in his whole body. The way he cowered for a moment, but only a moment. His hands clenched into two fists. They returned to their relaxed state on their stomach perch, and the benign smile found its way back to his mouth, but the effect was ruined.

"Good-bye, Mr. Keats," I said. He didn't speak again.

I stand here now, in the hospital, watching this unknown woman on the gurney. I don't know her, not really, but I do know the man who had her. I've seen his kind again and again. I know his eyes without ever having seen his face.

And it bothers me.

It bothers me that I have a better idea of who he is than of who she is.

"Well, this is a fine kettle," Callie exclaims.

Sam is on his cell phone a few yards away.

"Changing your plane tickets?" I ask her, nodding toward him.

She makes a face. "Work call, honey-love. Lord knows how that's going to end up."

Callie calls everyone "honey-love," often to their great annoyance. Sam flips his phone shut and comes back over to us. His face is serious.

"That was Hickman," he says to Callie. "There's a situation."

"I thought Hickman was running things," Callie protests. "What was he going to do about this 'situation' when we were in Bora-Bora?"

"Well, we're not in Bora-Bora, honey. I called him, he didn't call me." He glances around, taking in Alan, James, Tommy, and me. "Are you really telling me you think we're hopping the next plane?"

She pouts, which elicits a roll of the eyes from James, who is watching. "That's hardly the point, Samuel."

He takes her hands in his and brings them to his lips. "It's just a hostage scenario, Calpurnia. It'll keep me busy until you sort this out."

She searches his eyes. "And if this doesn't sort out? If it turns into something that requires canceling the honeymoon altogether?"

He smiles. "We knew we were marrying each other's jobs too. This is who we are."

She purses her lips. "Fine. Go play guns with the boys. But don't get shot, and I expect a honeymoon-level performance tonight, regardless of circumstance."

"That's never a problem," he growls.

"Okay, then, Husband. Off you go."

He kisses her on the lips, hard. "Bye, Wife." He trots off down the hallway.

Callie flaps her hands in her face, pantomiming the need to cool herself off. "Goodness! That man knows how to get my furnace burning."

"Cool your jets, Jezebel," I say, smiling.

James exhales in a noisy, exasperated sigh. I turn to him with an inquiring look on my face. "You have something to add?"

"Why are we here? Just because some woman shows up at Callie's wedding screaming doesn't make it our concern."

"Your compassion is touching, as always," Alan says.

James ignores him. "Our mandate doesn't cover us picking up random cases."

"It's not random," I say.

James frowns. "How's that?"

I pull the note from my pocket and show it to them. I tell them about the text message.

"Great," Alan mutters, handing it back to me. "*Follow the line of inquiry.* Another one who likes to play games."

"Think about it, James. She was dropped off at a wedding filled with FBI and other law enforcement personnel. Do you really think that was a coincidence? She's a message."

He shrugs. "Even so. We don't mobilize for every threatening letter that appears in the mail either."

"She's not a letter, honey-love," Callie says. "She's a person."

He waves a hand dismissively. "Different form, same intent. My point stands."

"I can argue its possibility as a direct threat against us, as well as the obvious kidnapping," I say. "That would put it under our purview."

"Semantics."

I smile. "Ah, but I'm the boss, which isn't just semantics, James. If I want to make the argument, I will."

A sucking-lemons sour expression appears on his face and stays there. "What's going to be the deciding factor on you making that argument?" he asks.

"What she has to say." I talk seriously now, pushing all banter aside. "Think about it, James. We've seen this kind of thing before. Combine that with the note and ask yourself: What do you think the chances are that she was his first? Or that, if she was, she'll be his last?"

The sour expression is replaced by something more contemplative. I've gotten his wheels turning. "Fine," he mutters, walking away.

"He's our rock, in his own way," Callie says, looking at James.

"How do you figure?" I ask.

"He's uncaring and unthinking. As constant as the wind."

"Good point."

Tommy approaches. "Sorry to interrupt, but I was thinking about going to pick up Bonnie. This isn't really my show."

"You'll take her home?"

"And feed her," he says, smiling.

I grab his tuxedo lapels and pull him down to me. I plant a kiss on his lips. "That'd be really great."

"Okay, then." He extricates himself from my grasp and leans over to give Callie an unexpected kiss on the cheek.

"What was that for?" she asks, startled.

"Congratulations," he says. "I wanted to be the first to say it. And don't forget."

"Forget what?"

He jerks a thumb toward the room where they're working on our Jane Doe. "That that's not what you should remember about today."

He smiles and saunters off. I watch him go, wistful and a little horny. Gallantry in men can have that effect on me.

"Nice guy," Callie says.

"Yes, he is."

I know he'll go and get Bonnie and take her home and cook her something delicious. They'll probably watch TV together or play a board game. Or perhaps they'll both read, enjoying each other's proximity.

I'd forgotten what it was like to have a partner in life. Tommy's been there all along, it's not like his support is a new thing, but it hits me now at an oblique angle. Life is about inertia. The necessities of the day to day pull us along, against our will or otherwise. The alarm clock wakes us, the child needs to be dressed and fed. We have to down enough coffee to be awake and alert, and we need to look presentable (more so if you're a woman), all the while checking the watch or the clock on the wall. If it all moves perfectly, we fulfill these obligations with time to spare.

But some mornings the kid's got chicken pox, or the dog is barfing on the carpet, or the car has a flat tire. Sometimes we (or he) forget to buy new coffee, so we're forced to do all this on no caffeine, and so we buy horrible drive-through coffee and spill it on the new skirt as we're driving too fast because we're grouchy and uncareful and running behind. The day starts bad and the boss is in a shitty mood and the computer on the desk breaks down.

This is most of life. The day to day. The majority of life is mundane, interspersed with moments of joy and pain that act as markers on the road. It's a challenge. But when you have the right partner, like I did with Matt, you develop a rhythm, a way of balancing each other's weaknesses, so that even on the catastrophic mornings you can pull it off. Maybe he takes the bullet and arrives late to work and gets the evil eye from his boss so you can arrive refreshed and awake and caffeinated. The next time, it's your turn. You still take the hits, but you divide the pain, and at the end of the day, you commiserate together in your foxhole and call it a home.

I guess I have one again.

The doctor appears, shaking me from my thoughts. He looks tired but frowns as he takes in Callie and me together. I guess this is the first time he's had a moment to process our appearance.

"You guys come from a wedding?"

"That's right," Callie says, flashing a smile. "We got to the 'I do's first, thankfully. How do I look, honey-love?"

"Beautiful," he replies, simple honesty born of exhaustion. "So, your friend in there is in bad shape. She's been severely dehydrated, which is the probable cause of some of her delirium. She has thick, repeated scarring on her wrists and ankles. I'm no expert, but as you said," he inclines his head to me, "I'd guess she's been kept in restraints for a long time."

"How long?" I ask. "Can you tell from the scarring?"

"That's very inexact. People heal at different rates. A general rule of thumb is that the red appearance of a new scar fades to white anywhere from seven months to a year. It's only an estimate, but based on the color and thickness of her scars, I'd guess we're talking years."

I thought the same, but somehow it seems more horrible coming from someone else. More real.

"Go on," I say.

"She's obviously underweight, but she doesn't appear to have been starved. There are signs of whipping on her back, as well as other places. There are also a few marks that look like electrical burns."

"So she's been tortured." Alan says it as a statement.

"I think so," the doctor replies. "Now, as to the question of sexual abuse, I did a preliminary exam and saw no signs of that. No recent or older tearing of the vaginal walls or the anus. No signs of biting. I was, however, able to tell that she's given birth."

I start at this. "What? How?"

"She has a C-section scar. That and stretch marks. They're not new."

"Wonderful," I mutter. "So where's her child?"

"Anything else?" Callie prods.

The doctor hesitates. "She's too white," he says finally.

Alan cranks an eyebrow at this but says nothing.

"I'm sorry?" I say.

"Some people have naturally fair skin. This woman's pallor is unhealthy. Almost grayish. I don't see signs of anemia, but her eyelids are white, and when the scars are taken into consideration, I'd guess she's been denied access to sunlight for a very long time."

"Jesus," Alan mutters.

"I've drawn blood to check for vitamin D deficiency in addition to all the other blood work we'll run on her. That's all I have for now."

"Thanks," I tell him, which sounds lame and inadequate, but then, that's always the case.

"The lack of sexual violation is very, very strange," James says. I hadn't noticed him approaching. "Long-term imprisonment and torture of a female for other than political reasons almost always has sexual motives."

He's right. You go through the work to follow a woman, to learn her routine. You watch her, you hunt her, and then you take her. You chain her wrists and ankles, you whip her back hard enough to leave permanent scars, but you don't rape her?

"Of course, it could have been done in a noninvasive manner," James muses. "He could have drugged her. Or he could have forced her to submit. To feign willingness."

"True. Though that doesn't fit with the torture. The other question: why release her? Why release her to us? Anyone else here still think that was coincidence?"

"Unlikely," James says.

"I agree with that emotion," Barry says, speaking up for the first time. Barry is a first-grade detective for the LAPD. He's also a friend and was at Callie's wedding. He followed the ambulance to the hospital like everyone else. "Someone smart enough to take her and keep her for this long didn't make the mistake of letting her go near a collection of law enforcement personnel without a reason. *Follow the line of inquiry?* He knows what we'll do and wants us to do it."

Barry is a very good cop, with good instincts. He's an interesting mix of a man. He's in his mid-forties, he's heavy without being fat, he wears glasses, he's bald, and he has one of those homely faces that become cute in the right light. For all his physical failings, he's always dating pretty, younger women. They're drawn to him, and I know why: In spite of his jokes and his larger-than-life personality, he has the still, watchful eyes of a hunter of men.

We don't acquire many of our cases by choice. There are areas of specific FBI jurisdiction—kidnapping, bank robbery, crimes committed on federal property—but in most cases, homicide in particular, we have to be called in by the locals. They have to ask for our help. Barry is one of those few who doesn't let politics influence his thinking when it comes to what's best for a case. If he thinks we'll help solve it, he'll ring us up. We've worked together on a number of occasions to clear some difficult cases. Who-gets-the-credit is never a game we've bothered to play.

I think about all of this now and size him up with renewed interest. He senses it and raises his eyebrows in query.

"What?"

"You know what. I probably want in on this one. I don't think I'll have a jurisdiction issue since it appears to be a kidnapping, but if I hit a bump, can you help?"

Barry can help with almost anything he wants to help with. His clear rate is unparalleled. He scratches his head, thinking.

"It's not a homicide, so it's not mine."

"I just need you to put in a good word with someone, Barry. I don't think I'll have any difficulty claiming the case if I want it, but . . ." I shrug.

"It's always a good idea to set up your interference running in advance," he finishes for me.

"Yes."

"I'll talk to my captain about it. Play up the kidnapping angle and how that's all yours, all the time."

"Thanks."

"Don't mention it. Besides, no one is going to want this. It smells like *unsolved* from a mile away."

"We'll see."

"Yeah, I know. Anyway, I have to get going. I have a pretty hot date later tonight."

Callie scowls. "You set up a date on my wedding day?"

Barry smiles at her. "You're still the most beautiful girl in the room."

She sniffs. "Apology accepted, then."

He tips his fingers in a salute and saunters off.

"This is bullshit," James says, shaking his head in disapproval. I ignore him.

"Callie, let's get her fingerprints and run them. Maybe we'll get lucky and she'll be in the system somewhere." I look at her and blink at her wedding gown. "Do you have a change of clothes?"

She taps her cell phone and smiles. "I'll call Kirby. She'll bring me everything I need."

"Still at your beck and call even after the wedding? That's hard to believe."

It wouldn't be an overstatement to say that Kirby is governed by her own self-interest.

"We have something she needs," Callie says.

"What's that?"

"People who know all about her but like her anyway. Even assassins get lonely, Smoky."

"I suppose." My cell phone rings.

"Barrett."

"Smoky, I need you to come to the office." It's AD Jones.

"Now, sir?"

"Right now."

"Yes, sir. I'll just stop by my house and change and—"

"No stops on the way. Get here soonest."

I glance down at my sun-yellow maid of honor dress and sigh.

"Yes, sir. I'll be right there."

## CHAPTER FIVE

The man stares at the email on his screen and begins to shiver. He can't help it. The terror is instant and absolute.

The email says:

You've run out of chances. I left you something in your backyard.

There's no signature to the email, but none is needed. He knows who sent it.

*God, oh God, why didn't I do what he asked?*

He glances toward the rear of his home, where the sliding glass door leads into his backyard. A feeling of dread speeds up his heart, making it thud in his chest. Hard, too hard.

*Am I having a heart attack?*

He glances at the email again, then back at the sliding glass door. He closes his eyes.

*Pull yourself together.*

He stands up and walks away from the computer in his downstairs office. He leaves the email up on the screen. He's aware of every step he makes across the walnut hardwood floor. He's almost counting them.

*This little piggy had a nightmare, this little piggy stayed home, this little piggy burned in hell forever . . .*

It's going to be bad.

He knows this because he knows the man he's dealing with. Well, no, that's not quite accurate. If he really knew, in that deep-down kind of way, he would never have failed to hold up his end of the bargain. He edits the phrase: He knows the man he's dealing with *now*.

He arrives at the sliding-glass door and peers through it. It's late morning, and the sun is wrestling the clouds for dominance. He has a large backyard, filled with the overwatered green grass that Californians favor. He sees it right away and squints.

What the hell is that?

It looks like a black vinyl bag, with a . . . straw? Is that a clear straw poking out of it?

The thudding in his chest gets harder, if that's possible. Something worms around in his brain. Black vinyl bag . . . he has a word for a bag that looks like that, doesn't he? Yes, he does. Yes, indeed.

*Body bag.*

He swallows bile and slides the door open. He walks across the concrete of his patio. He's barefoot, and the grass is damp and cool against the bottoms of his feet. He hardly notices. The bag holds all his attention.

It is shiny in the sun. A heavy-duty zipper runs the length of it. The straw (because he can confirm that now) is clear tubing, poking through a hole that was made in the bag.

*Don't open it!*

The voice in his head is loud, a fearful shout. It's probably good advice.

He gets down on both knees in the grass, oblivious to the dirt and water stains that are soaking into his khaki pants. He reaches for the zipper. His hand hesitates above it.

*Last chance. You can still turn back.*

He gulps down a breath, grips the zipper, and opens it halfway before he can think about it any further.

He sees her face and he staggers on his knees, almost swooning.

"Dana!"

The words expel from him in a kind of low gasp, as if he's been punched in the stomach.

She's there. The straw is taped to her mouth, the tape covering her lips. There is something very, very wrong with her eyes. They're clear but empty. Nothing intelligent stares back at him.

"God, oh God . . ." he whispers.

She was supposed to go on a spa trip yesterday. Two-day affair, a little getaway. She didn't call last night, but he hadn't been worried. He'd had too much on his mind.

"Sorry, honey, God, I'm sorry, let me get that straw out of your mouth." He's babbling and he knows it but is helpless to stop.

He removes the tape as gently as he can, and pulls the tubing from her mouth.

Her mouth falls open and stays there, slack. Drool runs from it as she stares, unblinking, at the sky. There is a smell coming from the bag. It takes him a minute to place it. He recoils when he does. Urine and feces.

"Dana?" he askes, not really hoping for an answer.

Her throat works a little, and he thinks she might be responding. He leans forward, ignoring the stench from the bag.

"Honey?"

She belches, once, long and loud. She smacks her lips and resumes her drooling.

He skitters backward on his hands and feet, trying to put distance between himself and the horror of it. He falls onto his back in the grass and finds himself staring up at the sky, which is blue, and the sun, which has broken from the clouds. It's shaping up to be a beautiful day in Southern California.

He flips onto his hands and knees and begins to vomit into the overgreen grass.

# CHAPTER SIX

Weekend or not, the FBI is a beehive. I ride up on the elevator to AD Jones's office with three other people. They all stare openly at the dress. Nobody cracks a smile. I guess they realize it might not be all that funny. There are only so many reasons for an FBI agent to get ripped away from a wedding, after all.

I think about the woman as the numbers climb toward my destination. The look of terror in her eyes has stuck with me. It was such a desperate expression. I shake my head to clear it and focus on why AD Jones would have called me here with such urgency. He's not the type to make up emergencies.

He's been my shepherd, my teacher. He saw something in me from the start and fostered it. That's his way. He's one of those rare things in the FBI executive strata: someone more interested in results than in politics.

The *ding* tells me we've arrived. I take a deep breath and head out into the hallway. I make a right turn and see Shirley, his longtime receptionist. She's about ten years older than I am and is a short, professional woman with twinkling green eyes that belie her stern outward demeanor.

"How was the wedding?" she asks, not missing a beat.

"It was great. Right up to the point when the car pulled up and dumped the screaming woman out onto the parking lot."

She gives me an uncertain smile and a shrug, as if to say, *What can you do?*

"So who's in there, Shirley?"

The smile grows sour. "Director Rathbun."

My eyebrows shoot up in surprise. "Really? Do you know why?"

"Not a clue. Good luck, though."

I glance down at the dress again and sigh. "Oh, well," I mutter.

"Knock 'em dead," Shirley says, her eyes twinkling more than I like. She, apparently, sees plenty of humor in the situation.

I go to the door of the office, take a deep breath, and open it. I enter and see both AD Jones and Director Rathbun standing. They don't look like they've been talking. They look like they've been waiting. Off to the right I see another figure I recognize. Rachael Hinson. She's blonde and stands about five feet five. Her face is a blank sheet of paper, her eyes, watchful. She holds a BlackBerry and wears a Bluetooth earpiece and is murmuring to herself quietly as she speaks to someone on the phone. Hinson is Director Rathbun's assistant, or hatchet woman as I think of her. She's the go-to gal, the one who knows where the bodies are buried, because she did the burying.

Samuel Rathbun sees me and cranks up the wattage, smiling his trademark politician's smile and holding out his hand for me to shake. I glance at AD Jones, whose eyes slit briefly in a go-with-the-flow gesture. I return Rathbun's smile and shake his hand. Firm, of course, but not too firm.

"Thanks for coming, Smoky," he says. "I know you were busy." He smiles again, crinkling his eyes and indicating my dress, the picture of good humor.

"I live to serve, sir," I chirp, earning a look of warning from the AD.

"Glad to hear it," Rathbun replies, either not getting the sarcasm or choosing to ignore it. "Let's all take a seat."

AD Jones sits down behind his desk. Director Rathbun and I sit down in the chairs in front of the desk, angled slightly to face each other. Hinson remains in the background, murmuring to herself in the shadows.

I take stock of the Director of the FBI. I can't help it. He's a political animal, but he's still the boss of bosses, so he inspires a little bit of awe. Samuel Rathbun is in his early fifties. He's got dark hair, cut Bureau-short (but stylish) with just the right amount of salt and pepper left in. He's handsome enough for his type. Not honest enough for me, but I'd guess the Hinsons of the world find him desirable. He's reputed to be ruthless but fair, although the fair will get tossed aside if needed to save his own ass. I don't really hold this against him. He exists on another playing field, answering to the president and the attorney general and the like. He keeps us funded. I imagine that requires a unique mind-set.

I have no complaints about my own brief brushes with him. He's been pretty straightforward, and he, too, seems results-oriented. He used to be a cop before joining the FBI and, like the AD, worked his way up the ranks. He has my grudging, if cautious, respect.

"I'll get right to the point, Smoky," he says.

"I appreciate that, sir."

"We're going to be forming a national strike team tasked with solving serial murders, child murders, and abductions, stuff like that. I want you to head it up."

I stare at him, nonplussed. Of all the things I could have expected hearing when I walked into this office, this is the last I would have conjured.

"Say that again, sir?"

He smiles at my surprise. It's a more genuine smile than the earlier ones. I guess he understands. He relaxes, settling back into his chair. "Post 9/11, the whole mandate of the FBI has been shifting. We're being asked to focus our attention on terrorism, and that's where the majority of our budget is heading. There's a lot of pressure to force locals to solve their own serial crimes and to reduce the FBI duties to simple areas: profiling, CODIS, ViCAP. Support activities as opposed to active investigation."

CODIS is the Combined DNA Index System. ViCAP is the Violent Criminal Apprehension Program. Both are FBI-maintained and -administered databases that exist for the collation of evidence. CODIS indexes DNA evidence collected in the investigation of violent crimes throughout the country. ViCAP houses all the specific details of violent crimes, the hows and wheres and whats. Both are searchable and invaluable, but neither requires FBI involvement on the ground.

"The idea being floated," he continues, "and it's a serious one, gain-ing steam, is to eliminate your function in all field offices. I'm talking about every state. The personnel would be retasked to antiterrorism, and the weight of investigation would be left to the locals."

"With all due respect, sir, that's complete bullshit." I can't help the profanity. I'm stunned and outraged. "Local cops, by and large, are very good at what they do. Or they at least have someone who is. But it's been proven, time and time again, that FBI assistance can be crucial to the apprehension of serial offenders. That isn't a statistic that can be credibly disputed. If they dismantle the network, we'll be cutting our effectiveness. Strike team or no strike team." I shake my head once, furious. "It'll take longer to catch the killers, and people will die as a result, sir."

He raises his hands in surrender. "I know. I happen to agree with you." His face grows serious, and I get the idea that he does agree with me, and deeply. "Listen, I'm not saying it will come to pass. What I'm saying is, there are people—uninformed people—who'd like it to. They're making noise about duplication of activities, reassessment of priorities. They have opponents, of course, but . . ." He shakes his head. "There are a lot of them, and they're in positions of influence."

"Why now?" I press. "Not to downplay it, but quite a few years have passed since 9/11." A little sarcasm leaks into my voice. "Besides, I thought Homeland Security was supposed to be the solution to all our problems."

"Bureaucracies are slow and politicians are careful, Smoky. No one wants another 9/11, and not as much time has passed as you seem to think. Pearl Harbor influenced politics and policy for quite a while. Not to mention, the plans to wind things down in Iraq have quite a few demanding beef-ups in other areas."

"Have to replace that preemption with something," I mutter.

He gives me a look of warning. I try to look suitably chastised. "I don't have certainty on how it's going to shake out. That's why I want to create a strike team. Call it hedging our bets. If the idiots win, the strike team will be there, and I'll have made it an indispensable feature."

"So even if they get rid of my position in the field offices," I say, understanding, "they won't be able to touch the team."

"That's right."

"And you want me to run it? Why?"

He pauses for a moment. He seems reluctant to say what he's going to say next. "Because you're the best, Smoky. Statistically. Believe me, I looked. There are some other agents out there who are very, very good at doing what you do, but you're the best we have." He gives me a wan smile. "You win the title. Not to mention that you have a great story. The national media will eat it up. Female agent, lost her family to the job, soldiers on, and is the best at what she does. Sorry to be crass about it, but you can't buy that kind of public relations. Even the face will work in our favor."

I stare at him. Part of me can't believe that he's saying what he's saying. Part of me wants to slap his face, to tell him he can shove it, that the memory of Matt and Alexa aren't toys for him to play with. But a certain tenseness in his posture, a kind of poised waiting, gives me pause.

"You're testing me, aren't you?" I ask. "Bringing up my family and my scars like that. You wanted to see if I'd lose it."

He relaxes again. I notice that Hinson has stopped her murmuring and that those ever-calculating eyes are fixed on me.

"What I just said is the truth, Smoky. How I said it . . . that's not my style. I can be a real prick—the job requires it—but I generally have a little more class than that."

"But others won't."

"Correct."

Now it's my turn to relax, to lean back and consider. I turn to AD Jones, who has remained silent throughout. "What do you think, sir?"

He doesn't respond for some time. He seems tired to me, tired in a new way that I haven't seen before.

"I think the director is right," he finally says. "You are the best. And his motives are clean." He sighs. "Bad times are coming for some parts of the FBI, Smoky. Maybe this will all be averted, but I'm for saving what we can if they're not. You should think about it."

I turn back to the director. "I'm not saying yes yet. How would it work, if I did?"

"Once I get your agreement, I'll go to the attorney general. He's on our side." He hesitates. "So is the President. He can't afford to alienate the members of his own party pushing for this, not with an election year coming up, but he's a good politician and the strike team gives him air cover. If the network is dismantled and retasked and a bunch of ten-year-old girls get killed because the locals were inept . . ." He shrugs. "The President can say he opposed it from the beginning and that he had the strike team formed to shore up the loss."

"I'm talking about logistics, sir. I have a child, a fiancé. I have my team."

"We could keep you based in Los Angeles for now. Other than getting your name in the news whenever possible, you won't have any political interface. You'd start out directly under me."

"And later?"

"No promises. Ideally you'll end up centrally located at Quantico, but we'll have to see."

"And my team?"

"Oh, we'd uproot them with you. They'd form the strike team." He nods at Rachael Hinson. "Rachael's done a pretty intensive workup on what's behind your success. It's her opinion that your existing team is as vital as you are."

"She's right," I say, looking at his number two with newfound respect.

"Functionally, your purview would be nationwide. Since we currently still have our network functioning, you'd be called out only on the most high-profile crimes. If the worst-case scenario comes to pass . . ." He shrugs again.

"We'll be juggling murder across fifty states."

His silence is my answer.

"What do you mean exactly by 'getting my name in the news whenever possible'?"

"Well, there are two points to creating this team. The primary—and largest—one is pragmatic. If they dismantle your function within the field offices, we'll still have a way to put boots on the ground. The second is to create goodwill and general awareness of how vital it is for the FBI to have such a team. We highlight your story and past successes. We do the same with future successes. Self-preservation of the team would be the first goal of that kind of PR. A hopeful third would be to lay a foundation for later reconstitution of the network." He smiles, and for the first time it looks tired. A few less teeth are flashed. "Of course, as I said, perhaps we'll be lucky and none of it will come to pass."

"If it doesn't? What happens to the strike team?"

"We'll cross that bridge then."

I sit back and consider everything. It's too much to answer sitting here and now, of course, but the idea itself . . . It makes me look at the director with new eyes. Maybe there's more than just a nice suit sitting across from me.

I run a hand through my hair. "How long do I have to give you an answer?"

"Twenty-four to forty-eight hours. Seventy-two on the outside."

I gape at him. "That's nuts. All due respect, sir."

He nods again, looking tired again. Perhaps more irritated now. "You're right. But it's the way it is."

"Why?" I venture, a final question.

"Because everything in this town takes too much damn time, Agent Barrett. Because both the President and I have our share of political enemies, and we need as much of a head start as we can get. Because I said so!"

He stops there; his good humor is gone. There are times to challenge your boss, and there are times to let it go.

"I'll let you know, sir."

# CHAPTER SEVEN

I ride the elevator back down to my office and find James, Alan, and Callie there. Callie is out of her wedding dress, but both James and Alan are still wearing their tuxedos.

"Where have you been, honey-love?" Callie asks.

"AD Jones's office."

I guess I look preoccupied. "Heavy stuff?" Alan asks.

"The heaviest. Where do we stand on our Jane Doe?" I'm not ready to open this can of worms with them yet. I need a few minutes to recover from my own shock before passing it along.

"I got her printed," Callie says. "I'm going to go down to the lab, where I'll take digital photographs of the prints and feed them into the system. I'll have a search going in the next hour and then I'm going to head home, assuming that's okay."

"That's fine. Alan?"

"Jane Doe woke up and had to be sedated again. She shows signs of vitamin D deficiency and calcium loss, probably attributable to a long-term lack of sunlight and milk. The doctor says she has scabs on her arms, legs, and skull from picking and scratching at herself. It's a behavior you see in meth addicts or the mentally ill." He lifts the ends of his lips in a bare nod to a smile. "Same difference. She's missing some teeth, and most of the rest are looser than they should be."

"Why?"

"He's only guessing, since he's no dentist, but he figures bone loss. Apparently vitamin D is needed for proper calcium absorption by the body."

"Jesus," I say, processing the ramifications.

"Yeah." He consults his notepad. "We already know about the whipping. Doc also confirmed the evidence of electrical scarring. The perp shocked her, probably with a car battery or something like it. *Workmanlike* was the word he used."

James frowns. "What does that mean?"

"He went for areas of concentrated nerve endings or areas that would cause psychological trauma. Nowhere else, and nothing too severe."

"Punishment," I murmur.

James glances at me, absorbing this.

"Go on," I tell Alan.

"No drugs found in her system. No other identifying marks, no tattoos. He estimates her age at early to mid-forties. No broken bones, though she does have some old calcification on her left wrist and a couple of left ribs. He says she probably broke them when she was a child."

"That will help with an ID," Callie observes.

"We hope." He closes the notepad. "One strange thing. She has good muscle tone."

"Which means?" I ask.

"Her captor probably made her exercise."

"This is starting to sound like purposeful imprisonment," I say. "No evidence of sexual abuse—though we'll have to hear from her to be certain about that. Torture, but not excessive. He fed her, made her exercise. He kept her alive."

"Which begs the question," Alan says. "Why let her go now? And why us?"

We're all silent. No one has an answer.

"First goal is to identify her," I say. "He took her for a reason, however he treated her. Knowing who she is might be the key to figuring out what that was." I take a breath. Prepare myself. "Now. Let me tell you about my meeting with AD Jones and Director Rathbun."

I give them a detailed account, explaining everything. They're quiet, taking it in. When I finish, only Callie has any immediate comment.

"What a curveball day it's been. I don't think I'll have trouble remembering my anniversary date."

Alan sighs. "So let me get this straight. The powers that be, in all their wisdom, have decided we spend too much money and personnel on catching criminals instead of terrorists?"

"Essentially."

"So they're tossing around the idea of centralizing everything? Doing away with the NCAVC coordinator postings in all the field offices?"

"That's right."

"Fucking idiots," he mumbles.

"I agree," I say. "But it may be the hand we're dealt. The strike team is Director Rathbun's solution to preserving at least some of what we do. Without the formation of the strike team, if this all comes to pass, there'll be no on-the-ground FBI involvement in serial murders. Our contribution will become limited to faxing locals profiles and answering ViCAP queries."

James shrugs, standing up. "The director's reasoning is sound. Let me know what you decide." He heads to the door to leave.

"James, can you wait a moment, please? I'd like to bounce some things off you about this perp. Start putting a face to him."

"Call me on my phone or wait 'til tomorrow. I'm late for something important." He exits without a backward look or another word.

"Charming," I mutter. "Callie? Any idea what you'll decide?"

"Sorry, honey-love. I'm a married woman now. I need to consult with my man." She smiles lasciviously. "Preferably after an extended sexual encounter."

"Let me know. About the job, I mean," I say, smiling.

Alan cocks his head at me. "What about you, Smoky? What are you going to do?"

"I honestly don't know." I sit down in a chair. My crinoline billows around me, and I feel ridiculous and tired and overwhelmed. "I need to talk to Bonnie and Tommy and do some thinking." I sigh. "I don't know. James is right. The reasoning is sound, but . . ."

"It's not all about logic."

"Yes."

"I hear that." He picks at his lower lip, pensive. "I'm no spring chicken, Smoky. Neither is Elaina. If they end up wanting us to uproot and go to Quantico . . . I don't know. Not sure we'd be up for that."

Callie nudges his shoulder. "Pshaw. Age is a state of mind."

"And my mind is in a state." It's meant as a joke, but there's something else there, something hidden and reluctant.

"Callie, why don't you go ahead and do what you need to do at the lab. I'll see you tomorrow morning. Call me if anything turns up on the fingerprint search."

Her eyes go back and forth between Alan and me. She understands that I'm trying to get her out of the office.

"Don't have to tell me twice," she sniffs.

"Hey, Callie," Alan says.

"What?"

He smiles at her, and it's a big, warm Alan-smile. "Congratulations, honey."

She grins and then she curtsies. "Why, thank you, sir." She turns and heads out the door.

"She's happy," he observes once she's gone.

"Yes. I really think she is." I turn my attention to my friend. "But you're not. What's going on?"

He looks off, taps his fingers against the desktop. Sighs. "This is a big move for me, Smoky. Like I said, I'm no spring chicken. I told you a few years back, I've been thinking of retiring. Having more time with Elaina."

"I remember."

"I'm not saying I'm decrepit, but the truth is, it's harder to get up in the morning than it was ten years ago. I'm in okay shape, but my doctor says my cholesterol is too high and I need to lower my blood pressure a few notches. Elaina had that cancer scare."

"Do you really want to hang it up?"

He shrugs. "I'm not sure. That's the problem—my ambivalence. Never used to feel that way. I lived for the job." He gives me a mirthless grin. "Not like I chose it for the great hours and pay. I like catching bad guys, and when it's good, police work is the most exciting job there is. Sure, there were times I considered quitting before. Strings of unsolveds, or really terrible cases with dead kids, or whatever. Depression is a part of the package. But something would always pick me up and get my blood moving again. I'd catch the scent. You know what I mean."

"I do."

"Lately I'm finding it harder and harder to get excited. It's not that I feel down, and *bored* isn't the right word either. More like I feel . . . full." He nods once. "Yeah. Satisfied. Maybe I've caught my quota of bad guys, and the world can keep on turning without my help."

Some part of me is envious, hearing this. I've thought about leaving the job. Of course I have. But my motivations have always been based on despair. The idea of a future where you could feel like you'd done enough? Unfathomable. I long for it conceptually but am unable to picture it emotionally.

"Well," I say slowly, "you know I'll support you whatever you decide."

"I know."

"But let me ask you a favor."

"Shoot."

"If I decide to go with this—and that's not a certainty—can you at least stick around while we're still based in Los Angeles? I understand your qualms about that possible future move to Quantico. That's a big one for me too, but for now we'd be here." I indicate our sparse office furnishings and roll my eyes. "In all our glory. But if this happens, I'd need you in the beginning, Alan. I really don't think I could do it without you. Not at the start."

He's silent, regarding me. I wait him out. It's a comfortable silence, not unlike so many we've shared. I've worked with this man for years. We've commiserated over corpses. He's held me when I cried. He knew Matt and Alexa and loved them both. He was at their funerals, by my side, dressed in black and shedding tears without shame. He loves Bonnie and likes the heck out of Tommy. Alan is some of that rare connective tissue that still links my past and present. The idea of him leaving, of watching his back as he recedes into a life that would include so much less of me, makes me feel both sad and fearful. Twelve years is a long time to know anyone. Doing what we do, it's a lifetime of friendship.

He grins at me, and I know he's going to say yes.

"Couldn't do it without me? That's enough to get my blood going again. For now."

# CHAPTER EIGHT

I'm almost home and am pleased at just how much of a relief this is. This is the way I used to feel. Home was my sanctuary, the place the shadows couldn't come. It's taken a while, but it's become that way again.

It's a different home, of course. Tommy and Bonnie are not as innocent as Matt and Alexa were. They've both seen murder, and Tommy has killed people. Funny thing is, the differences don't make me long for the past. I find them appropriate, even comforting. Civilians in my life have too hard a time.

I see my exit approaching, and I allow myself to consider all the current uncertainties for one last time tonight. They won't be allowed past my threshold.

What am I going to decide about the strike team?

Another:

What about the secret Tommy and I are sharing?

The last.

What about the secret I'm not sharing with anyone?

No answers arrive. I hear the sound of my tires against the pavement, the wail of the radio turned down low.

I pull into my driveway and do as I'd promised: I stuff the uncertainties away.

"Welcome home," Tommy says. His eyes are troubled, and the kiss he gives me is perfunctory, distracted.

I allow myself a moment of selfishness, a second to feel irked and disappointed that I couldn't just walk in to find sunlight and smiles. Then I push it aside and do my job as a partner.

"What's up?" I look around. "Where's Bonnie?"

"Something happened," he says. "Let's sit down."

Fear flashes through me. My hand finds my weapon, an almost unconscious gesture. "Is it Bonnie? Is she hurt?"

He reaches out and covers my gun hand with his own. His touch is gentle. "Nothing like that. No one is hurt. But let's sit down anyway."

I allow him to lead me over to the couch. I'm still jumpy. Tommy is generally a rock. The petty challenges of life that tend to pique me, like getting cut off on the freeway, lukewarm coffee, and long bank lines, don't faze him. Right now he's nervous and deeply troubled. This frightens me.

"Bonnie did something," he finally says. "Something bad. She feels terrible about it, which is why she told me. It happened a few days ago, and she's been holding it in, but she broke down when we got home."

I close my eyes and almost breathe a sigh of relief. This is old, familiar, comfortable territory. Kids do bad things sometimes; dealing with it is part of parenting. Tommy's never raised a child, so it caught him off guard. I open my eyes and put a hand onto his knee to reassure him.

"What did she do? Shoplift? Beat up another kid?"

His eyes level on mine. "She killed a cat."

I blink. "Sorry?"

I'm sure I didn't hear him right.

"She killed a cat. A stray she found. She brought it into the backyard two days ago and shot it in the head with the twenty-two target pistol you keep in the gun safe."

"How'd she get the combination to the gun safe?" I ask, though of course it's not the most important question. The important question belongs to something unreal.

"She guessed it. Alexa's birthday."

Stupid, I think to myself. Stupid of me, not Bonnie.

"Did she say why?"

I'm amazed at how level my voice is, how normal. We could be having a conversation about a casserole.

"She did. But I want her to tell you."

He looks away and can't meet my gaze. This cuts through my shock. I feel a stirring of fear in my stomach, a dark churning. "Tommy. You tell me."

He shakes his head. "No. I need you to hear it from her. I want you to be watching her when she says it."

"Why?" Now I can hear the fear, hear it in my voice. It's bubbled up and found its sly way into my vocal cords.

He takes my hands in his. "Because," he says. "I believe her. I think you will too, but only if you're looking into her eyes while she tells you."

I yank my hands away. They're shaking.

"Go see her. She's waiting for you in her room."

I'm standing outside Bonnie's door, hand raised to knock. I lower it and grip the knob instead.

She killed a cat. Shot it in the head. Whatever the reason, she's lost her right to privacy.

It feels like a meaningless gesture, but this again is familiar territory, and it comforts me. I steady myself and turn the knob. I open the door.

Bonnie is lying on her bed. She's staring at the ceiling. Her face is expressionless, but she's crying. She doesn't turn to look at me when I come in.

"Bonnie." I keep my voice firm but gentle.

"I'm sorry," she says.

"Sorry isn't going to cut it, honey. I need you to sit up and explain this to me."

She wipes her eyes with the back of her hand. The sigh she emits sounds so old, so . . . *bone-weary* that my heart skips a beat. It makes me want to go over there and take her in my arms, but I restrain myself. This isn't the time for comfort.

She struggles to a sitting position, her legs dangling down from the bed. Her eyes remain averted.

*God, she looks like Annie.*

Her mother and I met when we were both fifteen, just three years older than Bonnie is now. It seems like an impossibility of time ago. I feel almost no connection to the me-of-then; too much is too different. But then I look at Bonnie now, and the band of unreality disappears. I find myself cheek to cheek with my fifteen-year-old self. Mom dead, Dad struggling, me hurting but also so very alive, everything bright-edged and multicolored and dramatic. Songs could still make me cry when I was fifteen. I had no scars on my face and no calluses on my soul.

"So what happened?" I ask my adopted daughter, fearing the answer but knowing I need to hear it all.

She shifts on the bed. She lifts her head, catching my brown eyes with her blue ones. The ghost of Annie stirs.

"I needed to know what it felt like."

I frown. "What? Killing a cat?"

She looks down again. Nods.

"Why?"

"Because . . ." She hesitates. "Because that's what they start out doing."

"Who?"

She lifts her gaze to me again, and the bleakness there shocks me. Each eye is a desert landscape, rocks and sand and wind.

"You know. Serial killers." She drops her eyes, ashamed.

I am silent. I'm having trouble thinking, much less speaking. If she'd slapped my face with an open hand, she couldn't have poleaxed me more.

"So . . ." I say, drawing the words out not by choice but because I can't help it, because I feel like I'm running in a nightmare, churning through taffy or thickening mud. "You shot a cat in the head because serial killers start out by killing small animals?"

"Yeah."

I don't try to keep the desperation out of my voice. Or the amazement. "But why, honey? Why would you want to do what they do?"

"To help me understand them. So later I can catch them." She whispers it. She sounds lost.

Maybe she is.

The slowness I'd been stuck in is dissipating. I can hear the thick metronome of my heart beating again. For some reason I think of Hawaii, of what I had thought of as God's heartbeat thumping against the shore.

"Look at me, Bonnie." It takes her a moment, but she does as I ask. "So? How do you feel about it? Did it help you?"

The bleakness, if anything, increases. More tumbleweeds. Scoured stone. A little hint of rain, as tears begin to pool at the edges. "No," she whispers. "It didn't help me."

I don't let up. "How do you feel about it?"

What I see next isn't bleakness or grief or even misery. It's despair. The tears begin to roll from her eyes, thick tears, creating unbroken streams that drip from the sides of her face and her chin to patter on her arms and her blue jeans. "I felt evil. I felt bad. I felt like . . ." Her eyes close, and self-hatred spasms across her face. "I felt like the man who killed my mom."

I want to go to her. Everything I am wants to grab her, yank her close, and make her safe. I want to tell her it's okay, she's not evil, to forgive herself. Something stops me.

*It's not enough.*

I'm not sure where this idea comes from, but I don't question the truth of it, because the voice is me and I recognize the feeling it brings. It is the same feeling I get when I realize something about a case or a perpetrator, when things that had been disjointed and strange suddenly fit together.

Bonnie lost her mother to a madman. She watched as the man broke Annie, raped her, gutted her. Then he took Bonnie with gentle but insistent hands, and he tied her to the screaming corpse, face-to-face. I've never really been able to imagine what those three days might have been like for anyone, much less a ten-year-old girl.

She's gone from screaming in the night and mute to sleeping through the night and speaking. She's learned to smile, and she has a friend or two.

Sure, there are things I don't like. She's told me that she plans to do what I do when she grows up. She wants to hunt the monsters. There's a certain stillness to her too-old eyes sometimes, a piercing sadness in her gaze. I find her watching the sunrise every now and then, and I worry. But these things always go away. The resilient thirteen-year-old always comes back, so I accept her injuries and her oddities. For God's sake—how could she be otherwise?

But this is different. This is a crossroads. It is a touchstone. I don't know how I know it, but I do. Either I save her here and now, or she'll keep swimming away from shore, farther and farther out, until one day she'll be in a place where I can't reach her. I see what Tommy wanted me to see. Bonnie's not a monster. I get that.

*But . . .* the voice whispers, and I nod to myself, inside, and complete the sentence:

But she could be.

I know this because I've been there myself. There is a dividing line, a place where trying to understand the monsters becomes too much understanding, where knowing becomes drowning. I've swum out to where the water is no longer blue. I've felt the black leviathans shiver against my naked feet, chuckling and slimy. There comes a time where I start to see too many similarities between them and me, and too few differences. More than once I wasn't sure I'd find my way back to me. I always have, but my swims began in my twenties. Bonnie is only thirteen. She's still forming. A decade is a lifetime of change at this age.

She hunted down a cat and shot him in the head, because she wanted to feel what the monsters feel. Her tears and her brief despair aren't enough. They won't ensure her survival as herself.

I try to push away all the protectiveness I feel for her, the desire to wipe away her tears. It's not easy, but it's not as hard as it might be for some, I guess. One of the things you have to learn in order to interrogate suspects is how to set aside your own reflex humanity. The rapist, the killer, the thief—they're all people. Once caught, they tend to collapse, to pull into themselves. Half of what makes them formidable is the mystery of who they are. What you're left with, most times, is something pathetic. Something that looks miserable, something that weeps.

It's only natural to experience feelings about that. You have to overcome it. "We all have a little bit of cold granite inside us," Alan told me once. "Some more than others. A good interrogator learns how to flip between being as loving as the suspect's own mother and as merciless and unreachable as God. It's all manipulation and a little bit inhuman, so you gotta find that cold granite part of you and bite into it. Let it hurt your teeth a little."

I find it now and bite down hard.

"Do you remember what your mother looked like when he was cutting her?" I ask Bonnie. I'm simultaneously amazed and dismayed at the level I've managed to find; there is no solace at all in my voice. I sound like a bored, slightly hostile drive-through attendant.

Her eyes widen. She doesn't reply.

"I asked you a question. Before she died and you were tied to her body, do you remember what your mother—Annie—looked like?"

"Yes," she whispers. She's staring at me, unable to look away, like a baby chicken watching a snake.

"Tell me. How did she look?"

She pauses for a long time. "She looked like . . ." She swallows. "I never told you something about that night, Mama-Smoky. Something he said to her. When he put the knife on her the first time, after he made her scream, he told her she could choose."

"Choose?"

"Yes. That anytime she wanted, she could tell him to take me instead and he'd stop cutting her up."

Something bottomless opens up in my soul.

"She was screaming, you know? He gagged her, but it hurt her so bad. She jumped against the handcuffs he used, and her wrists and ankles were bleeding, they were bleeding so much. He danced to the music he put on, and he laughed sometimes." Another swallow. Her eyes still fixed on me. "So this one time—you asked me how she looked—so this one time, while it was happening, I saw it in her eyes. It was only there for a minute, but I saw it."

"What?" I prod her, still biting on that cold granite. Shoving her face into the darkness of it.

"She wanted to give me to him. Just for a moment. She wanted to give me to him, and she hated herself for wanting that." The sound of loss in her voice, at that moment, is heartbreaking. She shakes her head, seeing the image, not fully able to believe it but knowing it was real. "She died hating herself for that, Mama-Smoky." Bonnie hugs herself and starts to rock, back and forth. She moans a little, and the tears, which have never stopped, stream a little harder.

*No no no no no,* I want to tell her, *she didn't die hating herself. She died loving you.*

I resist this urge. We're not done yet. I don't know what *done* is, just that I'll recognize it when we arrive.

"So here's what you need to understand, then, Bonnie," I tell her, and I'm still amazed at the absolute disinterested *cold* of my tone. "Listen close, because I need you to get the differences here. What you did and what you are not. Both are equally true. What you are not is evil. You are not the same as the man who did that to your mother." I lean forward now, fixing her with a heartless, baleful gaze. "But when you killed that innocent cat? When you hunted it down, caught it, brought it into our backyard, and put a bullet into its head? At that moment, what you did to that cat was no different than what that man was doing to your mother. You say you want to do what I do in memory of your mom?" I sneer then and hate myself for it, because it actually makes her flinch. I bring my face close to hers, close enough so she can feel the heat of my breath. "She took the pain to save you, Bonnie. When you killed that cat, you spit in her face."

Hey eyes widen more than I would have thought possible, and her face goes white. There is a space of horrified silence, and then Bonnie's breath expels from her chest, as though she'd just been punched in the stomach. She lets out a low moan. It's a hushed, soulful thing, the voice of misery.

*Now we're done.*

She scrabbles back on the bed, fisted hands to her mouth, shaking her head back and forth, back and forth, horrified at herself, at what she did, at the truth of it. This time, I go to her. She fights me, but I grab her and clutch her to me, not letting her get away no matter how hard she tries or how much she pummels. Eventually she stops resisting, and her arms wrap around me and she just cries. Sobs and sobs and sobs. I cry too. In the midst of my own mix of relief and self-hatred, I lean down and give her the truth I'd denied her earlier.

"When your mom died, honey," I whisper into her hair, "she wasn't hating herself. She was loving you. Don't let him take that away from you."

I glance up at some point and see that Tommy is there. I wonder how much he saw. He watches for a little while longer, his gaze unfathomable, and then he gently closes the door, leaving us alone.

Bonnie has wept herself to exhaustion. She's in my lap, too big to fit comfortably but unwilling to let me go.

"I really am sorry," she says.

I stroke her hair. "I know you are, honey. Believe that."

We fall into silence again. She sighs once, and I continue to stroke her hair. I glance out her bedroom window and see my old adversary: the moon. *So . . . we meet again.* The attempt at humor topples to a soundless death.

"Listen, baby," I say after some more time has passed. "There's nothing wrong with you having a goal to do what I do when you grow up. I mean, it's not the career I'd want for you, but if you still want it when you're older, I'll support you."

"I'll still want it," she says.

"But there have to be limits, Bonnie. That's part of the secret and the safety net. There's a huge difference between us and them. We can understand them, but we'll never be them, you follow?"

"I think so."

"Here's the thing you have to understand: They can pull you under. They can suck the life and the soul out of you, and once that's done . . ." I search for a metaphor. "Think of yourself as a lighthouse. No matter how foggy it gets or how rough the sea, the lighthouse will guide you home. Well, if you get too close to them, if you go too far, the light can die. You don't become what they are, but you lose yourself."

She's quiet for a time, thinking about this. "If the light goes out," she asks, "can you ever get it back?"

"Almost never." I put a hand under her chin, angle her face up to mine. "That thing you did with the cat? That's the kind of thing that puts the light out, honey. You understand?"

She nods. I let her chin go, and she snuggles back into my embrace. "So what do I do?"

"You learn to balance. Look, honey, regular people, they know how to enjoy life. It's more natural for them to look for the good stuff than the bad. It's harder for people like us. We have to force ourselves to engage in the good stuff. Even when we don't want to. The thing is, even if you have to force yourself in the beginning, somewhere along the way you'll find yourself having a good time."

"But how does that work for *me*?" she asks, and I'm pleased to hear the impatience mixed with the pleading. I cracked her, but I didn't break her. Thank God.

"Well, let's see. Balance and Bonnie. Okay, here's an example. You told me you wanted me to take you to the shooting range, right?"

"Yes."

"Well, fine. I'll agree to do that every other week. On the weeks off, you have to find an extracurricular activity at school to take part in. I don't care what it is. Band or track—I don't care. Just something any other thirteen-year-old would do."

"Sounds boring."

"It might be, at first. But you'll be surprised. There's an old acting trick. If you make yourself start laughing, at first it's just going through the motions. It'll feel silly, sound silly. But you almost always end up laughing for real. This is like that. Besides, it's really a part of your current goal, anyway."

"What do you mean?"

What *do* I mean, exactly? I can feel the idea swarming within me. It's something I understand innately but have never had to put words to.

"Our biggest advantage over the monsters isn't that we know how they think, honey. That's not so hard. It's that they can never understand how *we* think." I kiss the top of her head and whisper again into her hair. "They can't understand how we can love each other so much, and they know it. That's what they hate us for the most. Love is the light."

Bonnie is finally asleep. I'd lain in bed with her as she tried. She kept waking, checking to make sure I was still there. I waited until her sleep was certain, and then I disentangled myself and crept back to my own bed.

I remove my clothes, which smell of salt: the sweat from Bonnie's troubled forehead and the wet from her tears. I crawl into bed next to Tommy, naked, and reach for him.

"She okay?" he asks.

"She will be."

"You okay?"

I shake my head, realize he can't see that in the dark. "Not really. Can you make me okay?"

He pulls me to him and kisses away my tears, then his lips find my lips and later we come together in that sweetest way. Afterward, I am lying with my head on his chest, listening to the gentle *thump thump* of his heart and the slow, even sound of his restful breathing. He's fallen asleep after sex, the man way. I'm headed in that direction but take a last moment to look at the moon and whisper some words to the God I'm not sure I'll ever really reconcile with.

Thank you for showing me how to reach her, I think, my eyes beginning to flutter. Keep doing things like that, and we might have a truce.

It's probably my imagination, but the moon seems to disappear behind a cloud at that exact moment, and I imagine it's Him, the Him I doubt more than I believe in, saying, *You're welcome.*

# CHAPTER NINE

His father sat him down on the living room couch one year. He patted the seat next to him.

"Move closer, Son. I have something I want to show you."

The Boy complied, sitting on the old couch, with its faded plaid print. Everything in the home was the same: serviceable, not tattered but faded by use and by age. They were neither poor nor rich, but his father had known the harshest kind of poverty, so they kept things until they died.

His father picked up a large book from the coffee table and placed it on his knees. There was a photograph on the front. A bunch of melting clock faces.

"Read what it says on the front aloud," his father instructed him.

"*The life and works of Salvador Dali,*" the Boy said, mispronouncing it as Dahl-eye. His father corrected him, and made him say it again.

"Dali was a painter. Some think he was nuts; many think he was brilliant. I think he was brilliant."

The Boy knitted his brows, looking for the lesson in this.

"You mean he was smart?"

"Smart is knowing your multiplication tables. Brilliant is casting a different light on the world."

The Boy frowned, struggling with the concept. "I don't get it," he admitted.

"Some people look out at the world and they see it differently from other people, Son. They try to share that sight with us, through paintings, or poetry, or the classical music we listen to sometimes."

"Like Beethoven? Like the Ninth?"

He loved the Ninth. In his plodding and single-minded life, it was light through a prison window. It made his blood move faster.

"Yes, exactly like that."

The Boy looked at the Dali book with new interest.

"And you're saying this man does the same thing with his paintings?"

"I'm saying he does the same thing for me with his paintings. You might not feel that way."

Confusion set in hard. In his world, Father was always right.

"That doesn't make any sense, sir. How can I see something differently from you?"

"I'm raising you to be strong, Son. There's a world out there full of ways to be weak. It's true, the road of strength is simple, single, and narrow, so in most things I teach you, there's just one way. You follow?"

"Of course."

"But when it comes to this," he gestured at the book, "or to the music or poetry, it's not as clear-cut. And that's okay." His father rubbed a hand across the book, a loving gesture that the Boy had never seen and rarely felt. "Dali's paintings talk to me. They may not talk to you. The point, though, what I'm trying to tell you, is that you need to find the ones that do."

The Boy pondered this, struggled with it, could come up with only one question.

"Why?"

His father turned to him, his gaze serious. "The basic key to survival isn't toughness, Son, it's speed. Thinking and doing and killing faster than others. You'll never be as fast as you can be unless you've found the ones that talk to you. I don't know why it's so, but it's so."

Why didn't you say that in the first place? is what the Boy thought but didn't say. "Find the one that talks to you, Son, because it'll make you quicker. But don't fall into the trap of thinking that it proves anything. It's an x-factor, like a vitamin that works but we don't know why. We read the poems, and we listen to the music, and they make us faster, but neither one is evidence of the soul." He leaned forward, like a dark tower, overwhelming the boy with his presence and his blackness. "There is no soul, Son. There's only meat. Never forget it."

"Yes, sir."

And he never did.

# CHAPTER TEN

I wake up exhausted but not unhappy. It's the wrung-out but comfortable feeling of satisfaction that comes from doing good work.

Some part of me had known, I suppose. I'd let certain things slide when it came to Bonnie, because of her past, and that was a mistake. I feel I'm on the right road to correcting that error.

Tommy is already gone from our bed. This is the case most mornings. He is one of those infernal morning people, who wakes at 6:00 A.M.—or earlier—and lands on both feet, ready to go. He likes to run in the morning, which is a nightmare scenario for me. Sometimes I'll wake up as he's putting on his sweats and watch with a single, bleary-but-appreciative eye.

I listen with an ear and sniff the air. I hear a faint murmur of voices from downstairs and smell the delicious aroma of frying bacon. It's enough of a motivation to get me out of bed. Tommy cooks a mean breakfast.

I stumble my way into the shower and turn it up to high and hot. This is my bliss place. Six years ago or so, Matt gave me a serious shower upgrade as a birthday gift. A contractor gutted the old vinyl one and installed a double-headed, temperature-controlled, marble-tile-and-glass wonder. There's even a seat, where I can sit and watch the steam build as I wake up or shave my legs. I love it every morning, and today is no exception.

Each showerhead has its own spray control. I put both on pulse, which delivers a wonderful light pounding spray. I stand and rock a little as the water pummels me, a somewhat goofy smile on my face.

If we do move to Virginia, installation of the same shower will have to be part of the deal.

My head is beginning to clear. Generally speaking, it takes me about thirty minutes to really arrive in the present. The shower gets the ball rolling and coffee seals the deal.

I wash my hair, turning one of the heads to spray, which delivers hard, almost sharp jets of water onto my scalp. The temperature is as hot as I can take it. Cold showers are for the insane.

I finish with some reluctance and proceed to get myself dressed. Black slacks, white shirt. I pad back to the bathroom and perform my bare nod to makeup. I've never been much of a makeup gal, less so now than before I was scarred. I pull my hair into a ponytail and secure it. Back to the room. Black jacket, flat pumps. Shoulder holster. Open the gun safe (need to remember to change the combo tonight, I think), grab my Glock, work the slide, then jam the magazine home. I triple-check the safety. I've been paranoid about this ever since I heard about an agent blowing two of his toes off. I pull the charger out of my cell phone and the phone gets clipped to my belt. My ID goes inside the inner pocket of the jacket. One final check in the bathroom mirror, and I decide I'm fit to face the world.

I grab my purse and head down the stairs. The breakfast smells are getting stronger, and my stomach rumbles in reply. The scent of coffee makes my nose twitch in anticipation.

Bonnie's heard me coming. She meets me at the bottom of the stairs with a fresh cup, something she hasn't done in a while. Guilt, I decide, has its upside.

"Thanks, honey."

"You're welcome." She looks a bit worn but stable. I have the idea she's feeling a similar exhaustion to mine—wrung out in the right way.

I sip the coffee and crinkle my eyes in an approving smile. "Yum." It earns another smile, and she goes to the kitchen and grabs three plates and glasses and utensils to set the kitchen table.

Tommy is working at the stove. He's wearing a red-checkered apron, a look and design that remind me of Betty Crocker cookbooks. I first saw him wear it in his own apartment. It was all he was wearing, and we barely made it through breakfast before I attacked him.

I walk over, stand next to him, and place a hand in the small of his back, that comfortable spot. He moves some bacon over onto a paper towel to drain the grease. It sizzles deliciously. "How do you want your eggs?" he asks. "Fried or scrambled?"

"Fried today, I think."

"We aim to please." He nods toward the refrigerator. "Bonnie fresh-squeezed some orange juice this morning."

"My favorite. Wow."

He gives the slightest shrug. "She's pretty helpful right now."

"Did you guys talk about last night at all?" I murmur, low enough that Bonnie can't hear me.

"Nope. I doubt we will either. But I think everything is okay, for now."

I lean against the counter and sip my coffee and watch as she sets the table. She catches me watching and gives me yet another tentative smile.

"Yes," I say to Tommy. "I think you're right."

"For now," of course, remains operative, but that's life.

"All ready," he announces, using the spatula to scoop everyone's eggs onto a serving plate. "Can you get the bacon?"

I transfer the now less-greasy bacon from paper towel to actual plate and carry it over to the dining table. Bonnie grabs the pitcher of OJ from the freezer. Tommy adds a plate of toast, checks everything over, and nods once, satisfied. "Let's eat," he says.

The room is filled with the sounds of people too busy eating to talk: clinking of utensils against china, the crunch of bacon being bitten into, the quiet slurp-and-swallow of orange juice and coffee disappearing into stomachs.

I'm on my second cup of coffee, and between the shower, the great breakfast, and the relative harmony of my home, I'm feeling awake and alert and refreshed. I eat the last of my eggs and push my plate forward.

I rub my stomach in an exaggerated way and roll my eyes heaven-ward. "Awesome." I sigh.

"I agree," Bonnie says. "You cook a good breakfast, Tommy."

"Mom told me a man who can cook would always make a favorable impression with the ladies. I guess she was right."

I check the clock. Bonnie will have to leave to catch the school bus in about thirty minutes. Time enough to tell them both about my offer from Director Rathbun. It's a bit of a skydive, but scheduling, for this family, is difficult.

"I have something you guys need to know about," I say. "Something I was offered." I give them the full rundown, leaving nothing out. When I finish, both of them are quiet. I scan their faces nervously, looking for any signs of upset.

"Well?" I ask. "What do you think?"

Tommy wipes the corner of his mouth with the paper towel in his hand. "Bonnie's the one with the time crunch," he says. "You and I can talk after she catches the bus."

I turn my attention to Bonnie. "So?"

"What would change?" she asks.

It's the perfect question, really. The key one.

"Well . . . I guess not much in the beginning. We'd still be living here." I frown. "No, that's not right, is it? We'd be covering the whole USA, so I imagine even though we'd be living here, I'd be traveling more. Kind of like last year, when I had to go to Virginia. Later, if this becomes permanent, we might have to move to Virginia."

She nibbles on her toast. "What's Virginia like?"

I don't have a detailed answer to this question. I spent twenty-one weeks in Quantico, Virginia, for my training, but I don't think Quantico is a good demographic. It's on 385 acres of woodland. Breathtakingly beautiful in the fall, surprisingly mild in the summer, at least when I was there. Humidity was higher than California, for sure, and rainfall was scattered but always welcome. I was gone before the winter.

"It has four seasons," I say. "Snow in the winter. Trees with the red and yellow leaves in the fall. Nice summer. Beautiful spring, I guess, though I wasn't there for that." I struggle to put words to the faint memories. "Everything feels older, but not in a rundown kind of way. California has a newer feeling to it. The East Coast has more weight."

"I'd like to see it," she says.

"Of course, honey. I promise, if this all comes to pass, we'll take a trip out there."

She brushes her hands off over her plate. "Okay, Mama-Smoky."

"Okay what, honey?"

"I'm okay if we have to move. And I think you should do this job."

"Why?"

"What you do is serious. It's important." Her voice is grave. She means what she's saying, maybe more than a thirteen-year-old should "mean" anything. "Your boss is right. You're the best person for the job. If that's true, then you have to take it. It's your duty. And it's my duty to help make it okay for you."

I have no immediate response to this. Duty? She throws the word out with certainty and intensity. It's another look into the direction her mind is growing, and it makes me wonder if agreeing to do this would be all wrong, after all.

"I haven't decided yet, but I'll let you know." I check the clock. "Time for you to go."

She collects her backpack and I walk her to the door. The bus stop is only a block away. She turns before she leaves and gives me a hug. "I love you, Mama-Smoky," she says.

This I can handle. I hug her back. "I love you too, baby. Don't forget what I said about the extracurricular activity."

"I won't, promise."

Then she's out the door and I watch until she disappears at the curve of our street. I close the door and sit back down at the table. Tommy has poured me another cup of coffee, bless him. He's nursing his own and gives me a little smile.

"She's something," he says.

"Something? What's with all the 'duty this' and 'duty that'? Sometimes I think it would be better if I hung it up altogether. Quit the FBI and just concentrated on her."

He studies the inside of his cup, takes a sip, then studies me. "I'll back your play whatever you decide, Smoky. You want to quit the FBI and be a mommy? I'm with you. You want to head up this strike team? I'm with you. If you don't want to work, we won't need your income, and if we move, money won't be a problem."

One of the things I found out about Tommy as our romance progressed was that he is, if not rich, financially stable. He isn't cheap, but he is thrifty. He struck out on his own as a security consultant after leaving the Secret Service and has done very, very well for himself. We can't rent private jets for weekend jaunts to Las Vegas, but money isn't a meaningful issue. I have my own assets too. The house was paid off by Matt's life-insurance settlement and is worth a lot more than what we originally paid for it, even with the current housing-market depression.

All of that is nice, but it's not what I need to hear from him.

"But what do you think I should *do,* Tommy?"

He smiles at me and reaches out a hand to stroke my cheek. "I think if you quit working you'll go crazy. It's still in your blood. One day it won't be, but for now it is. When I first joined the service, and for a long time after, that's how it was for me. I had to leave when I was ready. You're not ready."

"And Bonnie?"

He sips from his cup and looks off into the distance. "People don't come in boxes with ingredient listings, Smoky, so we'll never know for sure how Bonnie is going to turn out. That's life. There are a few things I do think. I think she needs to go to therapy. I understand why you haven't taken her there before, but it's time. In my opinion."

I sigh. "You're right. I just have trouble trusting anyone else when it comes to dealing with her."

"I know. But get over it."

"You said 'a few things.' What else?"

"What you did last night was on the money, Smoky. As long as you're on the case as her mother and don't let that slide, I think you'll be doing the right thing. I'm not convinced that it would be any better for Bonnie to have you around all the time, if you weren't working. In some ways, it might be worse."

"Why?" I ask, intrigued.

"She needs a balance. What happened to her, and to her mom, did happen. We can't unmake that. On the one hand, exposure to what you do runs the risk of keeping her attention on it too much, leading to things like the cat incident."

"But on the other hand?"

He shrugs. "On the other hand, I think watching you do what you do, seeing you put away the kind of men who killed her mom, is therapeutic. Cathartic. It gives her a goal. It's a balancing act, a darn shoddy one, but I think it's more helpful than harmful as long as we keep that balance."

I grin in spite of the gravity of the conversation; I can't help it. "'Darn shoddy'?" I tease. Tommy is a Boy Scout. Had literally been one. He never, ever uses profanity.

He doesn't respond to the humor. My stomach flutters a little at the determination in his eyes.

"I'll back you in either direction, Smoky, but I have one condition."

"What's that?" I ask, though I already know.

"If you decide to take the position, you tell them everything."

You don't even know what everything is, Tommy.

I keep this to myself. What he's asking is fair.

"Deal."

He shakes his head in the negative. "Don't be flip. I want your promise. Your oath."

Tommy flouts almost all of the Latin macho stereotypes, but now and again these oddities appear. Things like "your oath." I'd crack a joke about it if he wasn't so deadly serious.

Relationships are born of love but survive on compromise. Who was it who said that?

I reach over and take his hands in mine. Both are warm from our coffee cups.

"I promise."

# CHAPTER ELEVEN

"We have a hit on her fingerprints, honey-love."

It's the first thing I hear when I walk into the office. This is one of the good mornings, the well-organized kind. I am already well caffeinated and awake.

"Tell me," I say.

Alan and I had met in the parking lot and taken the elevator up together. James and Callie had arrived before us. Alan unscrews the top of his thermos and pours coffee into his mug. I gave him a coffee grinder for Christmas. He'd rolled his eyes at the time, joking that all the real cops grew up on Dunkin' Donuts and 7-Eleven coffee, but not long after he'd started bringing the thermos.

"I'm a junkie now," he'd confessed. "After fresh ground, everything else tastes like crap."

"Her name is Heather Hollister," Callie says.

I frown. "Why does that name seem familiar?"

"Because," she continues, "Heather Hollister was a homicide detective. From our very own LAPD. She disappeared eight years ago, without a trace. No body was ever found."

"I remember that case," Alan says, nodding. "Eight years? Jesus Christ."

I remember it too. "It was big news," I say, "and not just in the law-enforcement community. She was married, right?"

"That's correct," James pipes in. "Husband worked for an Internet service provider. His name is"—he consults his notes—"Douglas Hollister. They had twin sons, Avery and Dylan. They were two at the time." He looks up from his notes. "They're ten now."

It's an unnecessary statement, but I understand why he says it. James is human, however hard he tries to hide it. The concept of this woman being held for eight years is difficult to grasp. Her children provide the necessary contrast.

Avery and Dylan were two when she went away. They would have been riding tricycles and speaking in small sentences, disobeying and acting out, like all two-year-olds. When she disappeared, they were still three years away from kindergarten. Now they're closing in on the fifth grade or are already there.

I force myself to focus. "What do we know about the investigation that was done at the time?" I ask.

"Not much, I'm afraid," Callie says. "The FBI assisted, of course, but the primary investigation was headed by LAPD."

Of course it was. Heather was one of their own. No way they were ceding that to anyone else.

"Do we have any news on Heather's status?" I ask.

"I called the hospital from home," Alan says. "She's quiet now, so they're no longer sedating her. She still hasn't spoken."

I chew on a thumbnail, a bad habit that replaced smoking. I think it's a pretty good trade.

"Callie and James, I want you to collect all the case files from that investigation. Do not, under any circumstances, tell anyone why we want them or release her name to the family yet."

"Why?" Callie asks.

"Because," James says, already keeping pace with me. "Everything points to either someone who knew her or collusion with someone who knew her. How else do you take a trained homicide detective without leaving a trace?"

"Understood," Callie says. "What are you and Alan going to be doing?"

"We're going to go and see Heather Hollister at the hospital. Maybe knowing her name will help us reach her. She's the best witness we've got."

James stands up and heads toward the door.

"Wait!" Callie cries.

Everyone stops.

She smiles a sly smile. "Aren't any of you going to ask me how my honeymoon night went?"

James scowls. "Stop wasting time."

"Ready?" I ask Alan.

He downs the last of his coffee, rolling his eyes heavenward in what I could swear is a brief prayer of thanks. He caps his thermos and stands up. "Ready," he says.

Callie is pouting. I pat her on the cheek. "None of us is going to ask because we all know how it went," I tell her.

She sniffs once, but seems mollified and follows James out the door.


Alan and I are driving to the hospital, both lost in our own thoughts.

We have an almost exact time period to put to Heather Hollister's imprisonment. Eight years. It's mind-boggling. Too much to take in. I think of all the changes just in my own life in that time and I am aghast. She's missed everything.

I imagine there's an empty coffin in a cemetery somewhere, perhaps filled with trinkets placed there by her family, friends, and coworkers. A headstone, maybe? What would it say? *Heather Hollister, beloved wife and mother? Mother and wife?* Which comes first—the eternal battle.

"You want to talk to her, or should I?" Alan asks.

"Let's see who she responds to first. If she responds at all."

He nods his agreement.

Eight years. That explains the scars. The doctor said that she was sun-deprived. Did that mean he'd kept her in the dark the whole time? A shiver runs through me.

How would I deal with that? Eight years shackled in the dark?

"Badly," I murmur, before realizing I've said it aloud.

"What's that?" Alan asks.

"I was wondering how I'd deal with eight years of prison with no sun."

"Yeah."

The sun is pale, which reminds me of Heather Hollister's dusty alabaster skin. I decide to change the subject. "Did you give any more thought to the whole strike team thing?" I ask Alan.

"'Course I did. Talked to Elaina too."

"And?"

"She agrees. I'll stick with you on the start-up, if you decide to do it. After that, we'll see. No promises."

"Thanks, Alan," I say, and I mean it.

He gives me a sidelong glance. "You decided yet?"

"Not officially."

He smiles at my answer. "So that's a yes, then?"

"It's a probably."

"If you say so."

I stick my tongue out at him. "You know, it's funny, but I can't help thinking about the early women in the FBI."

"Duckstein and Davidson."

My mouth drops open. "You know about them?"

He fakes affront. "Hey, I have depth, you know."

"And Lenore Houston."

"Right."

Alaska Davidson, Jessie Duckstein, and Lenore Houston served in the "Bureau of Investigation" before it was known as the Federal Bureau of Investigation. J. Edgar Hoover took over the FBI in 1924. By 1928, all three were gone, at Hoover's behest. They were the last female agents until 1972, when Hoover died. Things are different now. More than two thousand women serve, and gender lines are largely blurred. Results speak loudest, doing what we do.

"I remember reading about those three women and how angry it made me."

"It should have. They got it even worse than the black man, and that's saying something. There weren't many, but even African American agents were doing investigations in the twenties, thirties, and forties."

"Now we've had an African American president who fought a woman to get the Democratic nomination," I muse. "Things change. I'm always kind of proud each time something like that happens for women. If that makes sense."

"'Course it does. I count coup sometimes myself. We're here," he says, turning into the hospital parking lot.

Counting coup, I think. Great phrase.

I whisk everything else from my mind and focus on the problem of Heather Hollister. We need to see if we can get her to talk to us.

We're in her hospital room, sitting next to her bed. I'm a little bit closer than Alan. Odds are, it was a man who did this to her. She might feel safest with a woman.

Her eyes are open, but I'm not sure if they're really seeing anything. They are roving, in constant, endless, nervous motion, flicking from my face to the fluorescent bulbs above her to the barred window on her left that lets in the light. It's outside that her gaze goes to most, I observe.

"Heather?" I ask. "Heather Hollister?"

The eyes flick at me, but she doesn't answer or show any signs of recognition. Her pallor is still ghostly. It's not the clean white of poured milk; there are too many scars. New scabs cover her shaved scalp and forearms, which will heal and then turn into scars of their own.

I watch as she chews her lower lip, biting hard enough once to draw blood. She winces and stops biting. A moment later, the behavior repeats. She breathes with her mouth open—quick, shallow breaths. The breathing reminds me of a cat in a hot car I saw at the mall one time. It was July, and the summer that year was sweltering. The cat was panting like a dog, and its eyes were rolling. The solution then was easy: I smashed the car window and removed the cat. I left a note saying I was from the FBI and giving my name and cell phone number and why I'd smashed the window. I said I was taking the cat to a no-kill shelter and even gave the address of the shelter. I never heard from the owner of the car, and neither did the shelter. The cat was adopted.

No windows here, I think, and she's no cat.

"Heather?" I try again.

She laughs, an awful braying laugh, like a donkey trying to speak human. I jerk back, startled by its suddenness. It stops just as suddenly, and the eyes go back to roving. Her right hand goes to her left forearm, and she starts picking.

"No, no, honey," I say, keeping my voice as soft and soothing as I can. I reach over to move her hand away.

"*Nooooo!*" she screams, jerking away from me. Her mouth opens a little and she juts her chin out. It's meant to be a gesture of defiance. It makes her look primitive, cavewomanish. I pull my hand away.

"Sorry," I say.

She starts picking again. The eyes go back to roving.

"She's not ready," Alan says.

I want him to be wrong, but I know he's right. Some part of me—the selfish, ugly part—wants to shake her, tell her to snap out of it. It only lasts a second, though.

I reach into my purse and find a business card. I show it to Heather. "This is my card, Heather. It has my name and my number on it. I'm from the FBI, and I want to find the man who did this to you. When you're ready to talk, just ask for me." I stand up and lay the card on her bedside table, at the base of the humongous lamp. "Let's go," I say to Alan.

I don't think she even notices that we've left the room.

"What's the verdict, Doctor?" I ask.

Dr. Mills appears to be a decent guy. He's in his mid-to-late thirties, balding early, and he looks like he's probably tired all the time, but I sense genuine care there. I tend to be sensitive to that kind of thing.

"She's got various vitamin and calcium deficiencies. We're working to correct those. She needs to put on some weight. Aside from that, she has no other major physical problems. I expect her to bounce back." He sighs. "Mentally? That's another story. I've asked for a psych consult, which will happen this afternoon. She's obviously in the middle of a psychotic episode. I'm fine keeping her where she's at temporarily, but she needs medication and psychiatric help."

"What about the picking thing?" I ask. "Biting her lips?"

"I'm actually encouraged by that."

Alan frowns. "Come again?"

"She stops after doing superficial harm to herself. Look, I've had people in here who have cut off their own noses; I had a guy who said he was a reincarnation of van Gogh, which is why he'd chopped off both of his ears with a set of gardening shears and sent them to the object of his affection. Heather knows when to stop. That's a good sign."

"You'll let us know of any change? I left my card on her bedside table."

"Of course. And please find out if she had a general practitioner. If I can get her old medical records, I'd appreciate it."

Alan stops and turns as we're walking away. "Two ears? I thought van Gogh only cut off one?"

Dr. Mills shrugs. It's a tired shrug, to go with his tired face. "He said just one didn't work last time."

Callie calls me as we're getting onto the freeway. She talks as I watch the hills of burned grass and fire-withered trees roll by. The last few years of wildfires have been especially hard on Southern California.

"Heather Hollister's partner on the job died of a heart attack last year," she begins, "but I have the case files."

"What did you tell the locals?"

"I told them that profiling was an ever-evolving science and that we're going over old cases with a new eye in the hopes that we'd see something we missed before."

"Where are you now?"

"About twenty minutes from the office."

I check the exit sign to see where we are. "We'll see you there in thirty." I hang up. "Callie got the case files," I tell Alan.

He nods. "Good. Let's get some meat on this bone. I feel like a dog gnawing air."

# CHAPTER TWELVE

Callie holds the case file as she sits in her desk chair. Alan nurses his coffee, while James sits with both arms on his desk, hands folded, like a schoolboy. I'm standing at the dry-erase whiteboard, marker in hand.

This is one of our methods, started on the first day of the first case we all worked together. I remember that day now, for some reason. I was nervous, not quite thirty, uncertain. I'd been involved with the FBI for years, my responsibilities steadily increasing, but this had been a quantum leap. I was now a boss, in charge of life and death and catching the creatures so concerned with these things in Los Angeles. I felt vulnerable and terrified.

I'd overdressed, wearing an expensive tailored blue business outfit, which I never wore again. James had just shocked me with some caustic remark. Alan was huge and imposing and not yet friendly, because he was checking me out, trying to decide if he should be taking orders from an agent with a lot less experience than he had. Callie was . . . well, Callie. Quick-tongued and more beautiful than I'd ever be. As a team, we started out slow and halting, gears grinding like a teenager's first attempt to drive a stick shift. It took some time, but we found our rhythm. The board became our shared mind.

"Let's start at the beginning," I say. "Tell us about Heather. What kind of cop was she?"

Laying out a case graphically like this helps us see the whole picture. It's not unusual to walk into this office and find all of us sitting, staring at the whiteboard like it's a religious artifact.

*"Heather Hollister,"* Callie reads. *"Got a BA in criminology and then went into the police academy. Graduated a week after her twenty-third birthday."*

"Thinking ahead with the criminology BA," Alan notes. "Helps later when she applies for detective. Smart."

"Or driven," I say. "She was certain she wanted to be a cop right out of high school. Civic-minded or something else?" I look at Callie. "Anything in her file?"

Callie flips through Heather's personnel file. She nods. "There is something here from her psych eval. Her father. He owned a tire shop in Hollywood. He was killed during a robbery when Heather was twelve." Callie sighs. "My, my. Mother solved the need for income by remarrying an abusive husband. He beat on her regularly—her name was Margaret—until Heather was sixteen. Heather had the presence of mind to take video of her stepfather beating up her mother. She took the video to the detective who'd been investigating her father's murder." She pauses, reading ahead.

"And?" James asks, impatient.

"Hold thy horses. Things get murky here. Something about . . . apparently the video was thrown out of court because of the way she acquired it. . . . Margaret wouldn't testify against her abuser . . ." She frowns, reads on a little further, and then her face clears. "Ah. There's a notation here from the evaluator. A paraphrased snippet of conversation.

"So what happened to your stepfather?" "He went away." "He died?" (SUBJECT SMILES HERE) "No. Detective Burns talked to him and he decided to leave us alone after that."

Callie looks up from the file, smiling.

"I can read between the lines," Alan says. "Detective Burns, and maybe some of his friends, had a talk with the stepfather that probably involved severe bruising and promises to make his life a living hell if he didn't clear out. Street justice."

I write two things on the whiteboard: *Became a cop because father killed.* And: *Detective Burns connection.*

"We need to find Burns," I say. "He took an interest in the family, Heather in particular. He'll have insight." Something else occurs to me. "Did the psych ask Heather if the stepfather ever abused her too?"

Callie puts her finger on the page and skims through the notes. Stops. "Yes, he asked. She said no. She said he basically ignored her. Mommy got all his love."

"Lucky," James says. "Statistically, she was at risk of sexual abuse."

All debate and bias aside, stepchildren are more likely to be the victims of abuse than genetic children. It's called the "Cinderella effect," and, though controversial, I've seen it proven out in my own experience. Younger children are the ones most likely to suffer heavy physical abuse to the point of death, while older children are the biggest targets of sexual abuse.

"Did they ever solve her father's murder?" Alan asks.

Callie flips back through pages in the file. "No."

"And?" I ask. "Did the evaluator take that up?"

"Oh yes. It was a big concern for him." She flips pages, one and then another. "He spent quite a bit of time on it."

"What was his conclusion?"

"He concluded that her father's death had driven her to become a police officer but that he was satisfied it wasn't an obsession. The usual blah de blah about how the police force, as a group, had become her father figure. The matriarchy—Mom—had betrayed her, so she identified with a largely patriarchal group like law enforcement."

"I see some truth to that," James says.

"She was driven," I say, "but not obsessive. Driven to what?"

James considers the question. "Competence, for one," he answers. "Competence, as a law-enforcement officer, would be very important. She empathizes with the victims, so shoddy work would be anathema to her."

"Her sense of injustice would be highly developed," I say, picking up the thread, "the little guy getting the short end of the stick. Really, if you think about it, she'd have to be obsessive to some degree. Not about her father's murder, maybe, but any case she was on would get her full attention. Unsolveds would weigh on her. She'd be the kind of cop who takes case files home with her."

"All of which bears out in her personnel history," Callie says. "She was in patrol for the required four years and did very well. Numerous commendations, almost all of them unsolicited and from citizens. The only complaints from that time are from other cops."

"Detectives, right?" Alan asks.

Callie looks up at him, surprised. "That's right. How did you know?"

"I know the kind of cop she was. See, patrol is usually first on the scene, but they're not investigative. It's their job to contain things and turn it over to the relevant detective squad. Patrol does all the grunt work, but they're not generally a part of the investigation." He shrugs. "You get a cop like Hollister, she's a pit bull. Gets her teeth in and can't let go. She feels like the detectives aren't giving a case the attention it needs, she bugs them about it. Maybe she goes out and does interviews she wasn't asked to do or digs up some new evidence. Some cops appreciate that. It's all about the solve, the victim, so no problem." He grimaces in distaste. "But you get the few assholes that are caste-oriented. It's about territory and status, and they don't appreciate someone in patrol doing more than what they're supposed to, regardless of results." He smiles. "They usually go on to become police commissioners."

"What happened after the four years in patrol?" I ask.

"She was promoted to detective. She started in juvenile crimes and was there for almost two years. She went from there to vice."

"Mom to whore," Alan says. "Nice to know some things haven't changed since I was in the LAPD."

"What do you mean?" I ask.

"She got put into juvenile crimes because she was a woman. They figure women will relate to the kids better because women are mommies, so forth. Then she was put into vice, which can be a great unit to build a jacket with, but I can guarantee you she didn't start on the plum side. They stuck in her some thigh-high boots and a miniskirt, and she was out there catching johns."

"True," Callie confirms, "but our pit bull didn't let that stop her. She forged relationships with other prostitutes over a year period. She parlayed that into a medium-size bust of a human-trafficking ring. People took note, and somehow she ended up in homicide."

"Burns," Alan says.

"The detective?" I ask.

He nods. "He was her hook into homicide. She had the chops, of course, but that's almost never enough. You need someone watching out for you too. Putting in the good word. I'd bet money that for her, that was Burns."

"Be that as it may," Callie continues, "homicide is where Heather really hit her stride. She had a very good solve rate." She raises her eyebrows in appreciation. "Very good. She was promoted to second grade on merit within six years." She looks up from the file. "Just before she went missing."

"How old is she?" I ask, wondering why I hadn't asked this question before.

Callie consults the file. "She's a hair past forty-four."

"If she's been gone for eight years," James notes, "she was abducted when she was thirty-six. Her sons were two, meaning she waited until she was thirty-four to have them."

"Not so old," I say.

"No," he allows, "but it keeps with the profile of career coming first. She waited until she'd been in homicide for almost four years. Until her position was secure."

"Tell me about her marriage," I say.

Callie goes back to the file. "Douglas Hollister. Systems administrator for a nationwide Internet service provider. One year older than Heather. They met when she was twenty-six and she was still in uniform. His car had been stolen; she was the reporting officer. They were married two years later."

"Was he looked at in the initial investigation?" James asks. "He should have been."

In all crimes against persons, you investigate family first. Sad but true.

Callie puts down Heather's personnel file and picks up one of five large folders.

"Those all case files?" Alan asks.

"Yes," Callie replies.

He whistles. "They pulled out the stops."

Callie opens the file and leafs through it. Finds something and stops. "The investigating officer was . . ." She stops, surprised. "My, my. The investigating officer was none other than Detective Daryl Burns." She continues reading. "Yes, it appears he zeroed in on the husband. The husband even filed a complaint at one point."

"Why?" Alan asks. "Besides the obvious reasons?"

"There was trouble on the home front, apparently. During the initial interview, Hollister had said that all was well and lovely in the marriage. That was a lie. Burns found that Hollister had been consulting with a divorce attorney and that Heather had hired a private investigator."

"The investigator turn up anything?" Alan asks.

Callie pulls a letter-size manila envelope from the file and opens it. She removes the contents and lays them on her desk. We all crowd around. It's a stack of photographs, 8×10 black-and-whites, five in total. They show a man entering a hotel room with a woman. As they enter, he's wearing a tie and a furtive look. As they exit, he's laughing with the woman, and the tie is stuffed in his side jacket pocket.

"Douglas Hollister, I presume," Callie murmurs.

I pick up one of the photos showing him from the front and study it. He's a handsome enough man, in an unremarkable way. Short hair, suit fits well enough to tell me he goes to the gym. He has a pleasant, easy smile. It's the kind of smile that women like, because it belongs on a solid, trustworthy man.

The woman is attractive as well, though not breathtaking. I'd guess she's about the same age as Douglas Hollister, with a little weight around the middle and a hairstyle that's five years too old. She's looking up at him as he laughs.

"She adores him," I say. I show the picture to James. He nods.

"This was a love thing, not a fling," Callie says, after her own observation. "She's not a young hottie-body. Definitely housewife, not coed."

I flip the photo over and see a date stamp there. "When was Heather abducted?"

"April twentieth," Callie replies.

"One month after these photos were taken," I say. "I can see why Burns was suspicious."

I walk back over to the whiteboard and write on it: *Husband/Affair,*

*PI photos one month before abduct.* Then: *Husband consid. divorce, consults attny.*

"Let's get back to the husband. I want to hear about the abduction."

"*Subject's car was found in gym parking lot, eleven fifty-three P.M. Car keys discovered on the pavement, near the door. No other signs of struggle. No witnesses.*"

"She had the keys in her hand, ready to enter her car when she was taken," James observes. "He surprised her."

"What was she doing there?" I ask Callie.

"Once-a-week kickboxing–cardio class."

"When did the class end? Does it say?"

"Of course it does, honey-love. They traveled down all the same mental paths as you. The class began at seven and ended at eight. The gym was only ten minutes away, and according to the husband she was always prompt in returning home. When she hadn't answered her cell phone or arrived home by eleven o'clock, he called her partner."

I raise an eyebrow. "Three hours? Why'd he wait so long?" I pause. "Ah. Right. I'll bet he said that he wasn't all that worried because she was a cop."

"Point to you," Callie confirms.

"Where'd she park?" I ask.

"It doesn't say."

"And no one noticed anything?"

"No. Too busy feeling the burn, I suppose."

I shake my head. "Whoever took her was confident and accomplished. Maybe overconfident, certainly a risk taker. A well-lit parking lot not long after the class let out? Daring."

"Strike the *well-lit*," Callie says. "They noted that all three of the lights nearest where Heather was parked were out. Expertly vandalized."

I turn to Alan. "She's a cop. How would she think and how would he use that against her?"

He ponders this. "It's a tough one. She worked homicide, so she'd know that the moment she climbed into a vehicle with him, her chances of survival would be lowered. I guess if I were him . . . I'd stick a gun in her back and tell her if she said a word, I'd shoot her. Cops know better than anyone that you listen to a man with a gun. You cooperate and wait for an opening."

"He'd obviously studied her life or had been given details about it by the husband," James says. "He could have used those against her. *My partner has your husband and kids at home. Come with me quietly or they die.* Pure conjecture, but the point being, there are ways."

"Still daring," I say.

"Yes and no," James replies. "Sunset in April is seven-fifteen, seven-thirty, or thereabouts. It would have been dark; he'd taken the lights out. The women coming out of the class would be tired, thinking about getting safely to their own vehicles and home. How many rapes occur in supermarket or shopping center lots after dark?"

"Tons," I admit.

"Their attention would be on themselves and making a beeline to their cars. He comes up to Heather, puts a gun to her back, and employs quiet but convincing verbal threats to get her into his vehicle. He would have told her to act natural, not to make a sound." He shrugs. "Daring, yes, but not the riskiest plan possible if he was confident and aggressive."

"She probably dropped the keys herself in that scenario," I say. "She'd know her car would be found and that the keys would make it clear it was an abduction."

I mark the relevant info on the whiteboard. "What happened next?" I ask Callie.

"Too much of nothing, I'm afraid. It's as if Heather vanished into thin air." She flips a page. "It seems the detective on the case dismissed the idea that it was random fairly quickly."

"Why?" I ask.

"I'm not sure, but—" She sweeps a hand to indicate the piled folders. "There's lots more to read. They went after the husband very hard, but there was nothing to hang him with. No trace of money transfers to or from accounts belonging to him. Nothing found on any of his computers or laptops, either at work or at home. There were large-sum life-insurance policies on both of them, but neither had been taken out recently."

"Was she ever declared dead?" James asks.

Callie flips through the folder pages. She finds nothing in the first or second folder, then stops near the end of the third. "There's a note, newer than the rest. From a year ago. The husband had her legally declared dead seven years after her disappearance. And get this: He collected on the life insurance just two months ago. Seven hundred thousand dollars plus."

"And then she reappears?" I say. "Some coincidence."

It's not, of course. I walk over to the board and write: *Wife held until life insurance payout/then reappears.* I circle it. Twice.

"Did the husband get remarried?" I ask.

"Yes indeedy," Callie says, smiling a shark smile. "To she of hotel-room-photo fame. Three years after his wife went missing."

*Husband marries mistress,* I write, then: *PATIENT* in big block letters. I circle it two times as well.

"He did it," I say, "or he's in collusion with whoever did."

"Amen to that," Alan says.

*Follow the line of inquiry,* the note had said. That's starting to make sense.

"James, Callie, I want you to go through these files with a fine tooth comb. Put together a detailed timeline and a database of all the relevant information. I'm looking for something that will give us the basis for a new warrant."

"This is so much better than Bora-Bora," Callie mutters.

"Alan, you and I are going to go and see Douglas Hollister. Somehow I don't think the reappearance of Heather was a part of his plans. Let's drop that bomb on him and see how high he jumps."

"Good idea."

My cell phone rings. "Barrett."

"Smoky." It's AD Jones. "I need you to come up to my office. Pronto."

"Yes, sir." I hang up. "Okay," I say, "who has answers for me about the whole strike-team scenario? Alan, you and I have already talked. James?"

He scowls at me. "Were you deaf last night? I already said: The reasoning is sound, and whatever you decide is fine with me." He goes back to the file he'd already begun to dig through.

I mime a neck-wringing gesture in his general direction. "Callie?"

"I talked to my new husband. After softening him up with my—"

"Hey!" Alan warns.

"—cooking," Callie says, batting her eyelashes at him. "Why, what did you think I was going to say? Anyhoo, we both agreed, I'm in at the beginning. If it comes to moving to Quantico, we'll have to reevaluate." She tilts her head and eyes me with speculation. "What have you decided?"

"I don't know. Thanks, though. All of you."

"As if we'd leave you to flounder on your own," Callie chides. "You should know better than that."

"Well, thanks." I turn and head to the door leading out of the office.

"Cooking?" I hear Alan say. "My ass."

"Actually," Callie purrs, "it was my ass that was cooking, honey-love."

# CHAPTER THIRTEEN

"Sit down," AD Jones tells me.

He's already seated. It's the same battered leather chair he's had since I've known him. It matches the man. If forced to come up with a single word to describe my boss, it would be *workhorse*. He lives to do what he does, to plow the fields. He doesn't do it for the glory. He does it for the pleasure of a well-placed furrow.

"I thought I had forty-eight hours, sir," I say, once seated.

He waves his hand. "I wanted to talk to you myself. Without the director here. Sorry to blindside you like that, by the way."

"I figured you were probably as surprised as I was, sir."

He bobs his head. "I was. The director showed up, serious-faced and sans entourage, aside from that grim reaper he calls an assistant." He hesitates. "I put the screws to him on this, Smoky. I wanted to make sure it was on the up and up and not just a political power play on his part."

"And?"

"At his position, everything is political to some degree. But I'm convinced his motives are what he said they were. He wants to preserve what we can of the NCAVC network. You can take it relatively at face value."

"Okay."

"The reason I wanted to see you, though, is to give you a little primer. Some schooling. If you decide to take him up on his offer, and I think you probably should, he'll be running you personally. There will be things about that that are good, and there will be things that are bad. Then there'll be things that you'll need to watch out for."

"Let's start with the good, sir."

He grins. The AD has always had a great smile; it takes at least ten years off his face. "Well, no one's going to want to fuck with you. The resources of the FBI will be open to you. The director is going to have a vested interest in the success of the team, and I can guarantee you that everyone will know that ahead of time. Expect red-carpet treatment and a better budget than you're used to."

"Sounds pretty good so far."

"You'll have a lot more altitude in general. That pays dividends in many ways. Power is power. Which leads us into the bad."

"I was really enjoying the good, but okay."

"Power and position bring envy. There will be people who resent you and your team being given what they'll view as a plum assignment. They'll be rooting for your failure and watching you very closely. Misstep, and I can guarantee you that someone will be there to report it. On the darker side, you should watch out for actual sabotage of your efforts. I'm not talking about big, destructive stuff. Think death by a thousand cuts. Little fuckups or bumps in the road of coordination that are designed to make you look bad."

"Seriously?"

"You've been lucky enough to work in a good environment, with a good team and a good boss. You haven't had to deal with enemies on the job. That's going to change, and if you don't accept it and watch out for it, you'll get eaten up."

I sit back and consider this. It's a lot to take in, but I know better than to doubt the AD. He's rarely, if ever, given me bad advice.

"What else?" I ask.

"The director might be the most ruthless man I've ever met. He's a political animal, but I can tolerate him because he's a cop too. He knows the reality of what we do, and I admire what he's trying to put together here. But you need to remember one thing, Smoky. If it ever comes down to a him-or-you proposition, he'll give you up in a heartbeat. Gunshots at dawn and no cigarette." He leans back. "Which is why you need to keep an eye on him and put aside a little leverage if you can find it."

"Leverage? You mean blackmail."

"No, I mean leverage. This is the FBI, Smoky. We don't blackmail anyone." He winks at me. "Let's just say, if you're lucky enough to witness the director bending the rules or cutting corners, however frivolously, it's my opinion you should document it and stick it in a floor safe somewhere."

I stare at him. "Jesus, sir. What kind of world do you live in?"

He sighs, rubs his face with both hands. "Not all sociopaths are serial killers. Some of them are politicians and administrators. Granted, the director doesn't fall into that category, but there are plenty at that level who do."

From a purely psychological standpoint, it makes sense. Narcissists are drawn to positions of power and prestige.

I venture a smile. "Appreciate the reassurance, sir."

The youth-creating grin returns. "You'll be fine. You're tough enough, smart enough. I never expected you'd work under me forever. You're overdue to move on up."

"Well, I haven't decided yet, sir."

He squints at me. "Save the bullshit for those who don't know better." He reaches into his back pocket and pulls out his wallet. He extracts a hundred-dollar bill. "I'll bet you a hundred bucks you take the position. If you don't, I pay up."

I glance down at the bill held out in offering. I look away. "No thanks," I mumble.

He cups a hand to his ear. "Sorry? What's that?"

"Give me a break, sir."

He puts the bill away and returns the wallet to his back pocket.

"Last thing, and then on to current business." There's a change in his demeanor, a slight softening that's rare to see in this man. AD Jones is an old-school guy, strong and silent, share your feelings with the mirror, hide them from everyone else. "If you ever need anything—advice, someone to talk to—come and find me."

"Thank you, sir. That means a lot."

"Of course, when the time comes, you'll have to stop calling me 'sir' and start using my first name."

"That's a tough one."

"Start practicing. Now, bring me up to speed on the woman who crashed Callie's wedding."

I tell him everything. He's silent throughout, as he usually is, listening to the whole story before asking questions of his own.

"You haven't told anyone yet who she is?"

"No, sir. Alan and I are planning to go and drop the bomb on the husband this afternoon."

"Negative. You go and brief this detective—what's his name?"

"Burns."

"See him first. He has personal connections to both your victim and your suspect. He might be able to help you get both of them talking."

It's good advice. "Yes, sir."

"Keep me in the loop. And let me know when you're ready to give the director your decision."

Back in the office, Callie and James are buried in the files. James is on the computer while Callie dictates a timeline to him.

"Ready to go?" Alan asks me.

"Change of plans." I explain.

He nods his approval. "The AD's right. It makes sense."

"Yes. But I'd prefer to meet him outside the precinct. I want to keep this under the radar. Heather's ordeal is going to be a huge story, and the last thing she needs right now is a pack of media wolves baying at her hospital-room door."

"True. I'll get him on the phone. Maybe we can meet him for waffles."

Alan's love of waffles is as pure and constant as Callie's love of miniature chocolate donuts.

As he makes the call, I walk over to the whiteboard and ponder the facts we know. Heather Hollister has lost everything. Eight years have passed. Her husband is remarried; her sons are three years away from being teenagers. The world has changed. When she was abducted, September 11 had not yet happened. We were not at war in Iraq. There were no hybrid vehicles on the road. Most people still accessed the Internet via dial-up.

Which would I prefer, I wonder? Eight years trapped in darkness and coming out to find Matt remarried and Alexa in college? Or what I have now?

I shift from one foot to the other, uncomfortable that my answer is not immediate. If I am a selfless mother, shouldn't I wish Alexa alive under any circumstances?

Her face comes to me, the morning of the day she died. It was at breakfast. She was eating her cornflakes. Matt had woken up late and was still in the shower.

"Daddy's lazy this morning," she said.

"Late's not the same as lazy, honey. And don't talk with your mouth full."

A mischievous look passed over her face, and she suddenly grinned, so that streams of milk and bits of cornflakes ran from the corners of her mouth. "Garrrr!" she cried.

"Gross!" I said, laughing in spite of myself.

She got the giggles, resulting in milk coming out of her nose, resulting in howls of laughter. We were still snorting by the time Matt got downstairs.

"What's going on?" he asked, bemused.

"Nothing," I said. "We were just talking about how lazy you are."

"Laaaaaaaaaazy Daddy," Alexa said, giggling some more.

Pragmatism had taken over not long after that. Matt and I needed to get to work; Alexa needed to get to school. A day like any other. But I like to think I would have remembered that morning, whether it was the last one we all shared or not. It was a good memory, whatever the context of time.

Alan puts down the phone. "He's going to meet us at the IHOP in Hollywood in an hour. Best waffles so far, there."

I follow him out, glancing one final time at the whiteboard.

Yes, I think, happy to find certainty in my answer. I'd take eight years of isolation if it meant Alexa was still alive. I really would.

I can only hope that Heather Hollister will find a similar comfort.

# CHAPTER FOURTEEN

"She's really alive?"

Daryl Burns is sixty years old and looks every minute of it. He's got short, thinning white hair and a jowly, hound-dog face, which is pock-marked with acne scars. Nature dealt him a sloppy look; he's countered by being a neat, impeccable dresser. The suit is off-the-rack quality—no surprise on a detective's salary—but he's obviously had it tailored. His shirt is pressed and his shoes are shined. He's about five-nine and has kept himself in shape. I look for a wedding ring. The finger is bare.

"We ran her fingerprints, Detective," I reassure him. "It's her."

He leans back against the booth seat and runs a hand through his hair. "Jesus," he says. He takes a sip from his coffee. We'd both de-clined the waffles, but Alan got a stack of four and is downing them while he watches Burns.

"I have to warn you. She's not in good shape. It's one of the things we could use your help with."

"What do you mean?"

"Her experience has left her in a psychotic episode. She's awake, but she's uncommunicative and we're not really sure if she's aware of her environment. Agent Washington and I tried to talk to her but got nowhere. You have a personal connection."

His eyes sharpen. "Why me? Why not the ex-husband?"

"Like you, we think the husband was involved. The fact that she's appeared just two months after he collected on her life insurance can't be a coincidence."

"It's not. He did it or he had it done. That's one thing I've been certain of from day one." It's said in a flat tone, a statement of fact.

"We're going to go scare the shit out of him shortly," Alan says after swallowing a mouthful of syrup-soaked waffles.

Burns's grin is unpleasant. "I'd love to see that."

"Come along, then," I say. "But I'd like to keep things quiet for now."

"I can agree with that. Heather doesn't need any cameras in her face."

Alan pushes away his now-empty plate somewhat wistfully. "I worked in LAPD," he says to Burns. "Ten years."

Burns nods. "I heard of you. Good things."

"I'd like to take the lead on questioning Douglas Hollister, if that's okay with you."

We don't really have to include the LAPD at this point. AD Jones had agreed with my original assessment—Heather was basically an unsolved kidnapping, and the fact that she'd been brought to Callie's wedding was an arguable threat to FBI personnel—but from the beginning, my team has always taken a cooperative stance with local law enforcement.

"Appreciate you asking. As long as I get to watch him sweat, I'm happy."

This dance aside, Alan dabs his lips with a napkin, crushes it into a ball, and tosses it onto his empty plate. "What can you tell us about everything?"

Burns laughs. "Everything?"

"You've known her and her family since she was twelve," I say. "You were the lead in the investigation when she was abducted at the age of thirty-six. You probably have the longest continual relationship with her of anyone besides her mother."

"Including her mother, actually. She died three years ago."

One more thing she's lost forever.

"Point is," Alan continues for me, "we don't know what's going to end up being important. We take everything we can get and sort out the good from the bad."

"I understand." Burns takes a sip from his coffee. His gaze is fixed on something from the past. "I met Heather when she was twelve. I was twenty-eight at the time. I'd been in homicide for two years, on the force for eight."

"Quick rise," Alan observes.

"I had a hook," Burns agrees. "My father was a cop. His ex-partner headed up robbery–homicide." Another sip of coffee. "The thing I remember is how different she was from her mother. I don't like to speak ill of the dead, but the mom was always weak. It was just one of those things you could tell, you know?"

"Yeah."

"Not Heather, though. She was strong. She was grieving, but she was also angry. Got in my face from the get-go. Didn't want to know *if* I was going to get the guy who shot her father, but *when*. Asked for my card and my number and told me she'd be calling regularly—which she did."

"What did you tell her when she called?" Alan asked.

He sighs. "A whole lotta nothing. We didn't have anything to go on. Her dad owned the store and was working alone. No witnesses. It was a robbery gone wrong, probably by a jumpy amateur, so I was hopeful. Someone comes in to steal a few bucks and ends up committing murder, they're going to feel guilty. But nothing ever came of it. None of the local skells or my usual informants knew anything. Not word one."

"Unusual," Alan says.

"Yeah. Made me think maybe it was someone from out of town, passing through. Regardless, I never gave up, but I never got anywhere either. One day, about two years later, Heather calls me. She asks if we can meet. I say sure. I have her come to the station and then I take her for a Pink's hot dog. She'd never been there. I thought if I wasn't going to give her good news, I could at least give her a legendary hot dog at a famous location."

Pink's is an LA institution. It's a slice of history. Paul Pink set up a hot-dog stand—a large-wheel pushcart—in 1939, at the corner of La Brea and Melrose. Back then, that location was considered to be "in the country." In 1946 he constructed a small building on the same spot where the hot-dog stand had stood, and it's still there today. The walls inside are covered with photos of all the movie stars and other famous people who've come there over the years.

"Heather has always been what some people call 'focused.' I think she was that way before her dad's murder. A lot of people like that become antisocial, misanthropic, no time for the small stuff, you know?"

"We know," I say, thinking of James.

"Not Heather. I knew she had something on her mind and that she wasn't really all that interested in Pink's, but she took the time to look at all the photos and to ask me about the history of the place. She was fourteen by then, and I remember it struck me."

Unusually thoughtful for any teenager, I think.

"She finished the hot dog before she even got around to what she wanted to ask me. 'I need you to be honest with me about something, Mr. Burns,' she said. I agreed I would be. 'Do you think you'll ever get the man who killed my father?'" He's watching his coffee, an expression of dissatisfaction on his face. "I considered lying to her. But I decided against it. She deserved better. 'It's always possible that something will happen, one day,' I told her. 'People get older and start talking because they think they've gotten away with it. Someone hears what they say and repeats it to a cop later. It's happened. But if you're asking, do I think that I'm personally going to catch him by doing what I do and being a good detective? In that case, I'd have to say no, I don't.'"

"How'd she react to that?" I ask.

"Better than I would have." I can hear the admiration in his voice. "She said she understood, and then she thanked me for being honest with her. Made me glad I had decided not to lie, because I got the idea she already knew what the truth was. She didn't talk for a while, then she asked for another hot dog. I could tell there was something else on her mind and that I needed to let her say what it was in her own time." He smiles. "She enjoyed the second hot dog more honestly than the first. There was no talking, but neither of us was uncomfortable. That silence is where we became friends."

He shoots us a speculative eye. "Some might think it was suspicious, a male cop getting friendly with a fourteen-year-old girl."

"The thought had occurred to me," Alan says.

I look at my friend in surprise, because it hadn't occurred to me. The truth of the relationship between Burns and Heather is written all over the old cop's face, in the frustration that's evident when he talks about not being able to solve her dad's murder. It's evident in his voice;

when he talked about her thoughtfulness, I'd heard more than admiration. I'd heard the pride of a father or a doting older brother.

Alan is usually much better at reading people than I am. Why'd his mind go there first?

Burns seems to take it in stride. "Yeah, well. We all have our problems. I'll be honest about the ones I have so you can be clear on the ones I don't. I can relate to Heather because I had a sister who died of leukemia when she was twelve. I was nine." His lips compress in sorrow at the memory, even after so many years.

"Second thing," he continues. "I had a gambling problem for a bit. I never lost the kids' college fund or anything like that. It was the opposite, actually. I was a poker player and I was really good. It started to take over my life. Playing forty-eight hours straight on my time off and then heading into work wired and with no sleep." He smiles, as though this isn't an entirely bad memory. "Might have been fine if I was making a living doing it, but I wasn't. I was wrecking my life at home and cutting into the job." He shrugs. "So I got a handle on it and that's it. Nothing off about my relationship with Heather Hollister. Not once, ever. We clear?" He looks at Alan, not me, as he asks this.

"We're clear," Alan says.

"You said she had something else to say?" I ask, trying to put this train back on the tracks.

"Yeah." The smile that replaces the mild defiance in his face tells me this is a better memory than the others. "'I want to become a policewoman,' she told me. 'Will you help?' Just like that. She was looking me right in the eyes as she did, determined, ready for a tough negotiation." He finishes his coffee and pushes it aside. "Heather was always strong, like I told you."

"What'd you tell her?" Alan asks.

"I told her the first thing she needed to do was graduate high school with good grades. Then I told her she should go to college, get a degree in criminology. My master plan, you see, was to steer her in the direction of doing something that would pay better and be safer. I figured eight more years of school, life, maybe boys, whatever, and some of that fire would cool. She was fourteen. I couldn't imagine her on the streets in a blue uniform, and I didn't want to." He shakes his head, still surprised by the past. "I misjudged her, like so many. She did exactly what I told her. Showed up when she was twenty-two and told me she needed help enrolling in the police academy."

"What about this thing with her stepfather?" Alan asks.

I watch Burns closely. His face doesn't shut down. It goes mild, the barest hint of a smile tipping the edges of his lips. Like most cops, he's an accomplished liar. If he still had coffee in his cup he'd be using it as a prop, taking a careful sip to show that he's not troubled in the slightest by Alan's question. "Pete? What about him?"

I touch Alan's leg under the table, and he lets me take over. "Burns. Our only interest in anything is Heather. We can guess what happened to the stepfather, and we couldn't care less. But did you ever consider the possibility that he might have had a hand in what happened to her? Ultimately, she's the one responsible for him going to court and having to move on."

"Yeah, I considered it."

"So? Tell us about him."

Burns grabs his water glass in a familiar, proprietary way that makes me think he wishes he was sitting at a bar counter. His expression is contemptuous. "Pete was every stereotype you could imagine. Small, weasely guy who got off on beating women because he was too cowardly to beat on anyone his own size. Blew into town a few years earlier and worked odd jobs. Margaret met him—I don't remember how. He sized her up the way guys like that do. He could smell it." He takes a drink from the water again, making me think of whiskey. "Thank God, Heather wasn't weak. Or that he wasn't one of the big ones."

I know what he's saying. The adage *all bullies are cowards* is wishful thinking. Some of them are brutes, huge men who are anything but cowardly and just enjoy using size to enforce their will.

"How old was Heather when Margaret married him?" I ask.

"Fourteen going on fifteen. I didn't know anything about him or what he was doing, until Heather came to me. I was, let's say, pretty angry. I'd taken a personal interest in this family. They'd been through enough, and here comes this piece of shit, like a vulture smelling an easy meal."

"She had a tape?" I ask.

He nods. Another admiring smile wipes away the contempt and anger. "Smart girl. She brought it to me, and I did the right thing and got him arrested. A good lawyer got the tape excluded." Burns turns the words *good lawyer* into bitter cuts of sarcasm.

"What did you do?" I prod.

He sighs. For all his anger, this memory tires him. He's not ashamed of it, but he's exhausted by the world that made it necessary. "I grabbed a sorta friend of mine, a retiree who shall remain unnamed but who, let's say, had always been flexible in his methods of interrogation on the job, and we paid ol' Pete a visit. Margaret was out at the movies with Heather." He glances away, and I see the first, smallest hint of shame there.

"Heather knew?" I say. "She knew what was going to happen?"

"As I said. She was a smart girl." Another whiskey sip of ice water. "We didn't knock. We waited ten minutes after we saw Margaret drive off with Heather, and we walked right in. Heather had left the door unlocked for us. Pete was sitting in his armchair, wearing a wife-beater and nursing a beer." He shakes his head. "The guy was such a cartoon. Maybe he saw domestic abusers on TV shows or in the movies and patterned himself after them. I don't know. Anyway, my friend-who-shall-remain-nameless walked over, grabbed Pete by the hair on his head, and yanked back. The armchair toppled over backward, and we went to work." He flexes a hand unconsciously. Sense memory.

"We didn't talk for ten minutes. He must have recognized me, but I imagine that only made him more afraid. We worked him pretty good. Not good enough that he wouldn't be able to walk out on his own, but we hurt him.

"Once the ten minutes were up, and he was curled into the fetal position and had pissed himself and was crying like a baby, I had the talk. I told him he was going to get out of town, right now, tonight. I told him if he ever touched Margaret again, I'd kill him. I told him if he ever touched Heather, I'd kill him slow. I told him if he ever showed his face around here again, I'd kill him. I told him if he filed a complaint against me, no one would believe him, and I'd kill him." He gives a little shrug. "Basically I told him I'd kill him."

"Did he go?" I ask.

"Oh yeah. He couldn't leave fast enough. I even brought him some money to stake him. Two thousand dollars of poker winnings. I'd do searches for him on occasion. Nothing ever turned up." He looks at me. His eyes are back to being troubled. "So? You think he could have had something to do with Heather going missing? I looked, but I never found a connection. Never found Pete, as a matter of fact. No records of him coming back into town at that time or later, no one saw him at any of his old haunts, nothing."

I consider it. The whole story is fascinating, both terrible and cathartic. Heather's complicity is disturbing, of course. I have only a sketch of "Pete," delivered by a man who hated his guts. But even so . . .

"I doubt it," I say. "I can't rule him out one hundred percent, but he doesn't sound like an intelligent planner. This is too advanced for him."

Burns stares down at his illusory whiskey water. "That's a relief."

"I understand why you focused on the husband and Pete," I say, moving things back to the investigation. "But were there any other suspects?"

"There was one." He sounds reluctant. "Heather's boyfriend."

"She was having an affair?" I ask.

He sighs. "Yeah. Nice guy by the name of Jeremy Abbott. He worked in real estate, divorced, around the same age as Heather. They'd been seeing each other for about six months."

"Was this before or after she suspected her husband was cheating on her?"

"Don't know. I found out about Abbott through her email."

"Why was he ruled out as a suspect?"

Burns looks confused. "You didn't read it? In the file?"

"We're still getting caught up," I say.

"Then get ready for a shocker. Jeremy Abbott went missing the same night as Heather. His car was found in his driveway, still running. Driver-side door was open and one of his shoes had come off."

"*That's* why you never considered it random," Alan says.

Burns nods.

"Douglas Hollister is looking better and better," I mutter.

"He never turned up?" Alan asks.

"Jeremy?" Burns shakes his head. "Not a sign. Just like Heather. Disappeared from the face of the earth."

I glance at Alan. He nods back at me.

"What?" Burns asks.

"We're wondering if Jeremy might show up soon too."

# CHAPTER FIFTEEN

The day is California-perfect. The sky is blue from horizon to horizon, and the sun shines down with a gentle warmth. It's a day for T-shirts and blue jeans, sunglasses optional. Parents and surfers alike will be looking at this day and thinking about the weekend, hoping that this honey keeps on falling from the sky.

We're on the way to see Douglas Hollister, and I'm excited about it. Not the excited of a kid going to the comic book store, but the excited of a meat-eater getting ready for a live meal.

I have developed a picture of Heather Hollister. Like me, she lost a parent early in her life. Like me, she was called to this job. To being a cop. Our reasons were different; she wanted justice for the world in exchange for the lack of justice for her father, whereas I was lured by an inner siren song.

By all accounts she was very good at her job. She hadn't let her obsession destroy her. She found time to marry, to have children, and to care for the victims she ran across as a detective.

Now she's lost her husband and her children. The life she knew is gone. Our stories couldn't be more different and yet the same.

I feel a kinship for her that's put an ache inside me, a longing that I recognize. It comes when empathy with a victim crystallizes to a painful, sharp-edged clarity. I care about every corpse that becomes my responsibility. Each was a life, replete with hopes, dreams, boredom, laughter, tears, day to day. I know this about them all, but with some, I can see it like I can see the hills next to the highway through the window as Alan drives.

Paul Rhodes is a writer I like a lot. He can be a little uneven at times, but there was a passage he wrote in one of his books that summed up this idea for me, this encapsulation of the uniqueness that each of us exists as, even though the stories of our lives are the same stories that have rolled on forever:

Every man thinks his dream deserves worship. It came from him, him, there is no other him; thus, it must be unique.

God says (in a booming, wrathful, surround sound voice, fit to shake the rafters of the world): FOLLY!

And man trembles.

God hunkers down in his white robes and puts an arm around man's shoulders. It's an ineffable embrace, of course; mother's milk, father's thunder, joy to build the world.

God says (not unkindly), Now that I've got your attention, listen up:

Every dream has been dreamt before, a thousand by ten thousand times. Those desires you deem unique have been attached to a million dreamers before you. They woke each day to wage the wage-war, to fight for survival for themselves and those they loved; to don a good suit, to drink a rich wine, to find themselves sweating that evening in the clutches of someone beautiful. The dream is never new, my son. Only the dreamer.

God smiles the sunrise.

Oh man, sweet child, how I love your folly.

They say any idiot can have a child, and that's true. The biology is the same. The outline of the story is the same. But the real truth is, none of them is the same. People make every story different. Only the world-weary really believe otherwise.

Tommy and Bonnie will never be Matt and Alexa. That's okay. They are themselves. They are the same idea when viewed from a distance, but listen closer and you hear it: Both songs are sung in a different tone, both are rich and beautiful, both are extraordinarily themselves.

I see Heather this way now. I perceive her not as a female victim with some similarities to myself but as a unique individual who added more to this world than she took away. I believe that her husband, Douglas Hollister, murdered not her body but her life.

We're on our way to see this man, and I'm hoping that our visit brings him sorrow.

"You think Burns will keep his cool?" Alan asks.

I turn my gaze from the passing hillside and my thoughts of Douglas Hollister's doom.

"What's that?"

"Burns. He seems a little amped up. I'm worried."

It was true. Burns was practically licking his chops, just thinking about biting a nice big juicy metaphorical chunk out of Douglas Hollister.

"I think he'll be okay. He's been a cop for too long. It's not like he's going to kill Hollister right in front of us."

Alan slides a look at me, then back to the road. "You hope," he says.

Or maybe I don't, I think but do not share with him.


Douglas Hollister lives in Woodland Hills, in a nice, newer two-story. The exterior is an off-white faux-adobe, with light wood accents at the windows. The front yard has a single adolescent tree. The rest is green grass, cut short. Attractive, cute even, but unimaginative. It has the look of any of a thousand homes that were thrown up during the housing boom. Hollister's been here with his new wife, Dana, for only three years, so I'd guess they bought at the height of the market.

"What do you think about Dana Hollister?" I'd asked Burns.

"I think she's clueless and that she loves the guy," he replied, echoing our thoughts when we'd first viewed the black-and-white photograph of them coming out of the hotel room. "She cheated with him, so I hold that against her, but she always struck me as not being the sharpest knife in the drawer. Dumb more than malicious."

He filled us in on the other facts. Dana Hollister had worked in real estate for a few years, a career she started not long after she and Douglas met. She'd done okay but had quit a year ago, after the housing bubble burst. Now she was trying to start up her own business.

"Keepsake store or something like that," Burns said. He checked his watch. "She should be there now. She's open every day, as a matter of fact. Hardworking, I'll give her that."

"You still keep pretty close tabs on them, then?" Alan asked.

"'Til he's suffering in prison," Burns had replied, his voice as flat as a machine.

Alan parks next to the curb in front of the house, pulling up so that Burns can ease in behind us. I notice a white Honda Accord in the driveway. We climb out and I wince at the sudden cold turn the air has taken during the short drive. February in Southern California remains capricious, as always.

"How do you want to work this?" Burns asks, coming up to us.

"He's already going to be on his guard when he sees you," I say to him. "That's good. I'll introduce us, and Alan and I will show him our FBI credentials. That should make him even more nervous. After that we'll let Alan run things."

Burns squints at Alan. "I heard rumors about you. You're supposed to be some kind of ass-kicker when it comes to interrogation."

Alan shrugs. "It's all just science, really. Body language, eye movements. Anyone can learn it."

"Anyone can play golf too," Burns says, "but there's only one Tiger Woods."

"Putting him on the defensive is good," Alan says, "but our vocal tones need to be soothing. Body language, nonconfrontational. Like we're coming to give him some bad news, not as if we think he's any kind of a suspect." He glances at Burns. "You think you can handle that?"

"Don't worry. I'll try to look contrite."

"Good. We get him to let us in. I'll do all the talking. Let me sit closest to him. I need to be able to watch him when I tell him that his wife is alive. The most important reaction is the one he has right after I deliver the news."

We walk up to the door. It's a simple gray concrete walkway. The driveway, I notice now, had been redone. Laid with brick or something like that. A number of the houses in my neighborhood have done something similar, but I hate the look. Paint your house, plant a tree, put in a beautiful garden. Driveways? They're for getting your car from the garage to the street.

"Let me knock," Alan says.

He raises a huge fist and pounds the door so hard it shocks me a little, and I was half expecting it. He waits a moment, winks at me and Burns, and then knocks again, practically bending the door inward.

More time passes than I would have expected. I'm watching the front windows; no one's pulled back a curtain to see who's knocking. I have no sense of anyone staring through the peephole.

Alan shrugs. "Nothing to do but knock again."

I brace myself as I see him getting ready to really lean into it. He hammers the door so hard I almost laugh out loud, except that none of this is funny.

Alan lifts his fist again, but Burns holds his hand up. "Wait. You hear that?"

I don't hear anything, but maybe Burns has bat ears. Then I hear it. The soft *swish swish* sound of socks against a wood floor. We all straighten. The sound stops and the peephole darkens.

"Yes?" It's a man's voice.

Alan glances at me. We want to make him nervous, but later, after he's let us into the house. A woman's voice will be better for now.

"Mr. Hollister?" I ask.

"Yes?"

"I'm Special Agent Smoky Barrett, from the FBI. We need to talk to you, sir."

A long pause.

"Sir?" I query.

More silence. Then:

"Hang on."

We hear the deadbolt turn. The door opens and Douglas Hollister stands before us. He has some gray in his hair now, and weight has settled into his face and around his middle, but not too much. If anything, he looks more fit than in the hotel photo. Perhaps, before today, he looked happier too.

But not right now.

Right now he reminds me of Al Pacino in *Scarface*. He looks like he just buried his head in a gigantic pile of pure cocaine and breathed deep. His eyes bounce from me to Alan to Burns, then back to me. There are bags under those eyes. He's unshaven and, from the brief scent I catch, unbathed as well. I glance down and see something stranger: One of his feet is missing a sock.

He smiles, but it's a parody, something hideous, as though it had been commanded at gunpoint.

"Can I help you?" he asks, his voice squeaking a little. He clears his throat, gives us the death's head grimace again. "Sorry. Can I help you?" A little better this time, but he's started to sweat. A line of small, fine beads has formed at the hairline.

I show him my ID, as does Alan. "My partner, Alan Washington. And you know Detective Burns."

The slightest hint of a new emotion breaks through the barely suppressed terror. It shows only in his eyes, and only for a moment, but I catch it before it's gone. Resentment, a brief petulance, the *this is all your fault* of a four-year-old child.

"What's this about?" he asks, turning his attention back to me.

"We have some important news, sir. May we come in? I'd prefer if you were sitting down for this."

His eyes widen, and he wrings his hands. For some reason, it seems contrived. "Is it Dana? Did something happen to her?"

I reassure him with my reassuring smile, well honed. "No, sir. Can we come in?"

The nonthreatening and deferential manner of my approach seems to be working. He's relaxed a little. He runs a hand through hair that's probably needed to be washed for days. "Sure. Sorry. Of course." He steps aside so we can enter, which we do. "I'm a little out of it. I've been ill and I was napping. I thought the pounding on the door was from a dream."

"Sorry about that, sir," I say, giving him my "shrug" smile, the one that says, *What can you do?* "It's a habit we develop. You see, if we knock hard enough and no one answers, we can assume they're either hurt or dead or possibly drugged." I'm making this up on the spot, but right now it's all about feeding Alan's observation machine. I know he's watching every tic and eye movement Hollister makes.

Hollister stares at me, taking in the idea of needing to learn to knock hard enough to determine if someone's dead or just sleeping. "Wow," he says.

"Where can we talk, sir?" I ask, prodding him gently.

"This way," he says, turning and walking toward the back of the house.

We follow, and I take in the surrounds. It's a beautiful home in that SoCal way. Light-hardwood floors polished to a mirror sheen. Vaulted ceilings with no acoustic popcorn. Recessed lighting. A stairway with wood railing and beige carpeting leads up to a second floor. It's a big house. I'd guess five bedrooms. Probably three up top, including the master, and two downstairs. Nice.

We pass the kitchen, which is spacious and gleaming; granite countertops and stainless-steel appliances shine. It's not cold, though, I notice. There are knickknacks and plants and mismatched doilies. It's not the kitchen of a neat freak. The refrigerator door is covered with various things held down by various magnets. A *God Bless This Home* plaque hangs on the wall.

We reach the living room, which matches the rest of the house. A fifty-inch plasma TV faces a large sectional couch. I see an Xbox and a stack of games. A DVD shelf is filled with DVDs stored in agreeable disarray. A fine layer of dust covers the coffee table, probably three or four days' worth.

I recognize this house. It's the home of busy people, doing their best to balance time in the fight against entropy, and not doing a bad job. Sloppy imperfection is everywhere, but it never overwhelms, and the place is never dirty. I find the same thing every night when I get back to my own house.

Hollister indicates that we should sit on the couch. Alan puts himself in the position closest to Hollister. Burns sits next to him. I stay standing. Nothing like a little unevenness to keep things uncomfortable.

I glance into the backyard as Alan begins speaking. It's a big backyard, devoid of trees but filled with lush green grass.

"Something happened yesterday, Mr. Hollister," Alan says. "Do you remember what day your first wife went missing?"

"Heather?"

"Yes, sir."

Hollister thinks about it, still sweating away. "Um . . . let's see. It was after her cardio class. Middle of the week. Wednesday. Yes. Wednesday. Why?"

"Where were you at the time?"

A flash of anger passes over Hollister's face, but he answers without hesitation. This is solid ground for him. "I was at home."

"What were you doing at the time?"

Hollister's quiet, remembering. "I was watching a movie. My sons were asleep. I was watching . . . *Dirty Harry*."

Alan smiles. "Clint. My man. What's your opinion? You think he was better as an actor or a director?"

Burns gives me a sideways look. I ignore him. He doesn't know what Alan's up to. I do.

Hollister seems as mystified but answers. "I think he's better as a director. I love the *Dirty Harry* movies and the westerns, but he really came into his own as a director."

"I agree. Which do you think is his best movie? As a director, I mean?"

Hollister considers it. Of course, the fact that he's answering any of these questions at all makes me almost certain he's guilty. The guilty, when confronted with an interrogation situation, jump at any chance to bond. They think being friendly will make us trust them more. Hollister is too desperate to be liked by Alan to wonder why the subject is Clint Eastwood.

"*Mystic River,* I guess."

"Your wife Heather was found alive." Alan shifts gears without bothering to acknowledge Hollister's answer.

You could hear a pin drop. Hollister stares at Alan. He swallows once, a huge, nervous gulping, like a gagging fish. "She was found?" he finally says. "W-where?"

I frown. *Found?* Not *found alive*? Odd choice of words.

"She was pushed out of a car into a hotel parking lot. My colleagues and I were attending a wedding there. We think he chose that location because of its proximity to a large group of law enforcement."

"Large group? What do you mean?"

Again, Hollister's questions are very, very strange.

"Almost everyone attending was either FBI or LAPD."

Hollister looks away. His eyes find me and then dart in another direction. He's sweating more profusely now. I peer closer. Sweat stains have actually appeared on the underarms of his shirt.

"Wow," he manages. "I don't know what to say. This is kind of shocking."

Kind of?

He points a finger at Burns, and his face twists in righteous indignation. "See! I told you I didn't kill her. You kept persecuting me, but she's alive. She's fine."

My mouth almost falls open. "I wouldn't say she's fine, sir. We think she's been held in isolation for eight years. She's in a psychotic state. Fine? I'm not sure that's the best selection of words."

I sense Alan's eyes on me, warning me off. I rein myself in.

"You're right," Hollister says, holding a hand up in commiseration. "I'm sorry. I feel like a pinball in a pinball machine right now. It's just . . ." He puts his hands together between his knees and looks down at them. "Eight years is a long time. When Heather disappeared, it nearly killed me. Then I was accused of being the one responsible for her disappearance and maybe her murder." He looks at Burns. "I know you were just doing your job. I apologize for my outburst."

"No problem," Burns says, playing along, though I can sense his tenseness.

"Where is she?" he asks. "Is she injured? Can I see her?"

All the questions now that he should have asked from the start.

"She's still being examined," Alan says. "So far, she doesn't show any signs of permanent physical harm, but her mental state is another matter. The doctors would prefer that she have no visitors right now."

I'm always amazed at how simply Alan can change his mode of speaking. In normal situations, he's very easygoing. A little bit of slang at times, a peppering of profanity. Man on the street. Now he sounds so formal, almost stilted.

"I understand," Hollister says, agreeing a little *too* quickly for my taste. "Do you have any idea yet? About who might have done this to her?"

This is the question he really wants answered. Alan waits, letting the pause hang a little too long as he stares at Hollister. "No," he finally says. "I'm afraid not. We're hopeful that Ms. Hollister can shed some light on things when she is ready to start talking again. If she's ever ready."

Hollister leans forward, ever so slightly. It's an almost imperceptible eagerness. "And?" he asks. "Do you think she'll ever be ready?"

God, I marvel. Either this guy is the world's worst liar or he's still too shook up to get his bearings.

Again, that too-long pause from Alan. He lets it go long enough now that one of Hollister's eyes twitches with tension. "That's an unknown at the moment, I'm afraid."

"I see," Hollister replies. He smiles again, that awful, desperate grin. "Does anyone want a beer?" he asks. "I sure could use a beer!"

It's utterly incongruous. Alan takes it in stride.

"We can't, sir, but thank you. We're almost done with what we came to find out—I mean, to do here. If I could just ask you to be patient a little while longer."

Alan's "slip of the tongue" was anything but. Hollister's eye twitches again at the words *find out*.

"Uh, okay," he says, staring at Alan. His mouth sounds as though it's filled with cotton, overdry.

"Is there anything you can think of that might help us, sir? Heather's reappearance is obviously a new development. Has anything happened in your life recently that might correspond to that? Has anyone contacted you, emailed you, left strange messages?"

"No, nothing like that," Hollister says.

"Anything at all you can think of?"

"No, I'm afraid not. That's the strange thing. Three days ago, everything was like it always is. Now everything has changed."

This is the truth. I can hear it in his voice. The problem is, again, in his choice of words. Three days ago is too long a window. Heather showed up yesterday.

Alan nods in sympathy. "That's how it goes sometimes," he says. "Sometimes we're sure we have all the bases covered, and then we make a mistake."

"Uh-huh," Hollister agrees, staring at Alan with a kind of dreadful fascination.

"Mr. Hollister, you have two sons, don't you?"

"Yes. Avery and Dylan."

"How do you think they're going to react to this?"

"I have no idea."

Douglas Hollister's affect has changed. His eyes have gone colder. His voice is flat. Why?

Alan's picked up on this as well. "Mr. Hollister, where are Avery and Dylan right now?"

"At a friend's."

Alan stares at the man and I know something is up. For the first time since we've arrived, he breaks eye contact with Hollister. He looks at me. He is very, very troubled. He turns back to Hollister. "Let me just confer with my boss for a few moments, sir, and then we should be out of your hair. You and Detective Burns can catch up in the meantime."

Hollister eyes Burns dubiously. "Yeah. Sure."

Alan gets up and walks me into the kitchen. "We have a problem," he says.

"What?"

"He's lying about Avery and Dylan being at a friend's. Why? Who needs to lie about where their kids are?"

I'm slow to arrive at the answer he wants, but when I do, I freeze. "You think they're here?"

Alan is quiet for a moment. "I think it's a possibility, which is not good. Hollister's obviously off the deep end. Something or someone's got him bugalooed. Last time I saw behavior like this with a suspect while questioning him in his home, it turned out he'd killed his wife just before we arrived. Took a long time to answer the door, just like Hollister. Know why?"

"He was hiding the body?"

"Close. He was washing the blood off his hands. The body was stuffed behind the couch while we were interviewing him."

"Jesus." I feel my hackles go up at the pure creepiness of this.

"What do you want to do?"

I focus my attention on Hollister, who's holding up his end of a terse conversation with Burns. Probable cause is the name of the game. He invited us into his home, but we're not here on a warrant. Evidence we can use is limited to what we can actually see.

"It's time to turn up the heat," I tell Alan. "We don't have a legal reason, yet, to search his home. If we do it anyway, we run the risk of whatever we find being inadmissible. Somehow, we need to crack him here and now."

"And if we don't?"

I study Alan. "What's your gut? Are the boys alive or dead?"

"Dead." He says it without hesitation. "He emptied out when I brought up Avery and Dylan."

"If you don't break him, I'll think of something."

Alan cracks his knuckles, watching Hollister again. "I think the direct approach is the one to take at this point." His voice is thoughtful. "I'll start by explaining neurolinguistics to him. Then we'll see."

We head back out to the living room. Alan takes his seat again. I remain standing.

"Sorry about that," Alan says.

"No problem," Hollister replies. He looks relieved not to have to continue his conversation with Burns.

"I want to talk to you about neurolinguistic interviewing, Mr. Hollister."

Hollister frowns. "Neuro what?"

"Neurolinguistic interviewing. There's a lot of technical jargon, but I'll simplify it for you. It's a way of finding out when someone you are interviewing is using their cognitive process and when they're remembering something. By cognitive process, I mean thinking. Creating an answer to a problem. Like, when I asked you earlier what movie was Eastwood's best directing effort, you had to review the movies you'd seen and then come up with an answer based on the data you have. You follow?"

"I guess."

"When you remember something, you don't have to use the cognitive process. It's a memory. You have to locate it. We access different parts of the brain for each function, and we have specific physiological reactions when we do that." He leans forward. "It's in the eyes."

The tic in Hollister's own eye starts again. "The eyes?" he repeats, somewhat moronically.

Alan nods. "Yes, sir. Most people, when they are remembering something, look up and to the right. When they're solving a problem, they generally look down and to the left. It varies, but you ask each kind of question and establish a baseline. You know why?"

"So you can tell when they're lying," Hollister whispers, hollow-eyed and dreadful again.

"That's right. If you ask them for a memory, and they access the cognitive function of their brain, that means they're lying. When I asked you to remember what day your wife was abducted, for example, you weren't lying. You were remembering." He shrugs. "There're other indicators, of course. Nervousness is an obvious one." Alan smiles. "You were already nervous and sweating like a pig when we arrived. You said you were sick and napping, but I don't think so."

Hollister says nothing. He's turned into the bird. Alan is the cobra.

"Here's the thing I'm really concerned about, Mr. Hollister." Alan moves closer, parting Hollister's knees with one of his own, creating an unconscious threat to his manhood. "When I asked you about your sons? When I asked where Avery and Dylan are? You lied to me. I could see it. And that bothers me—us—Mr. Hollister. Why would you need to lie about the location of your sons?"

Hollister's eyes have gone wide. His mouth is hanging open, though I doubt he realizes it. He's falling apart right in front of us.

"We're also trained to keep an eye on what we call 'affect,' Mr. Hollister. Do you know what that is? Roughly, it's the observable effects of someone experiencing a particular emotion or emotions. You can have a bored affect, a sad affect, so on." He moves in even closer, pushing his knee in further. It's now only an inch or two away from Hollister's crotch.

Hollister farts, once. He's unaware of it. It's a small toot, but it's telling. You see this, and sometimes belching, in a highly skilled interrogation. The person doesn't even have to be guilty. It's a physiological reaction of fear.

"Your affect when I asked you about your sons went from fearful to a near total absence of emotion. Do you know who I see that kind of reaction in the most?" He cranes his neck forward, so that his nose is almost touching Hollister's. "I see it in murderers."

"Gahhh . . ." Hollister says.

He is shattering now. Most people have no idea how devastating an interrogation can be. Men have fainted dead away when faced with nothing more than an accusation and a badge.

"Jesus, he's wetting himself," Burns mutters.

I see the stain spreading before the smell reaches my nose. Alan doesn't move.

"Where are Avery and Dylan's bodies, sir?" Alan asks.

Hollister doesn't reply. He doesn't have the presence of mind for words. He extends his arm and he points. Upstairs.

I waste no time. I leave Douglas Hollister to Alan and Burns and I race up the beige-carpeted stairwell to the second floor. The lights are on in the upstairs hallway. The walls are white and covered in a patch-work of framed and carefully hung photos. I was wrong about the bed-rooms. I see only two here: the double door of a master, and then a single door on the right at the end of the hallway. The other is a bath-room; I can tell because it's open.

I begin with the master. I open the door and am hit with the faint odor of feces. I curl my nose and pull my gun and enter. It's an unimag-inative but entirely acceptable room. A ceiling fan hangs above a king-size bed. There's a dark-blue accent wall, but the rest is white. All the furniture is wood, neither too old nor too new.

I'm never going to look at beige the same way again.

The humor doesn't dispel the willies, and I almost fire my weapon when I hear the sound. It's a snort, followed by a wet smacking noise. It's coming from the master bathroom. I take a breath and clear my mind and head toward it. I reach the door, which is cracked, and I open it.

I see Avery and Dylan Hollister right away. I had expected it, but still, my heart sinks. The floor of the bathroom is carpeted with a thick shag, all the way up to the separate tub and shower. One of the boys is lying on his side, his face turned in to the carpet so that only the back of his head and his ears are visible. There is bruising around his neck. The other lies faceup, on his back, his eyes closed and his mouth open. I kneel down and check for a pulse on the first boy, hoping but not really expecting to find one. Nothing.

The smacking sounds start up again, bringing me to my feet, gun raised. They're coming from the bathtub, which is a deep whirlpool tub. I inch over to it. I can see what I know to be a body bag inside the tub. A white tube sticks out of the bag. Suddenly the bag moves and a wet, gargling noise comes from it.

I holster my gun and climb inside the tub without thinking twice. My hands are shaking as I undo the zipper. The smell of feces is strong, but I ignore it. All I can think of is that someone's alive inside there, maybe injured, and time's an enemy. I push the flaps of the bag open and a horrible odor wafts out. I look down at the woman inside and I can feel the blood draining from my face. I feel dizzy for a moment.

I sit down on the edge of the tub. I want to call for Alan, but I seem to have lost my voice. All I can do is stare.

It's Dana Hollister; I recognize her from the black-and-white photograph. She's nude. Her eyes are empty and they stare into nothing, and her open mouth yaws, hungering at the level of instinct only, the plastic tube falling out and away.

"Dana?" I whisper.

No reply. She continues to stare without seeing. Drool runs freely from her mouth, and everything about her is a slackness and a void. Something terrible moves through me, a mix of grief and rage and misery. I kneel down next to her and open the bag farther. I don't care about the smell. I just want to touch her, so she knows she's not alone, if there's anything in her that is still aware. I reach into the bag and grab her hand. I cradle it in one of mine, and I reach out and stroke her forehead. There is no reaction. Her mouth opens and closes once, that smacking sound.

I notice a hole above her eye but within the socket, and a single full-body shiver rocks me.

Is that what I think it is? It's something I've seen before.

When the other boy—the one I hadn't checked yet because Dana had surprised me—cries out softly, I almost fall backward off the tub in sheer terror. I recover, and I crawl over to him and feel for a pulse. I find it, weak and thready but there. He coughs twice, and his eyes flutter.

"Alan!" I yell. "Get up here, please! Right now!"

I wait until I hear the heavy thuds of his shoes on the stairs, and then I let myself weep a little. Grief, anxiety, fear. I cradle the boy in my arms and thank God for his moans. They mean he is alive. Dana Hollister grunts once. The other child stares into the carpet with sightless eyes.

What we do is primordial.

# CHAPTER SIXTEEN

Dana and Dylan Hollister have been taken away in an ambulance. I've arranged for them to go to the same hospital Heather is in. Avery Hollister has been confirmed dead.

My grief has fled, brushed aside by a hot wind of rage. I want to go and rip the arms and legs off Douglas Hollister, to put his eyes out, to tear out his tongue.

I feel a large hand on my shoulder. "Now is the time to interview Hollister," Alan says. "He's been read his rights; he's not asking for a lawyer. If we're going to get it out of him, we should strike while the iron's hot."

If I close my eyes and listen hard, I can still hear the ambulance sirens howling in the distance. "Do you want to transport him first?"

"No. The more time we give him to think, the greater the chance he lawyers up. I've already asked him. He's agreed to be interviewed here. He even provided us with a video camera and a fresh tape."

"Why is he being so cooperative?"

"He's scared. He's not the one who did that to Dana."

I turn the ramifications of this over in my mind. "Let me make a call, and then, yes, let's do the interview here."

Callie is silent, processing what I've just told her about Dana and the Hollister boys.

"My, my," she manages. "What do you want us to do?" She's all business, flippancy put aside for now.

"Have James continue distilling the information from the case files. I want you to do a ViCAP search. We're looking for similar crimes to Dana Hollister's."

"You think he's done it before?"

"I don't know, but what I do think is that it's relatively unique. I think if he has done it before, it will definitely be in ViCAP and it will definitely be him."

The Violent Criminal Apprehension Program was established by the FBI in 1985. It was a stroke of genius and has lived up to its name. It's a cooperative endeavor. We provide participating law enforcement around the country with a form that can be filled out. I am always struck by the clinical contrast it provides to the reality of the horrors it records. It's filled with *if yes then go to item* . . . directions, like some twisted tax return.

*Were there elements of unusual or additional assault/trauma/torture to victim? Yes/ No/Unknown.* Assuming *yes* is checked, then question 88b follows, a laundry list of possible additional abuses: *If yes, indicate what elements occurred (check all that apply and describe).* Some possibles among many are: *Beat sexual areas with hands/fists, with objects; body cavities or wounds explored/probed; cannibalism; douche/ enema given to victim; skinned,* and, my personal favorite at the end of this impossibly long list of awfuls, *Other.*

The first time I read the form, I wondered about the people who'd come up with it. What would you have had to see to make that list? What would you have to know to ensure it was complete? I wondered then, but I know better now: I could rattle off most of the list from memory, based on the things I've seen myself.

Once filled out, the form is sent to ViCAP in Quantico. The information is entered into the database and then compared against the existing database to try to identify similar cases.

"Give me the pertinent information," Callie says.

I force myself to be as clinical as the form she'll be filling out. It won't be complete. That's not necessary right now. I explain what I want her to search for, the thing unconfirmed by a doctor but that I believe, in the gut of me, to be true.

She's silent for a moment. "Are you certain about this?"

"Not certain, but I'd bet my home on it."

"I'll get in touch with them right away."


If anything, Douglas Hollister seems calmer now than when we first knocked on his door. I'm not really surprised. This is something you see a lot with a confession. Hiding what they've done is stressful. One offender described it to me as a "huge building pressure with nowhere to go." Many are relieved when they no longer have to hold it in. One of the most common requests after a confession, from my own experience, is to sleep. They're finally able to relax.

He's seated on the couch. Alan has positioned the coffee table so that the camcorder can face him directly. Alan is seated nearest, with Burns to one side, as before. I decide to remain standing. I'm afraid to get too close to Hollister, afraid of what I'll do.

The sliding-glass door that leads into the backyard lets in the light. I think that it does not belong here, but the sun shines on everyone equally, I guess.

"Can I have a cigarette?" Hollister asks. "Do you mind? Dana didn't like me smoking, but I guess it doesn't matter now."

"It's your home, sir," Alan says.

His voice is all business without being cold. It's a part of the deal: cooperate and get treated with respect. Why? Because pragmatism rules in what we do. We want suspects talking, not silent. So even if we'd personally like to set them on fire, as long as they'll continue to hang themselves for the camera, we'll bring them sodas and light their cigarettes.

"They're in the kitchen," Hollister says. "Can I get them?"

"Where are they, sir?" Burns asks. He, too, is polite. I'm sure he wants to destroy Douglas with his bare hands, but he knows the tune.

"In the drawer to the left of the stove."

Burns gets up and returns in a moment with a pack of Marlboro

Reds and a green lighter. I feel twin pangs of hunger and irony shoot through me. I quit smoking almost four years ago, but stress can still bring out the craving. Marlboro Reds were my brand too. I watch him light up with an envy made greater by my hatred of him. He inhales deeply, eyes closing in a moment of brief bliss.

Alan pushes record on the video camera.

"This is FBI Special Agent Alan Washington interviewing Douglas Hollister in his home, located at . . ." He goes through the process of listing all pertinent information, including date and exact time, who is present, why we are there. Hollister smokes and listens, his eyes fixed on something in the distance. "Mr. Hollister, can you testify for the camera that I previously read you your rights?"

"Yes, I can. You did."

"And can you confirm for the camera that you've waived your right to have an attorney present for this interview and confession?"

"Yes."

"And can you further confirm that you're doing this of your own free will and not as the result of any duress or coercion?"

"Yes."

"Can you tell us why, in fact, you've agreed to this interview and taped confession?"

Hollister pauses, using the moment to take another pull on the cigarette. There's no ashtray, but he's beyond caring. He taps ash onto the top of the coffee table.

"I'm scared. The guy who did . . . what happened to Dana . . . he's after me. I've decided my best chance at surviving is being protected by the police."

"Thank you, sir. One last thing. You supplied us with this video camera?"

"I did."

"And you supplied us with the tape currently being used to record this interview?"

"Right."

"You confirm that we tampered with neither the camera nor the tape?"

"I so swear!" Hollister says, then giggles.

"Can you give me a contemporary affirmative answer, sir?" Alan's patience is endless, awe-inspiring.

Hollister stubs the cigarette out on the coffee tabletop and lights another. "Sorry. Yes, I confirm no tampering has happened."

"Thank you." Alan says nothing for a moment. I know he's collecting his thoughts, settling in for however long this takes. "Let's talk about Avery, Mr. Hollister."

Douglas seems to sink into himself. His eyes gain a furtive quality. "Avery."

"Avery was your son?"

"Yes."

"We found Avery dead in the master bathroom of this house, sir. He was strangled. Did you kill him?"

"Yes. Yes, I did." He sounds amazed.

"When did you kill him, sir?"

"Late last night."

"About what time?"

"I guess around three in the morning."

"How did you kill him, sir?"

Hollister puts one hand over his eyes as he speaks. He doesn't want to see us seeing him as he tells it. "I gave both the boys drugs to make them sleep. Told them it was medicine. I didn't want them to be awake and afraid when they died. I went into Avery's bedroom first. I didn't want to use a pillow to smother him—I wasn't sure about that. I was afraid it would take too long. I read yesterday on the Internet about the carotid arteries, about how you could use them to knock someone out quickly. I figured I'd do that first, in case the drugs hadn't worked right, just to make sure he was out."

Burns jots something down in a notebook. Probably a reminder to check the browsing history on Hollister's computer.

"I came in and sat him up and got behind him. He started to wake up when I put my arms around his neck. I don't know what happened. I thought I gave him enough drugs, but maybe he slipped some of the pills to his brother when I wasn't looking. Avery was clever that way." He swallows once, his Adam's apple bobbing hugely. "He just kept struggling. It wasn't knocking him out." The hand over his eyes remains. The hand holding the cigarette rests on one of his knees, burning away, forgotten. "So I had to do it the old-fashioned way. I let go of him and he was kind of freaking out. So I hit him a couple of times in the face, really hard."

"You used your fist?" Alan asks, probing for more details, guiding Hollister gently toward the hanging rope.

"Yeah." His breath hitches. "He got out half of one word. You know what it was? *Da-*, he said, and then my fist hit his mouth. God. He wasn't even totally awake."

"What happened next?"

"I started choking him. Hard. So hard. I've never grabbed anything that hard in my life. I remember I was kind of snarling, you know? Like this?" He draws his lips back from his teeth in a feral grin. The hand still covers his eyes. "I must have looked like a monster to him. He must have thought I was so angry. But I wasn't. My face wasn't contorted because of anger. It was effort. I was trying to make it go fast for him; I was squeezing so hard my hands ached and veins were standing out on my arms." The amazement is back in his voice, replacing the misery. "His face got so red. Deep black-red. His eyes were popped open and his tongue was out and he was pissing himself. God, it was horrible. I had his hands pinned under my knees, and I could feel his chest bucking against me. Then—it stopped. He stopped. Everything stopped. He was dead." He takes the hand away from his eyes. He draws on his cigarette.

I feel like killing Hollister. At least he's not crying. I'm not sure what I would do if I had to witness his crocodile tears.

"When did you move him to the bathroom?" Alan asks.

Hollister stubs out the second cigarette, lights his third. "Right after. I couldn't believe how much he weighed. Deadweight, they call it. Now I understand. He was so heavy. My heart was pounding so hard, and I felt like everything was very, very sharp. Do you know what I mean?"

"I think so."

"I moved Avery in and put him on the floor. At first he was just lying there, but then I turned his face in to the carpet. Because his eyes were open. I think it's bad luck to let them stare like that after they're dead. You understand? I was trying to be respectful. You understand?" He grins, ghoulish, insane. It fades. "It was too much. I should have gone right to Dylan, I should have finished him then, like his brother, but I just couldn't. I brought his body into the bathroom, but I was still too shook up from Avery to kill him. I needed time." He nods once, to himself. "Yes. I needed time."

Alan takes it all in stride. "Mr. Hollister, why did you kill Avery?"

Hollister stares off, considering this. It occurs to me that perhaps now, in the light of day, he's starting to doubt his reasoning.

"Sir?" Alan prods.

"I needed to run. I was going to have to empty my bank accounts and run. Live on a cash-only basis. That was no life for two young boys."

I've seen this kind of reasoning far, far too many times. It's the epitome of malignant narcissism. A father or husband is planning to either run away or take his own life. He decides it would be cruel to let his family go on without him, so he kills them. The truth is that he can't stand the thought of them despising him once he's gone.

"Why were you going to have to run?" Alan asks.

"I screwed up. I was supposed to pay him. I didn't. So he took Dana and . . . he did what he did to her." He grimaces at the memory. "He told me he was going to let Heather loose. Then he told me he was going to do to me what he did to Dana."

"Who is 'he,' sir?"

Hollister gets very quiet now. "You can learn to live with almost anything," he says. "As long as you don't have to deal with it on a daily basis, it's not that hard. The first few weeks and months might be difficult, but time sort of . . . covers everything with dust. Just like in the real world. The years roll by and dust covers everything, and then the dust turns to dirt, and then trees grow in the dirt. Soon enough, houses are put up, and no one has any idea that shiny new house was built on a graveyard."

He takes in a huge drag of smoke, which makes him wince and cough a little. "Heather and I started out in love. I really loved her. She was smart, she was kind, she was good in bed, a great mother. She was focused on her career more than I liked, but that wasn't a big deal in the beginning. At least that's what I thought. My mistake.

"Time passed. She changed, I changed, and I realized that she wasn't what I'd been looking for. I needed someone who'd be more attentive to me, to my needs. She needed someone who'd let her be married to her job.

"It wasn't one-sided either. She started seeing that faggoty real estate guy, Abbott."

More narcissism. He'd decided he didn't love his wife and had gone looking for her replacement but was shocked and enraged at similar behavior on her part.

"I got lucky. I found Dana. She wasn't a hot-body like Heather. But she put more care and effort into everything when it came to me. To her man." He smiles at Alan, a sickly smile. "That's what she used to call me. Her man. She was always a little heavier than she wanted, her body leaned that way, but she went to the gym for an hour every day except Sunday, because she wanted to look good for her man. She cooked meals. She never refused sex or used it as a weapon. That's what I wanted in my wife."

I wonder about the things missing in his account. Heather had been a strong woman. She wouldn't have knowingly married a caveman like Douglas, would she? Did he hide it? Or was it just one of those anomalies, the ones you see in couples sometimes? People aren't stereotypes; they are complex fractals, driven in the main part by things not visible on the surface.

Hollister has gone quiet, lost in his own remembering. Alan nudges him along. "What happened?"

"I had a problem. Heather was a bitch with a gun. She would have taken my sons and my house in a divorce. Dana said she'd stand by me, but, come on—what woman really wants a loser in an apartment? It was bothering me. I was losing sleep over it." He shoots me a hostile, volcanic stare. I assume it's because I, too, am a "bitch with a gun." "I even started to have trouble performing in bed! Can you imagine? All I wanted was to be allowed to love who I wanted to love, and she wanted to take away my sons, my home, and my cock!"

"Did you ever talk to her about divorce?" I ask. I should keep my mouth shut and let Alan do his thing, but I can't resist, because I am almost certain of his answer.

"Talk?" He laughs and waves me off. "I didn't have to. I knew how it would go."

I bite back the words I want to say. He never even bothered to talk to Heather. He'd already decided who she was and how she'd react. His decisions weren't based on his years with her. They were based on his own narcissism.

Maybe she would have let him have the house.

"What happened next?" Alan asks, reasserting control.

Hollister spares me a last, distrusting glance and turns his attention back to Alan. "I was staying up late a lot. I spent my time surfing the Internet. Just trying to keep myself amused. I found a website. It was all about guys like me, stuck with wives they didn't love. Wives getting ready to cut their balls off. There was a forum and a chat room, and I spent a lot of time there. It was a safe place to vent, to give each other advice. Every now and then some feminist would find her way in there. We called them *fem-cows*," he says, smiling at the memory. "The moderator would give them the boot pretty quick. It wasn't getting me anywhere, but I felt a lot more at home.

"Some of the guys who were there had already divorced their wives and were still hanging around to help those who hadn't. A few had gotten married again but to better, more traditional women. Russians, or South Americans. Thai. Anything but American women," he mutters. "God save us from the land of delusional fem-cows. Like one of the guys used to say, *If I see one more fat ass wearing sweatpants that say 'juicy' at the supermarket, I'm going to puke.*" He leans forward to make his point, jabbing a finger at Alan, completely caught up in his own sermon.

"You ever see a Russian woman out shopping? She wouldn't be caught dead in sweatpants. She puts on makeup the moment she rolls out of bed." He sends me another blistering gaze. "Anyway. Where was I?" He puffs on the cigarette. "That's what most of the men bitched about. So you can imagine how envious they were when I told them, no, I had the perfect woman, and she was American! Some of them couldn't believe it. I said, yes, I know, it's about as likely as winning the lottery, but Dana was the genuine article." He grins. "They got me, though. One of the long-term members told me that I should find out about her mother. So I asked, and you know what? Dana was a first-generation American. Her parents came over from Poland. The guys had a good laugh over that, but I didn't mind." He chortles at the memory. "*See?* they said. *She had a mother who knows how to treat a man.* It's true. I've met her mother and her father quite a few times since, and she's just like her mom."

If Alan finds any of this diatribe boring or distasteful, he doesn't let on. "So you were going to the forum and chat room regularly, and . . . ?"

"And one day I got a request for a private chat."

"Which is?"

"The regular chat room is public, a free-for-all. Everyone in the room can see what everyone else is typing. A private chat is opened in a separate window and is only visible to the two people talking."

"I understand. Go on."

"The guy's handle was Dali. I thought that was kind of strange."

"What was your handle?" I ask.

"TruLove," he replies, defiant.

I want to puke, but I say nothing.

"I hadn't seen this guy before, but there were always new members showing up. New victims of the fem-cows. We called them *the walking ball-less*." He grins at Alan. "Do you get it? Like the walking wounded, but—no balls."

Alan smiles politely. "Very clever. What did Dali say to you?"

"He said he could solve my problem. He said he could do it by making my wife disappear and that her body wouldn't be found until or unless I wanted it to be. I was suspicious, of course, and told him so. *You could be a cop,* I said. *I can prove I'm not,* he said. *Is there anyone you work with—man or woman—that rubs you the wrong way? Someone you don't like very much?*

"That was easy. Everyone has someone at work they don't like. For me, it was a woman. Not my boss but the boss of a department that interfaced fairly often with mine. Her name was Piper Styles—silly-ass name—and she was a bitch on wheels. One time she accused me of staring at her ass and threatened to bring me up on sexual-harassment charges." He makes a grimace of disgust. "She wore these tight slacks; of course I was looking at her ass! So I thought of her when he asked, and I told him about her. He asked me for the exact spelling of her name and a description. Asked if I knew what kind of car she drove, which I did—an emerald-green Mazda Miata.

"He told me something would happen to Piper in the next few days. Nothing fatal but something that would hurt her enough that I'd hear about it. *That will be my proof to you that I'm not a cop and that I mean what I say,* he said. I replied with a *Sure thing, friend,* or something to that effect. I figured he was full of it. *One more thing,* he told me. *Breathe a word about this conversation to anyone, and I'll kill Avery and Dylan.* Then he was gone. I was left wondering who it was

I'd just been talking to." He rolls the cigarette between his finger and thumb, regarding it. "I decided I'd wait to see if anything happened to Piper. Until then I'd keep my mouth shut, for my boys' sake. Just in case. He was probably a nutcase. Maybe he was one of the other members, playing a practical joke on me." He shrugs. "Better to play it safe. Avery and Dylan were my sons. I wasn't going to do anything to put them at risk."

The fact that one of his sons is lying dead upstairs, killed by his own hands, makes this statement ridiculous, but it's obvious he is as oblivious to this as he is to any of the other thousand holes in his logic. His rationalizations only need to satisfy him, not us.

"Did something happen to Piper Styles?" Alan asks.

"Oh yeah." For the first time since all this began, Hollister smiles his real smile, an ugly smile. "Someone broke into her home and used a knife on her face. Not just one side, like yours," he says, looking at me, "but both. It was in a few newspapers. He disfigured her for life." He smirks. "She never came back to work."

It's amazing how quickly he's let his true face show, the result of Alan's rapport making him feel safe and his own decompensation now that the need for a mask is off. What we're seeing now isn't what Douglas Hollister became but what he's always been. He never loved Heather. He is incapable of love. He probably married her because he hoped he could subjugate her strength in some way. When that didn't work, he found a submissive woman.

"So that's when you started to take him seriously?" Alan asks.

"Well, yeah. Wouldn't you?"

"I guess I would."

"He contacted me a few days later, again while I was chatting online. *Did you get my proof?* he asked. I said I did. Then he put the hook in me." He pauses. "I guess I should say, he handed me the hook and had me put it in myself." He puffs on the cigarette, no longer smirky or nasty. "You ever read *Faust*? The bargain with Mephistopheles?"

"Sure."

"There's the guy, Faust," Hollister says, telling us the story anyway. "He's an alchemist/scientist kind of guy. A seeker of truth. He's frustrated because he's reached the limit. Can't find out more about life, the universe and everything. The devil notices and makes a bargain: He'll serve Faust until the moment Faust reaches some highest point of happiness possible—then he gets his soul. Faust says, 'Sure, why not,' because he's certain that moment will never come. He'll get the devil's help learning the secrets of the universe, but he'll never have to pay the piper. Problem is, he does." He sighs. "Dali gave me a choice, but he didn't *make* me choose. I did that on my own."

Of course, I think, God saves Faust in the end, because He sees the value in Faust's striving. Faust's bargain, however misguided, was made in the direction of a worthwhile endeavor: acquisition of knowledge. Hollister sold his soul for a lot less.

"He told me," Hollister continues, "that he was going to give me a day to think about things. *If you decide to go on from here, he said, there's no turning back. We'll be entering into an agreement. You'll be making promises to me. Break a promise and there will be consequences.* Then he signed off."

"Did you think about it?" I ask, truly curious.

He contemplates me, not with contempt this time. There's some recognition from him of the question's value. "Not much," he admits. "I just wanted her gone. I think he probably knew that. He knew I was caught the moment he offered to help me. Everything else was just reeling me in."

He's probably right. Sociopaths tend to understand each other. Birds of a feather.

"What did he offer you?" Alan asks.

Hollister is getting tired. The adrenaline high of the last few days is wearing off. He's looking into the future now, I imagine. Years of a prison cell, with memories of his dead son's eyes, begging him for life. He takes a last drag of his fourth cigarette and stubs it out on the coffee table. He doesn't light another.

"He told me he could make both Heather and her boyfriend disappear. He'd take them away. He didn't tell me if he was going to kill them or not, just that no one would ever find them."

"I assume you were supposed to pay him something?"

"That was the brilliant part. I'd wait seven years and then get her declared legally dead, sans body. I'd collect on the life insurance and then he would contact me for delivery—in cash—of half the amount. It seemed risk-free. There would be no body, so no one could prove murder. Seven years would pass. That's a long time. People would have moved on to other things.

"*You have to do only three things,* he told me. *Say yes, live your life normally for seven years, and then give me my half of the insurance money when it comes.*" His grin is sickly. His pallor has changed even in the short time of this interview. He is pale, drained. "So I said yes. A week later Heather and her boy toy were gone. He only contacted me one other time, with a warning. *Remember—consequences,* he said. *Turn on me in any way, and terrible, terrible things will happen to you and the people you care for.*"

Now I'm finally seeing what happened. "You didn't pay him," I say. "I'm right, aren't I? The money came in, and you didn't pay him."

"Seven years had passed!" He speaks in a whine, like a small boy trying to justify himself. "We'd gotten on with our lives, we were happy. Hell, I'd kind of forgotten about him. Well, not forgotten . . . more like . . ." He pauses, searching for the words. "Like it never really happened. Like it was something I dreamed. You know? I mean, he never contacted me during that time. Never. And I had no way to contact him. He just didn't seem *real* anymore.

"Then one day he emails me and says it's time for me to pay up. Out of the blue." He shrugs, and it's a gesture of cautious amazement. "I deleted the email. One little button push. It scared me, but it also kind of made me feel *strong.*" A muscle in his cheek jumps. "I remember thinking, how do I know he's still got Heather? Maybe he killed her right off." His eyes dart back and forth between Alan and me. They are filled with petulance and self-righteousness. "There was a good chance he had nothing on me. I had a new life. That money belonged to *us!*"

I can withhold myself no longer. I should, but I can't. I walk over so that I am standing behind the video camera. I pause the recording and look down on him, mustering all the contempt I can find, which in this case is plenty.

"You're a shitty excuse for a human being, Douglas. You'd gotten on with your life? You were happy? Do you know what was happening to Heather that whole time? She was cuffed or chained and left by herself in the dark. For *eight years*! While you watched TV and fucked your new wife and went to Little League with your sons. You robbed her of everything. And why? Because you didn't want to be married to her anymore?" I put my palms against my eyes for a second, because I'm losing it. I steady myself. "I know I'm wasting my breath, but I want you to think about something, Douglas. Think about all the times you were sitting in this nice house, having a nice dinner, while Heather was naked and screaming in the darkness, probably not knowing why or if her sons were alive or dead or maybe in some dark room next to her."

He snarls then, a last defiance. Maybe he finds a surge of strength because I'm everything he seems to despise so much. "She deserved every minute for what she did to me. If it wasn't for her, Dana would be fine, and Avery would still be alive."

I gape at him, aghast. I've seen it before, of course, this kind of un- believable displacement of responsibility. A pedophile once told me, in all seriousness: *But they wanted me to touch them. If they want it, it's natural, and you can't fight nature, right?*

It's my turn to slump, to feel drained. I push the record button again. "Finish up with him," I tell Alan. "You can fill me in on anything pertinent later."

"Too much for you to handle?" Hollister sneers. "Just like all the fem-cows. You want the same job as a man, but you can't handle it when things get messy, when the pressure is really on."

I can't muster any anger. That's okay. Exhaustion fits my reply best anyway.

"Douglas, the problem I have isn't that it's too messy to confront. The problem I have is that you're so"—I look for the word—"unorig- inal. You caused so much pain, but in the end you're a caricature. Do you understand what I'm saying? You don't scare me: You make me tired."

He has no reply but hate. He shows it to me as he has throughout: with his eyes.

I turn and walk away, opening the sliding glass door and letting my- self out into the blessed freedom of the backyard.

# CHAPTER SEVENTEEN

"Burns called some uniforms to come and take Hollister away," Alan says.

I'm standing in the large backyard—which is much like the front yard, just a single tree and waves of too-green grass—looking at nothing. Trying to make sense of everything I just heard. "He really had no way of contacting this Dali?" I ask.

"Nope. Hollister never initiated contact. The perp always contacted him, either by email or cell phone. The emails were always from a free service provider, like Yahoo or Gmail. He tried calling back on some of the cell phone numbers when things blew up, but they were all out of service."

"They were probably pay-as-you-go phones." I sigh. "He's smart. Controlling the contact limits his exposure. He provides proof that he can deliver without ever actually meeting Hollister, and he doesn't disclose the payment details until it's time." I glance at Alan. "I'm assuming they never met?"

"Not once face-to-face."

"Right." I nod. "Clever."

"What's smart is waiting seven years. You know how much changes in that amount of time in a major metropolitan police department? People are transferred, fired, retire, chiefs come and go, not to mention all the new crimes being committed. Picking out a crime from seven years ago, unless it's something really memorable, is pretty unlikely."

It's true. The inexorability of it is terrifying. Seven years for a pay-off?

"It explains some things about Heather," I say. "The lack of over-the-top physical abuse. No overt signs of rape. Maybe this really is just a purely financial transaction for him."

"Pick her up, lock her up, toss some food in every now and then?"

"Maybe."

"What about the scars on her back?"

I consider this. "Perhaps they were just punishment. Again, there was nothing in them to suggest someone out of control. Eight years is a long time. Maybe there were times she rebelled, and he needed to show her who was boss."

"Like a dog." He curls his lip in disgust.

"It's cold," I muse. "There's a pathology there, but no passion. I don't know. It's odd."

It's difficult for me to accept finance as the sole motive. Seven years is one hell of a personal investiture just for money.

My cell phone rings and I answer. "Barrett."

"Another victim has turned up," Callie says. "Male, unresponsive, just like Dana Hollister."

My stomach churns. "Where?"

"He was left in the parking lot of a hospital in Simi Valley. He'd been placed in a body bag with a breathing tube. Some poor grandmother on her way in for a checkup on her hip replacement heard noises, went to investigate, and found him."

"Any ID?"

"Not yet, but this happened two or three hours ago. What do you want me to do?"

I put a hand to my forehead, just briefly. There's too much happening all at once. Dana Hollister in the bathtub, Heather Hollister in the hospital, Douglas Hollister in jail, Dylan struggling for life . . . I don't include poor Avery, because all that's left for him is the indignity of an autopsy and a burial. "What's happened on the ViCAP search?"

"Completed. There have been three other similar crimes reported in the last seven to eight years. One near Las Vegas, another in Portland, and the oldest in Los Angeles. The same marks in the eye sockets were there on all three of them, with the same mental unresponsiveness." She pauses. "As you suspected, all three had been given homemade lobotomies."

We don't have medical confirmation on Dana or the new John Doe, but I'm confident we'll find the same thing. Our killer is good, but he isn't flawless. Flawless would be remaining undetected. Leaving bodies behind is the same as a trail of bread crumbs for us. I hope.

"Honey-love?" Callie asks. "What do you want me to do?"

"I'm pretty sure I know who the new male victim is, Callie. Heather had a boyfriend." I explain to her about Jeremy Abbott.

"That would make sense," she agrees.

"The timing is pretty compelling. Find out if I'm right."

"What do you want James to do?"

"Keep him on the database. This guy's very smart. We're going to need to be detail-oriented to catch what he's missed."

"Speaking of the little beast, he's asking to talk to you."

"Put him on."

"I came across something interesting," James says without preamble. "The night Heather Hollister was abducted, an oddity was noted by the investigating officers: a series of car accidents, four in all, of vehicles exiting the parking lot the gym was in."

I frown, puzzled. "You mean a four-car pileup?"

"No. Four separate accidents, four vehicles, all unrelated."

"Strange."

"Too strange," he says. "I don't think it was an anomaly. I'm going to see if I can chase it down further."

Then he's gone, before I can reply, and Callie is back. "Ah, James, our James," she says, sounding wistful. "Can't live with him, can't kill him slowly enough."

"Do you know what he's talking about? This thing with the cars?"

"That would require him to give me the time of day. I'm off to see the man you think might be Jeremy Abbott." She pauses. "Is it bad?"

I consider Dana Hollister staring into the void. "It's one of the worst things I've ever seen."

"Curiouser and curiouser," Alan says, not in his happy voice.

I've just briefed him on my phone call with Callie.

"What's the game plan?" he asks.

I glance at my watch. It's closing in on four o'clock. The day has gotten away from us. The sun is a runaway horse. "We could go to the hospital," I say. "We can try to talk to Heather again."

He shakes his head. "I advise against it. Give her another night, and then go over there with Burns. Just you and him."

The Crime Scene Unit has arrived. Douglas Hollister has already been led away, cuffed and crying. Avery Hollister's body continues to decompose in the bathroom upstairs, awaiting the coroner. Dylan Hollister is at the hospital having his stomach pumped. I think of refrigerator magnets and suddenly I'm overwhelmed with a desire to see Bonnie.

"I want to go home," I say. "Is that weird? I just got back from vacation, and I guess we should go balls out on this, but I just don't feel like it."

"Nope. Not weird. That's the voice you need to listen to when it pipes up."

He's mentioned this before, in years past. The voice. He says it is your internal fuse box speaking, letting you know what your limits are.

*It has been a crazy few days,* I tell myself, beginning the necessary internal rationalization. *Bonnie's cat-killing, the offer from the director, Callie's aborted wedding celebration, and all that followed. I'm only human. Right?*

I yield to my own wimpiness.

"Let's go home."


"I'm going to stay here," Burns says. "Obviously. CSU will feed me anything they find right away, and I'll send it your way. I assume that will be a two-way street?"

"Scout's honor," I say, raising my three fingers in the time-honored salute.

"That's the Boy Scout salute. You're a girl."

I smile, in spite of my exhaustion. "We won't play any games when it comes to cooperation. You have my word."

"Good." He runs a hand through his thinning hair. "You want to hear something awful? I'm excited. All this, and I'm excited. Finally going to break this case open."

I force another smile, but I don't share his optimism. "Would you have a problem with letting our computer team go over his PC?"

"I don't, but computer crimes might. They're pretty open when it comes to cooperation, but they don't like having it taken away kit and caboodle."

"How about a compromise, then? I'll send my tech over to the LAPD, and they can work together on it. No turf wars that way."

"That'll work."

"Not to tell you how to do your job . . ." Alan says.

Burns waves him off. "Bull-pen advice is allowed, no offense taken."

"Your CSU should print the body bag that Dana Hollister came in. It's a good surface for prints."

The paramedics had lifted Dana's slack form out of the bag, which remained upstairs in the tub.

"You think he's that careless?"

Alan shrugs. "Devil's in the details."

"Consider it done. When do you want to try interviewing Heather again?" Burns asks me.

"Tomorrow mid-morning. Ten o'clock?"

"Let's make it ten-thirty. I'm going to be up to my asshole with this until late tonight. My captain will want a briefing at nine-thirty."

We agree and shake hands. Burns is still flushed with his grim, hopeful excitement. I understand it, but I can't find any of it in me right now.

Alan drops me off at my car. The parking lot is emptying out of cars as the sun meanders toward its setting place, getting ready to make the sky bleed.

"I think I'll go upstairs and rattle James's cage a little," Alan says. "You should just go."

"Thanks." Alan is my de facto second in command. Yet another reason I will miss him when he retires.

"One thing. In the interview with Hollister, I got the idea he was still holding something back."

"A lie?"

He squints, thinking. "Not so much lying as, maybe . . . omitting? Fuck, I don't know. It's just a gut thing."

"I trust your gut."

He pats it with his hand. "It's a good gut."

"Prodigious."

He grins. I envy his perfect white teeth, as I have so many times before. The last time I had teeth like that, I was fifteen. Then I started smoking, and now they are what I like to refer to as an "eggshell white." Alan's sparkle like all-natural veneers. "Good night," he says.

There's still a little bit of light in the sky when I pull into my driveway, a minor miracle. It's almost always the moon that ushers me through my front door. I climb out of my car, trying not to think much about the day.

I'd never have come home this early on a case even five years ago.

The guilt, I reflect, is a little like Catholic guilt. That feeling that you should be doing something or not doing something, even though the majority of the world wouldn't judge you for either. This is like that. I'm going to walk through my front door, into my house filled with the people who love me. I'm going to have a nice hot dinner, a heavenly cup of coffee, and then some conversation, laughter, television, bedtime, and possibly a little de-stress sex.

Avery Hollister, in the meantime, will be taken to the morgue. Heather Hollister will be picking at her skin and pulling out strands of hair. Dylan Hollister will wake up to a world where his own father killed his brother and tried to kill him. Dana Hollister will be trapped in her dark, soundless world, as will the man I believe to be Jeremy Abbott.

Douglas Hollister is going to jail, though.

I nod to myself. That earns me something.

As I walk to the door, I notice a white envelope, greeting card size, propped against it. SMOKY is written on it in block capital letters. I frown and look around. I pick up the envelope and open it.

Inside is a blank card on white stock, utterly featureless. I flip it open.

ONE LAST WARNING. DON'T COME LOOKING FOR ME. THERE WILL BE CONSEQUENCES IF YOU DO. LET IT LIE.

My heart stutters in my chest and my hand reaches for my weapon. I scan the front yard. The streetlights are beginning their dim hum as a timer tells them darkness is approaching. I try to swallow, but my mouth is too dry.

*He'd been here! At my house!*

The keys shake in my hand as I turn the lock. My hand shakes as I turn the knob. I can't help it.

*Hold it together. I need to tell Tommy about this, that's established, but Bonnie doesn't need to know anything.*

I close my eyes and take in a deep breath, hold it for a moment, expel it slowly. I do this again. I open my eyes. Better. I paste a broad smile on my face and enter my home.

Tommy approaches as I walk into the living room. He gives me a hug and a kiss on the cheek. Bonnie comes and gives me a hug and a smile. It's all very *Ozzie and Harriet* and surreal. We're turning into the kind of family that the men I hunt need so much to kill.

"Hungry?" Tommy asks.

I sniff the air and find that, yes, I actually am. "That smells amazing. What is it?"

"Just spaghetti. Secret's in the sauce."

"I can taste it from here."

"You'll get to eat it hot off the stove this time, instead of heating up the leftovers like usual." Another kiss. "Dinner's in twenty." Bonnie's returned to the coffee table and what looks like homework.

I go upstairs and change into my relaxed clothes, which can consist of such things as sweats or shorts, depending on the weather, and always—always—socks but no shoes. Tonight it's sweats. I finish taking the band out of my hair. I wear it up at work, but leaving it up at home can give me headaches. I close my eyes again and breathe. "Tommy!" I call. "Can you come up here for a second?"

"In a minute."

I wait, thinking as I do that you could set your watch to Tommy's "in a minute." He tends to mean what he says. I hear footsteps on the stairs and he enters the room, closing the door behind him.

"So you ready to tell me what's been bugging you since you came in the door?"

My mouth falls open. "You knew?"

He reaches out to touch my hair. He likes it down, like this.

"Smoky, when I was in the Secret Service, I would spend hours study-ing a crowd of five hundred people, looking for an indication of trou-ble. Do you really think I can't see when the woman I love has something on her mind?"

I scowl, irrationally irritated at being seen through so easily. "Why didn't you ask me about it, then?"

He shrugs. "Because I trust you. I knew you'd tell me when and if I needed to know."

"Simple as that?"

He contemplates me with loving eyes. "A lot of people think being together means you always have to know every single little thing that's going on with your partner. As if not being clairvoyant suddenly be-comes a failing when you're a couple. I think you should know about the important things, and you should be there when your partner needs you. All the rest is trust."

"That sounds a lot like the relationship between cops who are part-ners."

"There are worse relationships to emulate."

I frown. "So wait—do you have some secrets still? Things you haven't told me?"

"Of course."

I consider this. "And you're saying it won't hurt me or us for me not to know them?"

"Yep."

My first instinct is to reject this philosophy, but after I give myself a moment, I realize that he's right. I trust him. I'm not worried about any secrets he hasn't felt the need to tell me. "That's pretty cool, Tommy."

"Trust and privacy aren't mutually exclusive. We fell in love because of who we are as individuals. What would be the point of losing that individuality?"

I put my arms around his neck. "Give me a kiss. A good one."

He does. "Now. Tell me what you need to tell me."

I fill him in on the text message sent to me at the wedding, and I pull the greeting card out of my purse and hand it to him. He reads it and gives it back to me when he's done.

"What do you want to do?" he asks.

That's all. No fit of anger, no fist shaking, no oaths to hunt down and kill whoever's doing this. Just a level gaze and a simple question.

"I want to put Kirby on Bonnie, 24/7. That's my real concern in all this. I was fine when it was just a text message—well, okay, not fine, but it was just about me then." I shake my head. "This is different. He came to my home. I can't function unless I know she's safe."

He thinks, then nods his approval. "Kirby's very good."

"We'll have to pay her something, Tommy. I can't ask her to do full-time bodyguard work for nothing."

"That's not a problem. You talk to her and then have her call me about the financial details."

"What about you?" I ask.

"I'll guard myself." It's said in a way that indicates that's the *end* of that particular discussion. "I'm going to get the house brought up to snuff on security. The stuff you did after losing Matt and Alexa was okay, but it's time to go high tech."

I'd put double deadbolts on all the doors. At the time it had made me feel better, but—once again—it was only me then.

"I'm scared, Tommy. We're too happy."

He plays with my hair again, strokes my cheek with a knuckle, and then he takes my hand and heads toward the door, pulling me along with him. "Wine and pasta are great levelers," he says. "'Calm your stomach, calm yourself,'" he quotes.

"Who said that?"

"My father."

I let him lead me down to the promised peace.


Dinner is a happy thing. Tommy was right. It doesn't take away the fear, but I feel grounded again.

Bonnie is chatty and animated, talking about her choice for an extracurricular activity.

"Track," she says. "I think I could run pretty fast, and they have meets and everything. I like running and being healthy, and it's a good way to meet other girls."

Track coordinates too well with her desire to become an FBI agent when she grows up, but she's so obviously happy about her choice that I let it go easily, a butterfly on the breeze.

She doesn't even mention the other part of the deal—our time at the gun range. I'm sure it's on her mind, just as I'm certain she's not bringing it up now on purpose. I accept this manipulation with a kind of relief; it's very teenage, almost normal.

She helps Tommy clean up after the meal. He likes to hand-wash the dishes and refuses to let me do it.

"It relaxes me," he says.

The man wants to do all the dishes, all the time. Who am I to argue?

They work quietly, not speaking. Bonnie is very comfortable with Tommy's taciturnity.

I enjoy watching them when they don't know they're being watched. I give them a final, lingering glance and then go upstairs to our bedroom. I close the door and retrieve my cell from the bed where Tommy had tossed it. I dial Kirby. She picks up after two rings.

"Howdy, Smoky," she chirps. Kirby is almost always chipper, except when she's killing someone, and maybe sometimes even then.

"Good job on the wedding, Kirby," I tell her, meaning it. "Sorry it got interrupted."

"That's okay. I don't think I was feeling as bad as the bald chick."

"I can confirm that."

"I'm most pissed off about the cake. I mean, gosh, I really got a good deal on it."

Probably by flashing your gun and that kilowatt smile, I muse.

"What did Callie do with it?"

"She took two slices home. Two slices! That's all. Does that make any sense to you?"

"What happened to the rest of it?"

She giggles. "Let's say it was put to good use on a beach by a fire satisfying the munchies."

"I guess a man was involved?"

"Of course! I mean, what girl with any self-esteem eats wedding cake on the beach alone? Talk about pathetic pictures, you know?"

"I suppose you're right."

"So, boss woman. What's the job? Need someone fucked silly until they give up secrets in the throes of ecstasy? Or maybe you need someone to become extra-special quiet?"

Kirby's only half joking. I imagine if I asked her to kill for me, she'd do it without much concern. She'd kill and then head back out to the beach with a gosh and a giggle for some more marijuana, wedding cake, and man. Kirby is a creature of the now, and she doesn't question her own enjoyment of things. I envy it sometimes, but only sometimes. I'm happy with my current moral compass.

"I need you to guard Bonnie. It will be full time, which I guess means you'll need to pull someone else in to help. I'll let her know it's happening. She's too smart to do otherwise. She'd figure it out."

A brief silence tells me she's disturbed by this request. Kirby is the only person I know who's more inscrutable than Callie, but I've seen enough and become attuned enough to the minutiae of her variations to be certain that she cares about Bonnie.

"Someone threatened her?" Her voice is cool, mild, dangerous.

"Me. Someone threatened me." I fill her in.

"Hmmm . . ." she says. "Sure, I'll do it. It's going to cut into my sex life, but that's the biz."

"We'll pay you, Kirby, of course. Tommy said for you to call him about that."

"Puh-leeeeeeze! Your green stuff is no good with me, babe. You'll have to foot the bill for whoever I get to help me, but I won't accept a shiny thin one for anything else."

"Kirby," I protest. "That's a lot of time, and—"

She interrupts me. "You do know that I'm rich, right?"

"You are?" The thought had never occurred to me.

I can almost hear her rolling her eyes. "See, you think blonde means dummy, just like the rest of the world. Hella yeah, I'm rich! Solving all those problems with drug cartels in South America tended to leave cash lying around, if you know what I mean, plus I was playing them off against each other, selling information and my own special brand of silence to both sides." If she was here, she'd be winking at me. "Then there's years afterward working freelance. People pay a lot of money for what I do, Smoky. I'm what is known as *highly diversified*. Mutual funds, gold, Swiss bank accounts—you name 'em, I've got 'em. Then there's all the blackmail I have stashed away in case I need a really big infusion of cash."

What can I say? "I appreciate it, Kirby. I really do."

"No problema. Now, gotta ask the question, hate to but have to. If something does happen, how do you want me to solve the problem?" It's asked with the same level of unending cheer as all the rest of it.

"Lethally," I answer, without hesitation.

The penalty for messing with my family is death. This is a morality I no longer have the slightest quandary about.

Kirby takes it in stride, never missing a beat. "You betcha. When do you want me to start?"

"Tomorrow morning, if you can."

"Coolio. Then I'll call Tommy, hammer out the details, and head for the beach. One more night licking wedding cake off my current hunk of man before heading into the salt mines."

I hang up, feeling troubled and amused, which is par for the course when it comes to conversations with Kirby. She weaves stories of carefree sex with cheerful tales of assassination in a dance that leaves you wondering how much is true and if you should be worried about the state of your soul or hers or both.

An adage from my father pops into my head. *Chase the wind and you'll be running forever.*

It applies to Kirby. Either cut her out of your life or accept her as she is, because you'll never tame her. She's the wind.

# CHAPTER EIGHTEEN

"Killing another human being, man or woman, is like concrete and dirt," his father said when the Boy was sixteen.

The Boy always listened closely to anything his father said, but his interest sparked stronger now, not because of the subject but because of the hint of poetry in its speaking. Dad was not a poetic man. He enjoyed his Dali and the thundering violins of classical music, but those were anomalies as a means to an end.

"The airy-fairy squad tells us about things like wind and the sky. Feelings of freedom, all that jazz. Maybe they exist, maybe they don't. All I know is that you can't touch the sky or see the wind. But everywhere you look, far as the eye can see, you'll find concrete and dirt. It's real. You feel it against your feet or your car tires.

"Killing another human being is something you do against concrete and dirt. It's where the blood goes as they die and where the body goes after they die. It's where you'll end up too."

Dad had been looking off as they sat in the backyard. They were having a barbeque, just the two of them. It was the Fourth of July, and the sun was setting in a panoply of runaway reds. Dad held a long steel spatula and used it to turn over the burgers as he exposited on the subject of killing.

"The sea," the Boy said, without thinking, and then shut up quick, his ears going red to the tips.

"What's that?" Dad asked. "Speak up, Son. Once you say something, own it."

The Boy cleared his throat and straightened his back. "Sorry, sir, it was just a stray thought. You said it was everywhere, concrete and dirt, as far as the eye could see. But . . . not on the ocean, sir. There it's water."

Dad turned a burger and nodded. "True enough. But think harder, Son. What's all that water sit on?" He didn't wait for an answer. "Dirt. Throw a body in the ocean, and it sinks to the bottom, which is sand and rock. Even if that body gets eaten on the way down, whatever eats it dies and ends up there anyway." He peered at one of the burgers with a critical eye. Somewhere, a string of firecrackers went off. "You can escape the water, Son, but you'll never escape the dirt."

Dad was right again, as usual. It occasioned a surge of pride in the boy. He was lucky to have the father he had.

"Thank you, sir. I'll remember."

"Good boy." His father flipped another burger. "Someday, Son," he said, changing the subject without warning, as was his way, "you're going to be on your own, and you're going to start examining everything I've taught you with a more critical eye."

"I'll never question your lessons, sir."

"I believe you as you say it now. But things change, Son, people most of all. You're under my thumb now. One day you won't be. You'll likely stop sometime—a full stop, probably—and the key question will come to mind."

The Boy waited for his father to continue. When he didn't, the Boy realized he was waiting for a prompt. "What's the key question, sir?"

His father turned a burger. "The key question, Son, is: What makes him an authority on all this stuff?"

His father leaned back on his heels and gazed up at the sky. The Boy watched him and pondered. He didn't really get where his father was going with this. Question his right as an authority? That was crazy talk. He was an authority because he was Father. What other explanation was needed?

"You listen to me now because I'm the biggest piece of meat between us," Dad said. "Boys grow, Son. You might never be bigger than me, but one day you'll be stronger. What will you use to explain my authority then?"

"Sir—"

"Don't worry, Son. I'm not trying to make you agree to something that'll I'll punish you for later. Listen up and I'll get where I'm going."

"Yes, sir."

Father moved the burgers off the grill and put some raw ones on. "When I was a boy, we were poor. I'm not talking about missing a radio or a new pair of blue jeans. We had handmade furniture and an outhouse and didn't always know where the next meal was coming from. Mama helped make ends meet by whoring. Daddy was a no-good who drank every cent she couldn't hide.

"Daddy wasn't too particular about who he fucked when he got a drunk. I had a brother and a sister, and all three of us got the touch now and again."

He flipped a burger and the Boy listened, rapt and fascinated. Father had never talked about his own past before. Never.

"Mama died when I was fourteen. I was the oldest, but not by much. Sissy was thirteen, and my younger brother—Luke—was twelve. Daddy had no intention of getting a job or quitting his drinking, so he put us to work fucking for money, all three of us.

"Sissy was the weakest of us three. Always had been. She lasted two years before she got Daddy's shotgun and blew her head clean off." Father paused, staring into a memory. "I came in just after I heard the blast. Blood was in the air like a thin red fog. It was like dust when it settled, but it was wet." He stared for a moment longer, then seemed to come back to reality, reaching down to turn a burger as though he hadn't just traveled in time.

"Daddy had us bury her in the woods. He beat us and told us we were going to have to do her share now too. And so we did."

The Boy noted that his father's voice had changed. A strong accent had crept in, along with a rhythm and mode of speaking that had only been hinted at before. He had no idea where his father came from. He only knew the here.

"Luke went next. Some freak strangled him to death while he was fuckin' him. Daddy had me kill the freak too and bury them both in the woods. He went to beat me again, but I decided I'd had enough of all that." Father examined a burger, voice calm as he relayed these horrors. "So I killed him and buried him in the woods too." He paused, looking off. "That was the day I understood, Son: There ain't no such thing as the soul. I tried pretending there was, because my mama had lied and said it was so, and do you know what that pretending made me?"

"No, sir."

"Pathetic, boy! It drove me to try to love that man, in spite of all the things he done to me. It made me happy when he smiled at me, it even made me cry sometimes when he wouldn't love me back. I was like a puppy dog, begging for scraps at his feet, just a touch or a smile or a kindly spoken word. All the time thinking I needed it because I believed in such a thing as the soul." His father leaned forward and spat on the ground. "I learned the truth, and I never let it go, and I swore if I ever had a son of my own, I'd teach him right, so he wouldn't make the same mistake in his own life."

Firecrackers went off, but the Boy barely heard them.

"Anyway, I buried Daddy, and then I lit out and joined the army. I ended up at the hard end of the Korean War. Managed to fake my age and get in where the fighting went rough." Father paused, staring off into the then again. "I saw things you couldn't imagine, boy. Men firing rifles with their guts hanging to their feet. Cannibalism in the snow. A dead woman getting fucked 'cause the man raping her hadn't realized she'd gone and died." Father kept on staring, his eyes wider now, in some kind of wonder. "People think we were righteous then, and maybe most were, but there were savages in all that rock and bone too. Men-beasts who lived for war. I wasn't quite one of them, but I understood the notion."

His father turned to him then and looked down on him with a huge fierceness and intensity. It was a look from the void, and the Boy glimpsed, just for a moment, what a man-beast might be. Men who'd eat men and sell their children and have sex with the dead.

"So when that time comes, and you question what I've taught you and what makes me the man to say, remember what I told you today. It's because I been, Son. Been and done and come to know. There ain't no God in this world. I've seen that truth, right down to the dirt we walk on. There's just the eaters and the eaten."

The look continued until the Boy began to sweat because he felt an absence of his father in spite of his physical presence. He felt himself top-pling into the chasm that had opened up in his father's eyes.

Then his own voice spoke to him, like the voice of that God who didn't exist, huge and booming, full of authority and fire.

I am my father's son!

It was a sudden thought, random as a bolt of lightning, and as pow-erful. It flashed once, lighting up all the dark landscape inside him, and it brought a feeling of pride he understood and a sorrow he didn't.

He blinked and it was done. Father had turned away from him, back to the grill, where one burger had burned to black. Firecrackers ex-ploded somewhere.

"Burgers are done," Father said, his voice normal again. "Let's eat."

It wasn't the first time they talked about killing, or the last, but it was always the most memorable. For reasons he couldn't define, ever since that day he equated the coldness of death with the rich burst of cooked flesh in his mouth. Not as a point of sensory enjoyment but more as a sense of déjà vu.

He frequently thought of firecrackers when he killed.

# CHAPTER NINETEEN

"It's time for an answer, Smoky."

The director called me on my cell phone not long after my first cup of coffee and has arrived at this statement without much in the way of preamble.

"I'm still waking up, sir."

He chuckles. The condescending tone of it puts my teeth on edge. "Come on, Agent Barrett. You've already decided. I just need you to tell me what your decision *is*."

His confidence irks me, though much of that is the early morning grumps. Bonnie, in a moment of loving clairvoyance, brings me another cup of coffee. I roll my eyes heavenward in thanks. She grins and goes back to helping Tommy with breakfast.

"Fine, sir. My answer is yes. My team and my family are on board too, but everyone essentially said the same thing—their view may change if and when a Quantico move occurs."

"That's normal in any relocation. You'll lose some if that happens, there's no way around it."

"So what now, sir?"

"Now I do my job. I have a number of things to accomplish behind the scenes, including getting this whole idea approved and funded. We're still a few months away. I'll be in touch."

He hangs up, no *good-bye* or *thanks, Smoky,* irking me further. I scowl into my coffee and take a gulp, when I usually take a sip. The taste and the caffeine, as always, mollify me a little.

A knock comes on the door, and I groan. "Why?" I complain. I plod over to answer it myself, defying anyone stupid enough to come knocking this early to have *any* problem with my hurricane hair and frayed bathrobe.

I open the door to find a woman in her early forties. Age and personal style have cast her looks somewhere between pretty and matronly. She already has herself fully together this early in the morning; her makeup is perfect, her hair is styled, and she's wearing shirts and slacks with a thin sweater. The slacks are something I would wear, while the sweater reminds me of my grandmother. It's slightly surreal. Her smile is cheerful and blinding.

All morning people should be killed. Except for Tommy and Bonnie, of course.

"Yes?" I ask, keeping my voice on the neutral side of pleasant.

"Good morning," she says, saying it with that long *o* that I can't stand: *good moooorning.* It seems to be favored by overly cheerful people who come selling magazine subscriptions or God. "My name is Darleen Hanson? I'm on the current homeowner's association board?"

Another thing I can't stand: people who turn all their statements into questions.

I sip my coffee, fighting the urge to snarl. "Yes?"

She soldiers on, undaunted by my unfriendliness. "Well, now, we're a new board, and we want to get off on the right foot—a good start, you know? I think you'll agree that the last board was a little bit lax. Letting people leave their trash cans out on the curb for an hour longer than they should per the bylaws, things like that."

"Okay."

My one-word responses don't seem to be getting through to her. "Anyhoo, I'm sorry to bother you so early in the morning, but I have to get to work, as I'm sure you do too"—another blinding smile is flashed, a we're-all-in-this-together-aren't-we smile—"and I'm coming by to ask you for a little favor."

"Really? What's that?"

"Well, now, one of the bylaws states that vehicles need to be parked inside the garage. Leaving them out on the driveways everywhere is so unsightly, don't you agree? So if you could just start parking your car inside each night, we'd really appreciate it. Okay?" She ends with her biggest, most beaming smile yet.

I lean forward and look at my driveway. Yep, there's my car. I lean back again and sip from my coffee, staring at Darleen, who's waiting for a response.

I decide to be polite. This woman means no harm, I'm sure. She's asked nicely enough, and not once did her eyes widen at the sight of the scars on my face or flick with disapproval to my state of disarray.

"Listen, Darleen. I work for the FBI. There are times when I need to leave immediately, times when, quite literally, ten or twenty seconds can make a difference. So I'm more comfortable parking my car in the driveway. I'm sure you can understand."

She nods, smiles again. "Of course I can—and how interesting! Our very own FBI agent! But I'm afraid a bylaw is a bylaw, and you'll have to park inside. I appreciate your cooperation, I really do."

The smile remains, but something in the quality of it has changed. I have misjudged this woman. There's more steel than vapor behind that smile and those eyes, along with a touch of ugly busybodyness.

Cool. I can play this game, too!

I smile at her, nice and wide. I take a sip from my cup, wink, and say, "It's never going to happen." Then I close the door in her face.

I walk back over to the table, where Tommy and Bonnie are laying out plates of waffles and eggs and bacon. I have a warm, happy feeling in my stomach.

"Can't say that was well handled," Tommy remarks.

"Maybe not. But come on. Someone's going to try to tell me I need to park my car inside my garage?" I shake my head. "I don't think so."

"I happen to agree," he says, smiling, "but I know her type. You just started a war."

I grab a slice of bacon and bite off a piece, grinning at him. "Well, one of two things will happen in that instance. Either I'll beat her into submission, or you'll go and smooth things over with the HOA for me. If they're all women, you'll have them eating out of your hand in no time."

"Manipulative," Bonnie observes.

"Realistic," I assert.

She giggles, and I follow suit. Tommy shakes his head and sighs, but I know he's happy too. Nothing like some suburban politics to make us all feel, well, *normal*.

Normal's hard for this family.


"Will Kirby be coming today?" Bonnie asks me.

Last night, we'd discussed what was going on. I'd agonized over what to tell her and had decided, in the end, on full disclosure. I thought Bonnie could handle it, and I was right. She took it in stride, asking few questions and accepting both the necessity and wisdom of a bodyguard.

"You'll call her and tell her where to meet you," Tommy says to me. "After you brief her, she'll park herself near Bonnie's school."

"So that's a yes, honey," I say. "You ready for that?"

She shrugs. "Kirby's cool. And I guess she'll try to stay out of sight, right?"

"Do you want her to?"

She struggles with something. "I like Kirby, but . . . it's hard enough fitting in at school sometimes, you know? If she can stay back a little, that'd be great."

I kiss her on the top of her head, saddened by her struggles to assimilate, gladdened that she cares. "I'll tell her."

"Don't worry," Tommy says. "She'll only get close if something's happening."

"Didn't you say there'd be some other guy too?" she asks.

I nod. "Kirby can't watch you 24/7 by herself. Do we know who that's going to be?" I ask Tommy.

"No. She just said she had someone good."

"I'll make sure she introduces him to you," I tell Bonnie. After she introduces him to me. "Time for you to go, babe. Don't miss your bus."

She rolls her eyes. "I never miss my bus." She gives me a hug, goes over and gives Tommy a hug, grabs her backpack, and heads out the door with a final "Bye!"

I stare at the door once it's closed and I sigh. "You know the hugs are going to stop soon, right?" I ask Tommy, a little wistfully.

"Surprised they haven't stopped already," he says.

I scowl at his back. "Not helpful." He says nothing, but for some reason I get the sense that he's smiling. No one takes me seriously around here. "I'm going to take my shower," I say, flouncing off in high color.

Some mornings it's nice to play the princess. Almost comforting.


I'm enjoying the usual heavenly morning spray, eyes closed, when Tommy opens the shower door and appears naked next to me in the rising steam. He wraps his arms around me and hugs me to him. The contact is exquisite. The smell of apricot scrub hangs in the air.

"Do we have time?" he asks, a low rumble in my ear that makes me shiver.

I turn around, grabbing him in a way that makes him shiver too.

"Does that answer your question?"

He lifts me up, something that I never fail to find incredibly sexy. He grabs my ass and hoists me off the floor. I wrap my legs around his waist and we kiss while the water runs down our faces.

"Do you think we'll still be doing this in our sixties?" I ask him.

"As long as my back holds out," he murmurs, covering my neck with distracting kisses.

I giggle at his answer, but that dies away soon enough. Desire and laughter are kissing cousins, but they don't belong in the same room together.

# CHAPTER TWENTY

I walk into the hospital feeling refreshed and alert. It has been quite a morning, between the director's phone call and HOA Darleen, but coffee, hugs from my daughter, and some satisfying last-minute shower sex have lifted my spirits considerably.

Alan and Burns are waiting at reception. Alan's chatting with Kirby, who I'd called and asked to meet me. There's another man standing off to the side. He's thin and bald and watchful. He's listening to everything without participating in any of it, and something about him makes me certain that this is Kirby's second man. He seems mild enough on the surface, but I smell "predator."

Kirby spots me first and flashes one of those über-white beach-bunny grins. "Hey, boss woman!"

I smile as I walk up to them. "Hi, Kirby. Alan, Detective Burns."

Kirby frowns, cocks her head, and peers at me. "Hmmmmm," she says.

"What?"

"You have that freshly fucked look." She sidles up next to me and bumps me with a hip. "Did someone get lucky this morning?"

I'm mortified to find that I'm blushing. For his part, Alan smiles.

Burns watches it all, fascinated. "None of your beeswax. Can I talk to you outside?"

She winks. "Sure thing. Come on, Raymond," she says to the thin, bald man. "Time to go to work."

Raymond doesn't respond, but I get the idea he'll follow.

"I'll be right back," I tell Alan and Burns.

The three of us exit through the automatic doors. The sky above is covered in clouds. It's a gloomy morning, though that could change by noon.

"Smoky, this is Raymond," Kirby says, introducing us.

"Pleased to meet you," I say, not really meaning it.

Raymond doesn't speak, but he nods. Barely. He has green eyes. They contain a faraway look that I don't like.

"Raymond and I did some work together down in Central America," Kirby says. "He's got great instincts, and I trust him."

I don't, but I let it go.

"Bonnie had some concerns," I say. I tell her about our conversation at breakfast.

"Jeez," Kirby says, somehow pouting and rolling her eyes at the same time. "You'd think having a bodyguard would be, like, a status symbol for a kid or something. But, hey, no problema. We'll keep back unless we gotta kill someone, right, Raymond?"

Raymond nods, still wordless. I decide I've had enough of his menacing-silence act.

"I need to hear your voice," I say to him. "If you're going to guard my daughter, I need to hear your voice."

He doesn't reply. He glances at Kirby and raises his eyebrows.

"Uhhh . . . awwwkward!" Kirby says. "Raymond can't talk, babe. Someone tried to cut his throat a few years back. He lived, but his vocal cords are screwed."

"Oh. Shit. Sorry, Raymond," I manage. "Now I feel like a complete idiot."

Raymond reaches inside his jacket. He comes out with a notepad and writes something down. He hands it over to me. I read:

DON'T WORRY ABOUT IT.

Then:

If anyone comes to hurt her, I'll kill them. Guaranteed.

I hand the notebook back to him. It's a strange reassurance, this promise of murder, and disturbingly comforting. "Fair enough," I say.

What else *is* there to say?

"Cool stuff," Kirby says. "You have her school address?"

I'd written it down on a sheet of paper this morning. I give it to her.

"Raymond and I will go there now. We'll do the first day together, get the lay of the land, and then we'll figure out the best use of our time." She smiles, dazzling me. "Righty-right?"

"Sounds good."

"Right on!" she cries, lifting both hands, fingers configured in the universal horns salute of rock-and-roll lovers everywhere. They walk away like a spiritual Mutt and Jeff: the assassin who can't talk and the one who talks too much. I watch them leave and then head back into the hospital. I reunite with Alan and Burns.

"Interesting crowd you hang with," Burns observes. "Girl scared me, but at least she's cute. The undertaker-looking guy just gave me the creepy-crawlies."

"Me too," I admit.

Hopefully the bad guys will feel the same.


Heather Hollister's eye movements have slowed. They no longer dance over everything like a crack-addled ballerina, now they simply stare. She is lying on her back, arms folded over her stomach, staring at the white hospital ceiling. Her mouth is closed. Only the rise and fall of her chest and the occasional blink let us know she's alive.

Burns stands just inside the room, staring at her. His mouth has fallen open, and his eyes are filled with a heartbreaking blend of raw hurt and exhausted spirit. I imagine he is seeing her at twelve, staring up at him with solemn eyes, telling him to catch the man who killed her daddy. It was a promise he'd been unable to keep, and things have gotten far, far worse.

He moves toward her bed. He finds a chair, and sits down next to her. His movements belong on a much older man. He reaches over and takes one of her hands in his. Alan and I stand back, watching, feeling like intruders at a funeral.

"Heather, honey, it's Daryl Burns." He squeezes her hand. "Can you hear me?"

I imagine the faintest twitch of her eye.

Burns sighs. "I guess I really let you down, honey. I'm sorry about that. One thing I can tell you, though, is we got that snake that called himself your husband. Douglas was up to his ears in this."

This time I'm certain; I see the faintest tremor in the placid lake Heather's become. Burns senses it as well. He cranes forward.

"You can hear me, can't you? Come on, Heather. I know you've been through enough, God knows it's more than anyone could handle, but you can't stay locked away like this. We need you to help us get the man who did this to you." He's squeezing her hand, stroking it, and he looks more like a father to me than ever. "We need to get the bastard who cut off your beautiful hair, honey. Remember how you told me you had your dad's hair?" His voice cracks. I think that Burns is an old-school man, raised in the tradition of hiding your tears, but he doesn't even bother with an embarrassed glance back at us. He's too humbled by his own pain to care.

The tremor passes over her now without stopping, like a pile of windblown leaves dancing in circles, aimless but vital and sometimes even beautiful. It's a sign of life, however distorted, and Burns seizes on it as we watch.

"Heather? That's it, honey. Come on back. I'm right here. It's safe."

She blinks a few times, then faster. Her cheek twitches. She turns to look at Burns, and it's the motion of a skeleton turning on its own bones, like a creaky door. She opens her mouth and she laughs, a high, horrible cackle. It sends shivers down my spine. If birds were around to hear it, they'd fly off in terror.

"Saaaaafe . . . ?" she croaks. Then the laughter again, but tears follow as well, cascading down her cheeks. Her face glitters in its pain, contorted by laughter that's really just another form of screaming.

Burns gapes at it all, taken aback. He seems at a loss for what to do. He recovers quickly. His face sets into grim lines, but it's contrived, a man pulling on a mask.

"Knock that shit off right now, Officer Hollister!" he barks. "Wherever you were, you're not there now, and we need your help to catch the man who did this to you. Pull yourself together!"

It achieves the desired effect. The awful laughing stops. The tears roll on, staining the white bedsheets with water fingerprints. "D-Daryl . . ." she chokes. "I'm so so so fucked up. I'm sosososososoo fucked up." She grips his wrists with clutching, desperate hands. "Can you help me? I can't get out of my head. Can you help me? Please?"

His true face again, a gelid, flash-frozen grimace of sorrow. He gets up onto the bed and gathers Heather into his arms. She writhes against him, alternately boneless and spastic.

Heather's moans of despair draw the nurse into the room. She turns white at the quality of the shrieks and leaves. I guess she's more comfortable with physical pain than spiritual.

Alan and I say nothing. We wait, watching without watching, a trick of respectful distance you learn after the third or fourth or fifth time you deliver the news of death to a loved one in their own home. They collapse into the reality and you become an intruder. You can't leave, so you become a ghost instead. It's a terrible talent.

Heather's moans die down after a while. Burns continues to hold her as she quiets, patient with the gusts of grief that whip back up without warning. These become less and less frequent, turning into tremors, which crumble into sighs and, finally, silence.

We wait out the silence too. Comfort comes best in silence, in that wordless closeness only another human being can provide.

Eventually she lies back, and Burns takes his seat in the chair again. "Better?" he asks.

She nods, then shrugs, then scratches her arm and her head. She's a mess of constant motion. "I guess. Yes. Maybe. I don't know."

"Well, you're talking again. That's a start. Are you ready to talk about what happened?"

Her eyes widen. "I think so," she says. Her right cheek twitches three times. "I'm scared, Daryl. Maybe it will help, though. I don't know. I guess so."

Listening to her reminds me of a conversation with a methamphetamine addict, except that Heather has been overdosed on terror. Her fight-or-flight mechanism is set in the "on" position, and the switch is out of reach.

I know all about this feeling. About its constancy. After my rape, when I got home from the hospital, I couldn't sleep for a week. It wasn't just the pain of losing Matt and Alexa, I was also terrified. Every creak or wind moan got my heart racing. Adrenaline would spike through me at the sound of a car alarm. I wanted to crawl out of my own skin because it was on fire, but of course I couldn't, I could only scream inside the burning house of me.

I walk forward, putting a hand on Burns's shoulder. I make sure to face Heather, so she can see my scars.

"Hi, Heather. I'm Special Agent Smoky Barrett, with the FBI."

Her eyes jitter over me, widening a little as they grope past the scars.

"What happened to you?" she asks. There's a desperateness to the question that I understand: *Tell me something worse than what happened to me. Please.*

"A serial killer broke into my house. He raped me and tortured me with a knife. He tortured and murdered my husband and daughter in front of me."

I don't know if it's worse than what she experienced or not. I don't think you can qualify mental agony that way.

"What happened to the guy who did it?" A different kind of wanting laces her tone now.

"I shot him dead."

She hoots in laughter. "Good!" She licks her lips and repeats this in a firmer voice. "Good." Her eyes widen again. "Avery. Dylan. What about my boys? Can I see them?"

"We'll deal with Avery and Dylan soon, I promise," I answer, keeping my voice soothing, feeling traitorous and awful. "First, if you're up for it, I'd like to talk about what happened to you, and especially anything you can tell us about the man who did it to you. Do you think you can do that?"

The twitching again, one, two, three. "I think so. Yes, I can do it. Where do you want me to start?" She scratches her skull a little too hard, leaving a livid red mark.

"How about the night you were abducted? What do you remember about that?"

She squints. "That was so long ago . . . lifetimes ago. Crazy times ago. I tried to keep track of time, I really did. But it was so hard, because he never gave me any light." She says it again, emphasizing what he'd denied her. "Any *light*."

"The lights were out in the area of the parking light you were taken from, right?" I ask, pulling a thread from her free association and connecting it to a real memory.

She frowns. "Were they? Yes, yes, I guess they were. He did it. He's smart. Very, very, very, very smart. And cold." She shivers, picks at her left arm until it bleeds a little. "Too cold."

"You'd just come out of your cardio class," I remind her, keeping my voice low and soothing. I want to put her into that moment of her past while keeping the now as unthreatening as possible. "The police found your keys on the ground near your car. What happened?"

She cackles again. "That was smart of *me*. Most times he's the smart one, but that was smart of *me*. I dropped the keys so everyone would know I'd been taken and hadn't just run off." She says it with a child-like pride.

"That was smart, Heather," I agree. "You were smarter than he was at that moment, and it worked out just like you planned. Everyone knew you'd been kidnapped."

She nods, back and forth. "Yep. Yep. I was smart. He took me, but I was smart. He took me . . ." Her words trail off, and the twitching returns.

"How did he take you, Heather?" I ask. "Do you remember? Can you tell me?"

She turns her head to look at me. Her eyes and mouth are wide, making her look exactly like a scared little girl. "It was the whispers," she says, whispering herself. "What he whispered. He put a gun in my back and he whispered into my ear."

"What did he say?"

"He said I had to come with him right then and there or he'd kill me and then he'd go and kill Douglas and Avery and Dylan. He told me things about them, about where Douglas worked and about what doctor the boys saw. I believed him."

"Did you fight him?"

She leans back and sighs. "It didn't do any good. That was my plan, you see?" She nods, answering herself. "Yes, that was my plan. It was a *good* plan. I'd go along with him and watch for my opportunity." She chews on her lip. It would look pensive on someone else, and perhaps the same instinct is behind it here, but Heather continues until her lip begins to bleed. A thin line of blood runs down her chin.

"Heather," I say, reaching out to touch her.

She doesn't look at me, but it startles her out of the behavior. "What?" she asks.

"You were talking about fighting back."

She shakes her head. "It didn't work."

"What didn't work?"

"Fighting back. He put me in the trunk of his car, but he didn't tie me up or anything. When it stopped, I was ready. The trunk opened, and I was like, 'hi-yaaaah,' ready to go all kung fu on his ass, but . . ." She shakes her head again. Sighs. "He was ready. He sprayed pepper spray in my face and then he used a stun gun on me." The little-girl wonder stamps on her features again and the baldness adds to it, making her seem even more vulnerable. "You know what the scariest part was? He never said anything. He sprayed me and he shocked me and then he dragged me into that place and"—she swallows hugely, whispers—"threw me into the dark."

I go to ask another question, but she's been fully captured by the moment. She's not here, she's there. I stay quiet and wait for her to continue on her own.

"Have you ever experienced perfect darkness?" she asks. "It's hard to find. Douglas and I went on a trip to Carlsbad Caverns one time. They take you waaaay underground. At one point in the tour they talk about that, about perfect darkness, and then they turn out all the lights. It's incredible." She marvels at the memory. "You can't see anything. There's no ambient light of any kind. There's nothing for your eyes to adjust to. Just blackness." Another huge swallow. "The darkness in my cell was like that. Heavy. It has a weight, did you know that?" She nods, more in a conversation with herself than with me. "Yes, it does. You can feel the dark when it's complete like that. It slides against your skin. It gets into your mouth. You try not to let it, but if you close your mouth it just crawls in through your nose or your ears. You choke on it at first while you resist it, but it's just too much. One big gulp, and you drown." She twitches, twitches, twitches. "Except this drowning doesn't kill you. It goes on forever and ever and ever. It's like falling off a cliff for years.

"He didn't do anything for about a day. Just left me there in the dark. Then he turned on the lights. So bright. Yes, they were. So bright. I couldn't see anything, and I banged into a wall. Three blind mice, see how she runs." She giggles. Picks at her arm. "I was staggering around and heard the door open and then he used the stun gun again. I felt a prick in my arm and I went to sleep.

"When I woke up, I was naked and shackled and in the dark. The shackle was attached to a chain, which was attached to a wall. I had ones on my ankles and ones on my wrists, four of them, one two three four, so I could move around about half of the length of the cell.

"There was a speaker—something—built into the room. Sometimes his voice would come out of the dark. 'There are rules,' he told me on the first day. 'You eat every meal given unless you're sick. You exercise every day, without exception. Start with push-ups and running in place. Failure to comply with any of these rules will result in punishment.'"

She glances at me, a sly, knowing glance. "I didn't listen at first, of course. He brought some food and shoved it through a small opening in the bottom of the door, just like in one of those prison movies." She stops talking and stares. Moments pass.

"Heather?"

She jolts and begins talking again, as though nothing had happened. It reminds me of a needle jumping the groove on a record. "The only time I'd see light was when he brought the food. He'd unlatch the opening and place the tray inside. I'd have to get down on my stomach to eat. I loved the light so so much. It was kind of him to give me that, don't you think?"

My stomach rolls. She continues.

"I threw the food and he closed the opening. I sat there in the dark for a long time. Sometime later, I don't know how long, the blinding lights came on again. I couldn't see anything but white. He did the same thing as before, the stun gun and the needle. I woke up on my stomach, strapped to a table." She scrunches into herself like an abused child, trying to present as little body surface as possible.

"'You broke the rules,' he said. 'Now you have to be punished.' He didn't sound angry or anything. I really didn't get that feeling at all. He sounded like someone who had a job to do. Yes." Big nod, back and forth, happy to have put the right words to it. "He had a job to do." She pauses. "He used a whip on me. It felt like white fire, like someone was pouring lines of gasoline across my back and lighting them up. I screamed right from the beginning.

"Once he was done, he put some greasy stuff on my back, over the cuts. 'Next time you break the rules, the punishment will increase in duration by a third. And again the next time after that. And before you get any ideas—it'll never get bad enough to kill you.'

"I tried to ask him a bunch of questions. 'Why me? Why are you doing this?' Things like that." She pouts, picking at a forearm. "He wouldn't answer me, no, he wouldn't. He just threw me right back in that room in the dark."

Again her eyes slide over to me, and again that sly smile intrudes. "I took another five punishments before I believed him." The smile evaporates, replaced by wide-eyed wonder. "After that, I was a good girl. He never, ever hurt me when I was a good girl."

She seems to have wound down. I give her a gentle push. "Were you in the dark all the time, Heather?"

She's staring again.

"Heather?"

She jolts. "What? Oh yeah. Pretty much all the time. There was a toilet there; I had to find it in the dark and use it in the dark. The only way of marking time was meals. That's how I counted the days. Three meals was a day, and I'd count that. The problem was, there were times he'd be gone for a long time. Then he'd leave me dried food to eat, divided up into meal portions." She frowns. "I'd try and count the portions and divide by three and keep track of the days, but . . ." She sighs, her head falling forward in a gesture of futility. "I just lost track. Especially when I started talking to myself a lot and even more when I started talking to them."

"Who is 'them,' Heather?" I ask.

Her smile is beatific. It erases the look of insanity and suffering from her features, replacing it with a kind of peaceful joy. "My boys," she says. "The voices in the light that would comfort me. Without them . . . I don't know." She picks at her arm until it bleeds. "I might have gone insane."

I feel my stomach rolling again, not in revulsion but in horror. My greatest fear, since I was a little girl, was exactly this: to go crazy and not know it. I remember seeing that movie about John Nash, *A Beautiful Mind,* and not being able to sleep afterward.

"Heather," I ask. "Did you ever see the man who did this to you? Did you see his face or anything else that might help us identify him?"

The twitch in her cheek again, four times. She shakes her head. "Noooooo . . . all I ever saw was the dark, the dark and my light through the hole in my door." She grimaces. "You can see the dark, just like you can taste it. Everything gets more acute. I have bat ears now, did you know that?" She startles me by emitting a few high-pitched squeals—her imitation of a bat—which then dissolve into cackles. "And my skin . . ." She runs her hands over her arms, and I watch goose bumps rise. "It's all more sensitive." She squints at me. "But I'm seeing now. Am I really seeing? Or is this a dream?" She picks at the bloody spot on her forearm.

"It's real," I tell her.

She looks around, peering with care at everything in the room. She shrugs. "It doesn't seem real." She sighs, lies back. "I'm tired again. It's sleep time." She sits up suddenly, fearful. "Or is it eating time?" She reaches out to me, her hand shaking. "If I missed eating time, I'm sorry. I didn't know. You won't hit me, will you?"

I fight the welling tears and reach out to take her hand. "No one's going to hit you anymore, Heather. I promise."

She calms, but I can see in her eyes that she does not believe me.

"She's not in any condition right now to give us more than that," Alan observes.

We're standing outside Heather's room. Burns is silent, and he looks stricken. I feel tired already. The day is young, and we've only just started foraging through the sticky meat locker this perpetrator left for us. Heather Hollister could easily be the least of it.

"I agree," I say. "Still, she helped. We know now how he took her and how he treated her. It's going to help us with his profile."

"Profile?" Burns croaks. "I'll tell you what his profile is. He's a dead man."

Neither Alan nor I respond. We could give him the lecture about death threats in our presence, but we won't. We empathize.

"What's next?" Alan asks.

"I'm going to call Callie and see if she's confirmed the ID of Jeremy Abbott. Then we'll go and check up on both him and Dana."

"I'm going to pass on that," Burns says. "I'll keep Heather company for a while. If you need anything, call me."

He looks old again, ancient and bent. Burns is one of what I call the old guard, a brand of man that seems to be dying off in the world today. Built not of stereotypes but stone: heavy, strong, enduring like a mountain. Alan has these qualities, as do Tommy and AD Jones. Burns looks cracked, fissured, crumbling at the base.

"Call us if anything changes with her," I tell him.

He nods and reenters Heather's room.

"I don't think her outlook is good," Alan murmurs. "What happens when she finds out one of her sons is dead?" He shakes his head.

How would I deal with it? Eight years shackled up and locked away in absolute darkness, unable to track the days, without the benefit of human contact?

"It depends on her. You never know, she could bounce back."

I don't sound convincing.

"It's confirmed," Callie says to me. "The man in the hospital is Jeremy Abbott."

My heart sinks. More bad news for Heather.

"Good work. Alan and I are going to see Dana Hollister and Jeremy now. What else is happening there?"

"James has almost finished the timeline and collation of the case files. He's also discovered some interesting things about the car crashes."

"He can fill us in when we get back. In the meantime, can you get in touch with LAPD CSU and get briefed on what they found in processing the Hollister home? Oh—and get hold of Leo Carnes. We're going to need his expertise on this case."

"Anything else you want to add to that laundry list?" she complains. "When I say, 'I live to serve,' I'm talking about others serving *me*."

Finally, something that makes me smile. "We'll see you soon."

The doctor attending to both Dana Hollister and Jeremy Abbott looks like a teenager with old eyes. His blond hair and baby face contribute to the effect; I'm sure he gets plenty of jokes about being able to do surgery before he could shave.

"Both patients have had extreme damage to their prefrontal lobes," he says, confirming what I already knew.

"A homemade lobotomy."

"In essence."

Alan shudders. "Jesus!"

"I've seen this once before," I tell him. "A doctor did it to his wife."

"Then you're familiar with the prognosis," the doctor continues. "The damage is done. Mrs. Hollister got the worst of it, but Mr. Abbott isn't much better. Mrs. Hollister is in a vegetative state."

"*One Flew Over the Cuckoo's Nest,*" Alan mutters.

"That's right. She'll have to be cared for like a coma patient. She can't feed herself, she can't speak, she can't be responsible for her own continence. It's unlikely that she has any awareness of the world around her."

"And Jeremy Abbott?" I ask.

"He's operating at the level of an infant. He can't form words, and he wears diapers. He's able to eat and crawl, though, so his physical prognosis is better than hers. If you can call that better."

"What do you think he used to do this?"

"I'd imagine he got his hands on a classic orbitoclast—what laymen refer to as an ice pick. The diameter seems right, and I doubt they'd be hard to purchase. The procedure itself is pretty simple, though it would require some practice. The doctor who developed the lobotomy experimented on cadavers, using an actual ice pick from his own kitchen."

I look down at Dana Hollister's still form, lying on the bed.

"She's not aware of anything?"

"Probably not. It's hard to know for sure. There are accounts of coma patients coming out of long comas who remember snatches of conversations that occurred around them while they were comatose. When it comes to the brain and consciousness, we still have a lot to learn."

I hope that he's right, that Dana is living in a world of nothing, that she's not floating alone in the dark instead.

# CHAPTER TWENTY-ONE

"Tell me something I can use," I say.

It's late morning and we're back at the office, with my team gathered around. We've briefed them on our interview with Douglas Hollister, on Heather, on all the rest of it.

I thought, on the way back, about Avery Hollister screaming into the thick shag of the bathroom carpet forever. I thought about Jeremy Abbott screaming like a baby for his next meal. I thought about the possibility of Dana screaming inside her own mind, beating with futile fists against the darkness.

I thought about Heather too, of course. He'd let her go, but she was still trapped. She sat in a hospital room, picking sores into her skin, surrounded by light that wasn't real to her.

Murder is murder, and it's always a terrible, inhuman thing, but my monsters are less concerned with that end result than they are with the elevation of suffering. It's their successes in this regard that haunt me the most. Avery Hollister will bother me less than Jeremy Abbott ten years from now. I will not forget him, but he didn't suffer enough to earn a place in my personal pantheon.

"I have something on the car crashes," James says.

"Go ahead."

"Four cars were involved in accidents. I was able to locate the accident reports on each one. Every case reported catastrophic brake failure, and all were slightly older-model vehicles, ten to fifteen years old."

"That's a pretty high percentage for one parking lot," Alan says.

"It's an impossible anomaly," James replies. "Follow-up was done on two of the vehicles. Both were inspected under the auspices of the related insurance carriers and showed signs of deliberate tampering."

"You think he did it?" I ask. "Why? As some kind of additional diversion?"

"I'm not ready to give my hypothesis yet. Let me finish. We told you the ViCAP search turned up three other similar crimes. Bodies dropped off in bags, suffering from catastrophic prefrontal-lobe damage. I followed up on two of those cases this morning, the one here in Los Angeles and the one in Portland. Both victims were identified, and both victims had been missing for extended periods of time."

"That confirms his involvement," I say. "It fits his MO."

"Both victims in those cases were female, and both were taken at night in parking lots. One at a superstore of some kind, another from a bowling alley." He looks up. "I did a further search and found that multiple car accidents also occurred in both locations, on the same evening of each abduction. I haven't tracked down the data on the vehicles involved, but I'm confident we'll find they were sabotaged as well."

"Weird," I say. "Not exactly a foolproof diversion. How would he know when or if those particular cars would be driven again?"

"He wouldn't," James says. "It's irrational. This is a subject who apparently operates with great care and planning. The accidents are not only unreliable as a diversion, they are unnecessary. Taking the women in the parking lots is similarly risky. Why not take them at home? Illogic is a form of insanity, small or large. Why would he take this kind of risk?"

"Because he needs it," I say. "Not professionally but personally."

It's the only answer that fits, and it's a behavior we see in serial offenders all the time. Serial killers collect trophies, even though they know, if they get caught, those same trophies will assist in convicting them. They can't help themselves. They need little Cassie's Barbie doll (with the blood drops on it) or Grandma Barbara's wedding ring (kept on a necklace around her neck since her husband died, until the killer ripped it off her body).

"What's he need?" Alan asks. "Car crashes?"

"It's called symphorophilia, dear," Callie says. "Someone who is sexually aroused by accidents or catastrophes."

"Seriously? That actually gets someone's motor running?"

"It's a factual paraphilia," James confirms. "It's just a hypothesis, of course, but I think it's worth exploring. He seems to be a meticulous and careful planner in every other way. Why do something so illogical unless some personal aberration was involved?"

"Fine," I agree. "We'll throw it into the mix. So let's examine this guy further. What do we know?" I count off on my fingers. "One: He's highly organized and effective. Other than the possible—what did you call it?"

"Symphorophilia," James says.

"Right. Other than that, he exhibits no signs of being a disorganized offender. Two: His motivations, based on Douglas's testimony, *appear* to be financial."

"Money as the motive would explain the way in which he selects his targets," James offers. "In Hollister's case, the perpetrator didn't choose Heather—the husband did. There's no evidence of any personal ties, and I doubt we'll find any."

"Impersonal fits with what we know so far about how he treats them too," Alan says. "Granted, we've only heard from Heather, but I think we can take her at her word. The way she talked about him whipping her for punishment, it didn't sound like he was getting off on it."

"As the doctor said—workmanlike," Callie says.

I nod. "That's a good tag for this line of thinking." I go over and write it on the whiteboard. "So, organized, methodical, everything he does he does for a purpose. That's our current theory. The overriding purpose, for now, appears to be money. But is money just his excuse?" I shake my head. "What about keeping them in darkness and housing them for at least seven years. Is it sadistic?"

"I don't think so," James says. "I—" He stops, pondering. "I think that *was* a good word," he murmurs, staring at the whiteboard. "Workmanlike. Maybe that's everything to him. Pragmatism. No wasted motion. Waste is the thing you don't forgive." He looks at me. "Darkness enforces compliance over time by making the prisoner insane. It's incredibly efficient. It saves on electricity, it eliminates the need for assistance from others, and it breaks down the ability to resist.

Heather Hollister said that he told her to exercise daily. Why? Because he knew he needed to keep her alive. Why? Because of the possibility Douglas Hollister might renege on their agreement." He shakes his head. "I don't think it's about sadism. I think it's about maximum return on minimum effort."

"Heather said he didn't even bother to speak to her when he punished her," I allow, though I'm still cautious. "He took her, whipped her, told her it would be worse the next time, and stuck her back in her room. Where's the enjoyment in that?"

"There isn't any," James says. "Probably because it *is* a business, and she was just a commodity."

"Maybe," I mutter. Something else occurs to me. "Why does he need to keep them alive as insurance against the husbands? If it's all about efficiency, isn't killing them more efficient than all the work involved in keeping them alive?"

"I considered that," James says. "I still think it fits. The whole point of releasing the victims, going with the financial theory, would be to punish the husbands. To draw attention back to them as suspects, similar to what just happened with Douglas Hollister. That being true, it's a much safer hedge on his bets to keep the victims alive until he collects his money. It keeps doors of possibility open, in terms of exposure or threat of exposure, that would be permanently shut if he killed them."

"Could make sense," Alan agrees. "If you think about it, the usual assumption would be that the victims were already dead, right?"

"Of course," I say.

When a female is abducted and never shows up again, the odds are that she's been killed. This holds true in almost every case, from simple kidnapping to rape attacks.

"So, if their corpses turn up seven years or eight down the road, it's a surprise, and it'll get the gears of investigation turning, but it fits with the existing expectations. Showing up alive?" He raises his eyebrows. "That gets attention."

"It fits," I say, "but I think there's something else here. Exposure may be a part of the reason he keeps them alive, but it just doesn't feel like the whole. I'm not sure why."

James nods. "I agree."

I mark all this surmise down in abbreviated form, including the question mark that stands for the thing James and I both sense but can't prove. These are things we feel, not things we know, but that's the way of it.

"Why lobotomize them?" Callie asks.

I cock my head, considering. "Could be pragmatism, again," I say, continuing James's theory of our perpetrator's mind-set. I'm still reluctant, but I can't deny that it's making more and more sense. "A lobotomized victim can't be a witness."

Alan frowns. "But how does that guarantee the husbands get punished for not paying? They can't talk about their abductor, but that means they can't point the finger at their spouses either. Doesn't seem to fit with the whole more-doors-left-open idea."

"We need more data on the prior victims he's left for discovery," Callie says, making a note. "My guess would be that he arranged the husbands' downfall in some fashion. It's not the kind of thing he'd leave to chance."

"What about Heather?" I ask. "I realize I'm the one who put up the idea, but if the whole point of the lobotomies is to leave no witnesses, why'd he let her walk whole? Conversely, why do it to Dana? Up to this point, so far as we know, he hasn't engaged in any collateral damage."

"'So far as we know' is a key phrase there," Alan points out. "Also, maybe Dana wasn't collateral damage. Maybe she was in on it."

I think about that and nod. "Possible."

"He might just think he has nothing to fear," Alan continues. "Look, he had Heather for eight years, and what does she remember about him? Nothing. That might change if she ever gets back into her right mind, but I doubt it."

"Doubt isn't certainty, though," James observes, "and that doesn't fit with the profile we hypothesized. That kind of pragmatism wouldn't allow for any risk of discovery at all."

"Perhaps it does," Callie demurs. "Pragmatism and logic *should* allow for an evolving paradigm."

James frowns. "So?"

"Assuming the motive is financial, our boy would be constantly examining his existing paradigm, with particular attention to risk and reward."

"Again, I ask: so?"

"So, sweet James, letting someone rip you off is a high-risk, zero-return endeavor. It breeds future rebellion and thus lowers income. He's apparently dealt with this kind of defiance before, yet here it is again, in the form of Douglas Hollister. He could have taken stock and decided a different approach was needed."

"Such as?"

"Heather is *free*. Whatever state she's in, she's no longer imprisoned. Douglas, in the meantime, is heading for jail. Think about that. These men are driven by their hatred of these women. What better punishment than to change places with them?" She looks at the whiteboard. "How much would you like to bet that current customers got an email, or a phone call, or a text message, telling them what's happening to Douglas Hollister and to keep an eye on the news for confirmation? The risk is increased, certainly, but so is the reward."

"It's an interesting theory," James says, his voice grudging.

"Brilliant is a better word, honey-love. Go ahead, say it: *brilliant*."

"We haven't talked about the biggest anomaly," he says, ignoring her.

I raise an eyebrow. "Which is?"

"Why confirm his existence by sending a text message, leaving a note with Heather, and dropping off a card at your home? If he just wanted to harm Douglas, why reveal himself at all?"

It is an excellent question. Possibly the best question.

"Maybe we'll get a better idea from finding out more about the prior victims," I say. "Callie, I want you to take that. Call up the departments involved and see if you can get them to send us the case files."

"It'll be my pleasure."

"The quickest way to a disorganized offender is through what drives him," James says. "Victimology. The quickest path to this kind of offender is going to be method."

"Good," I agree. "So let's examine the requisites for our boy." I walk over to the whiteboard and find a clean section. *METHOD/ REQUIRED,* I write. "Let's stick with the financial motivation and look at the most basic factors. What does he need to do what he does? What's the foundation?"

"A client," James says.

"Good." I write *CLIENT* on the whiteboard under *METHOD/ REQUIRED*. "How does he find a client?"

Alan scratches his head. "He found Douglas Hollister in a chat room for dissatisfied men. He finds them on the Internet?"

"That's the most logical route these days," I say, writing it down. "The Internet's a big place. How does he decide where to start?"

"All kinds of ways," a voice says, interrupting us.

I glance over and grin when I see Leo Carnes. "Hey, Leo!" I walk over to him and give him a hug. It's not big-boss professional, but Leo is a friend. He's also one of the best computer-crimes agents we have.

"Got rid of the earring, I see," Callie teases.

He gives his left earlobe a self-conscious tug. "They're not really very cool anymore, unless you're Tommy Lee or someone like that."

"Suits you," Alan says. "Welcome back."

Leo helped on the case of Annie, Bonnie's mother. He looked younger then than he does now. He's only twenty-seven or twenty-eight, but he's already getting that certain wariness. I showed him his first murders, helped him sidle up close with real evil. It changed him. Other things are different too. He's wearing a tie now, and his dark hair is cut much shorter.

Leo's gone FBI on me, I think, and I'm both amused and saddened.

"Anyway," he says, embarrassed by the attention, "you wanted to know how he'd go about finding clients on the Internet. It's not that hard if you've got time and patience."

"He's got that in spades," Alan says.

"If I do a search on, let's say . . ." He sits down at a workstation. His fingers fly over the keyboard, as comfortable with it as my hand used to be with a cigarette. He starts an Internet connection and opens a browser. "Let's do a search on *antifeminism forum*." He types it as soon as he says it, and the page loads. "See? Eighteen thousand four hundred possibles. Let's scroll through these. . . . Here's one: *fightmisandry.com*."

"Misandry?" I ask.

"Hatred of men," James says. "Or boys."

"What's that got to do with feminism?" I ask. I recall Douglas Hollister's rant from yesterday. "Ah . . . I understand. Feminists hate men, right?"

"That's an oversimplification," James says. "The idea behind a site like fightmisandry.com is going to be based on the concept that feminism has ceased being about equal choice and has instead become a forum for being broadly 'antiman.'"

"And you know about this how, my dear homosexual?" Callie asks.

James only recently came out to us, and if this were anyone other than Callie and James, I'd be terrified at the sexual-harassment suit possibilities. But Callie would never say it if she actually thought it would hurt James's feelings.

"Unlike some people," he replies, not looking at her, "I'm constantly working on my academics. Intellectual stagnation isn't just slothful, it's unattractive."

Callie laughs. "Good one."

"Look at this," I murmur, reading the menu of the site Leo called up. "There are options for real-time chat, forums, social groups, buddy listings—wow." I stand back up, rubbing my lower back. "Lot of passion on this subject."

"I can understand it," Alan says. "Equality is equality, and I've always been cool with that. But men as the villain? That's not equality, it's hate, and that seems to be the direction of radical feminism today."

"With everything we see," Callie says, "how can you say that? When's the last time we were chasing a woman who rapes and kills men?"

Her back is up, and I see Alan ready to return the salvo.

Here it is, I realize, bemused. A version of the argument that led Douglas Hollister to our mystery man. Watch and learn.

Alan stabs a thick finger at her. "See, that's exactly what I'm talking about! Serial murderers are not what I'd called a representative cross section of the male population. But, hey, since they're usually men, men must be beasts at the core, right?"

"If it walks like a duck . . ." Callie says, shrugging.

I watch as Alan struggles to lower his blood pressure. The effort to do so is the essential difference between an Alan Washington and a Douglas Hollister.

"Look," he says, his tone reasonable without being conciliatory, "I've never bought into the boys-club mentality of law enforcement. I've never cared who carries the gun, man or woman, black or red or white. I'm fine with a female president and women CEOs. What I'm not fine with is being categorized by my gender. That's no different than me assigning traits to you because you're a woman, right?"

"I suppose," Callie allows.

"Well, that's what radical feminism has skewed toward, in my opinion." He emphasizes the last three words, with more than a little bit of irony.

"I love you, honey-love," Callie says, reaching out to pat his cheek. "Always have, always will. And Lord knows I'm the last to ride the horse of political correctness. But—taking a cue from our current psycho, speaking pragmatically—a man criticizing feminism is always going to be suspect, just as a white man criticizing any black movement would be."

"I can see that." He gives her a sly grin. "So, really, what you're saying is that we're brothers and sisters under the skin. We've both been oppressed by the white man, right?"

Callie sniffs. "Speak for yourself."

Their differences resolve easily, because the element of psychosis is missing. Callie and Alan can argue, even on a subject they feel passionately about, and walk away friends. Douglas and his pals could not.

"Thank you for the live case study," I say to them. "Now let's refocus. What you were saying, Leo, is that he could search for clients any number of ways."

"Yep," he says, bobbing his head. It makes him look young in spite of his suit and tie. "The Internet is about a limited number of things, at its core: information, communication, and community. You can find anything on the Internet if you know how and where to look and are patient. *Anything,*" he says.

"There's a big difference between venting and taking action," James says. "Most of the men in those forums are going to be talking, not doing. It seems very needle-in-a-haystack, even if he did narrow it down to a site like this one."

Leo considers this. "He could write a program, have it do searches against a set of regular keywords within the chat. For example, *bitch, cunt, dead, kill her*—anything that might point to an interest in or intent to harm. He could also put out bait—forum posts or, in the live chat, hints that he wishes he could do away with his spouse, and wait for kindred spirits to reply."

"Possible, but unlikely," I say. "That leaves too much of a trail."

"Then I'd go with the 'bot concept," he says.

"'Bot?"

"Sorry. Short for robot. In this case, an automated software program. It runs on its own, either on a timer, being told to perform a specific function every $x$ seconds, or in response to input. For example, you can insert a 'bot into a chat room. It'll look like a live person, but it's not. It's just a program. It can be set up to give a response to a query, so that if someone initiates contact, the 'bot would have a canned reply ready."

"Like?"

"It's been popular in promoting porn sites. You create a profile for a hot twenty-year-old with big gazoongas." He reddens. "Sorry."

"No, I think 'gazoongas' is the technical term," Callie says. "Please continue."

He clears his throat. "You create a profile for an attractive young woman. She's not real. It's fiction. The 'bot is inserted into a chat room full of single guys looking for girls, and you assign that profile to the 'bot."

"They think the program is the girl," Alan says, catching on.

"That's right. So, of course, all eighty of the guys in the chat room send her a *hey, you come here often?* instant message. The 'bot is programmed to respond to any query with: *Hi, sorry, I'm away from my computer for a sec, but you can come and see my naked pics and chat with me live at . . .* You see?"

"Men are stupid, that's what you're saying?" Callie asks. "A sound hypothesis."

"How would that approach benefit our guy?" Alan asks.

"Well, it wouldn't, not really," Leo allows, "but there are other things the 'bot can do once it's in the chat room."

"Searches," James supplies.

"Exactly. Back to the timer concept. The 'bot is inserted into the chat room and told to search every five milliseconds for any of the following terms: *bitch, cunt, whore, hit man, death,* and to alert the program operator if one is used by anyone in chat. If he really wanted to be advanced about it, he could have the 'bot send a generic reply to the originator of the keyword. Something like *I hear that.* It's not that hard."

"How secure would that be for him?" I ask.

"If you do it right? Very. If we're watching and waiting and the ISP is cooperative, maybe we could trace something like that—*maybe.* But you have to understand, most providers don't keep any logs of chats at all. Privacy is a huge issue, and you can't be competitive if you're not providing it. Many providers who have instant-messaging services, for example, have option settings for full encryption, and these days, full usually means full, as in government grade."

"But we can wiretap if we need to, right?" Alan asks.

"Not necessarily. There are two different services out right now in the instant-messaging arena that are essentially impossible to, quote, 'wiretap.' They use a combination of encryption and peer-to-peer architecture—" He waves his hands in a gesture of dismissal. "I don't need to get too technical. Suffice it to say that in those two cases, even if the company wanted to cooperate with us, they wouldn't be able to."

"Let me guess," I say. "Those two are the most popular."

He nods. "Anonymity is everything. Most of it isn't illicit. People just like their privacy. They want to talk and not worry about Big Brother—us—listening in on them. The problem is, the pedophiles and terrorists support it too."

"What about before the Internet?" James says.

Leo shrugs. "Not my area, sorry. But he could have been using the Net for a long time, anyway. Chat rooms have been around for a while, and BBS's—electronic bulletin board systems—were already popular in the late seventies. He could have been operating on a primitive version of what we're talking about for the last twenty-five years if he was really tech-savvy. A little longer, even."

Monsters, casting nets into the information sea. Pulling the nets back in, filled with their catch of the hate-filled and the hungry.

"Good, Leo," I say. "Now I need you to follow up on this hypothesis of yours."

"Shoot."

"The LAPD Computer Crimes Unit has taken Douglas Hollister's computer. I want you there, peeking over their shoulders. Fill them in on your theory and scour his computer for evidence to back it up. I want the name of the website he used to visit."

"That shouldn't be a problem. LAPD CCU is a good unit. They know what they're doing, and I'm on good terms with them. Geeks are competitive but not all that territorial."

"We also have three other abduction victims who were . . . returned. We're pretty sure it's the same perp. We're going to be liaising with the departments involved, and this may lead us to other Douglas Hollisters. If so, we'll need to fine-tooth their systems too."

"Just let me know. Is that it?"

"We work here," Callie chides. "Real work. We don't get to sit around all day parked on our posteriors, sipping coffee and perusing Internet porn. Chop chop."

Leo gives her a sympathetic smile. "Envy is tough."


"So I was thinking," Alan says.

Leo has left, and we are back to the whiteboard, back to our list, scrawls in black and blue marker that look disconnected, maybe a little bit deranged, like puzzle pieces cast onto a coffee table. We stare at them and talk about them and fumble to find and add new pieces. A finished puzzle is always the same: a face, with a name written below it.

"Our perp keeps things simple. He searches for men who want their significant others taken out of the way," he says.

"What about unsatisfied wives who want their husbands gone?" Callie interjects.

"Possible," I allow, "but not really pragmatic. Roughly sixty percent of spousal murders are committed by men, so they're the largest demographic." I smile at Alan. "Skewed target group acknowledged, no man-hating intended."

"No problem. Back to my thinking. He finds guys who want to take that extra step. A divorce won't do it either, because they don't want to split the money, or they don't want to share the kids, or just because they hate the wife so much. He cuts a deal with the husbands: Take out life insurance on her, if you haven't already, and I'll grab her and hold her. No one will ever find a body because there's no body to be found, and seven years later, you declare her dead, collect the insurance money, and give me my split."

"That sounds right," I agree.

"So what does he do with them after the seven year period is up?"

James's sigh is both dismissive and derisive. "He kills them, of course. He kills them and disposes of the bodies in a decisive way, so they'll never be found. Maybe he cremates them, or cuts them up and feeds them to pigs, but whatever he does, it's not a productive line of questioning."

"Really, smart-ass? Then what is?"

"The same as before: methodology. We have an idea now of how he selects his victims. We know from Heather Hollister's interview how he treats them. The next logical question is: Where would he keep them?"

"Well . . ." I say, thinking. "We have three mutilated victims in three different states: California, Nevada, and Oregon. Do we think he has different holding houses in each state?"

"Absolutely," James says.

"Why?"

"Because it's the most pragmatic solution. The longer he travels with his victims, the greater the risk of getting caught. Much easier and much safer to house them locally."

"I agree with the princess," Callie says.

"These would be places that he'd own," I say. "Rentals would be risky too. No good having to take an ax to the landlord because he dropped in for a surprise cup of coffee."

"Agreed," James says.

"So what kind of properties would we be talking about?" I ask.

"Remote," Alan says. "Either because it's literally remote, like out in the boonies, or figuratively remote, as in no one's around or no one gives a shit."

"Warehouses?" I ask.

"I don't think so," Callie replies. "There are too many variables in a warehouse district. Squatters, or fires, or drug busts because someone is growing the wrong kind of nursery. He'd want something dedicated, something no one else could interfere with."

"I can think of all kinds of things to fit that bill," Alan says, "but if I were him I'd probably just have it built. Concrete building on private land, add the custom stuff—steel cots and eye rings for the shackles—myself."

"How would he keep an eye on them when he travels?" I ask.

"Video surveillance is something you can watch over an Internet connection now," Callie says. "I know because Sam has been installing a number of them at our house. They transmit an image to your computer, and you can access the feed from anywhere in the world as long as you have a connection to the Net."

"Sam's a little paranoid, huh?" Alan asks.

"Careful. I think of it as careful."

"We're cutting too wide a swath here," I say. "Even if Alan is right, so what? I'm not sure how we'd go about doing a statewide search for concrete structures built by individuals and, if we did, what it would net us. We don't know where he's located."

"Geographic profiling might help," James says. "He's a commuter, but it can't hurt."

Geographic profiling is essentially a mathematical process that attempts to predict the most likely location of a serial offender, and it's based on the same bedrock as the rest of what we do: Behavior is everything.

One suggestion is that there are basically two types of offenders: the commuter and the marauder. The marauder is a localized offender. He commits his crimes in a geographically stable area. The marauder is the best candidate for geographic profiling.

The commuter is mobile or transient and commits his crimes over large distances. He tends to be a complex hunter who can cross cultural and psychological boundaries. He's the hardest to pin down with geographic profiling. Son of Sam was a marauder; he was caught because of parking tickets. Bundy was a commuter; he was caught because he wouldn't stop killing and the evidence and his own decompensation caught up with him.

Geographic profiling is relatively new but has been steadily building its own database of interesting behavior tidbits. When lost, for example, men will go downhill while females will go up. I didn't believe it when I heard it but am assured it's true. Another: A right-handed criminal who has to scram in a hurry will run to the right and discard weapons to the left. Geographic profiling is a controversial, complicated, but sometimes useful tool.

"I'm not sure how useful it will be in this case," I say. "Four victims only, in three different states? Not too many variables to plug in there."

James shrugs. "We should do it anyway."

"You have someone in mind?" I ask.

"Dr. Earl Cooper. He's a little annoying, but he knows his science."

I stare at the whiteboard. It stares back, mocking me with silence and incompleteness. I wonder about the other Heathers, women stuffed into darkness and kept there until they can no longer see the light. I stand up and grab my purse.

"Let's go see the man."

Motion is motion. Stillness is death.

## CHAPTER TWENTY-TWO

Dana Hollister listens to a loud hum that never goes away. It's as if someone picked a single note and is singing it with forty mouths. It's taken over her world, that hum.

Most of the time it runs over her like water, and she is submerged. There is light and there is the hum and there is no thought.

But every now and then, the hum stutters.

These are millisecond flashes. Once, the hum stuttered and she thought a single word:

*I,* she thought.

Then the hum returned, drowning out even the idea of the rest.

A stutter comes now, longer than the others. She swims up inside herself, from the bottom of a lake filled with syrup.

*The man,* she thinks.

*The man bending over, a needle in my eye. Something is seen.*

The humming is coming, a roar in the distance.

*Something is seen that's important. Something about the man.*

*I should tell them.*

*Who is them?*

*Who am I?*

*I—*

The hum covers her, and she is nothing again.

# CHAPTER TWENTY-THREE

Earl Cooper, as it turned out, came to see us. He's standing in our office, something from another time.

He's wearing a cowboy hat and boots and a flannel shirt and a pair of battered blue jeans. He's a short man, about five-seven, and he's broad in the chest but thin in the waist. He's sixty-two years old and looks every minute of it. He has a craggy face, a huge nose, and, to top it all off, a handlebar mustache that's been waxed at the ends. It's a good face, unique, made by its wearer rather than the other way around.

The eyes sparkle with intelligence and have a depth of distance that tells me he's seen things, done things, gotten dirty in the living of life.

Once you get past all of the exterior apparel, it's the eyes that reveal the most: This is a vital, intelligent man with a touch of the maverick and a dash of the sad.

"Pleased to meet you," he says to me, with a bare smile as he shakes my hand. "Heard about your work. Sorry about your family and your face."

It's so brief and so genuine that I can take no offense from it. "Thank you, sir."

Earl Cooper seems like a "sir" to me, the way some older men just naturally are. He's an elder, a teacher with experience to be listened to, and it's draped all around him like a cloak of quiet certainty.

"Young James has a quick tongue, but he's pretty sharp. That's why I put up with his back-talking. He came to a forensics symposium I was speaking at."

"Where are you from, sir?" Alan asks.

"Texas. Place near Dallas. But I come out here three months of the year to consult and lecture. Pays the bills and keeps me occupied."

"Are you a cowboy, Earl?" Callie teases.

He grins at her, and it lights up his face. "Me? Naw. I'm just an academic who wears cowboy boots. I do some shooting, though."

"What kind?" I ask, interested.

"Handgun," he says. "Nine mil is my gun of choice." He rolls his eyes. "Some of my contemporaries think that's sacrilegious, but I don't give a hoot. I looked for a gun I liked and that was the one."

"I use a Glock," I tell him, pulling my jacket aside so he can see it.

He nods in approval. "Nice weapon." He squints at me. "You any good?"

"Good?" Callie says. "Honey-love, she's a natural gunfighter."

"That a fact?"

"I'm competent." Shooting is one of the few things I don't bother to be modest about. "I did some comparisons based on my own scores at the range. I'd probably rank within the top hundred in the world if I competed."

"For women?" he asks.

"Top hundred, period."

He grins again, delighted. "That's something I'd like to see! Most of the boys involved in the gun game are good enough, but there's a few that'd be pretty upset to be bested by a woman. You should compete sometime."

I grin back. I like Earl Cooper. "Maybe I will."

"Have we had enough bonding time?" James asks, rancorous and impatient, as always. Maybe we dislike James, when we dislike him, because he's our conscience. "Can we get to the matter at hand?"

Earl curls his mouth down. "Curb it a little, son," he says.

"I'm not your son," James retorts. "And there are other women locked away in the dark out there, just like Heather Hollister was."

Earl sobers at this and nods. "Ah yes," he says, his voice soft. "The impatient hunter, the one who can never put down his gun or take his boots off. I used to be just like you, son. You better learn to turn it off or one day you'll burn out."

"The business at hand," James says, practically grinding his teeth.

"Give it up, Earl," Callie opines. "This is who James is, sad but true."

"I guess I knew that. Fair enough, young Jim, we'll get to the meat of the matter. What can I do for you all?"

I brief him in detail on the case. He listens intently, rolling his mustache at times, asking questions at others. When I finish, he is silent for a while, staring at our Sanskrit scribbling on the whiteboard.

"Well," he drawls finally, "I'm not sure how much help I can be, but I'll tell you what I see and then I'll take all the data home and give it a figure."

"That's all we're asking," I say.

"What do you know about what I do?"

"Just the broad strokes. Callie is our criminologist. She's pretty conversant in general forensics, but we bring in experts like yourself for the specialized fields all the time."

"Fair enough. Geographic profiling is the bastard stepchild of profiling," he says. "In other words, for many, the jury's still out. With good reason. There are a lot of factors that can throw a wrench into the works. The main one, in your case, is a lack of data. Geographic profiling is all about data. Number crunching, variables. Your boy has dropped four people in three different states. He selects his victims via the Internet. That's unhelpful.

"We operate with four basic types in geographic profiling, when it comes to offenders. We have the hunter. He looks for his victims in his home territory. He's the one my kind of profiling works best for. We have the poacher. He travels away from his home to hunt. He's smarter, he knows you don't shit in your own backyard. You have the troller. He's an opportunist. He's most likely your disorganized offender. He sees what he likes while he's out doing something else and he acts on the impulse. Then you've got the trapper. He lures the victim to him, controls the situation."

"There's a lot of overlap there," I observe.

He nods in agreement. "Very good, Agent Barrett. That's correct. The troller can operate in his own home area, like the hunter, or he could only troll when he's away from home. The traveling salesman as rapist, so to speak. The poacher can create a kind of 'new home territory.' He thinks he's being smart by choosing his victims from somewhere else than where he lives, but then he gets comfortable with that particular area and only draws from it. He could also be unconscious of the decisions that drove him to choose that 'away' spot.

"That's one of the principles that underpin geographic profiling: We tend to operate in our comfort zones, knowingly or not. The theory, then, is that location—both of abduction and dumping—tells us something important about where an offender lives. A famous and simplistic example is the case where bodies were always being found near railroad tracks. It pointed to an offender with an on-the-move, drifter mentality. That helped narrow the search and, though it wasn't the only factor, contributed to finding the perpetrator, an illegal immigrant who'd been deported numerous times before."

Listening to him, I guess that Cooper is probably a lecturer in demand. He has a laid-back but engaging way of speaking that makes you feel as if you're just having a conversation. Sitting in the living room, feet up on the coffee table.

"The key with your boy and me, if I'm any help at all, is going to come down to distance. There's a difference, you see, between perceived distance and actual distance. If any of you have ever walked toward the mountains on a horizon or tried to swim across a lake to the other shore, you'll understand what I'm talking about. They look close, but you could walk for days before you reached those mountains or swim 'til you drowned and never reach that other shore.

"It works in reverse too. A killer might think something is just too far when it's actually too close to home. It helps to know method of transportation—in this case a car—as that gives us an idea of his mobility range."

"It sounds like a drifter is easier to catch with geographic profiling than a man with a car," Alan says.

"That is a fact," Cooper agrees. "It's unhelpful that your boy is operating in different states. Still, the distance factor might turn up something. In relation to the abductions, I mean."

"How's that?" Alan asks.

"Where he took them, how he took them. He's a pragmatic man. What does that tell you?"

I nod, seeing it. "That he's not going hundreds of miles away," I say. He smiles. "Kee-rect."

"But that's not always going to be under his control," Callie says doubtfully. "His victim choice is limited by need—the needs of his clients. He can't know where they're going to be located."

"Good thinking," Cooper says, "but not so fast. Los Angeles proper—the city, I mean—is somewhere around forty miles wide. Hell, Portland is only about a hundred forty-five square miles to Los Angeles's four hundred seventy, and it's not long after you leave the city that you can be out in the middle of the woods."

He turns to the whiteboard.

"The parking-lot angle is a good one. I think you're right. He's taking them there because he needs to feed his little sexual sideline of making the cars crash. That's behavior. Combined with geography, it tells us what? What are you missing there?"

It's a gentle probe, a teacher's insistence to look. We all stare at the whiteboard, James and I most of all. I see it first, a forehead slapping moment.

"How does he see the crash?" I say.

Cooper smiles.

"Right," James says. "He has a victim. He can't very well sit there and wait all night for the crashes to occur. He can't count on the media—too many variables, might or might not be newsworthy."

"So?" Callie asks.

"So," I reply, "he'd set up a way to record it."

Cooper tilts his head at me in acknowledgment. "I'm no gadget genius," he says, "but I'd think his options in that regard would be limited. How long would a battery-operated system last? If no Internet's available to pipe it to his computer, how many hours can a stand-alone system record? I'd look for local hotels and neighborhoods nearby with wireless capabilities—on the most recent crimes. The older ones . . ." He shrugs. "I can't say. You'll have to ask one of them tech boys I'm sure you have on the payroll.

"As far as my neck of the woods goes, get me copies of everything. Here, the Oregon and Nevada cases. I need your notes too, anything that might or might not be relevant. I'll stir it all up together and add some eye of newt and a little finger-crossing, and we'll see what I come up with."

"You'll have it all today," I tell him. "We really appreciate your assistance."

He tips his hat at me. "No promises."

"You've already helped," I tell him. "You've given us some new things to look at."

After Cooper leaves, I give James the job of gathering copies of everything Cooper needs. He accepts this task amiably enough, for James.

"The spatial-distance angle is interesting," he allows. "As is the linkage with the theory of symphorophilia."

"Interesting," I agree. "Now let's turn it into something we can use. Callie, you help James with this. Alan, please give Leo a call and find out where he's at with the LAPD." I glance at my watch. "I'm going to bring the AD up to date."

Not just on this, I think. I need to talk to him about the other thing. It's time to let someone in on the secret, now that I know the changes the future will bring.

# CHAPTER TWENTY-FOUR

AD Jones regards the ceiling of his office, pondering everything I've just told him.

"So you think he was telling the truth?" he asks. "You think he has more victims stashed?"

"I think it's likely, sir, if we operate on the theory that it's a financial model. No victims, no money."

"Probably not a shitload, though," he muses. "He wouldn't want to risk drawing too much attention."

"Perhaps," I agree. "Then again, there's kind of a mutual code of silence. He probably records and keeps copies of everything that goes on between him and his 'clients' in case something goes wrong."

"A dead man's switch."

"Sure. That and the whole I'll-ruin-your-life-if-you-renege thing. Douglas Hollister tried to screw our perp, so he got buried. That's a pretty convincing deterrent."

"How's Heather Hollister?"

"Not good. Some part of me wants to say she's better off than Dana, or Jeremy Abbott, but I don't know."

"She's better off." He says it flatly. "You should know that better than most. If she's tough enough, she'll pull back from the edge. If she's not, she won't. At least she's got the chance."

"You're right," I say, "I guess it just creeps me out. My two biggest fears as a kid were getting locked in the dark forever and going crazy but not knowing I'd gone crazy."

He smiles. "Maybe you're already crazy now, and you just don't know it." He indicates his office with a sweep of his hand. "Maybe none of this exists, and you're sitting in a padded room somewhere in a straitjacket, imagining it all."

I give him a withering glare. "Not funny, sir."

His grin tells me he feels otherwise. "And the other boy?"

"He's alive. He'll probably be turned over to social services, until and if Heather comes out of her funk enough to claim him."

"So what's the plan of attack?" he asks.

"Maybe Earl Cooper will help, but at the moment I think our best leads are the Internet aspect and the car crashes."

"I assume you're planning a sting on the Internet end of things?"

"I'm considering it, sir. I'll know better when Leo gets back."

"And the crashes?"

"If James is right and it's a sexual need, he probably won't have been able to limit himself to feeding it only when he's performing an abduction. There should be other instances. I think it's important. In most ways this offender appears to be incredibly disciplined and careful. The paraphilia is a deviation from that. It could be one of the places where he makes mistakes." I shrug. "It's a stretch, but it's what we have."

He thinks about it. "Good," he agrees. "You should also look into Internet communities on the car-crash angle."

"What do you mean?"

"Every fetish and weirdo perversion out there probably has a community of some kind connected to it. Pedos do. Places to share photos and experiences. If Cooper is right and he records his exploits, maybe he shares them too."

I blink, surprised. "That's a good idea."

"I still have a few. Your current plan of attack sounds good. I agree with assuming that his motivation is money. It might not be the only reason, but Hollister's testimony and everything else we know supports the concept. Proceed as planned." He leans back in his chair and laces his fingers over his stomach, gazing at me. "Now, tell me why you're really here."

"Sorry?" He's right, but I resist being readable as a reflex action.

"Come on, Smoky. I know you. I can tell when you're distracted. You had something else on your mind the whole time you were briefing me."

I meet his gaze with a miniature defiance, then I look away and sigh. "I told Director Rathbun I'd take the job."

"I know. I think it was a good decision."

I still am not looking at him. "I think so too. But there's a complication. Well, I don't know if *complication* is the right word. Let's call it a variable. I need your help. Your advice on what to do about it in context."

"If I can help, I will. What kind of variable?"

I feel myself shiver inside, a mix of nervousness and fear along with a yearning. It's a secret. I've felt that way about it from the first. I'm not sure why I felt that way, but it was too visceral an emotion to ignore.

I force myself to meet his gaze again, and then I force myself to say the words, the words I haven't said to anyone yet, not even Tommy.

"I'm about two months pregnant, sir."

He stares at me. He says nothing for almost a half minute. I can't tell if he's shocked or just thinking. His fingers remain laced on his chest, his hands still relaxed, unmoving.

"Well," he finally says. "Are congratulations in order?"

There's a cautiousness to the question that I appreciate. Maybe this is one of the reasons I wanted to talk to AD Jones about this first, because I knew he'd have the exact kind of empathy that I needed.

It's the question I've been asking myself since the middle-of-the-night pee test and have continued to ask since the blood test confirmed it.

Is this a good thing? Am I happy about it?

"They should be," I say. "But I don't know."

"Why?"

I study my mentor and wonder about answering that question. AD Jones has known me longer than anyone in the FBI world. He watched me come up, and he was there when my life burned down and blew away. He's seen a lot, but there are things he hasn't seen, because of the type of relationship we have.

AD Jones has never seen me cry. He hasn't had to hold me while I screamed. His support has been absolute, but it has been either silent or spoken gruffly. And I've been grateful for it.

"I was pregnant," I tell him. "Before Matt and Alexa were killed."

"Okay," he says.

Not *Really?* or *Oh my God!* Just *Okay,* and then waiting. It encourages me.

"No one knew. I was still turning it over in my mind, you know? Trying to decide how I felt about it before telling Matt. Then . . . what happened, happened. When I was lying in that hospital bed, I decided I was going to go home, get my affairs in order, and kill myself. The thing is, I knew I couldn't pull the trigger if I still had that baby in my stomach. Twisted, I know." I swallow, ashamed. "So I ended up aborting the baby." I sneak a look at him, afraid of what I'll see, but all I see is patience. "Later, when I decided I was going to live, I had so much regret about that decision. So much . . . I can't . . ." I shrug, defeated in my search for an adequate phrase to encompass that feeling of self-loathing and despair. "I pushed it down, kept it secret, and life moved on."

I look down at my belly and touch it. I imagine it growing, as it did with Alexa. I remember what it felt like, those stirrings of life. Amazing and crazy and frightening and humbling. "So here I am again. I get another chance. There's no way I'm getting another abortion, that much I know. But it would be a lie to say I'm not scared, sir."

"I understand, Smoky," he says. "I really do. You've lost a lot. Fear's natural." He cracks a crooked grin. "What's the old saying about paranoia?"

"You're not paranoid if they're really out to get you?"

"Yeah." He gets serious. "People are out to get us. Every day. Maybe they're not actively pursuing us, but somewhere in this great nation of ours, at this very moment, someone is at the very least turning the idea over in their head. Pregnancy makes you vulnerable, that's a fact. Then, a baby . . ." He shakes his head. "I envy those who are courageous enough to have children. At the same time, I'm relieved I don't have to worry about my children, if I had any, being used as a weapon against me."

"That's part of it."

"Have you discussed this with Tommy?" he asks, then catches

himself. To my great surprise, he blushes a little and clears his throat. "Sorry, that's an assumption on my part. Is Tommy the father?"

My mouth drops open. "Sir!"

He looks embarrassed again. "I'll take that as a yes."

"Jeez. What kind of hussy do you think I am?"

"So?"

I sink back into my chair. I feel like a kid in the principal's office. "He doesn't know. I haven't told him yet."

He squints at this answer and scratches a forearm. "Well," he says, "I guess it's really your business. You're not married, after all."

In for a penny, I think. I blurt it out before I have time to stop myself.

"Actually, we are married, sir."

Now his mouth does drop open, to be replaced soon after by a genuinely happy smile. "No shit?"

"Really and truly. Hawaii wasn't just a vacation, it was a honeymoon."

"Congratulations! Why didn't you tell me?"

Time to sink back into the chair again.

"Well, I haven't told anyone, sir. You're the first. To be honest, Tommy and I have been fighting about it a little."

"He wants to spill the beans and you don't?"

"Something like that."

He seems about to say something but closes his mouth. "I can understand your reluctance, I guess. I kept my second marriage a secret for almost three months. I didn't want to jinx it."

"Exactly! You understand where I'm coming from."

The quality of his next smile is full of affection but a little bit sad. "But that's all bullshit, Smoky. That second marriage failed like the others, and it wasn't because I did or didn't tell anyone about it. Don't get superstitious about it. Bottom line, I wasn't willing to give my marriage the same priority I gave my work. You and Tommy are a good match in that regard."

I feel the great reluctance again, the push and pull of trying to decide what to reveal.

"It's not just that, sir," I say, my voice quiet. "I'm afraid if I say it, if the world knows, that he'll be taken away from me."

"Maybe he will," he replies without hesitation. "That part's not up to you. I'm not talking about religion and higher powers, just truth. One of you will eventually die, and barring a plane crash or something similar, one will die before the other. That's life, Smoky. We live and then we die, and the only uncertainty is how much time goes in between."

I've heard these words before, of course. Inside my own head. I know the truth of them, and I can even feel it, a little. But my heart has its own legs, and it wants to run in the other direction.

*Fearful hope,* that's my phrase for it. Up to now everything has been organic. Tommy and I came together naturally, windblown, like people who tripped and fell into each other's arms; Bonnie came to me via Annie; but—and here is the linchpin of it all—I didn't ask for any of it. Tommy chose me. Bonnie was left on my metaphorical doorstep. They were given; I didn't take.

Marriage is different. It's a choice, a stand, an act of defiance against a life of loneliness. I took that stand once without fear, but the water of life has run far and deep since then.

"What can I say, sir? I'm terrified all the good stuff is going to come crashing down again. I took it for granted once. It was an invulnerable life. Alexa would grow up and make me a grandmother. Matt and I would watch each other's hair turn white. That all changed in an instant."

"You want my advice?"

"Kind of."

He laughs at that, something just south of a chuckle. It pulls a reluctant smile to my own lips. "My advice is to go down fighting. Life kicked your ass once, and almost for good. You survived; now you have a husband again and not just one child but the possibility of another. So shout it out. Be proud of it. Challenge fate and flip a bird toward heaven. Hold what you got tight, and tell the world it's yours. Whatever you decide, stop shying away. It's just not your style, and it's boring as shit."

I grin at my mentor, at my quasi-friend. "Pretty good pep talk, sir."

"I have my moments. Now, I'm sure you're wondering how this will go over with the director."

"A little, sure. I don't think a big, fat pregnant agent is what he had in mind for the poster."

"Probably not. My advice is not to tell him, for now. He's going to be out there selling his idea to the President and various budget committees. He's going to use you as a key selling point. Hopefully, by the time he finds out you're pregnant, it'll all be too far along for him to switch horses."

"Pretty devious."

"That's the world at this level. Better get used to it. Anything else you need to talk about?"

"I don't think so."

He waves me away, his voice gruff again, impatient again, not as an insult to me but as a way of showing that nothing's changed between us, that I revealed what I revealed and am regarded as I was before. "Then get going. Catch this loony."

"Yes, sir. Thank you, sir."

"My pleasure, Smoky. And that carries forward into the future, even when I'm not your boss anymore. Maybe especially then."


I get on the elevator to head back to the office, feeling cleansed. The things inside me had built up pressure. I was unaware of just how much until I let fly with AD Jones, a lobbing of emotional hand grenades that he'd taken with assurance and aplomb.

Maybe we'll be real friends when he's not my boss.

I touch my belly. I like that idea.

I like it a lot.

# CHAPTER TWENTY-FIVE

"Attention, everyone," I say. "Before we go any further, I have an announcement to make."

"Do tell," Callie says.

Alan puts down his pen and waits. James gives me a sour glance and continues working.

"Tommy and I got married."

Alan's eyes widen. "God damn!" he says, laughing. "That's great! When?"

"We did it in Hawaii."

"And just how long were you going to keep this a secret?" Callie asks, her tone and expression severe.

"Just until now."

"I'm displeased," Callie says. "Very displeased. You've cheated me. Us."

"How exactly did I cheat you?"

She looks heavenward, a prayer for patience with fools. "Do you not remember my wedding?" she asks. "Picking out dresses, flowers, a cake, a ceremony? Don't you think we'd enjoy doing something like that for you?"

"Maybe. I guess."

"No. No maybe." She shakes a finger at me. "It's a fact."

"After all," Alan snorts, "look how great your wedding turned out."

"Keep quiet," Callie orders him. She turns back to me. "You need to have a real wedding."

I shrink, dismayed. "What? Why?"

"Because that's the way these things are done," she says, her voice frosty. "We don't gallivant around, slipping rings onto each other's fingers and getting some civil servant to sign a paper, and call that 'married.' It's not right."

"Love is just a chemical reaction designed to encourage propagation of the species," James declares, without looking up from what he's doing. "Weddings are a colossal waste of money."

"Really?" Callie says. "If it's all about propagation of the species, then how do you explain homosexuality, honey-love? Those of you who wear the ruby slippers?"

He shrugs, continuing to work, not missing a beat. "I don't know. My theory is that it's a chemical imbalance or some kind of genetic abnormality."

Callie says nothing to this. Alan and I stare at him.

*Is that what he thinks about himself? That he's defective?*

James senses our attention. "Oh, are you all feeling sorry for me now? Worried about my self-image? Don't be. I have a lot of value to the species. It's just not in the baby-making area."

"This is all very uplifting," I say, "and I appreciate the offer, Callie, but it'll have to wait."

She points a stern finger at me. "This isn't over." Now she smiles. "Having said that, and now that you're properly chastised: congratulations. It's about time he made an honest woman out of you."

"No kidding," Alan says. "Congratulations."

"Yes, yay, wonderful," James says, exasperated. "Let's get back to work."

For once, James and I agree on something.

"Alan, did you talk to Leo?"

The door to the office opens before he can answer, and Leo walks in.

"He's going to tell you he has all the information from Hollister's computer," Alan tells me.

"LAPD CCU did a good job," Leo affirms. "They scoured his hard drive and were able to resurrect quite a bit of data. People make the mistake of thinking a simple delete means the file's gone."

"So?" I ask.

He points to the computer at Alan's desk. "May I?"

He sits down, connects to the Internet, and opens a browser. He types in a URL: http://www.beamanagain.com.

"This is the website Douglas Hollister spent the most time on."

"*Beamanagain?*" Alan says. "What the hell is that?"

"You have to separate the words," Leo explains. "*Be a man again.*"

The layout of the site is simple, not graphics-rich. A menu of options is listed on the left side. I read them aloud.

"*Forum. Bitch Stories. Brother Stories. Bitch Photos. Bitch Chat. Brother Chat. Books.* Wow."

"I spent some time looking through this already," Leo says. "The site is built around a pretty simple philosophy: American men are being emasculated by American women and the radical feminist movement. It says that American women have, over time, been changed by the feminist movement into narcissists and ballbusters—their words, not mine—and that American men have bought into this and accepted the idea that they are fundamentally bad. They call it the *brute paradigm.*"

"Which is?" I ask.

"Essentially that men are brutes. They're genetically programmed to be brutes, and they can't be trusted to be masculine men because masculine men rape and subjugate women."

I scan the menu. "Let's see the photos first."

He clicks that option and a new page loads, filled with thumbnails.

"From what I could tell, there are basically two reasons photographs are posted here," Leo explains. "One is simply to put a face to a story."

"*This is her, the bitch that ruined my life,*" Callie fills in.

"Exactly. Then there's a whole other kind of photo, and it dovetails with another point that gets brought up on this site a lot: the idea that American women let themselves go."

"As in . . .what?" I ask. "They get fat?"

"Get fat, wear sweatpants to the grocery store, et cetera. It's generally image oriented and ties into the later complaints about withholding sex as a weapon."

"You seem very well informed for someone who's been studying this subject for only a morning," Callie observes.

"I'm a quick learner," he says, undaunted. "Anyway, the guys on this website lose their credibility early."

"Why?"

He shrugs. "Too much anger, which becomes hate in a lot of instances. If you have a thesis, it should be provable on its own merits. The guys posting here don't make a good argument for men. They end up perpetuating the stereotype they're protesting."

"Show us some examples of what you're talking about with the photos," I tell him.

"Ummm . . . here."

He clicks on a thumbnail of a woman with a large, round face. A page loads, and it's a series of three pictures. One is of the woman in a grocery store. She looks like she's having a rough day; she's wearing sweats, and her hair is barely brushed. She seems tired. She's overweight but not obese. The next is a more professional photograph. The woman is smiling. She's made up in this photo, and her hair is styled. The last is the most unflattering. She's lying on her back in bed, sleeping. Her mouth hangs open. Her right arm is thrown to one side.

Underneath the photos is a paragraph. It reads:

"When I married this bitch twelve years ago, she was hot. Skinny, took care of herself, and was into everything in bed. We'd fuck 'til the sun came up some nights. Three years in, we had our son, and that was the end of happiness. She let herself get fat, she quit work to take care of the kid, and, worst of all, she became a whining narcissist. Sometimes I watch her sleep or eat and it's all I can do to keep from puking. I've asked for a divorce, and in true bitch form, she let me know that she's going to take me to the cleaners.

"Pretty angry," Alan murmurs. "Let's see another."

Leo clicks the photo of a smiling blonde woman. The page loads. The woman is in a bikini bathing suit, standing on a beach. The sun is out, and she's laughing. She's in her early twenties, effortlessly beautiful, endlessly happy.

The paragraph under her photograph begins:

Inside every hot American woman is a harpy waiting to be let out. Sally and I have been together for fifteen years, married for ten of those. In the beginning, we had a great time together. I'd go so far as to say that everything was perfect. We traveled the world together, backpacked through Europe, smoked hash in Amsterdam. She was always up for adventure, and the sex was great—she was smoking hot in her twenties, and she doesn't look too bad now. Then we finished college and got married and settled into life. She started watching feminist sitcoms that degrade men and quote *empower women* unquote (all that "you've come a long way, baby" bullshit). The changes were slow and subtle, but what it boiled down to is that she started treating me like the enemy. We fight all the time now, and we haven't slept together in years. She accuses me of cheating constantly—even though I haven't. When I try to defend myself, she attacks me and says that I'm full of shit, all men are scum who cheat, etc. Sometimes she cries for no reason, and it will last for days; other times she can get so rageful that it literally scares me. One time she grabbed a kitchen knife while we were fighting. I've tried to be the good guy again and again. I've tried to talk to her, but when I ask her what's wrong, she just tells me I'm a "fucking man and would never understand what's going on with her." I've had it, and I'm going to ask for a divorce.

"Sad story," Callie says. "Too bad he hasn't sought out professional help."

Deep, sudden changes in personality always have root causes. The woman this man is writing about could be bipolar and it's just now manifesting, or she might have experienced a trauma in her life that she hasn't revealed to him, such as a rape or an abortion or some other personal loss of magnitude. Perhaps she's remembered something from her past that's come back to haunt her. There's always the possibility, of course, that he's leaving out details and that he's the source of her trauma.

Assuming his account is factual, this is the story of a woman in crisis, not a woman out to "destroy men." Callie's right. It's tragic.

"That's actually a fairly nice one," Leo says. "Most of them are like the first: bitch this, bitch that, she got fat, she won't have sex anymore, et cetera, et cetera. *Bitch Stories* on the menu takes you to more and much longer versions of the same."

"We get the idea," I say. "Let's look at the forums."

He navigates to the forum index page. There are three different forums to choose from: *General Discussion, Man Talk,* and *Bitch Talk.*

"I think we get the idea on *Bitch Talk,*" I say. "Let's take a look at Man Talk."

Leo clicks and the forum opens. A list of thread subjects appears. I scan them and see one called *Reclaiming the Right to be a Man.*

"That one," I say.

The page loads.

Men today are marginalized without even knowing it. They have come to accept that they are "the brute," "the abuser," "the rapist," and worse, that these qualities are inevitable and can be reversed only by women. We accept today that we do not hold the keys to our inner selves, that it is the wife or girlfriend who holds the key, and that we must listen to her as our most important teacher.

That men have been brutish in history cannot be disputed. That women have been treated poorly by men, even oppressed, cannot be disputed. But this has gone beyond a dialogue about aberrant behavior; it has instead become the accepted indictment of all men everywhere. John Bobbitt is the image held up, not Leonardo da Vinci. Ted Bundy is the example of "the lows that men can sink to"; Beethoven is not similarly held up as the "heights that men can rise to."

Because we love our mothers, we have come to accept this image and the inherent guilt that goes with it. There are men who have never touched a woman in anger that live in fear of the possibility they might.

So let's discuss—what are some things we can do to reverse this process in ourselves? How can we reclaim not our brutishness but our masculinity, which—current opinion aside—does not contain brutality by default as its birthright?

"This is a long thread," Leo observes. "This first post, the one that starts the thread, is two years old. There are almost two hundred pages of replies and discussion."

I scan down through some of those that most immediately followed this post.

One reads:

It's hard for me to admit this, but I read your post and I cried. It was pretty unexpected. See, I'm a decent guy. I was married for ten years, and I have two children, a boy and a girl. I love them to death and I really work to be a good father. I never cheated on my wife. Yeah, I know, a lot of guys say that, but it's really true. I had my temptations, but I never felt the pull strongly enough to actually stray.

My marriage fell apart about two years ago. I see a lot of guys on this site are pretty angry, but that's not my scene. We fucked up the marriage mutually, and the real basis of it is that we should never have married in the first place. We weren't marrying each other because it was what we most wanted. We married each other because it seemed like a good match. It "looked right."

To make a long story short, I read your post and I cried because I realized the basis of making that decision was exactly what you wrote about. Cheryl was a good woman, and I needed a good woman in order to be a good man. God, what heartache I could have saved us both.

"I'm starting to understand," James says. "This site is built on a set of dichotomies. Brother Talk is more philosophic. It involves in-depth discussions on the subject of masculinity, as opposed to Bitch Talk, which is more of a full frontal assault on women and feminism in general."

"That's a pretty accurate summation," Leo agrees.

"I can see how that would help our perp," I say. "He's not interested in posts like the one we just read. He doesn't want the grief; he's looking for the hate."

When it comes to the relationships between men and women, it always seems to be the extremes that rule: love or hate, no in between.

I've had a complicated relationship with the war of the sexes for most of my life. I was raised by a father who treated me less as a female and more as a human being. My father was a dreamer, a man who'd tilt his head up in wonder to search for the blue sky peeking between the tree leaves. He appreciated simplicities, the small things, and he tried his best to transfer this understanding to me.

My mother was the one who loved the dreamer but kept her head out of the clouds. She anchored him to the ground with a mix of love and anger so that he didn't float away. The problem with Icarus men is that they forget the sun can burn, that even if they manage to escape the earth's atmosphere, space is cold and dark and deadly.

I landed in between the two of them. I have my mother's anger, but I'm capable of my father's wonder, and the truth is, when I think of my parents, I see myself more through my father's eyes than my mom's. His eyes said one thing to me: *You can be anything you want, and I'll love you.*

He let me shoot guns at eight, even though he hated them himself. He didn't bat an eye when I told him, during high school, that I planned a career in law enforcement.

The men in my life, those successors of my father, have all been good men, not intimidated by my dreams but loving me for them instead. We've used our strengths to fill in for the other's weaknesses, and not because we were trying to prove something. I don't cook, because I never learned, not because I'm trying to make a statement about women's duties in the home. When Matt and I were married, I cleaned the toilets, not because it was "my job" but because Matt begged me to. Cleaning toilets truly grossed him out; I had no problem with it. It was a love thing, not a man–woman thing.

Still, I haven't been immune. I wasn't just a woman when I joined the FBI, I was a woman-child, and physically small. This made me a target to some.

The most significant encounter was with an old-timer by the name of Frank Robinson. He was over fifty years old and had been with the Bureau since he was my age. I was assisting on a case in an administrative capacity, and Frank was either second or third in command.

At one point after a briefing, I found myself alone in the conference room with him. I was gathering up papers and putting them into folders. Frank was sitting in his chair, leaning back, chewing on the cap of his pen while eyeing me thoughtfully.

I tried to ignore it, but he kept staring, so I stopped what I was doing and confronted him.

"Do you need something, sir?" I asked.

He smiled, and I saw the shades of ugliness there. The hints of a leer.

"I was just remembering why I never liked having young female agents in the Bureau."

"Why is that?"

He stood up, downed the last bit of coffee in his Styrofoam cup, and let the leer fly. "It's distracting. Always wondering the same questions. Satin or lace? Natural or shaved? Big clit or little?" He licked his lips and the next words were practically a purr. "And the most important question of all: Does she swallow?"

I remember how shocked I felt in that moment. How violated. He wasn't touching me, but he was. His hands were all over me, even though they were hanging there at his sides. I felt myself blushing and hated my face for the betrayal. In the midst of it all, his eyes, drinking my reactions down.

Everything I'd dealt with up to that point had been essentially harmless. Less harassment than hazing, testing me to see what I was made of. I'd push back hard, give as good as I got, and that would be the end of it. This was different. It was a direct assault based on a perceived imbalance of power, and it was overtly sexual in nature.

I was young and unscarred then. I hadn't taken a life yet, and my proximity to the low men I'd later hunt was still more than once removed. My gift of seeing was just a seedling, but it had begun to put out shoots. It was taking dark root in the dark cellar part of me, and on that day, it spoke.

Robinson had done fairly well in the Bureau, it whispered to me. He'd spent years in financial crimes, doing excellent work, but had fought hard for entrance into the Behavioral Analysis Unit. His work there had been less than exemplary. Sufficient, but not stellar.

*It's the work of a distracted man.*

The whisper was like a caress in my mind, and in that moment I knew who Frank Robinson was. His actions had exposed a need. The thing inside me had taken it close, battened on it, and delivered him up to my knowing.

"I understand now why you wanted to be in the BAU, Frank," I said to him, "and why you've played second fiddle there."

His eyes narrowed at that. I walked up to him, got close, so that I had to tilt my head up to see his face. I was absolutely unafraid.

"Yeah? Why's that?"

I remember how I smiled at him, how I knew it was a cruel smile, an unfrightened smile, a grin of satisfaction powered by certainty.

"You're a voyeur, Frank. Some part of you likes what you see. The part that makes you go home at night and masturbate, thinking about what those men do to those women." I leaned into him, even closer, still smiling, unable to stop myself and not wanting to even if I could. "Do you ever take a case file home, Frank? Maybe copy some photos? I'll bet you do. I'll bet you have a folder hidden away in your house, full of victims' photos you've cherry-picked along the way."

His face turned ashen—with anger, yes, but also with a glimmer of fear. I was like a shark smelling the blood, not just hungry but enraged. He'd violated me. I was returning the favor, and a slap wasn't enough. I wanted to turn him inside out.

"You're not a real monster, Frank, I know that. I doubt you've ever raped anyone. But you feel the pull, don't you?" I nodded at him. "That's why you said what you said to me. Catharsis through sublimation."

"Cunt." It sounded like he'd been punched in the stomach.

*I bet your cock's limp now!* I remember thinking, ugly and satisfied, my meanness a brightness, like a bitter penny.

He backed away, heading toward the door. I watched him all the way out, still grinning like a jack-o'-lantern. He'd turned once to look back at me, and I saw something new there, an incredibly complicated mix of emotions and tiredness and oldness. There was respect, and anger, along with shame and fear and a certain thoughtfulness. Behind it all, like a child peeking around a door frame, was a younger Frank, from a time when he was still clean. I saw he could remember that time and yearned for it. I'd reminded him that he had a mother.

That was the first time I truly understood the difference between a bad man and an evil man. Frank put in for retirement a week later.

I've been blessed and cursed, depending on viewpoint and circumstance, with unique insights into the truth of human beings. I've been raped by a man, but I've watched a video of a young girl giggling as she strangled cats and buried them in her backyard. The overwhelming majority of those I chase are men, but I once arrested a woman who cooked her six-month-old in the oven because he "cried too much."

I am not blind to the differences between men and women, but I have seen the truths: The capacity for violence is there in all of us, and there's a world of difference between the flawed and the evil.

It's this knowledge that let me keep doing what I do after Sands's assault. I was worried that I'd be driven by rage, or a desire for revenge, and that these would cloud my judgment. I was relieved to find that I was driven instead by my desire to save the flawed and not by a need to destroy the evil. It's a small thing to say, but the difference inside your heart is immeasurable.

"Let's take a look at the chat," I say.

"Which one?" Leo asks.

"*Bitch Chat*. I imagine that's where he found Douglas Hollister. Douglas doesn't strike me as the philosophical kind."

Leo clicks on the menu option and the chat loads into the browser. A long list of names appears.

"Pretty active place," Alan says.

Callie leans forward. "Look at the names. USAWomenSuck. Single4life. NotYrBalls. I continue to see a theme."

"Some chats require a log-in to observe the conversation. This one doesn't, so you can watch without participating," Leo explains.

I read the back-and-forths, fascinated at this subculture of aggrieved man–boys.

Marriage is just another form of prostitution.

You got that right. My wife actually had a system. If I worked on the honey-do list, fucking was an option. If I completed it, sucking was an option. If I sat and watched the game, nothing was an option.

What did you have to do to get her to swallow?

Find another woman!

LOL!

"Charming," I observe.

The dialogue continues elsewhere.

Thing is, I still hope sometimes to find a decent woman I could spend my life with. Does that mean I'm a pussy?

Various responses fly:

Yes!

Pussy!

Not really. We all hope for that to some degree. If we say otherwise,
we're lying. But the odds of you finding an American woman who's not
a cunt-on-wheels is pretty slim. You should look outside the U.S. if and
when you're ready.

Mail-order bride? I don't know.

Russian women, Romanian women, Thai women. All of them know how
to treat a man. And they're all looking for American husbands. Supply
and demand goes the other way, in those places.

This is just one of three or four conversations going on in the chat.

"Why are some of them silent?" I ask Leo. "I see some names that
are just sitting there, not typing anything."

"They're probably PM'ing—private messaging. One of them can
double-click the name of another, and a separate chat window will
open up. Then they chat privately. No one else can read the conversation."

I scan the names and their activity. "Quite a few of those, I guess."

"The really personal stuff generally takes place in PMs. Anything
you say here can be read by anyone." He sweeps a hand to indicate all
of us. "Including law enforcement. In sex-based chat rooms, for example, you rarely see anything steamy going on out in the open. People
come in to the primary chat to flirt; they use PMs to . . . you know."

"The word you are searching for is *fuck,* honey-love," Callie purrs,
teasing him.

"Right," he says, blushing a little. "Point being, the same applies
here. If someone isn't comfortable talking about something out in the
open, they'll ask for a PM."

"You talked about 'bots," I say. "You said they could be programmed to respond to a private message."

"A canned response, sure."

"Then why don't we just go down the line of names there and start
clicking? We should be able to tell who the 'bot is, if there is one,
right?"

"If I were him, I wouldn't have set up a canned response for just that reason. He'd assume someone like me could figure it out."

I frown. "Won't a lack of response raise a red flag too?"

"Not really. It's fairly accepted that if someone doesn't reply to your PM, they're either not interested in talking to you or they're already busy."

"So much for easy," Alan says. "If we want to find him through the Net, we're going to have to develop a real cover for this one. The whole enchilada."

"What's that mean, exactly?" Leo asks.

"One of us is going to have to make himself an enticing target for our perp," Alan explains. "That means developing a full identity that will stand up to scrutiny. It means coming up with a name, backed by verifiable information, and a cell phone that he can call and that's traceable to that identity. So on."

"It means having an address that matches the identity," Callie chimes in. "In case he has some way of tracing the Internet provider you're using. Mostly," she says, "it means a lot of research. Reading all the 'manifestos' of the very lovely men from this website, wading through hundreds of forum postings. Et cetera and on."

"I get the house and cell phone, but I don't really see the need for research. Things seem pretty straightforward here." Leo smiles. "Just put on my wife-beater, drink some beer, and say 'bitch' every now and then, right?"

"Wrong," I tell him. "What you're talking about is a stereotype, and it's a common and sometimes deadly mistake in undercover work. A stereotype is a two-dimensional view. You need to exist, when you adopt an identity, in three dimensions."

"For example," Callie supplies, "you are a computer nerd, yes?"

"I suppose."

"Well, then, all I need to do is put on a pair of horn-rimmed glasses, grow some pimples, and know the difference between an IP number and a DNS server, right?"

"Okay. I get it."

"Who do you want doing this?" Alan asks me.

"You and Leo. It needs to be men doing it. I might miss something unconsciously as a woman. I want you as a backup. Leo's too inexperienced. No offense, Leo."

"No, you're right. I'll feel better if Alan's there."

"Shit," Alan grumbles. "But that means I'll be stuck."

"Why?" Leo asks.

"He might have seen my face at the wedding, when he dumped Heather Hollister. If he's watching the house, and he sees me, the jig's up. Which means you'll be doing all the shopping, roomie."

"Wait," Leo says, "are you saying I'll have to *live* there? Full time?"

"Of course."

"But how do I explain that to my girlfriend?"

"You lie."

"Lie?"

Callie pats him on the top of the head. "Ah, I was once young and naïve too. Yes, honey-love, you're going to lie. Tell her something exciting. You're being whisked away on a top-secret mission; you might not come home alive. That'll cover you and perhaps get you some hot good-bye sex too." She winks. "Women love secret agents."

"Fuck," he mutters.

Alan claps him on the shoulder. "Think of it as an adventure."

Leo nods glumly. "What do you want me to do about the other stuff?" he asks me. "Liaison with CCU and the past cases?"

"Those go on hold for now. You said the LAPD CCU was competent enough."

"Okay." He sighs, resigned to his fate.

"Division of duty," I say. "James, you stay on the job of getting those files to Earl Cooper."

"He'll have everything by end of day."

"Good. Callie, I want you to do all the legwork of setting up the identity and location. You know who to liaise with. I'd like to have things in place by tomorrow."

"Shouldn't be too difficult. It doesn't have to be fancy. We can have him work from home, so we won't have to contend with building a workplace cover. I'll have to find him an ex-wife. That might take a little longer."

"Find someone who's not on the radar yet."

"A promising, fresh-scrubbed graduate to be. I'm on it."

"What are we going to be doing in the meantime?" Leo asks.

"Research," I say. "Lots and lots of research."

"There's different ways to approach it," Alan says. "My opinion,

the best is to look for the things you can agree with, empathize with."
He points to the website, which is still sitting on the computer screen.
"Find something in there that makes sense. Align the rest of it to that.
That's what a guy coming to the site's going to do. He didn't come here
to find out everything about everything."

"He's there to find the solution to his own problems," Leo finishes,
getting the idea.

"Exactly."

"Everyone know what they're supposed to do?" I ask.

Silence is assent.

"Let's get to it."

We work late into the afternoon, each of us at our respective computers, reading over forum postings, lurking in the chat rooms, looking at
the photographs.

Sex is here, and so is rage, but most of all, below it all like a toxic
river, is the pain. The anger is the top layer, the loudest voice, the most
visible, but pain is the fuel that drives the engine.

When rage outstrips agony, you have murder, and it's this that I
search for on the website. There are men, few and far between, who
have long since passed the point of simply feeling their pain. It is their
anger that drives them, anger that has mutated into rage. It's a subtle
thing, but as I read, the small tics become signposts.

One man writes:

God, sometimes I hate my ex-wife. I wish she'd just fuck off and die.

Anger is present but has not yet taken over. He is still grieving, not
raging.

Another man writes:

Feminists have all but destroyed the culture of manhood. We need to reclaim our right to be men, and fuck the women who disagree.

Angry, but this is anger toward a principle, not a person.

Then there are the ones I'm starting to the think of as "the dark
men."

I lie awake sometimes in my bed at night thinking about her. About what she did to me. She fucked my best friend. She filed for divorce and got custody of my kids. She took my house and half my income. I live in an apartment, and I go to work every day, and I'm angry. I come home and eat alone, and I'm angry. But at night? When I'm in my bed and thinking about her? Sometimes I close my eyes and pray to God, or wish to the wishing genie, that she'd have a stroke, right now, or crawl into a bathtub and slit her wrists, or have a heart attack. I wish her dead. I actually lie there and try to will it to happen.

That's an obvious example. There are subtler, even darker ones. Such as:

God took a shit, and there was a woman. Sows, every one of them. The sow who took my son from me, I watch her from my car after work every night. I sit outside, parked, and watch that bitch.

"This is tiring as hell," Alan laments, standing up to stretch and groan. "I've never seen such a collection of whiners in my life. I mean, what's the problem? You want to be a man? Be a man! You want to think differently than the quote *feminists* unquote? Think differently! No one's putting a gun to your head."

"What about the ones who lose their kids? You don't think we have a system skewed toward the mother when it comes to custody?" Leo asks. "Just playing devil's advocate."

"There are countries where the kid goes to the father by default. You think that's right?"

"Not especially. I think custody should be based entirely on who is the fittest parent and not biased toward gender. Women are considered a safer bet as a parent. Why?"

"That's good, Leo," I say. "Sounds like you found one of your points of agreement."

He smiles, showing me that his comments had been more intellectual than passionate. "I saw their side of the argument, but the jury is still out."

"Who raised you?" Alan asks.

"My father, mostly." He looks uncomfortable. "Mom was a drunk."

"How would you feel about incorporating that into your cover?" Alan asks.

"Okay, I guess. Not pleased, but okay."

"That's the point. A good cover has just enough truth in it to make it believable. If you can incorporate things that give you real emotional response, response you don't have to fake, so much the better."

"Are we ready, then?" I ask Alan. "To build the cover?"

"I think so. I've read plenty. Leo?"

"I have a pretty good understanding of it all."

"You seem to have a pretty strong connection with the child-custody aspect," I say. "Sorry to get personal, but in the interests of motivations for your cover . . . I'd guess you object to the bias for the mom based on your own experience as a child."

"That's fair. Dad is the one who held the family together, fed us, clothed us, made sure we went to school and did our homework."

"Good, that's good," Alan says. "That's exactly what you're going to use for your cover. You are a newly divorced, disillusioned twenty-eight-year-old."

"Twenty-nine."

"Right, twenty-nine-year-old with a baby face, got it," Alan teases. "You were raised by a solid, dependable father and an alcoholic mother."

"Who physically abused you," I interject.

"My mother never abused me."

"I'm glad to hear it, but here is where the narrative veers away from the truth and into the profile we need. Your mother abused you physically. She did it when your father was not around, and you hid it from your father."

"Why did I hide it?"

"Because you were trying to keep the family together. You still loved your mother, and your father had said, many times, that if things got much worse, he was going to divorce your mom."

Leo's face reddens. He looks away.

"Hit a nerve there?" Alan asks.

He seems to shake himself. "Dad always called Mom 'a woman of trouble and fire.'"

"What did he mean by that?" I ask.

"It meant that she was full of life, and full of trouble, both, together." He bites his lower lip, pensive. "I remember one Saturday, I woke up and Mom was sober. I guess I was about twelve. I walked into the kitchen and she was awake, not hungover, and she'd made me breakfast. A great breakfast. Pancakes and bacon and fresh squeezed orange juice. I'd never had fresh squeezed orange juice until that morning. I remember drinking it and thinking it was the best thing I'd ever tasted.

"After breakfast, Mom asked me, out of the blue: *Leo, do you know how to dance?* I didn't, of course. I was pretty geeky, and I told her as much. She grabbed my hand and took me into the living room. *It's never too late to learn!* she laughed." He pauses, remembering. "Mom had a great laugh. Anyway. She put on one of my CDs, and we spent the afternoon dancing. Dad was on a double shift, so we were all alone." He picks at the knee of his pants, glum. "I wasn't a great dancer by the end of it, but I've danced ever since. Mom started drinking around dinnertime. She was angry by six, crying by seven, and blitzed by eight. Fresh squeezed orange juice and dance lessons, followed by vodka and puking and tears, all in the same day. Trouble and fire."

"You need to tell that exact story when you're on that site," Alan says. "It's real, son. So it'll ring true."

"I understand."

"The child end of things is more problematic," I say. "We can't pull a child into this operation."

"I have an idea on that," Leo offers.

"Go ahead."

"What if my ex-wife had an abortion?"

I resist the urge to put a hand to my own stomach. "Go on."

"What if she got an abortion prior to the divorce to avoid child-custody issues?"

Alan whistles. "Yeah, that could generate some hate."

"It could tie in with my whole story," Leo continues, picking up speed as his certainty increases. "My dream was to raise my own child in a good home, with a stable mother and father. She destroyed all of that."

"It's a good stressor," I agree.

"Just the kind of thing to bring a young man out of despair and into a nice, simmering rage," Alan says. He claps Leo on the shoulder again. "Good work, son. You're a natural."

We spend another hour working out the details. A good cover is not so much about the big picture. It's about what one of my teachers at Quantico used to describe as "moments of undeniable humanity."

*There are things you hear,* he'd said, *that you know are true. Moments of undeniable humanity. Like when a character in a book admits to us that he eats his boogers, or a husband fakes an orgasm, or a wife adds spit to her cheating husband's BLT. Perfection is not empathetic. We feel intimate with other strivers and failers; we're comforted to find that someone else also stole a dollar from Mom's purse.*

"An important aspect of undercover work," Alan says, "maybe the *most* important aspect, is patience. Criminals are a suspicious bunch of people. Their first assumption is that you can't be trusted, period. You prove otherwise by not seeming too eager, by just playing the part. You don't do anything out of the ordinary, until you do."

"What's that mean?"

"People are unpredictable. Being too predictable can be suspicious. The bank manager who slinks off to put on women's panties is more believable than the bank manager with a drinking problem."

"Why?"

"People like drama, I guess. Point is, every now and then, you throw a curveball. Not a big one, just enough to show them, yeah, this guy's human. A key one can be to break an appointment. If he says, *Meet back in the chat tomorrow at two o'clock,* you agree and then don't show up 'til four or maybe not until the next day. When he asks why, you say, *I fell asleep,* or *I got too depressed to move,* or *I went to a movie.* It pisses him off, and that's real, you see?"

"I'm starting to."

Callie bursts into the office, carrying a stack of documents and with a young woman in tow. The woman is about the same age as Leo. She's around five feet four, with dirty-blond hair down to her shoulders and a trim figure.

"I have what we need to get started," Callie announces.

I raise an eyebrow. "That was fast."

"Don't discount the power of my charm." She drops the documents down on the desk in front of me, ignoring Alan's snort. "Driver's license, Social Security number, bank accounts with a minimum of money in them—you're not a rich boy, Leo."

"Good, that'll make it easier to get into character."

"Your name is Robert Long. You dabble in freelance computer

consulting and are trying to break into day trading—so far unsuccessfully."

"So I'm a quasi-loser."

"A dreamer, honey-love, someone who walks the path less traveled. Think positively. This is your ex-wife, the ex-Mrs. Robert Long. Her real name is Marjorie Green. She just started in the financial crimes division. Her cover name is Cynthia Long, née Roberts. Being smart, as I am, I thought you could come up with a nice story about the serendipity of her maiden name being Roberts while your first name is Robert."

"Glad to meet you, Marjorie," I say, extending my hand.

"Thank you, Agent Barrett," she says, shaking my offered hand. She's looking at me a bit goggle-eyed. "I know it's not professional of me, but I just wanted to say that I'm a huge admirer. I've studied your career and your cases." She smiles shyly. "I'm not a stalker, just a fan."

"Well, thanks. I appreciate you taking part in our operation. Has Callie briefed you?"

"To a degree."

Marjorie Green is one of those subtle women, the ones I secretly tend to envy the most. She looks younger than she probably is, but she radiates a mix of unself-conscious assurance and lack of ego, an air of quiet, unprepossessing confidence.

"We'll fill you in. Let me introduce you to the others."

Everyone is welcoming and friendly, except for James.

"We have a house," Callie continues, when the introductions are complete. "Both the title and the mortgage will be in place by tomorrow morning, held in the names of Robert and Cynthia Long. I went with leaving a fair amount of equity in the home."

"How much?" Alan asks.

"More than a hundred thousand."

"Good. It'll give credibility to Robert Long's need to get the wife out of the way."

"Nothing makes more sense when it comes to murder than money," Callie agrees. "They both have a good credit rating to go with the Social Security number, and there are credit cards with minor balances on them for both. Use them sparingly and make sure you keep all your receipts."

"I assume you have a place for Leo too?" I ask.

"Of course. Being the slighted young man, he's in a so-so two-bedroom apartment. All utilities, including Internet and the rest, will be activated tomorrow. Ah, and a joint life-insurance policy as well. Five hundred thousand dollars on each of you."

I shake my head in amazement. "Jesus, Callie. How'd you manage to get all of this done so fast? This normally takes at least a week."

"I am owed many favors by many people. And I have my numerous male fans, of course."

"Puh-leeeze," Alan says, rolling his eyes. Marjorie watches it all, bemused.

"Additionally," Callie says, pinning Alan with a scowl, "I told them it could count as a belated wedding gift. It's called incentive."

"However it occurred, good job."

"Thank you."

"When are we going to start?" Marjorie asks.

It's a good question, and I give it careful consideration. As Alan had said, the bugbear of a good undercover operation is a lack of patience. There are probably a number of women out there, locked away in dark rooms, losing their minds and picking their skin until it bleeds. He'd warned us about coming after him, and we need to ensure that our actions do not endanger any living victims.

"Tomorrow," I decide. I look at Alan and Leo and Marjorie. "That work for you?"

"It works great for me," Marjorie says, obviously excited about her first undercover experience.

Leo and Alan both nod, resigned to their fate.

I give Leo and Marjorie my full attention. "You have to operate on the assumption that you're being watched, every day. When you're on this assignment, you're not allowed to call family, wives, husbands, girlfriends, boyfriends, anyone. Success depends on assuming the identities we're developing for you." I pause to give weight to what I'm about to say next. "The consequences of having your cover blown go further than your own safety. We're operating on the assumption that his threat is real, that he has other prisoners. If he thinks we're getting too close, he could decide to kill them. Do you understand?"

"I understand," Leo says, face and voice sober.

"Yes," Marjorie replies.

"Good. Then let's get Marjorie up to speed and finish building your covers."

# CHAPTER TWENTY-SIX

I am at the prison, watching Douglas Hollister as he sits across from me. The rest of my team are busy at their assigned tasks; I want to spend some time with Hollister, so I can continue to fill in the picture of the man who's behind all this.

We still know remarkably little about our perpetrator. He's done an excellent job of hiding himself from view, whatever his anomalies in that regard. He's kept contact at a minimum, controlled all points of communication. He's mutilated most of our best witnesses, and Heather Hollister is too damaged to be much help right now. Douglas Hollister is the most tangible link we have.

I take some time to study Hollister before speaking. He's a broken, beaten man. It permeates his body language and his silence. He stares down at his own hands, meeting my eyes only once, when he entered the interview room. He's aged overnight; his skin is sallow, and his face sags in exhaustion and depression.

"Why are you here?" he asks, listless.

"Two reasons. I want to talk more with you about the man you dealt with. And I wanted to see how you were adjusting to prison life."

He raises his head at that last. "Adjusting? Is that a joke?"

"Not at all."

He snorts, but it's halfhearted. "I'm trapped in a building filled with rapists, murderers, and thieves. Almost all of them are bigger and stronger than I am, and almost all of them are unfriendly. How do you think I'm doing?"

"Has anyone threatened you?"

"Not overtly. But it's coming. I can feel it."

"You can request protective custody."

"Oh sure." His tone is derisive. "Someone told me about that. You're put in another building with a different set of rapists and murderers and thieves, except now you have a target on your back forever, because everyone assumes you're a snitch. No thanks."

"If it comes down to a choice between that or death, I'd advise you to choose that, Douglas."

He sighs, rubs his face rapidly with both hands, as though he's trying to wake himself up from a hangover or a nightmare. His skin glows red from the rubbing, then returns to its normal color. "I'm not all that concerned with living or dying right now. Why should I be? I killed one of my own sons, and the one who lived will know that eventually. Dana's a . . . thing now. And Heather wins, after all. Death? I really don't care."

*Heather wins?*

I fight the instinct for anger. However many years I spend with sociopaths, with all their malignant narcissism, they still have the ability to surprise me. They have a twist in their mind that I can't understand in the root of me.

"You will," I say. "You feel that way now, but it will pass."

"How do you know?"

*Because I know you. Because you care more about yourself than any other human being in the world. Because you are what you are pathologically, by reflex. You couldn't be otherwise any more than you could choose to stop breathing.*

"Because I'm familiar with the phenomenon of shock," I tell him instead. It's a true-enough answer. "I've dealt with men and women in your situation. Suicide or death wishes are a common first stage. Survival asserts itself eventually."

"Really?"

The self-pitying sound in his voice makes me want to say ugly things, to hurt him in his weakness. *Poor baby,* I want to say. *Is life unfair for poor widdle you?* I slam down the window on these thoughts and continue to wear my own mask.

"Really. Just hang in there, and don't close any doors you might need to open later, okay?"

"Yeah," he says. "Thanks." He raises his gaze to mine and I witness naked gratefulness. Who knows if it's real or calculated?

"You're welcome. Let's talk about this man, this Dali. Are you willing to do that?"

"Why not? He's the reason I'm here."

"That's exactly right," I say. "You don't owe him anything."

He seems to take courage from this idea. He sits up straighter and nods to himself a few times. "Yeah. Yeah. Fuck him. Okay. What do you want to know?"

"When you talked, did he ever explain what his name meant?"

"Dali?"

"Yes."

"I never asked. He wasn't the kind of man you question a lot."

"Fair enough. What else can you tell me?"

Hollister frowns, thinking. "He was very careful about giving me any details. I never spoke with him face-to-face, only by cell phone and email, and those numbers changed regularly. He was always the one to initiate contact. I had no way of reaching out to him."

"How about his voice? Was there anything distinctive about it? High-pitched, low-pitched, rough, smooth, anything?"

"Sorry. He used some kind of voice scrambler. It made him sound like a robot when he talked."

I bite my lip, frustrated. "How long were you posting and chatting on that website before he first contacted you?"

"On beamanagain.com?"

"Yes."

He considers it. "Not long. A week and a half? I think that's right."

"What kind of things were you saying just before he contacted you?"

Hollister gives me an appraising look. I glimpse the first return of shrewdness. "Why?"

"Just trying to get a full picture."

The barest smirk ghosts his fetid lips. I prefer the beaten-down Douglas to the man I see returning to himself now. Sometimes the mask slips.

"It was pretty specifically after I said something along the lines of *I wish I had the guts to just make her go away.*"

"You said it that openly?"

"Sure. I was just one of a bunch of other guys venting. I didn't feel like I was risking anything."

"That's when he contacted you for a private chat?"

"Right."

It makes some sense, I think. No reason to tiptoe around something like this. When you're selling kidnapping, torture, and murder, you have to be aggressive. Dali would watch for the indicators of more than mere discontentment and then he'd approach and be blunt about it. Most of the time, I bet, he gets turned down. The majority of the human race is all bluster when it comes down to the nitty-gritty of harm. It's one thing to say to your wife, "I wish you were dead," and another thing entirely to bury an ax in her skull and dump her body in a lake. The distinction might seem a hop and a jump to the uninitiated, but in reality the difference is a distance from here to the sun.

"Then what happened?"

"Exactly what I said when the black man was interviewing me. Dali told me he could make my problem disappear. He offered proof and he warned me that if I breathed a word, he'd kill Avery and Dylan."

"Why'd you agree to go ahead? What was the tipping point?" I ask the question without really thinking about it. It's the common need, the most visceral one: a desire to understand *why*. We need why; it helps us sleep at night. Too many times, there is no why, there's just madness.

Hollister seems to have a need to understand it himself or perhaps to make me understand. He leans back in his chair and ponders my question. The silence in the room settles in as I watch him struggle to unravel his own reasoning.

"I just . . . I guess I just didn't see any other way out. Divorce meant giving her my house and my sons and half my money for God knows how long. This was a way for me to get the happiness I deserved." He points to his chest and the expression on his face is hurt, bewildered, petulant. "I deserved to be happy too."

I think I hate the ones like him the most. The serial killer is a simpler, more honest monster. Ask them why they did it, and their answers boil down, in the end, to the same thing: *because it makes me feel so very, very good.*

Douglas Hollister and his ilk live in a world of mirrors that reflect their own rightness and rationalizations back to them. They're worse, in some ways, because they're too close to the rest of us. They lack the elegance of the serial killer's mandate. Why'd he do it? For money. For a house. Because he is a spoiled, failed, psychotic child.

"Did Dana know, Douglas? Was she in on this with you?"

His face falls, and his eyes grow hostile. "No. Fuck you for asking."

*So she was another victim of your narcissism, in the end.*

"Thanks for your time." I stand up and head toward the door.

"That's it?"

I turn to him. "Just one more question, Douglas. Are you happy now?"

I'm pleased by the rage that profuses his face. I've grown crueler, and I question it less and less. Should I be worried?

I reach my car without an answer. By the time I hit the highway, I've forgotten the question.

# CHAPTER TWENTY-SEVEN

"I knew it," Bonnie says to me.

Tommy and I look at her, then at each other.

"You did?" I ask.

We're sitting at the dinner table. Dinner has long since been enjoyed, the dishes washed and put away. I'd told Tommy about my revelation of our marriage when I arrived home, and his happiness gave me the certainty that I'd done the right thing. He'd pulled me into his arms and held me there.

"Thank you," he'd said. "I hated having to hide something I'm so proud of."

I haven't dropped the pregnancy bomb on him yet. I am reserving that for, well—now. Or shortly. First we have to finish our sheepish confession to Bonnie.

She smiles and reaches out, taking one of Tommy's hands and one of mine. "Of course I knew. You guys aren't good at hiding when you're really happy. I thought about the Hawaii trip and put it all together."

"Smart girl," I say, my voice wry. "So?"

"So what?"

"So what do you think? How do you feel about it?"

"Oh." She grins. "I think it's about time."

Sometimes it gets to be that easy.

I pull my hand away and clear my throat. "Well, uh, I have some other news too."

I suddenly feel as though I'm naked on a stage, with a spotlight blinding me. My throat feels rough, and my heart is pounding in my chest.

"Smoky?" Tommy asks. "What is it?"

"Well, you see . . ." I clear my throat again, and now I'm getting angry at myself. "Oh, for God's sake. Look, I'll just say it, okay?" I take a deep breath in, then: "I'm pregnant."

Neither of them reacts, not at first.

"What's that?" Tommy asks. He seems dumbfounded.

"I said, I'm pregnant. We're having a baby. Your baby." I sound defensive. I hate it when I sound defensive. It's fear, not fight. Fight is better.

They both fall into silence. I grind my teeth. I'm starting to get pissed off and more afraid at the same time.

"Well? Don't either of you have anything to say?"

Tommy sits back. His jaw is slack. "I'm going to be a father?"

There is wonder in his voice, only wonder, and I know then that it's all going to be okay. Terror flees, replaced by a relief that exhausts me, the bottom of the adrenal bell curve. Bonnie stands up and comes over to me. She hugs me, wordless. She clings to me, not letting go, and I worry for a moment what it means. Is she scared? Jealous? Sad?

She pulls away and wipes tears from her face.

"What is it, honey?" I ask.

"That's just . . . so *cool*," she says, choking a little.

I laugh and she laughs as well, and then I'm crying too, so now we're both crying and laughing, as Tommy watches and repeats:

"I'm going to be a father? Holy *shit*."

We stare at him in shock.

"Tommy," I say. "Did you just use profanity?"

His eyes swim toward me, here yet not here, happy and disbelieving at the same time. "Did I?" he asks. He stands up, the chair sliding back on the wood floor. He walks over to us and he takes us both in his arms, Bonnie and me, equally.

"I love you both very much." His voice is rough, like unsanded wood. He hugs us to him with certainty and tenderness, that mix of sorrowful strength all good men seem to carry around with them. "This is great news."

Tommy, my man of few words. Sometimes shorter is not just better. Sometimes it's the best of all.

"Listen to me, honey," I tell Bonnie. "This is important."

"Okay."

"The first thing you need to know is, the moment you stop really listening to me, the moment you put your attention on automatic or start acting like you know everything or get impatient with my direction in the slightest way, we pack up and leave. Got that?"

"Yes."

Bonnie and I are at the shooting range. Raymond, Kirby's undertaker friend, sits outside in the parking lot, watching and waiting. He reminds me of a frog. Perched, quiet and harmless, until a fly buzzes by, then the fly is consumed and quiet harmlessness resumes.

We'd gotten past our tears and happiness. Well, maybe not past the happiness, but at least the giddy side of it. Tommy is at home, searching the Internet for a book on pregnancy and childbirth. I considered trying to dissuade him but gave it up in the end because, in truth, I like that he's doing it. This isn't going to be the walk in the park it was when I was in my twenties. The thought of Tommy boning up on the subject brings me comfort.

Bonnie and I had already made our appointment for the range tonight, and there's no way I'm breaking it because of my announcement. I've never had to juggle two kids, but something tells me it would be a bad precedent to set.

I've been shooting at this range in the Valley since I can remember. Its owner, Jazz, is an ex-marine sniper with eyes that are warm up front but cold in the back. He doesn't have to let me bring Bonnie here, but he's made no bones about it. I guess he approves of her teething on gunmetal.

Bonnie has big hands for her age, and they're strong, so I've decided to start her with a 9mm. We'll work our way down from there as needed. Jazz rents guns at his range, and I chose the Sig Sauer P226 for her to begin with. It's a 9mm that's somehow always felt light and comfortable to me, and it's an accurate weapon. I prefer the Glock, but mostly because it's the gun that found me first. Jazz set us up with a ten-round-capacity mag, one hundred rounds of ammunition, some paper targets, and our eye protection and earmuffs.

"Earmuffs go on before we enter the range," I continue. "They never come off while we're on the range. You could go deaf, no joke. Protective lenses stay on at all times while you're on the range, without exception."

She nods, and I'm mollified by the rapt seriousness on her face. It's apropos. I pick up the gun.

"This is a double-action weapon. What that means is that you don't have to pull back the hammer prior to firing. Just pulling the trigger will cause it to fire. Not only for that reason but especially because of it, you are never—and I mean never—to have the weapon pointed anywhere but down the firing range when it is loaded. You are never—and I mean never—to point the weapon at anyone, including your own foot, regardless of whether you think it's loaded or not. Do you understand so far?"

"Yes."

"You are to eject the mag and place the weapon down each time you finish firing."

"How do I put in and eject the mag?"

I look at Jazz and raise my eyebrows, asking permission. It's a firm rule that you never walk off the range with a mag in your weapon. I was here when someone forgot this rule, and I watched as Jazz held a .357 on them and asked them to lie down on the floor. No one got shot, but it made an impression on me.

"Go ahead," he says, watching it all with a passive interest.

I show her, sliding the empty mag home and then releasing it. "Got it?"

"Can I try?"

I hand her the weapon and watch as she examines it carefully, along with the mag. She takes her time, not putting on a show of pretending to understand how it all works. "What's this?" she asks, pointing at the decocking lever.

"Kind of like a safety."

"No," Jazz says. "It's a decocking lever. Not a safety. Apples and oranges."

He's right, of course. I'd been trying to dumb it down for Bonnie, to keep it simple, but the old rule is always the best rule when it comes to guns: If you're not smart enough to understand your weapon, you're not smart enough to use it safely.

"Many handguns have what's called a safety, honey, that you can put on manually. The P226 has a decocking lever, which lowers the hammer of the gun safely. That way, when you travel, you don't have to worry about the hammer coming down by accident for any reason. But," I continue, emphasizing this last, "it also means that this gun is basically always ready to fire."

"Decocking lever," she repeats, nodding. "How do I engage it?"

Jazz raises an eyebrow and smiles. "*Engage.* Good word."

I show her. She practices it a few times. "I got it."

"Okay, so load the magazine."

It takes her a moment, as she's going slow and is observing everything as she does it.

"Good. Now, use your thumb to pull down on the slide catch lever. Here, honey," I say, pointing it out to her.

She does, and the slide snaps forward into the battery. "Like that?"

"Yep. There you go. If the magazine was full, your weapon would be loaded and ready to fire."

Bonnie pulls the trigger back, and I hear the *click* as the hammer hits home. I grab the gun away from her.

"Never fire a weapon off the range, loaded or not!" I snap at her.

She's surprised at my anger but doesn't quail the way I'd like. Jazz sees this and walks from behind the counter. He comes over to Bonnie and stands above her, looking down at her. Jazz is not a big man, but he personifies intimidation. There is a calm and quiet coldness that surrounds him. Bonnie's mouth falls open as she looks up into his dead-fish eyes.

"You ever do that again in my shop and you're going to be in a lot of trouble," he says, full of patient threat. "You understand?"

She gulps, swallows. "Yes," she manages.

"Yes, what?" he asks.

"Yes, sir."

He nods. "Good." He ambles back over to his side of the counter. "Now, the two of you get on the range and leave me alone."

Bonnie and I put on our protective lenses and head toward the double doors that lead to the indoor range.

"Put your earmuffs on," I tell her before opening the first door.

She hesitates. "He's scary."

"A little, yes."

She glances back at Jazz, who's writing something on a stack of receipts. "He's killed people," she says. "I can tell." She slips on her earmuffs and gives me a beaming smile before I can think of anything pithy to say to this. "Can we go and shoot now?"

We're riding home in the dark that's never really "the dark" in Los Angeles. There's too much ambient light from all the megawatts we throw around in this city for that. Darkness here comes in pools, little islands of blackness where the monsters hide and where all the bad things happen. Women get raped in the spaces where the streetlamps don't reach; their bodies get left in the night shade of trees, with perhaps a naked foot poking out to be silvered by the moon.

Bonnie wasn't a natural, but she did just fine. The loudness of shooting a handgun surprised her at first, which is a common reaction. Her eyes went wide and she nearly dropped it. She caught me watching and pulled herself together, determined to show no fear. One hundred rounds later, she was getting very comfortable with the whole process. Her fingers weren't strong enough yet to load a full magazine, but that will come in time. Her accuracy was so-so. Jazz brought in a step stool for her to stand on, to make her more even with the target, and that helped.

She asked me to shoot a little before we left. I had brought my Glock with me, and I took it out of its case and obliged. She watched as the target disappeared to the end of the lane.

"You can really hit it that far out?" she asked.

"Uh-huh. Watch."

I never think much about shooting, and I never have, not after my first thousand rounds or so. It's something that comes best naturally, like walking or breathing. The more I think about it, the less accurate I become. I keep it instinctive now.

I like to draw and shoot, not as an Old West emulation but because that's often the truth of things. I stood facing the target, heart rate slow, relaxed, hands at my sides. My right fingers danced in their dangle, getting ready. Then I pulled my weapon and fired, eight shots, not the full mag, rapid-fire.

"One shot per second on the range, please," Jazz's voice said, coming over the loudspeaker.

I gave Bonnie a wink and a grin. I pushed the button to bring the target forward and was satisfied at the tight grouping. All center mass.

"Wow!" Bonnie said, goggle-eyed. "Do you think I'll ever be that good?"

"It's possible. With practice."

I'd shot a few more times, and then it had been time to leave.

"That was fun, Mama-Smoky," she says to me. "How often can we go?"

"Every other week, like I promised, as long as you keep your end of the deal. If I'm away, Tommy can take you too."

"I want to practice a lot. It's important."

She lapses into silence, and I sneak a glance at her. The determination I see in her face, as it goes from shadow to light to shadow to light, is as uplifting as it is disturbing. It makes me question again my decision to help her walk on this path.

"She'll walk it with you or without you," Tommy had said to me. "With you is better, I think."

I hope he's right, but who knows? Bonnie catches me looking at her and gives me a big smile.

"Thanks for doing it. I know you're really busy right now."

"You get my time when I have it, honey, always. Even when the new baby comes."

"I'm not worried."

"That's important to me, babe. I love you. I don't want you ever thinking you're second fiddle for me."

"It'd be pretty selfish of me not to be happy you get to have another baby, Mama-Smoky. I know you love me. I love you too. Actually, I'm pretty excited about it."

"You are?"

"I always wanted a younger brother or sister."

"Me too," I admit. "Which do you hope for more: a brother or a sister?"

"A brother," she replies without hesitation.

"Me too." I laugh. "I don't know why."

"Little boys are cute."

"Let's hope."

She fiddles with her lower lip, thinking. "We're turning into a real family now, aren't we? You and Tommy are married, a baby on the way. Wow."

Wow, indeed. I decide it's time to spring my other surprise on her. "Honey, Tommy wanted me to ask you something."

"What?"

"He'd like to formally adopt you. He's been thinking about it for a while, now, but we needed to get married first."

She stares at me, blinking. Once, twice, three times. "He . . . he wants to be my father?"

"Very much. But only if you're comfortable with that."

"Comfortable? Is he joking? That'd be awesome! I've never had a dad."

Bonnie's biological father was a flake. He'd left Annie in the lurch and died a few years later in a car accident.

"You tell him when we get home, then, honey. It'll make him so happy."

"Really? It will?"

I reach over and caress her chin with my hand. "Of course it will. He's never been a dad either."

Tommy and I are lying in bed, drifting, not so much toward sleep as simply drifting, two lovers in a rowboat, floating on a windless lake. My cheek is against his chest, while my hand lies farther down, nestled against his penis—for comfort, not for sex. His eyes are half lidded, but I know he's awake.

"She was genuinely happy about me adopting her," he murmurs.

"I think *ecstatic* is the word."

Silence.

"Never thought a child would be so happy to have me as a father."

I lift my cheek onto my hand so I can see his face. "Seriously?"

"I don't mean it like that. It's not that I thought of myself as unworthy or anything. It's just . . . to have her not only say yes but to be so happy about it . . ." He sighs. "I can't explain it."

I smile and lie my head back on his chest. "I think I understand."

"I did a lot of reading tonight about babies," he says. "Ordered some books." He clears his throat, perhaps a little self-conscious. "I want to understand everything."

"The books help. Up to the birth. After that, we're on our own."

"I don't care if it's a boy or a girl, by the way."

My hand pauses in its slow caress of his lower belly. "Really?"

"Yep. I know most guys want a son, and that would be fine, but I honestly don't care. I just want a healthy child that we raise together."

"I'm afraid we're going to get punished for being too happy." I don't mean to say it. The words come of their own accord.

He strokes my hair. "I understand."

I snuggle into him, finding comfort in him speaking those two simple words and no others. He didn't try to reassure me or pooh-pooh my fears.

We drift again, and I feel him slip away. Tommy usually falls asleep before I do, just as he wakes before I wake. His breathing is slow and steady, and I feel the reassuring beat of his heart against my ear.

I reach down and run a hand over my belly.

*Are you in there, whoever you are? No arms, no legs, just a lump of cells, I guess, but I'm going to talk to you a little, anyway. I want you to know that I'm going to take care of you. I'm not going to let anyone hurt you or take you away from me. I have a new rule, baby. Do you want to know what it is?*

My stomach gurgles, and I take this as an acquiescence.

*Anyone who comes after me or my family personally? They don't get to go to jail after doing that. Not anymore. The price for that is death, pure and simple. Okay, baby?*

No gurgle this time, but that's okay, because I'm drifting differently now too. My eyes are heavy, and I close them and drift off, one hand on the place where my child grows, the other on the man who helped to make it.

# CHAPTER TWENTY-EIGHT

"I've set up some software that lets you log in to our computer," Leo says. "You'll be able to watch what we're doing as though you were the user. That's how you can follow along with the chats and so on. I've also got a webcam on so we can talk over the microphone."

Leo and Alan have taken their places in "Robert Long's" apartment. Marjorie is ensconced in the house as Cynthia.

"Cynthia's not working yet," Callie had briefed us. "Since we needed the cover-up and running so quickly, I decided that we would go a similar direction with the ex-Mrs. Long as we did with Robert. She's trying to decide what to do with her life. In the meantime, she'll go to the gym, get her hair done, read, all those activities the well-kept woman engages in."

I peer at the image on my own computer. "It's like being right there," I say, impressed.

"This technology has come a long way," Leo agrees. "You should be able to read everything as we type it. I'll be keeping logs as well, so you can catch up on anything you miss, as needed."

"Have you registered with the website yet?" I ask.

Alan's voice comes through the microphone. It's odd to be having conversations while staring at a monitor. "Yep: Hurting2105. Hurting 1 through 2104 were taken."

"That's a lot of pain."

"Or whining," Alan says. "Anyway, we're ready to get started."

"Go ahead."

Law-enforcement undercover work is not that exciting, unless you're a narcotics officer. Most of it is not about the moment of the criminal act but the day-to-day living that surrounds your cover iden-tity. You have to eat, and sleep, and make bank deposits, and pay bills. You have to see movies and decide between popcorn and licorice. You have to buy toilet paper. All of it done under the assumption that every move you make is being watched. You play your part and hope that the moment of action comes.

I watch as Leo surfs to the beamanagain website.

"Should I log in to chat?" he asks.

"Take it slow," Alan counsels. "Let's see what's happening on the forums first. What's the hot topic of the day?"

Leo navigates to the General Discussion section of the forums. "This is a new one," he says.

I lean forward, squinting a little to read what he's talking about.

"You'll need to use the software connection if you want to follow the chat," Leo says. "But you should just read the forums yourself, in your own browser, since everyone reads at different speeds."

"Good point," I allow.

I open the other browser window and get myself onto the website. I navigate to the forum. The top posting Leo had pointed out is entitled *More housework, better sex?*

"That sounds interesting," I murmur.

I click on the topic and begin to read.

A recent study found that when men and women feel the housework is divided evenly, the couple's sex life is better. The study noted that it wasn't important that the housework was factually divided evenly. Only that the parties involved felt that it was. Discuss.

The next posting:

PUH-leeeze. Who did that study? A woman, right?

LOL.

The next, from the poster who started the thread:

Heh. Yeah, I thought the same, but it turns out the study was done by a man.

The responses continue.

Well, hell, I'll vacuum if it will get my knob polished. Small price to pay.

Another poster jokes:

Fine, but I don't do windows unless my salad gets tossed.

Ick. That's gay. You want your turdhole polished, go find a fag forum.

Up yours!

The original poster steps in again, attempting to mediate.

Guys. We fight enough with women. Let's not use this site to fight with each other. Back on topic, please.

I read through the back-and-forth of the thread. Much of it is harmless banter, some of it is more thoughtful. There is only the occasional venomous remark.

The cunt I live with wouldn't fuck me if I hired a live-in maid.

Or perhaps the most disturbing:

All I know is she won't have sex with me and hasn't for four years. I've tried everything. I finally had enough of her shit. The other day I jacked off into her shampoo bottle. Then I went and got her a hamburger and added some "extra mayo" of my own. I almost laughed when I asked her how it was and she said, "It's delicious!" She's gonna swallow my cum and have it running down her face whether she likes it or not.

"I'm going to post a response," Leo says. "Something I read yesterday would be appropriate here, and it would start to fill out my profile and give me some credibility with other members of the site."

"Go ahead," Alan says, "but let me read it before you post it."

I peruse other threads as he types. A few minutes pass.

"I'm done."

"Let me see," Alan says. I wait as he reads it. "That's pretty good, Leo. Where'd you get that?"

"I picked up some books. I also ordered a few from the site's online bookstore, in case the perpetrator has a way of watching that."

"Good thinking," I chime in.

"Go ahead and post it."

A pause. "Done," Leo says. "Smoky, if you refresh the last page of the thread, my posting should be visible now."

I hit refresh and watch as the page loads. I scroll down to the bottom and see a posting by Hurting2105.

I read a book recently that discussed the differences between men and women and their desire for sex. It said that, by and large, it's true: Men want sex more often than women do. Yeah, yeah, I know, that's nothing new. But there was one thing the author said, an observation that I thought was really insightful. He said: Men tend to want sex when they are under stress, while women tend to lose interest in sex when they are under stress.

I think that's true and might explain a little bit of what that study found.

Anyway, is that God's idea of a joke or what?

"Very good, Leo," I say.

"Thanks."

"I have to agree with the writer of that book," Alan says. "That is pretty insightful."

"Speaking from personal experience, Alan?" I tease.

"No comment."

I refresh the page. "Hey, you got a reply."

It says:

Good contribution, newbie. I read the same book, and I agree, it's an excellent observation.

"How can he tell you're a new guy?" Alan asks.

"Check out the line under my handle. See?"

I look for and find what he's talking about.

"Post count," I say. "One."

"The guy who replied—IronJohn2220—he's got a post count of over five thousand," Alan says, and whistles. "Too much time on someone's hands."

"What's next?" Leo asks.

"Let's post your story," Alan replies. "Smoky, we're going to go with the Brother side of the website and stay out of the Bitch sections for now. Leo is going to be a reluctant hater, rage on simmer."

"More sad than angry," Leo supplies.

"I assume you already have the story drafted?"

"Just cut and paste," Leo says.

"Go ahead."

A moment later, he tells me I can find the story online.

My name is . . . actually, let's hold off on telling you my name for now. Just call me John or Jim or Joe. I'm no one special, that's the point. I've been reading through all of your stories, and I see that now.

I met a girl that I thought would be mine forever. I'm twenty-nine, and I met her when I was twenty-two. Young love. I thought she was everything you could possibly want in a woman. She was attractive without being model-beautiful, she was quiet but not weak, she had her own mind but was interested in what I thought too.

Good melding of the traits of the real-life Marjorie, I think.

We didn't tumble right into our wedding either. We took our time. Kept separate places at first. Made sure we were sexually compatible—which we were then. She wasn't slutty, but she was up for trying anything once. She wouldn't let me finish in her mouth, for example, but she'd use her mouth to get me up to that point. Compromise a guy could live with, you understand? I've always thought I have a healthy sex drive, as much as the next guy, but I don't have any particular fetishes. I guess that's not the case for some men, but it's the case for me.

We finally moved in together, again taking it slow. We were both aware of the statistics on divorce. She grew up in a single-parent home, raised by her mom because her dad was a loser who was never around. I grew up with two parents, but in name only. My mom was a mean drunk who used to hit me when my dad wasn't around. We were in no hurry to screw things up by getting married. We took our time.

We lived together for almost a year before I proposed, and she agreed. I thought, Why not? We were really compatible. We shared the housework, we pooled our money and paid our bills, we had similar tastes in furniture and drapes—which is to say, I didn't care and she did. We were happy, and we felt good about having taken it slow, about being sure we were making the right choice.

Even our wedding was a careful affair. We kept it simple and cheap but still made it special. We got married by the ocean, on a spring day. She looked beautiful, and I didn't look half bad myself. Her mom came, and so did my dad. My mother did me the favor of staying away. We liked to joke that nothing changed except that we were both wearing rings now. We didn't have a honeymoon. I guess we were both a little superstitious, not wanting to jinx it. We got married, spent the weekend at home, screwing our brains out, and went back to work on Monday.

I want to share a moment from that weekend. I know a lot of guys on this site are really angry, and I see a lot of talk about women being "bitches" and "cunts" and stuff like that. And I understand it, I really do. But I'm just not there right now. I can feel that anger, deep down inside (or maybe not so deep), but I'm still not comfortable calling her those names. In spite of everything she did to me.

It's still too fresh, you know? It still hurts too much. Anyway, maybe that moment I mentioned will explain a little.

It was Sunday morning. Early, like, 5:00 or 6:00 A.M. I woke up for some reason, I don't know why. The TV in the bedroom was on, and the whole place smelled of sex and sweat. I remember coming out of my fog and hearing an infomercial playing in the background. Something about getting rich in real estate. I opened my eyes and turned my head, and she was lying on her side, cheek against the sheets, watching me.

I remember looking into her eyes and seeing, really seeing, that she loved me. It was there, as naked as we were. It took my breath away.

"What is it?" I managed to ask her.

She reached over and stroked my cheek. She didn't say anything for a few moments. "I was thinking about us fifty years from now," she said. "Thinking about you with white hair and wrinkles."

"Nice," I joked.

"No," she said. "I mean it. Life is short and long, both together. We've made a choice, driven by the hope that we'll be better than our parents were. A leap of faith. I woke up next to you and I was looking at you and I realized, yes, I made the right choice. We're going to make it." She came to me then, snuggled under my arm, put her head on my chest. "I'm so happy," she said.

We didn't talk any more, but, God, I remember how good I felt at that moment. She drifted away while I lay there with my heart bursting in my chest. I was twenty-five, and my life had begun. Corny, I know, but that's how I felt. It was like I could see the future, you know? A thousand moments like this one, years and years of sharing the same bed, waking up to say things to each other that no one else would ever hear or know. I had a partner, a second self, someone who'd always be on my side.

It was the first time in my life that I can remember not feeling alone. She gave me that. She took it away later, that and a whole lot more, but she gave it to me first.

Those first two years were probably the best years of my life. We had our fights, but that was expected. We fought about money, and chores, and sometimes we just fought because we were rubbing up against each other and that makes you bark. I remember one time, I went out and bought a new set of drinking glasses. We'd seen them at the store together, and I really liked them but she didn't. I went ahead and got them anyway, and, man, was she pissed! We were screaming to high heaven, and she ended up smashing one of the glasses in the sink, so then I took her favorite coffee cup and broke it against the wall. We were both shocked at ourselves and ended up kind of standing there, hands to our mouths, going "Oh my God . . ." and then laughing 'til we cried at our own silliness.

We always made up, made love, and learned from our fights. It was something we'd actually do—sit down and talk once we were calm and try to understand the other person's viewpoint. We'd admit where we were wrong and the other was right, and then we'd come up with a compromise.

Neither of us had an awesome job, but we were making enough money between us to buy a house. It was a lucky purchase too. It's worth more now than what we paid, in spite of the market. We set up that house together. We were frugal, and that was part of the fun of it. We went to secondhand stores and garage sales, buying bookshelves that didn't match the coffee table that we'd bought somewhere else. We had three or four different kinds of silverware, none of them a full set. Sometimes we'd make a weekend of it. We'd pack a picnic lunch and a thermos of coffee and we'd spend two days driving through the San Fernando Valley searching for treasures in other people's castoffs. We'd find a park when we were hungry and spread a blanket and just . . . stop. Look. Take in the sun and the sky and the grass. Sometimes we'd talk about the future, about the kids we wanted to have. We agreed that a son and two daughters would be ideal, but a son was on the agenda, period, and then on other days we'd talk about grandchildren, or whether we'd get a Lab or a collie, and all of our other zillion plans. It took us some time, but we built the inside of that house together. We made it a home. It wasn't the prettiest, and nothing matched, but it was ours.

It was an adventure. I felt good. I felt like I'd found my place in this life. I was set.

One day, without warning, everything changed.

I came home and she said we needed to talk. She was so calm, so reasonable, I remember that clearly. Not a sign of grief. She talked to me like an adult would talk to a difficult child, and she proceeded to destroy my life in what was almost a monotone. She'd fallen out of love with me, she said. It wasn't my fault, she said. It was a gradual thing, but she was sure of it now, she said. She wanted a divorce. She wanted the house. She also said—and this is the worst of all of it—that she'd gotten pregnant a few months back but got an abortion. Because she knew then, already, that she was going to want to get divorced, and she didn't think it was a "good idea" to have a baby if we were no longer going to be together. She said all of these things, one after the other, cool as a cucumber, just stating the facts with no embroidery. It was as if she was reading from a list that she needed to get through.

I should have said something then. Something smart, or cutting, or deep. But I couldn't talk. It's not that I couldn't think of anything to say— I couldn't speak. The pathways from my brain to my vocal cords had shorted out.

Looking at her, I felt like I was staring at a monster. Which was part of the problem. Because she couldn't be a monster. This was the woman

I loved, the one who'd told me, in the middle of a sunrise, that we were going to make it. This was the woman I'd built a home with. I had trusted her absolutely, with every single tiny part of me. And now here she was, sitting across from me, calm, collected, almost mechanically cold, telling me it was over.

When I did manage to finally engage my mouth, I didn't say anything worthwhile. It was pathetic. I cringe when I think about it now. The whining, desperate sound of my own voice. I asked her if there was someone else, and she assured me that there wasn't. I asked her why, what I had done, and I remember what she said, because I could really tell that it was true. As much of a stranger as she'd just become, as hard as she'd blindsided me, I still knew her enough to know that she believed what she was saying.

"I woke up one day and what I felt for you had gone flat. I waited for that to change." She shrugged. "It didn't. I realized it never would. I can't live the rest of my life feeling that way, and you shouldn't either."

I begged her on my knees to go for marriage counseling. She refused. Nothing I said or did could get through to her. She was closed off to me. I guess that's the final point of all this, why it hurts so much for all of us. When a woman gives herself to us completely, when she lets us inside, it brings us to life like nothing else. When that's taken away, we're somehow lonelier than we were before we met her.

I came to this site because, quite frankly, I'm a mess. I have trouble sleeping. I go through times when I miss her and times when I wish she was dead. I've had feelings of rage that frighten me. Mostly, I'm just in pain. Right, wrong, indifferent, I'm just in pain. I'm not ready to call her a bitch, not yet. But I'm getting there.

That's it. Sorry to ramble, but I feel safe here, and I needed to say it all.

I finish reading and sit back in my chair. "Wow," I say. "I'm impressed. That's going to make an impact."

"We spent a lot of time crafting it," Leo says. "It's a little long, but we wanted something that would resonate with the men on this site and that would be sure to get a lot of attention. It's already generating discussion."

"Where?"

"There's a place below each story where members can post their comments. Reload the page and you'll see the ones that have already been posted."

I refresh the post, and I see four. The top one begins:

Great first story. Honest sharing. You really spoke to me with that one, buddy. Really and truly. I loved my wife too, before she kicked me in the balls. It's always easier getting hurt by a stranger. Just hang in there. It will get better, I promise.

Then:

Don't let anyone make you use the word *bitch* until you're ready, brother. This is about you, not other people. You work through it the way that's best for you, period.

Next:

Good first post. Strong stuff.

And finally:

You won't say it, so I'll say it for you, brother. She's a bitch. A fucking cunt. I'm sorry if that offends you. That's not my intent. But I'm more sorry that you went through that. People say that men have commitment problems, like it's a male-only condition. Bullshit. Women are just as wired to be twisted as we are. It's not a "man condition." It's a human condition. A man who did to a woman what your wife did to you would be called a bastard, or a motherfucker. So I'll say it again: She's a bitch. A cold, fucking cunt.

"I think we left our mark," Alan observes.

"Good job. Now what?"

"Chat room?" Leo asks.

"Go ahead," Alan replies.

I switch views now, watching in real time as Leo clicks on and logs in to the Brother Chat room.

"We'll lurk for a bit," Leo says.

"Lurk?" I ask.

"Just like it sounds. We watch but don't take part. It's pretty common for newbies. Good manners, even. You sit back and observe and try to learn the rules. Every group has its standards by which you're judged and its own rules of etiquette. Violate the first one, and nobody will take you seriously. Violate the other, and no one is going to talk to you. I already see a rule for this chat room that's unusual for chats in general."

"Which is?"

"Most chat rooms are quick back and forths. Just like real conversations. This chat room has a lot of soapboxing. That's strange enough in and of itself, but the real shocker is that the others in the chat room actually shut up while that's going on. There's no heckling, no stepping on each other's conversations."

I watch the screen. It takes me a moment, but I see what he's talking about. Right now a member who calls himself KingEnergy12 is preaching.

Misandry is not just being legitimized psychologically. It's being made law. The original intent of laws to protect women, as stated, was simply to raise the rights of women, not to lower the rights of men. But in practice, that's exactly what's occurred. We have created a society where a belief system about men has been inculcated as a collection of false facts. You see examples of it in every walk of life. Take a look at television sometimes. What kind of man do you see portrayed there? Let's see. You have the silly daddy, a kindly fumbler with the best of intentions but a few brain cells missing. He's guided through his own stupidity by his wiser wife, who is endlessly patient with his genetically programmed inabilities. You have the man's man. He watches sports, farts and laughs about it, and lives to hog the remote and slam back those brewskies, baby! He's trained young in all the ways to get the stripper glitter off his clothes, and he lives by the rules of *look but don't touch*, or *touch via lap dance but don't fuck*. His (again) wiser wife puts up with her Neanderthal because she knew what she was getting into when they got married, and, besides, he comes through in the clutch. Other luminaries include the wife-beater (Lifetime channel, anyone?) and the pedophile.

We're inundated with stories about the deadbeat dad, the husband who raped his wife, the stepfather who sexually abused his stepchildren. Women, meanwhile, are celebrated everywhere. The female boss who is a cunt-on-wheels is defended with the phrase *a driven and demanding woman is called a bitch, while a driven and demanding man is hailed as an example.* Well, I'm sorry, but a bastard's a bastard and a bitch is a bitch, ladies. No one likes to be treated poorly by anyone, regardless of the gender of the abuser.

A few seconds pass without him typing anything further.
"I think he's done," Leo says. "I'm going to type something."
"Start simple," Alan says. "Take it slow."
Leo begins:

Hello, New here. I don't have a lot to say yet, but I had to speak up briefly. I'm going through a lot just reading the things on this site and watching the conversation in this chat. It's a strange feeling. I feel liberated on one hand and guilty on the other. Still, I'm glad to be here. That's all I wanted to say.

KingEnergy12 replies:

Welcome, brother. That guilt you feel? That's been educated into you. Men have been trained to feel bad about asserting themselves as men. If we do, we're sneered at, called "old-fashioned," "misogynists," or "woman haters." A man who claims his masculinity is a knuckle-dragger by default. It's all smoke and mirrors, brother. It's conditioning, nothing more, nothing less, and it will fade in time.

Leo types:

I hope so. I could really do with feeling good about myself.

Another member types:

Hey, I read your story. You just put it up today, right?

Yeah.

Wow, man. That was a hell of an account. I really appreciated your honesty, and I definitely felt your pain.

Thanks. It was tough to write all that, but . . . I don't know. I felt better after too. Not fixed, but better. Anyway, I have to go now, but I just wanted to say that I appreciate you guys being here, and the site, and what you have to say.

KingEnergy12 types:

Come back anytime, brother. You're welcome here, and you won't be judged.

Leo leaves the chat without replying.

"Good touch," Alan says. "Being a little bit nervous at the end."

"It's not like I'm totally clueless when it comes to online undercover work," Leo says. "I've played a pedophile before. This is harder."

"Why?" I ask.

"Being a pedophile was nothing like being me. It was an act from start to finish."

"Whereas this . . . ?"

"I don't see things the way these guys do, I'm not saying that. But . . . it's a little too easy to slip into this role."

"Dance with the devil, son," Alan says.

"Yeah." Leo sighs. "I like computer work better."

"You're doing fine," I say. "So what's the plan now?"

"He needs to do some day trading," Alan says. "Slow and easy."

"Give me a call when you go back into chat."

"You got it. Bye."

The microphone clicks off. A moment later, the connection to Leo's PC is severed.

I think about what I've read, what I've watched being typed in that chat room. Part of me feels for these men. I don't sense rage in all of them. Some simply seem confused, hurt. My hand finds my belly and I wonder: What if I have a son? Should I think about these hurting men, worry about what role model my boy should look up to?

The only answer I can find is Tommy. Tommy is unassertive about being a man. He just is one. His masculinity is a part of him, as natural as breathing, unconfused. I could do worse than raising a son to emulate such a man.

My cell phone rings.

"Barrett," I answer.

"Hey, boss woman." Kirby's cheerful voice—not much different from her killing voice, but comforting nonetheless. "Thought I'd report in, give you a little update on where your money's going."

"Tommy's money, you mean."

"It's all one big green pile now that you're married, right?"

I don't bother asking her how she knows about the marriage. "What's the briefing, Kirby?"

"So far, so nada. Nothing happening. No signs anyone is following her or even has eyes on her."

"That's good news."

"But not really, right?"

When a threat is out there and we know it, we'd rather it come out to fight than hide. We can win a fight. All we can do about the other is worry.

"No, not really."

"Well, don't fret about it, boss woman. We're on the job. Raymond's not much for company, but he's a good listener."

"You're not taking shifts?"

"I decided to add a few people. Raymond and I are on the evening watch, and a couple of my other buddies are there during the day. Nighttime is the right time when it comes to killing people, don't you think?"

"I suppose." I consider asking her about her "buddies" but realize maybe I don't want to know. Raymond was creepy enough. "I appreciate you taking the night shift, Kirby. You're right, it's the time of greatest threat."

And it'll let me sleep, knowing you're out there, watching us.

"No problema. Well, not *no* problema—it's cutting into my sex life, I have to be honest, but that's what friends are for, right? The guys'll just have to come in the daytime and get some afternoon delight. Law of supply and demand."

"You being the supply, I take it."

"Of course! Hey, did you see how I did that, a little intentional pun? 'Come' in the daytime?" She giggles.

"Good-bye, Kirby."

"Later, alligator!"

I hang up, shaking my head.


"Have we heard anything from Earl Cooper?" I ask James.

"He said he'll have something for us by late afternoon. He also said not to expect very much."

"Reassuring."

"Collecting facts," he replies, either missing the light humor or ignoring it.

"On that note: Tell me about the other victims."

"All women," Callie says, picking up a file from her desk and opening it. "Eight years ago, on June thirteenth, Elizabeth Harris was found on the steps of the Chatsworth police station, prefrontal lobes mutilated in the same way as our current victims. She'd been abducted a little more than seven years earlier, and her husband was the prime suspect."

"But the investigation stalled because a body was never found." I deliver it as a statement.

"That's correct. Her husband, one Marcus Harris, killed himself a few days after the discovery of his wife. He left a note, saying that he was 'sorry.' It was assumed that he was responsible for the mutilation as well as the abduction, and the case was closed."

"Strange." I frown. "If he was willing to kill himself, why didn't he say anything about Dali? What did he have to lose?"

"He had a daughter. She was twenty at the time. She went missing the day after her mother was found."

Something inside my stomach plummets into an icy abyss. "Was she ever recovered?"

Callie consults the file. "No."

"Dali probably gave him a choice," James says. "Keep your mouth shut about me and take the blame, or your daughter suffers the same fate as your ex-wife."

"He would have killed her after Marcus's suicide," I say. "She was no longer 'necessary.'" I exhale. "Well, we have an answer to the question of how Dali ensured Marcus would take the fall. What happened to Elizabeth?"

"She never came out of it. She died of a blood clot to the brain three years ago."

"Nothing came up when Elizabeth was found about Dali? He didn't text the cops or drop off a stray greeting card?"

"Not a word. The police assumed, understandably, that Marcus Harris had been keeping her somewhere all that time. They chalked the mutilation and suicide up to an unbalanced mind. The disappearance of the daughter confirmed, more than disproved, this."

"I'm assuming he had an insurance policy?"

"Four hundred thousand dollars. He'd recently collected, and all the money was accounted for. He hadn't sent any of it away."

"No notes," James muses. "Dali took care to remain hidden. The current circumstances remain a significant anomaly."

"Tell me about the next victim."

"Oregon, four years ago. November twelfth. Two patrolmen were on a coffee break. They came back out to find Kimberly Jensen in a body bag, which had been left in front of their cruiser."

"Bold," James says.

"Kimberly had been abducted from a supermarket parking lot— you guessed it—more than seven years earlier. She was thirty-five at the time. Her husband, Andrew, was—surprise—the prime suspect. She'd been having an affair and was seeing a divorce lawyer."

"I guess he'd collected on life insurance and kept the loot?"

"Greed is a bitch."

"Kimberly?"

"Inhaled her own saliva and developed pneumonia. She died."

"What about the husband?"

"Evidence fell from the heavens. Very fortuitous."

"What?"

"An electronic diary on his computer, filled with seven years of monthly entries, all about Kimberly and how he'd kept her confined. A storage space in his name complete with chains in the floor and Kimberly's DNA. Things like that." She smiles. "Andrew killed himself before the cops could pick him up."

"Starting to see a pattern here with the suicides."

She shrugs. "Cowards are cowards, the whole day long."

"No notes left behind, I assume?" James asks.

"Not a one."

I sigh. "Two for two on Dali staying off the radar. Next?"

"Hillary Weber, forty-five, found by tourists on a side street leading off the Vegas strip three years ago. Hillary had been taken like the others, and the husband, Donald, was in the cross hairs. He'd been in the middle of a contentious divorce and had a very busy little penis."

"Tell me one or both is still living."

"I wish I could. Donald crept into the hospital three days after she'd been discovered and finished Hillary off with a pillow. Then he hopped into a car and crossed the border into Mexico. There was no contact until last year."

"And?"

"They found what was left of Donald in the desert. His eyelids had been cut off and he'd been staked out nude, in the middle of the Mexican summer. There was no sign of the money."

"So," James murmurs, "kill yourself or go to jail, but if you run, he finds you."

"Did Dali plant any evidence?" I ask.

"Doesn't appear that way, but then, Donald moved very quickly, didn't he? I suppose he saved Dali the effort. And before you ask—no, Dali didn't leave behind any clues to his existence that time either."

"Three for three," I murmur. "The notes telling us he exists are the first." I glance at Callie. "Circumstances on these three victims seem to contradict your 'evolving paradigm' theory about why he let Heather go with her brain in working order. Somehow, I think death would be a sufficient deterrent for most of these men."

James shakes his head. "Strange. He's succeeded so far due to the simple elegance of what he does. Why change it now?"

"You sound like you admire him." Callie's tone is disapproving.

"Facts are facts, not admiration. Dali's brilliance is in the complete simplicity of his plan and his actions." He counts off on his fingers. "His clients never meet him. He makes them into coconspirators. He offers financial incentive. He limits his contact with the victims, so they can't describe him even if they did somehow get away. Look at Heather Hollister. He let her go, and she's unable to provide us with anything truly probative.

"The time element is crucial and also brilliant. A lot changes in seven years. People move, people die. Cops retire, move on, die. By the time the insurance money is collected, who's likely to be watching?

Even in the instances where he's been forced to punish for nonpayment, it's low risk, high reward, and, as you said, we can be sure that he lets his existing client base know what's happened, as insurance against similar actions on their part. Simple. Brilliant. Why change all that?"

"It doesn't make sense," I agree. "What are we missing?"

"I have no idea. I do have another anomaly, though. I spent time hunting through the Internet, looking for sites that cater to symphorophiliacs. There aren't many out there, and it took some looking. I didn't find anything—no still photos, no video footage—from any of the locations where we think he engineered car crashes."

"Perhaps he pervs in private," Callie says.

"Maybe," James allows, "but unusual. A paraphilia like that requires regular fulfillment. Sharing is a way of reliving. Something that unique . . . it's odd. How does he feed it?"

"So, no good news, then," I mutter.

"Not entirely true. I did a search for hotels nearby the crash sites—there was only one in a relevant mile radius. A room was rented there under the name of a Heather Hollister on the night of her abduction."

A thrill runs through me, picks up speed, then dies and blows away. "Seven years in a hotel room? There's not going to be any evidence to find. Even if there was, it would be tainted."

"Still," James insists, "it continues to confirm the profile. There's no reason for him to rent that room—and more, to use Heather's name—except to satisfy a desire."

"How does that help us?" Callie asks.

"It will help with his prosecution, when we catch him. If his need was that strong, there's no way he'll get rid of the evidence. He can't. Find him, and we'll find the photographs and video footage too. It's a fairly unique paraphilia, not something you'd find in the average household. It will tie him to the scene, and thus to Heather Hollister."

It's a thin bit of optimism, hardly helpful in the moment, but it's true nonetheless. As a prosecutor once told me, *Catching the guy is only half the battle. Keeping him caught is the other half.*

"I have another bit of news," Callie says. "We found a fingerprint on Dana Hollister's body bag, on the inside. I ran it through AFIS, and it doesn't match anyone known to be associated with this case." She grimaces. "Unfortunately, it doesn't match anyone else on file either."

"More strangeness," James says. "Strange that he'd be that careless, if it's him."

He and I stare at each other, more troubled than enlightened by this turn of events.

"Maybe he's decompensating?" I offer.

"That makes no sense."

"Oh pish. What a bunch of wet blankets you two are," Callie chides. "Maybe he's finally grown too big for his britches. Sometimes they get stupid."

"Maybe," I agree.

*But I don't think so.*

# CHAPTER TWENTY-NINE

Go on. The words read: Say it. You'll feel better when you do, I promise. It's liberating.

I don't know. Leo-as-Robert-Long types: I just don't feel right about calling her—or any woman—*that*.

That's just programming, brother. The radical feminist movement has conditioned men to be afraid. Let me give you an example. We all know the one word no man is allowed to say to a woman, right?

Cunt. Someone else types: The word of death.

That's right. Now: Tell me what similar word exists in relation to men?

No one types, the equivalent of dead silence in cyberspace.

There you go. That's what I'm talking about. How is that possible?

There are also probably ten times the number of pejoratives for women as there are for men. Leo says: We've spent more time throughout history putting women down.

Jesus. One of the men answers: You're truly brainwashed, aren't you?

Screw you.

Calm down, guys. The original typist soothes: We've all been where he is now, at least most of us have. Let me talk. You still there, Hurting?

I'm here.

Look, I read your story. Let me just ask you this: Are you angry at her? I want you to think for a minute before you answer. Really turn it over, and be honest. What's the best word for the emotion you feel?

Leo drags out the pause. He finally types:

Hate.

Good. Well, not good, of course, but it's honest. Now, why do you hate her?

Because. She stopped loving me for no good reason. She aborted my child without even consulting me. And she's become an emotional stranger with no effort at all.

Okay, Hurting. Now I'm going to ask you another question, and again I want you to really think about it. You ready?

I'm ready.

Here it is: What kind of woman does that?

The silence again. The cursor blinks on the screen, and I get the sense of a group of men in a medium-size room, watching, waiting, eager.

"Go ahead," Alan tells him. "This is why we came into this room. Time to cross the line."

They're in *Bitch Chat*. Alan had discussed with me whether I thought it was too early, but I dismissed this concern. "At the minimum, curiosity is normal."

Leo types, continuing to play up his reluctance: I guess only a bitch would do that kind of thing.

Good! You're almost there, brother. Take a breath, and step back. Look at the logic of what you just said. If a woman who'd do that kind of thing is a bitch, and that's true—then why on earth would you have any questions or qualms about calling her one?

Cursor blinking silence.

I'm starting to see what you mean.

Of course you are, brother. It's called truth. So?

So what?

So SAY IT. What is your ex-wife, brother? Not what kind of woman would do that, but what kind of a woman is she? What is she?

She's . . . a bitch.

Say it again!

She's a bitch. A fucking bitch.

What else?

A cunt. A lying, coldhearted, baby-murdering cunt!

Various encouragements are shouted by the others in the chat; at least, I imagine them as shouts. I see, in my mind's eye, that same group of men in that medium-size room. Some have faces contorted by rage, others are crying. All of them are shaking a clenched fist and shouting the words, again, and again. *Bitch! Bitch! Cunt!*

What about my personal favorite? I think.

I search and I find.

Whore. Someone has typed: Fucking whore.

I've always hated that one, even more than the sacrilegious *cunt*. I'm not sure why.

Leo types: God, I fucking hate her. I HATE HER SO GOD DAMN MUCH! I wish . . .

He stops typing, waits.

You wish what, brother?

"Wait a little longer," Alan coaches. "Make him pull it out of you. Don't be too eager."

Go on, brother. It's just us here. No one knows your face or your real name. Don't hold back. What do you wish?

Leo types in a blur of letters: I wish she'd fucking die.

Silence. Then:

We've all been in that place. Don't be ashamed. The first part of reclaiming your masculinity is being honest about your feelings for women. You know how you feel; they don't. Don't let them tell you how you're "allowed" to feel, right?

I gotta go. Thanks.

Leo logs out.

"That was good," I tell him. "Virtuoso performance. The hasty exit at the end was a good touch."

"Conflicted and full of hate," Alan agrees. "Just the right elements for a psychotic break. Hopefully it'll catch Dali's attention."

James is signaling to me.

"I have to go, guys. Let me know when you decide to go back into the chat."

"Will do."

The connection is severed. "What is it?" I ask James.

"Earl Cooper is on his way over to see us."

I stretch, trying to purge myself of the toxic mix of excitement and frustration. "Let's hope he has something helpful to say."

"I have some observations, but I'm not sure how useful they're going to be."

Cooper sits in one of our office chairs, relaxed but watchful. He twirls one end of his handlebar mustache.

"We'll take what you've got," I reassure him.

"Fair enough." He settles back, seeming to collect his thoughts. "Much of geographic profiling is about the concept of a 'mental map,' the cognitive image we develop of our surroundings. This 'map' is developed via experience, travel, reference points, so on. We all have safe areas, zones we're most comfortable or confident in, and those tend to be close to home, though not always so. You following?"

"I think so," I say.

"It's true often enough that the first killing is usually the most helpful when it comes to geographic profiling. I've interviewed a couple of bad boys who were correctly pinpointed by what I do, and I showed them how we found them. Each one said that it made sense. They killed close to home and dumped the bodies in areas known to them. They thought they were being clever, but when I showed them the facts, they realized that they were operating subconsciously within a very definite comfort zone."

"That makes sense," I say. "First-time killers haven't been emboldened by their success. There's a lot of excitement there, but there's also a lot of fear. Staying relatively close to home would be reassuring."

"That's right. Travel to a foreign country and you understand the concept real quick: We're most comfortable in familiar surrounds.

Here's an example: Which one of you has spent time around train yards?"

No one raises a hand.

"Well," he continues, "in that case, if one of you was to kill a man—or a woman—it's not likely you'd do it near the tracks. But one of the more famous cases of success in geographic profiling is the one I mentioned to you earlier, and it involved just that factor: All the bodies were found near train tracks."

"You mentioned this before," James says, sounding bored. "The perpetrator was a transient, right?"

"An illegal immigrant, actually, young Jim. It's a simplistic example, but a good one for our purposes. You had a man in a country that was not only strange to him, it was hostile by default. If he got caught, he'd be deported. So he hobo'ed, traveled by rail. When he started killing, it was only natural that he'd do it by the trains.

"Now, back to the lecture. So we all, knowingly and unknowingly, develop comfort zones. They're spatial, and they have degrees. You're most comfortable in your own living room. You're more comfortable in your backyard than your front. The local grocery store? Less comfortable than the living room, but you've shopped there plenty, so that's all right. The place you work every day is probably fairly safe. You form a mental map, and when it comes time to commit a crime, that mental map comes into play. You're going to consider the factors, control what you know: escape routes, what areas are most deserted, where does the light from the streetlamps end.

"Boiling it down to a greater simplicity, by way of example, let's say we have two neighborhoods right next to each other. One is a white lower-middle-class neighborhood. The other is predominantly black and poor, with a higher crime rate. A white man gets killed inside the white neighborhood, shot dead on his green lawn behind his white picket fence. What's the first assumption?"

"That one of the scary black people came over and shot that poor white man, of course," Callie says.

Earl smiles. "That's correct, little lady. What's the likely truth, based on what I've been saying?"

"That he was killed by someone on his side of the tracks," I say, getting it.

"Just so. Comfort zones."

"All very interesting," James says, conveying with his tone that he thinks anything but. "How does it help us here, now?"

"In due course, young Jim," Earl says, seemingly unaffected by James's misanthropy. Maybe he's used to difficult students. "We consider other factors too. We look at the abduction site and the dump site. We examine the likely escape routes and see what that tells us about him. So on."

I grimace. "I think I'm starting to understand why you said you might not be able to help much. We don't know who his first victim was. The abduction sites were built around the victim, not the perpetrator. And the dump sites were chosen for effect, not convenience."

Earl mimes tipping a hat at me. "That's correct, Ms. Barrett. Add to that mix the fact that he's operating in three separate states we know of and . . ." He shrugs. "Makes things a little tough."

"What can you tell us?" I ask.

"A few things. First: He's probably from the western seaboard. My guess would be Southern California or hereabouts."

"Why?"

"The victims we're aware of come from Los Angeles, Oregon, and Nevada. It's a broad area, but it's still a comfort zone of sorts. That's why I say Western Seaboard. I'm thinking SoCal because of the victim in Nevada. A perpetrator living in Oregon is less likely to stray to Vegas as a hunting ground than one who either lives in or grew up in Los Angeles."

"That actually makes sense," James allows.

Cooper ignores him. "You said the perpetrator is probably driven by finance as the primary motive, and I agree with you. Then why stay out here, where real estate's so expensive? It'd be cheaper to set up shop in the Midwest, the South, or some areas in the East. He probably tells himself he's here because it's a good victim pool, and there is truth in that, but I think he set up shop here because it's familiar territory."

"I can see that," I say, warming to this line of deduction.

"There are other things we can ascertain in the victim dumps. In both here and Oregon, he left the victims near the police. One on the steps of a police station. In Vegas, he left the victim on a side street.

That would suggest he's much more comfortable in California and Oregon than he is in Nevada."

"Which means he'd spend more time there, meaning we should concentrate our efforts in those two states, right?" I ask.

He smiles at me, tips that imaginary hat again. "Yes indeed. It's where he'll be most predictable. He'll stray away from the profile more in those areas outside his comfort zone."

"But if that's so," Callie says, "wouldn't that also be where he's most likely to make a mistake?"

"You'd think so, but no. He'd be far more careful in unfamiliar territory, whereas he'd be more relaxed—however infinitesimally or subconsciously—in those comfort zones."

"What else?" James ask, interested now.

"Prefacing all of this with 'in my opinion,' of course, I'd say that you can ignore all suburban neighborhoods. They're too small and packed too close together. Neighbors want to know you and your business. I considered the woods in Oregon and the desert in Nevada but rejected those. I agree with the idea that he'd keep an eye on his victims while traveling, and that requires that he be on at least the outskirts, where Internet connectivity is still available." He consults his notes briefly. "Business districts are a good choice, because people are by and large keeping their heads down. They don't own a business zone the same way they do the space where they live, and so they're less observant. It also would allow him to rent or buy the space he needs in the name of a business, giving his personal information another layer of protection. I considered warehouses, and while that's still a possibility, I don't think that's how he'd go. Warehouses tend to be in out-of-the-way areas—good for him—but they also have a higher probability of being the victim of attempted burglaries or squatters."

"Somewhere in between," James says.

Cooper nods. "Just so, young Jim. Those side streets, away from the strip malls and the main arteries. Where they put the business parks and such. That setting would fulfill his needs for privacy while keeping him within shouting distance of the streets and freeways, which he requires based on his abduction pattern. He's taken the victims we know of from what are essentially urban areas. That's an uncertain affair, and he'd want to get them back to his lair as quickly as possible."

"Urban areas seems so risky," I say.

"Yes and no. People tend to be more observant in your residential enclaves. If he's decisive enough—and it surely seems that he is—urban areas are better in many ways. You have the highways, you have the streets. You can get almost anywhere in Los Angeles, at the right time of day, within forty-five minutes."

"That's true," James says. "He timed these abductions mid-evening, which would be after most rush hours."

"Right again," Cooper says. He shuffles through his notes, seems to find his place. "Here we go," he continues. "He'd own the properties he's using. He doesn't want to have to deal with a landlord snooping around. The victim described concrete walls. That doesn't point to office space, though I suppose he could have bought the building and put in some aftermarket changes."

"That would leave a trail," James says.

"I thought the same. If I were going to do it—and keep in mind that we're in the realm of pure guesswork now—I'd buy a piece of land and build myself a small storage unit building."

"Personal storage?" I ask.

"Just so. Build it, but don't advertise, and make sure the front office is never open. No one thinks twice about places like that getting few visitors, or getting visitors at odd times of the day or night. They're generally gated off, and there are places where you can pull a car in and empty it out without anyone seeing a thing. Security-camera placement isn't unusual either."

"Or climate control," James adds. "More upscale places offer it as an option, for people who are storing climate sensitive belongings, such as paintings or books."

"It does make sense," I allow.

Cooper shrugs. "That's where my road ends, I'm afraid. Not sure if it'll help you much in the final analysis, and there's more guesswork than certainty there, but you asked and I answered."

I stare at the whiteboard, seeing it but not seeing it. My gaze unfocuses. *Workmanlike,* I read. *Torture,* I think. *Decisive.*

Something's knocking, wanting to be seen.

"I know that look," Earl says, his voice soft. "Whatcha thinking, Ms. Barrett?"

The vagueness coalesces.

"I'm thinking about a man with, so far as we know, a perfect record of abduction. He follows his prey, gets to know their routine, and then he swoops in and takes them cleanly. It's something you said. He's decisive. Confident." I look at Cooper. "Trained?"

James responds first. "Possible. These abductions are precision activities. You don't arrive at that level of competence naturally."

Earl twirls his mustache. "Military? Law enforcement?"

"It's just a thought."

"That makes sense as much as anything else. Still guesswork, but good guesswork, I think."

"We'll look into it." I hold my hand out for Cooper to shake, which he does. "Thank you, sir. I appreciate the insight."

"My pleasure. What's your next move, if you don't mind my asking?"

"I'm going to talk to someone I know who could do exactly what our perp does without breaking a sweat."

"He's ex-military, I take it?"

"She's an ex-something."

# CHAPTER THIRTY

Kirby comes into my office and takes a seat without being asked. She's dressed in jeans, a white button-down shirt, and tennis shoes. She puts her feet up on the desk and smiles as she chews her gum.

"What's up, boss woman?"

"I need the perspective of a professional."

"Professional what?" she asks. I can't tell if she's teasing me. Kirby lives in a state of perpetual unconcern, and, as usual, the only hint of what lies inside her floats transiently through her eyes. A certain watchfulness. A certain deadness.

"Operative. Killer. Whatever."

She grins. "Oh that. Sure, shoot."

"We're chasing a guy who could have had some training. It's just a theory, but I'd appreciate your perspective."

A hint of interest. "Tell me about him."

I brief her on Dali. Kirby is technically a civilian, but I imagine there are times in the past that she's had a security clearance higher than anything I'll ever see. She asks no questions throughout, just listens, intent. When I finish, she leans her head back and stares at the ceiling, chewing her gum.

"Well," she says finally, "I'd agree with your assessment that he might have had training. Smooth abduction in an urban environment, batting a thousand on not getting caught or noticed?" She nods. "That's some highly effective activity. You could learn stuff like that in the Special Forces branches, though it's always possible that he went directly into the private sector, like I did."

"What do you mean?"

"They're really funny about women in those branches of the military. It's the law, boss woman. No fems allowed. But I knew what I wanted to do from an early age, and if you're really extra-special motivated to get that kind of training—the kidnap and interrogate and kill kind of training—there are places you can find it, for a price."

"Like?"

"Central and South America. The Middle East. Israel. Shucks, right here in the good old USA. The CIA has a program or two, but you have to be a little bit too true-blue for my tastes."

"Let's say he did go the military route. How long does that take?"

She considers it. "Minimum of four years after joining, as an average. You have to be Mr. Perfect Soldier, be in tip-top shape, and pass various and sundry physical and psychological tests. Even then there's no guarantee of placement."

"Which branch would be most likely to prepare you for abductions?"

"Who knows? The truth is, it could be any one of them, depending on how they're tasked. Not to mention that someone in the Green Berets, for example, could always be cherry-picked for recruitment into the CIA." She grins. "It's all one big happy family in the end. Common goals and all that cool stuff."

I think about everything she's told me, factoring it in with my current picture of Dali.

"We know he's been operating for at least fifteen years, probably longer," I muse. "If he joined the military before he started his current 'career,' he'd be . . . what? Forty-five?"

"If he was lucky."

"The question is, did he decide to get trained so he could become a criminal or did the idea come after his training?"

"From personal experience, people like Mr. Nut Job and me tend to know what we are from an early age."

I cock my head at her. "You think you're the same?"

"Pish. There's no way he's as good as me."

I smile. "There's more difference than that."

"Maybe, maybe not. How are you so sure?"

"Two reasons. One, I trust you with my daughter. Two, you'd never do something like what was done to Heather Hollister, an innocent, a civilian, a mother. You have limits, Kirby."

She assesses me with those oft-dead eyes. "Once, down in South America," she says, her voice low and reasonable, a talking-about-the-weather voice, "the team I was a part of was captured by a group of paramilitaries. I'd been doing recon prior to the attack and capture, so they didn't get me. One guy stayed behind to guard their rear." A wink. "His mistake! I reached out and touched him, just like the old phone commercials. I needed him to tell me where they were, but, gee, he was *against* the idea, soooo . . . I pulled out his teeth with pliers until he changed his mind." She grins, and I force myself not to recoil. I'm disturbed less by what she's saying than by the lack of madness I see in her eyes. She's lucid now, she was lucid then; Kirby is entirely present in everything she does.

"He was a tough one; he held out through ten teeth. *Marathon Man* in spades. He told me what I needed and then I put a bullet in his head." Her gaze goes distant. "I caught up with them and found out that they'd executed the rest of my team." She shrugs. "So I executed them too. All ten of them. It took me five days, tracking them through the jungle. Picking them off at night, catching some while they were taking a pee pee, others while they were sleeping. One of them was yanking his little pud when I crept up behind him. He couldn't have been more than sixteen. I let him finish and then I watched him beg and cry like a baby before I blew his brains out."

She smiles, and it's a normal Kirby-grin again. The blue eyes that had been so dead and empty just a second before sparkle with mischief.

I've sat in badly lit rooms looking across the table into the eyes of a man who strangled children in front of their mothers. I've watched psychotics have involuntary orgasms as they related the grimmest details of rape and murder to me. These people have a darkness to them, a terrible gravity that cannot be faked. Kirby is Kirby, I have no illusions about what she is, but I know what she is not.

I reach over and pat her cheek, once. "You may be twisted, beach bunny, but you're not evil."

A space of silence, a drop of time where, for just a split second, I think I see something akin to gratitude roll through her eyes. It's there, maybe, then it's gone. She grins and pretends to wipe sweat off her brow. "*That's* a weight off my shoulders." She stands up. "We done here, boss woman?"

"We're done."

"Catch you on the flip side," and she's gone, leaving something always strange but definitely not evil in her wake.

My cell phone rings.

"Barrett."

"We got a bite," Alan says.


"The guy's screen name is Dali," Alan says. "He approached Leo via private message."

Dali types:

Do you hate your ex-wife?

It's asked without preamble or introduction.

"What do I say?" Leo asks. His voice is low, hushed. I understand. Dali can't hear us, but it's a visceral thing.

"I don't know," Alan says. "Something's off with this. It's too soon. Smoky?"

Alan's right. Everything that we've learned about Dali tells us that he's careful, a planner, driven by pragmatic necessity, not desire. Leo's been on this site for less than twenty-four hours. Why the rush?

"Maybe it was your story," I say. "Hell. I don't know. Take it slow. Answer him with a question."

"Like what?"

"Trust your instincts," Alan says. "Don't sweat it, son. I'll let you know if you start fucking up."

There's a beat of silence and then I hear Leo's fingers, tapping the keys.

Why do you want to know?

Good choice, I think.

I'm a freer of men from the prisons of women. I'm trying to find out if you're a man who wants to be freed.

How do you know I need to be?

I read your story. Very compelling. But there's a big difference, a world of difference, between being trapped and wanting to be freed. It requires a decision.

What is this? A self-help deal? Are you going to tell me how to harness my inner happiness or something?

I'm just a problem-solver. Go on, humor me. Answer the question. Do you hate your ex-wife?

"Go for it," Alan says. "But wait a few moments. Be hesitant before committing."

Three or four seconds pass before Leo types his answer.

Yes.

Yes what?

Yes, I hate her.

Why?

You read my story. I think it's pretty obvious.

The story is something you took time with, that you thought about before writing down. I want something more immediate. I've found that's the quickest way to the truth. Let me ask again, and this time answer without thinking about it too much. Why do you hate your ex-wife?

Leo waits before responding, and then:

Because she ruined me.

"Good," Alan encourages.

How did she do that? Explain what you mean by "ruin."

"This isn't as easy as I thought it would be," Leo says.
"You're doing fine," I tell him. "Get into character and let yourself respond as Robert Long.
He begins:

Before she dumped me and killed my baby, I believed in love. It's different now. I'll never love freely like that again. I'll always be suspicious. I'll always be afraid to trust.

What was worse? Revoking her love without warning or aborting your unborn child?

Leo doesn't hesitate.

There's no way she could have ever really loved me and then have done what she did. You understand what I'm saying? It means that everything was a lie. Our love was a lie. That's what hurts the most.

Thank you.

For what?

For being honest. It's the reason I contacted you to begin with. That honesty. It resonated in the story that you posted.

I just wrote what I felt.

Let me ask you another question. Just a hypothetical. Consider it a form of fantasy.

Okay.

How would you benefit if your ex-wife was gone?

Gone? Gone how? You mean dead?

No, no. This isn't literal. Just . . . gone. Aliens came down and sucked her up into a spaceship. How would you benefit from that, emotionally or otherwise?

Well . . . I guess I'd get our house, for one. We're both still on the mortgage and title. That's something.

What else?

"Take this very, very slow," Alan cautions. "Don't bring up the life insurance. Go to the emotional side now."

Part of me thinks . . .

Leo waits a few beats, letting Dali nudge him for an answer.

What?

That I'd be relieved. Her being gone would be some kind of huge relief. We're not together, but I know that she's still out there, in the same city. As unlikely as it is, it's still possible that I could run into her at the store or drive by her on the freeway. We're not together, but I feel her presence. If she disappeared, I think a weight would come off me.

I understand. I promise you I do.

Yeah, well. That and five bucks will get me a latte at Starbucks.

You might be surprised.

By what?

By the solutions I can offer. But we're not going to talk about all that right now. It's too soon. Let me leave you with something small, something to show you that I'm for real and not just another lunatic on the Web.

Go ahead.

Don't feel threatened by what I say next. I'm a friend, not an enemy, I promise.

Whatever you say, "friend." LOL.

Here it is: I know who you are, Robert Long.

"Holy shit, that was fast," Leo marvels. "How the hell did he do that?"
"Put that shock in writing, son, and see what jumps."

What the fuck! Leo types: How the hell do you know who I am? I thought this was all anonymous!

It is, Robert, it is. No one else you've met or talked to here knows your name. I know because of who I am and what I do. Remember what I said before: I didn't tell you this to threaten you. I offer it as proof, nothing more.

Proof of what?

Proof that, when I talk to you, I'm talking about the real world. We're meeting in cyberspace. But when we talk in the future

The typing stalls, suddenly.

Dali?

Wait.

"What's going on?" Alan mutters.
"Probably had to answer the phone or something," Leo says.

I have to go. Dali finally types: Good-bye.

When can we talk again?

No reply.

Dali?

Dali's screen name disappears.

"Damn," Leo says. "He logged off."

"Odd that he'd cut you off when he had you on the string," I say.

"Maybe we caught a break," Alan says. "Maybe one of his abductees broke out or something."

"Interesting insight into how he cultivates his clients," James murmurs from behind me. I jump in my chair, startled.

"Jesus, James! How long have you been watching?"

"I saw everything. He's very smooth, very smart. You see what he was doing there? He feels out the potential client via hypotheticals. He's careful not to talk about death or murder. It's all just a dream, a 'what if?' "

"Which lets him gauge where they're at without alarming them."

"It's more than that. He sets himself up as the dominant personality in the relationship but in the role of a confidant. You can trust him and he has the answers. It makes it easier for him to manipulate them, later."

"Slick," Alan agrees. "Guy's probably a great interrogator. He's laying a lot of subtle groundwork."

"Are we still worried that he reached out to me so quickly?" Leo asks.

"I don't know," Alan says. "Maybe he's just trying to fill a quota. He lost Heather Hollister, so he needs some new meat, right?"

"Perhaps," I allow. "But be careful, anyway. Let me know if he reinitiates contact."

"You got it," Alan says. The connection terminates.

I rotate my chair in James's direction. "So? What do you think?"

"The profile is contradictory. A careful über-pragmatist who suddenly changes what's been a perfectly acceptable MO. He leaves us notes telling us he exists—a first—he lets Heather Hollister walk intact, possibly leaves a fingerprint on Dana Hollister's body bag, and now jumps the gun with Leo." He shakes his head. "Strange. It could simply be the crazy factor, but it's troubling."

"The crazy factor" is a term we coined locally. It refers to the inexplicable mistakes and aberrations from the expected norm that we so often see with serial offenders. There is the rapist who never fails to use a rubber until one day he doesn't, the killer who always wears latex gloves but couldn't keep himself from licking a victim's thigh. Ask them why, and the answers won't be based on anything sane. *She was my first redhead,* the rapist might say. *All that red hair. I needed to feel it.* For the murderer, perhaps something more obscure: *I had to taste her to experience it fully. Smelling her just wasn't enough of her life essence, you understand?* We don't understand, no one can. The crazy factor.

"It's possible."

"Let me add to your discomfort, honey-love," Callie says from her desk.

"Great. What?"

"I ran the fingerprints recovered from the Los Angeles, Oregon, and Nevada cases against the unknown we found in the Dana Hollister case."

"And?"

"They're all from the same individual."

"All four?"

"That's right. The same unknown was present in each case."

I stare at James and see my own confusion reflected back at me. *What the hell?*

I throw up my hands. "Fine, then, let's treat it like a gift. Widen the search. Interpol, any databases we can think of that might help. I heard whispers that the NSA has been building a 'secret' database of their own. Covert operatives in various countries."

"Shot in the dark."

Interpol's database is so small that it generally returns an average of eighty percent in negative results, and the NSA tends to be pretty condescending to us, post 9/11 calls for cooperation notwithstanding.

"Still, try."

"Fine," Callie sniffs. "But it may take some time. I don't have any friends there."

"Imagine that," James sneers.

"Speaking of the crazy factor," I say, cutting off Callie's planned retort, "James, let's do a property search in Los Angeles, Portland, and Las Vegas. Confine it to commercial properties."

"What am I looking for?"

"Anything with *Dali* in the name."

James taps his upper lip with a finger, thoughtful. "I'll do some research on Salvador Dali as well and look for any permutations. Names of paintings, things like that." He frowns. "It's going to take some time, and it's likely to be pretty inexact. Not all records are computerized. The ones that are aren't necessarily searchable. We might find nothing."

"Or we might find something."

The office door opens and AD Jones strides in.

"Upstairs, Smoky," he says. "Now."

# CHAPTER THIRTY-ONE

"Am I in trouble, sir?" I ask as we ride up in the elevator.

He smiles. "Nah. The director wants to talk to you, and he's on a time crunch."

"He's upstairs?"

"In my office as we speak."

We exit the elevator and walk past Shirley into the AD's office. Director Rathbun is standing as we enter, and he walks over to me and shakes my hand. "Sorry to pull you away, Smoky. I understand you're handling a difficult case right now."

"Yes, sir."

"I'll keep it short. It's not official, but I have what I'd call basic backroom approval on the establishment of the strike team. From the president himself."

"Wow," I manage.

"You're going to have to get better than that before I put you in front of the press," he jokes.

"Or we could just skip that part, sir. I don't like talking to reporters."

"And most of the time you won't have to. I promise. In the beginning, though, once everything's done and the funding's approved, I'll need you to do a little bit of PR work. That's a part of the deal. There will be senators and congresspersons who want to be seen with you. The president too."

"Really?"

"Of course. My solution gives them an out, Smoky. At some point, an enterprising reporter will find out that funding and personnel have been cut for FBI nonterror activities nationwide. That's going to make a lot of people uncomfortable."

"Rightly so," I say.

"The strike team becomes the story the president and others get to tell to soothe that discomfort. We're not dismantling our NCAVC activities, you see, we're just changing them."

"Can I ask you a question, Director?"

"Anything you want."

"Off the record, what's your opinion about all this 'dismantling?'"

"I told you before, I disapprove. This is my effort to save what I can."

"Why do you disapprove?"

Anyone can tell you they believe in a principle. The test is: Can they defend it? It's a serious question. I want to see if he can give me a serious answer.

"Some people are convinced that increases in technology will take up the slack. They believe that DNA and fingerprints and all the rest are going to make profiling not obsolete but certainly less important. They feel that local police can provide the needed feet on the ground, and that our role can become both more centralized and more automated. I think this is a grave error in judgment."

"Why?" I press.

"For the same reasons you do, Agent Barrett." A faint smile. "I may be just a 'suit,' but I've kept my finger on the pulse. I'm aware of the work you and your team, and other teams, do. Forensics is and will always be invaluable. But there will never be a replacement for a group of people who are trained and experienced in understanding serial offenders. Unfortunately, what I think, and how I feel, is falling on deafer and deafer ears." He spreads his hands in a gesture of futility. "What can I say? It's inevitable. A storm is coming; I'm just trying to save what I can."

I search the director's eyes for any hint of a lie. I see nothing. Just a low-grade exhaustion at playing the politician's game, a brief vulnerability that disappears a moment later with a squaring of his shoulders and a flash of the trademark smile.

"Did I answer your question satisfactorily, Agent Barrett?"

"Yes, sir. Thanks."

"How long 'til we know something?" AD Jones asks the director.

"One month. Six weeks on the outside."

"So fast?" I marvel.

"Washington has a short memory. Right now the president's excited about this. Best to seize the moment while it's ours." His gaze goes serious. "Now, I need to know, before I really let the dogs loose: Are there any stumbling blocks I should be aware of? Anyone not on board? Anything at all?"

I fight to keep my gaze from sliding over to AD Jones. The alien in my belly stirs, but not really; I know that's a fantasy. He or she is still just a bare collection of cells. I consider Alan, both his age and his misgivings.

"No, sir," I say, smiling as I lie. "I think we're good to go."

"Glad to hear it." He checks his watch and nods to himself. "Good timing, then. I have to run. I'll let you both know as things develop." He shakes our hands and heads out the door.

"You're getting better at lying," AD Jones says, when he's gone.

"Lying and equivocation aren't the same thing," I retort. "Ask any lawyer."

"It's not a criticism. That's a skill you'll need to develop where you're going. In the meantime, we're all still here, so bring me up to date on this case."

I tell him everything we know. He interjects a few questions but is largely silent.

"Why do you think he let Heather Hollister walk without giving her a lobotomy?" he asks when I'm finished.

"I don't know. Maybe she personalized herself to him in some way. Maybe she looks like his mother. I'm not sure."

"What's your gut say?"

This is his way. He asks for our instincts, because his own got him where he is today. AD Jones trusts his people.

"Every sense I have of this guy so far tells me that everything he does is deliberate. His actions are driven by reason based on self-preservation, not emotion. Heather Hollister is a piece that doesn't fit, but only because we don't know how she fits yet."

"And the fingerprints?"

"Again, I don't know. If that's deliberate, I can't imagine why. It could be something as simple as him thinking the plastic on the body bags wouldn't retain a fingerprint."

He stares off, and I know he's calculating all the facts I've given him. "Okay," he finally says. "Sounds like you're on the right track. I agree, property records and the undercover op are the best paths you have at the moment. Keep me briefed."

"Yes, sir." I get up to leave. "One other thing, sir?"

"Yes?"

"I need to leave an hour early today," I say. I look down at my feet, embarrassed.

"Why?"

"Doctor's appointment."

He leans back in his chair, twirling a pen in his right hand. "Baby stuff?"

"First checkup, yes, sir."

His eyes pin me for a moment longer, and then he leans back over his desk again and starts working on the paperwork there. "Approved."

I beat a hasty retreat. I wonder at my discomfort on the way down in the elevator. Why do I care? What difference does it make that I'm going to see an obstetrician about being pregnant versus seeing a general practitioner about something more mundane?

The answer comes: *Because it makes me a woman.*

Being pregnant makes you a woman more than anything else. You can talk tough like the boys, wear a gun like the boys, even be a boss like the boys, but once your belly starts to show, everyone is reminded: You're not one of the boys and never will be.

Why does it matter? I ask again, and again the answer comes: *because of who we stand against.* Our strength, our guns, our organizational might, those are the things that keep the evil men at bay. It's not shame about being a woman, it's the maddening question: Would Sands have crept into my house if I'd been a male agent instead of a female one?

In my heart of hearts, I don't think so.

I touch my belly. It's a baby, it's hope, it's a future life, but what it feels like right now is a bull's-eye, outlined in neon, carrying a bullhorn and shouting out loud for all the world to hear, *This is where I'm weak! This is where I'm weak!*

*This,* it says, *is the place where you can hurt me the most. Shoot me here, and you shoot my soul.*

# CHAPTER THIRTY-TWO

The doctor I'm seeing is a serious woman—not serious in that way that makes a person unapproachable, not grave, but in that way that says you have all of her attention and she cares.

Meeting a new doctor, even though I'm not a fan of going to the doctor, is easier than meeting new people in general. When a doctor examines my scarring, it's usually frank and open, and I can be relatively certain the curiosity is professional. This doctor is no exception. Her name is Sierra Rand.

"Why did your parents name you Sierra?" I ask.

I'm buying time. Now that I'm here, sitting in this office, and she's sitting there, with her white coat, file folder, and pen, I find that I'm terrified. Seeing a doctor has suddenly made it all too real.

She seems to take it in stride. "My parents were big into hiking and camping. As the story goes, I was conceived in a tent on Mount Whitney, which is part of the Sierra Nevada mountain range."

"It's a pretty name."

"Thanks. They were just getting over being hippies when I was born. I could have been named 'America' or 'Freedom,' or something like that, so I have no complaints, trust me." She smiles. "Now, what can I do for you, Ms. Barrett?"

She's killed the banter, and it leaves me discomfited. No escaping now. "I'm pregnant."

She doesn't smile or offer congratulations; she doesn't frown. Her expression is a PhD study of the noncommittal. "How do you know?"

"The usual. My period stopped a little over two months ago, and my boobs got sore, so I did a home pregnancy test and it came up positive. Followed it up with a blood test to confirm."

She consults my chart. "On your intake form you said you've had a child before?"

"One."

"And is she healthy?"

"She was."

She frowns and puts the chart back down on her lap. "Was?"

"She was murdered by the man who did this to my face."

I see it then, as I've seen it before: the look of recognition. My story was splashed in the papers and on television. Instead of going goggle-eyed or, what I hate even worse, searching for the "right thing to say in this situation," she shakes her head. "I'm sorry, Ms. Barrett. I didn't put two and two together."

"It's okay. And call me Smoky, Dr. Rand."

"Smoky." The smile again, a nice one. "You're welcome to call me Sierra, but you should probably call me Dr. Rand. Studies have shown that patients trust their physicians most when they stay in costume. They just don't believe I'm a doctor if I don't wear the white coat."

I open my jacket a little and show her my gun. "Similar phenomenon. It doesn't matter how much I flash my badge; if I'm not carrying, people don't really believe I'm an agent."

"I assume you had an obstetrician. Can I ask why you're not seeing him—or her—about this pregnancy?"

"A him. Dr. Evans. To answer your question—superstition, I guess. The daughter he saw died. I don't want him having anything to do with this baby." I look down, a little embarrassed, maybe a little ashamed. "I know that's unfair, and really I don't blame him for her death, but . . ."

"You want a fresh start in every way."

I look back up, surprised. "That's right."

She smiles reassuringly. "There's nothing wrong with that, Smoky. The first thing we want to reduce in an expecting mother is stress. It makes sense not to be stressing about your physician, whatever the reason."

"Thanks."

"So, back to your daughter. Was she healthy? Any problems with the pregnancy or delivery?"

"No, Alexa was easy. I had minimal morning sickness and a four-hour labor. She was a healthy baby and a healthy child. She ran a really high fever when was six months old, and she cracked her forearm once when she fell off the jungle gym. Other than that, she was fine."

"Good. How about you? Have you developed any health problems since then?"

I take a deep breath and tell her what only a handful of other people know. "I had an abortion not long after my rape."

She takes it in stride, not even looking up from my chart. "Any complications from that? Infection, more bleeding than usual?"

"No."

"Have you been going to your gynecologist regularly?"

"Yearly pap."

"Excellent." She looks at me directly now. "Were there any physical complications resulting from your assault that I need to know about?"

"Just the scars. Everything he did was exterior."

"Okay. Now, I notice you didn't put down any medications, but I always ask. Some patients are more private than others. Are you on any antidepressants?"

"No. Thought about it, but no."

"What about birth control?"

"We were using the sponge. Can't recommend it now, I guess."

"So you're not on the pill?"

"No."

"What's the medical history in your family?"

"My mother and father both died of cancer."

"What about miscarriages, difficult childbirths, genetic defects?"

"I heard something about a great-aunt who gave birth to a son with a cleft palate. Other than that, no."

She makes a few notes and puts my chart aside.

"You sound like an ideal candidate for a healthy childbirth, Smoky. You're in good shape, at a good weight, with no history of blood pressure or heart problems, you don't smoke, and your first birth went well, with no eclampsia, diabetes, or clotting." She smiles. "There's no reason to expect you'll have any difficulties with this pregnancy. We'll keep a close eye on things due to your age, but I'm not concerned."

"What are the risks because of my age?"

"There's an increased risk of chromosomal disorders as the mother gets older, primarily Down syndrome. The statistics are debated. The worst-case scenario I've heard presented is as follows: at age twenty-five, a woman has roughly a 1 in 1,250 chance of having a baby with Down syndrome. At age thirty it's 1 in 1,000. At age 40 it's a 1-in-100 chance, and above forty-five it drops to 1 in 30."

"Jesus."

"I'm giving you this in fair disclosure, but keep in mind, seventy-five percent of all babies born with Down syndrome are to mothers under the age of thirty-five. We'll also, if you like, do a blood test that will look for markers associated with having a Down syndrome child."

"When would we do that?"

"It will depend entirely on you. The test is most accurate between the sixteenth and the eighteenth weeks, but there's no need to wait that long. First-trimester screens, when done properly, are ninety-five percent accurate."

"So I'd have plenty of time to decide, if it did have Down syndrome, whether I wanted to keep it." I sigh. "Great."

She reaches out to briefly touch my arm. "Smoky. There's no reason for you to think your baby is going to be anything other than healthy. I've delivered quite a few healthy children to women over forty years of age."

"And a few that weren't, right?"

"Yes. But those few women had all been tested and knew that they were going to be giving birth to a Down syndrome child. It was their choice, and they were no less happy about their babies than anyone else."

"Really?"

"Think about . . ." She hesitates. "Think about your daughter. Would you have regretted bringing her into the world, even if she'd had a birth defect like Down syndrome?"

It shouldn't be a startling question, but it certainly hits me that way. I think about it, about Alexa, my sweet girl. Would she still have been her, if she'd been born with a handicap? I close my eyes for a moment and her face comes to me, as I saw it on that last morning. I see her smile, I hear her giggle; most of all, I see the essence of her shining in her eyes.

Yes, I think. Alexa would always have been Alexa, in whatever form.

I open my eyes. "No, I wouldn't have regretted it. She would have been my baby, and I wouldn't have loved her any differently."

"Well, there you go."

This is a woman who chose her profession not because it would make her the most money, not to avoid the pressures of other medical disciplines, but because it was her calling. She loves what she does and has no choice about doing it; it's her fate to help bring new life into the world.

I think about Douglas Hollister strangling his own son. A parent killing his own child has never seemed more alien to me than right here, right now, in this woman's office. I touch my belly, and search for understanding, but it's unfathomable. How could I ever kill this baby?

"It won't matter." I say it as I know it, and I feel a surge of relief. "We'll do the test, but it won't matter. I want this baby, Doctor."

I'm mortified to find that I'm crying. I thought I'd put all these tears behind me. I'd settled into a new life, a new love, a new marriage. I'd recovered my ability to be flip and to let fly, to laugh on a dime and damn the torpedoes. The river of sorrow that had haunted me for so long had turned into a stream and then had dried to a puddle.

Apparently, some things can still bring the rain.

I thought I'd never have this chance again, and now I do, and I've just understood how much I want it, how deep that need, how great the ache.

"Sorry," I choke, unable to keep the tears from coming.

"Don't be silly."

I let the tears come.

I think about my search for the soul on the drive home. Everyone has their own answer. Father Yates, the priest at Callie's wedding, has his. The Buddhists have theirs. When I was a girl, I had mine. I had it with a certainty and innocence too powerful and too pure for me to consign to mere naïveté. Is there something we know when we're young that we forget when we're older, or is it all just a process of looking behind the curtain, finding that what the young call cynical the old call reality?

The question I've been asking myself most is: Why do I care?

I rub my belly, trying to sense the life growing there, to commune with it.

*I care because of you.*

*I care because of the truth I saw in Dr. Rand's office, that Alexa would be Alexa whatever her form. Is that proof of the soul?*

Nothing answers me, but I am content that I'm getting closer.

I consider going by the office but decide against it. Alan will call me if Dali contacts them again. James and Callie will call me if anything else develops.

"Screw it," I say out loud, and laugh. I'm a little giddy. Once again, my hand finds that spot on my tummy. "I'm going to be a mom again, baby. Young again at forty-plus. Can you believe that?"


We need milk, and I pull into the supermarket parking lot, humming "Blackbird" by the Beatles. Mom always loved that song. She could sing it too, high and sweet. I stare out through the windshield, remembering her sitting at Dad's feet, smiling and singing as he played the guitar. It makes me smile too.

It would have been nice if she could have known her grandchildren.

I'm not sure what it is right now that makes me think of her instead of Dad. Maybe it's because Mom always seemed to find it just a little bit harder to be happy, and when she did find it, she found it in her family.

I continue to whistle as I close the car door.

Something hard touches my lower back, and a voice whispers in my ear:

"Make a wrong move, Special Agent Barrett, and I'll shoot you right here and walk away. You'll die, I'll live. You know who I am, so you know that I'll do what I say."

I freeze in place. My heart starts to hammer so hard I think it's going to punch its way out of my chest. I feel slightly nauseated.

"Dali?" I croak.

How did my throat get so dry so fast?

"We're going to walk to my car. You're going to get in the trunk. Fight me and I will not only shoot you, I'll go to your home and I will kill your adopted daughter and your boyfriend. Do you understand?"

A million thoughts whirl through my head, things to say, bargains to make. The gun nudges me, pushing all that aside. "Yes," I whisper.

He reaches under my jacket and takes my weapon. He unclips my cell phone from my belt.

"Walk forward."

We walk no more than ten feet, arriving at a blue Toyota Camry. The trunk is already unlocked.

*How'd he know I'd be here?*

*He didn't. He was following me. Why?*

"Open it," he orders.

I comply.

"How long have you been following me?" It's a useless question, but as I peer into the darkness of the trunk, I think about Heather Hollister, living for eight years in the dark, and I am overwhelmed by terror, atavistic and instantaneous.

"Get in or you die and your family dies with you."

His voice is flat, emotionless, almost bored. It's the boredom that convinces me more than anything else. I scan the parking lot briefly. A man is walking to his own car, bag of groceries in hand. He's talking on his cell phone and pays us no mind.

I crawl into the trunk and whip around to catch a glimpse of Dali. His face is swathed in gauze. He pauses for a moment, looking down at me.

"People look away from a burn victim," he says, and then slams the trunk shut.

I hear nothing, and then I hear a muffled voice, followed by two spits that I recognize as silenced gunfire. More nothing, then some scuffling sounds and the car door slams. The engine starts. We're in motion.

It had to be the cell-phone man. He must have seen a guy with his head covered in bandages stuffing a woman into the trunk of his car. He said something and Dali shot him without hesitation. I have little doubt he's dead. Dali is a creature of precision and pragmatism, and it's only practical to become good with a gun.

I pray that someone's noticed all this, that a patrol car was driving by and saw it go down, something, anything. I put my hand on my belly and I pray to the God I don't believe in.

*I don't even know if you're there, but if you are, please, do something. I'm not asking you to part the Red Sea. He shot a man in a public parking lot, you know? Just give me a cop or a concerned citizen with a cell phone. Please.*

As time goes by, I understand just how far away we must be from the parking lot by now. I hear no sounds of pursuit. I slump into myself.

I go silent, smell the faint odor of gasoline, and try to get ready for the moment when he opens the trunk.

# CHAPTER THIRTY-THREE

The car slows down and stops. It idles, waiting. I hear the sound of something moving, something mechanized. A gate?

I'd tried to get some idea of how long we traveled. I was surprised at how difficult that was to do with no watch, in the dark. There's no sense of distance. I had tried to count the seconds but kept getting lost in my own fear.

The panic is crippling. I don't know if it's better or worse for me than it was for Heather Hollister. I have more training. I know what I'm up against. I've been under fire and have survived more than a single attack on my life.

None of it seems to be helping. Images of my rape and torture at the hands of Sands, images I thought I'd put to bed long ago, rise in my mind. My heartbeat is out of control and I'm close to hyperventilating.

I attended a conference once for law-enforcement personnel. It had various lectures on a variety of subjects: personnel, firearms, interrogation, etc. I attended one entitled "The Psychology of Fear: Conquering the Flight Urge in Combat Situations."

The speaker was a man by the name of Barnaby Wallace, an ex-Delta Force operative turned Special Forces instructor turned private consultant.

*The problem in most situations where fear takes over is a lack of training on the subject itself, or improper training. We've promoted the idea in this society that fear is found only in cowards, men who aren't worth the title of men. We've promoted the concept of being ashamed of fear. In World War Two the Russkies approached it from a more practical angle: You could choose between the guns of the soldiers behind you—which would kill you for sure if you ran—or the guns of the enemy in front of you, which you might still survive.*

*The history of the military is one of dealing with fear. We train soldiers to "obey orders, no matter what." Desertion is frequently a capital offense, punished by a firing squad.*

*What's it all show, though?* He'd leaned forward a little to emphasize his point. *Obviously, that fear is a natural response. In fact, in my years of command, it was always the fearless men who gave me the most trouble. They generally had a screw loose.*

The audience laughed, and you could sense in that laughter a low relief, as though we were all being given a sudden pass on some hidden shame, a time we'd felt fear and had to hide it.

*Fear is probably one of the oldest biological imperatives. It was developed to keep the organism alive. Fear demands flight from the stronger opponent, because, at the animal level, might does tend to make right. The bigger opponent will generally be the winning opponent.*

*Things have changed. We can think, and because we can think, we can create advantages that nullify the size or superior armament of the enemy. At this level, fear still serves a purpose, but only if we learn to harness it for our own ends.* He smiled. *Fight or flight, everyone's heard that one, and it's true. Fear was designed to encourage us to run, but it had a fail-safe: If running wasn't an option, it delivered the adrenaline we'd need to put up a good fight. So there's a flip side to fear. It tells you that you're in danger, that you need to get your shit together quick, and that you need to either retreat, or fight, or die.*

*So the first step of conquering your fear is to embrace it. It's telling you something.* Listen. *Don't resist. That's the first mistake, and it'll be the one that kills you. You'll be so distracted trying to push that fear aside that you won't notice the guy with the gun 'til he's right up on you. Fear freezes us first, and that's a problem in a combat situation.*

*You have to take fear out of the instinctive level. It's just an indicator, like a speedometer or your blood pressure. Apply your intellect to the indicator. Observe it. What's it telling you? Is flight the answer? Could be. How about fight? Maybe. Observe it, embrace it, intellectualize it. When you do that, fear becomes a tool, nothing more or less, and you lose no forward motion.*

*Stop treating fear as a defect or something alien. It's probably the oldest part of you.*

I close my eyes and force myself first to breathe and then to examine my fear. Why am I afraid?

Number one is the visceral answer: because of what Sands did to me. I've been in the hands of a madman before. It almost destroyed me. It's happening again, here, now, and the possibilities terrify me.

I examine this and throw it aside. It's neither pertinent nor helpful. Dali is not Sands. There's no indication that he's a rapist. His attitude with Heather Hollister seems to have been that of a zookeeper with an animal. He might beat me, but he probably won't fuck me.

My heartbeat slows a little bit.

Second: Heather Hollister herself. She wasn't a weak woman, but eight years alone in the dark drove her crazy. She was a strong woman, a competent, confident police officer; now she picks holes into her skin and talks in circles like a child.

I group this one with the third and fourth. Third: Dana Hollister. What if he decides to lobotomize me in the same way? What if he makes the darkness last forever? And, finally, fourth: He could just decide to kill me.

These things, on the advice of Barnaby Wallace, I embrace. They're real. They make sense. They are things that could actually happen and thus are the problems to solve.

My heartbeat and breathing have both returned to normal.

*Thanks, Barnaby. You go on the Christmas list, if I make it out of here cognitive.*

So, fight or flight? Which makes the most sense in this situation? I tick off the factors in my mind. He's got the weapons, which gives him a distinct advantage. If he's had military training, he'll be conversant in close quarters combat. The most troubling thing is his experience. He's been doing this for years. He knows what to expect when that trunk opens.

*Flight, then. But how?*

I remember what Heather Hollister said. She'd been ready to jump out and attack when the trunk opened. She'd been pepper-sprayed and stun-gunned for her efforts. It was the most obvious tactic, and the first one he'd be braced for.

*Jitter-step.*

It was one of Kirby's words. She'd challenged me to a little hand-to-hand combat one weekend, and I'd accepted. I prefer my gun but am aware it's not always an option, and I knew my jujitsu could use some serious updating.

We had a good time, and Kirby, as it turns out, was a good instructor. She was skilled but never brutal, and she was able to explain everything she did. At one point I thought I had her. I'd caught her from behind, in a headlock, and she was straining hard to escape. She suddenly relaxed, sagging, then strained again, then sagged further, then strained again. It was confusing, and I found myself off balance, struggling to anticipate and react. In the midst of this calculation, she went from straining a little to a huge burst of resistance that threw me off utterly. She surged forward and flipped me over her shoulder. I landed on my back, hard.

Kirby had grinned down at me as I struggled to catch my breath. *Jitter-step, Smoky-babe. One step up, one step down, one step up, one step down, and then, just when they think they've got your rhythm, make it two steps, see?*

The car moves forward again.

I decide to make my move as I'm climbing out of the trunk, when my back is to him. It should be when I seem the most vulnerable and off balance. I'll pretend to struggle with the exit, as though I'm lightheaded or faint. I'll try once, fail, try twice, fail, and on the third time, rather than fail, I'll kick back, catch him with a foot, and run.

I hope.

The quality of the sounds has changed. They are subtly deeper, as though they contain an echo.

A garage. We've pulled in to a garage.

I take a few deep breaths to steady myself and chant one of the phrases Barnaby used later in his lecture. It had seemed cheesy at the time, but it helps me now.

*Fear serves me. I do not serve fear.*

The engine stops. A pause. I hear a door opening and the muffled sounds of footsteps against a hard, smooth surface.

The trunk pops open slightly, a crack of light. There was no key in the lock, so he must have used the remote on his key fob. Smart.

"I'm going to open the trunk door halfway. I'll throw in a pair of handcuffs. You'll put them on. If you make a single move I'm uncomfortable with, I'll hurt you. Do you understand?"

"Yes."

The trunk opens a little more but not completely. The handcuffs are thrown in.

"No tricks. Put them on tight or I'll hurt you. Do you understand?"

"Yes."

He sounds bored, as if he's reading from a prepared script. Just a job, done it a hundred times, same old same old.

I ratchet the cuffs onto my wrists, ensuring that they're tight.

"Okay, they're on."

The trunk opens fully. He's standing behind the car, relaxed but alert. He holds my gun in one hand, pointed at me. The other holds a can of what I assume is pepper spray, also pointed at me.

We're inside a concrete structure with a roll-up door. The door is up and I can see night sky and a fence behind Dali. Freedom.

"You're going to climb out of the trunk and stand with your back to me. I'll walk you forward. You'll go where I direct you. If you make any sudden move, I'll shoot you. I'll injure you if I can, but I'll kill you if I have to. Do you understand?"

"Yes."

"Climb out."

*Now or never. This is the chance. Jitter-step.*

I struggle to get out and fail.

*That's one.*

I take a quick breath, steady my nerves, and get ready to try and fail again.

He sprays me with the pepper spray before I even start. It hits me in the worst way: directly into my open eyes and down my throat. The pain is immediate and excruciating. I scream as my eyes burn, and then I can't scream because I'm coughing uncontrollably and retching. He continues to spray me, he won't stop, and I'm unaware of him, of the car, of the fear, because everything is about the agony I'm in.

He kicks me so that I fall back into the trunk, and then he slams it shut.

I cough and retch in the dark. I scream when I can. My skin burns anywhere the spray touched it. I rub my eyes, but that only makes it worse. The pain is more terrible than anything I've ever experienced, not in terms of its intensity but because of its inescapability. Nothing I do lessens it, nothing will make it stop.

I burn in the dark, and writhe.

I have no idea how much time passes. Time is measured in suffering, in its lessening, and finally in its ending. Somewhere in the part of my mind that's still capable of rational thought, I guess that an hour must have passed. I'm covered in sweat; my face drips with tears and snot. I've vomited on myself. My muscles are weak, and I'm filled with a deadening mixture of lassitude and despair.

A hand pounds twice on the trunk.

"We're going to try this again. If you attempt to do anything other than what I've told you, I will give you the same again. Do you understand?"

"Yes," I whisper, my voice trembling with fear and hate.

"Do you understand?"

He couldn't hear me. The hate rises.

"Yes," I say, louder. "I understand."

What else is there to say?

The trunk opens. The scene is the same as before. The night sky behind him, the gun in my face. I gulp in cool night air. I tremble, and hate that I tremble.

"Go on," he says. "Get out."

I shake as I climb out, no funny stuff this time. I stand with my back to him. He places a hand on my shoulder. The gun settles into my lower back.

"Walk."

I walk, aware that the night sky is receding behind me. Is this how the others felt? Is it always the same? The bored voice, the instructions, the fading stars? I think it probably is. Dali is pragmatic, soulless. He doesn't deviate from what works.

My eyes are still burning, though it's tolerable now. I try to take in my surroundings as we walk toward a door. I see gray concrete walls, floor, ceiling. The room we drove into was small. The ceiling can't be more than eight feet high. There's a single bulb. The door he's marching me toward is flat gray metal, windowless. Utilitarian. I note a camera in the upper right-hand corner.

Looks like Earl was right on the money, I think. Or close enough.

We reach the door.

"Open it," he tells me.

I reach out, turn the knob, open the door. Beyond is a concrete hallway, probably thirty feet long. It turns right at the end. There are three doors along the left wall, and it's all lit as unimaginatively as the room we're leaving.

"Walk," he says, still bored.

I move forward. I hear the door close behind us, and now I'm in a tomb. There are no sounds here, just silence and coolness. We reach the end of the hallway and turn to the right. There's a metal stairway.

"Up," he directs.

We march up and reach the second floor landing, which is the top.

"Open the door."

I turn another knob and open another door, and now we're in a new hallway, much more terrifying than the one below. This one has a series of ten doors on either side. These are made of steel, and there are no knobs on them. Padlocks and hasps secure them from the outside in three places. I swallow back bile as I note the locked openings at the base of each door.

*That's where he'll put the food through.*

"Walk," he tells me, and I walk, helpless to do anything else.

We come to the end of the hallway. As we pass each door, I have to wonder: Are there women in each? The last door stands open, waiting for me.

"Enter the room," he tells me.

I balk, and the gun pushes into my spine, reminding me of his promise. I have no reason to doubt him.

"Enter the room," he says again, that endless bored patience.

I walk forward. As I reach the threshold, he shoves me hard, and I stumble inside. The door begins to close immediately, taking the light with it. I scan my surroundings, seeing what I can: a bunk built into the wall, a toilet. Nothing else. I whirl around and watch as the door slams shut.

I launch myself against it. I can't help it.

"Let me out, Dali, you piece of shit! I'm a member of the fucking FBI!"

I mean for it to be anger, but it sounds like terror. He doesn't reply. I hear the locks being applied to the hasps.

"Dali!" I scream.

I can hear him walking away.

Then I hear nothing.

# CHAPTER THIRTY-FOUR

The darkness is, as Heather Hollister had said, total. I thought some light might come in through cracks in the door, but Dali's done something with all the seams to seal off any possible ingress of illumination. I hold my hands up to my face and stare at them. This is something my dad taught me when I was girl, when he wanted to get rid of my night-light.

"But it's dark, Daddy," I protested, eight years old and using my best little-girl-in-distress voice, the one that never failed to bend him to my will.

This time, he'd held firm. I saw my mother behind it.

"It's never completely dark, honey," he said. "Look, I'll show you. I'll turn off all the lights, but I'll be here with you when I do it, okay?"

"Okay," I agreed, doubtful.

He flicked the switch and everything turned to black. I felt the old panic rise, the same panic that told me to beware, there was something under my bed, something with the voice of a snake and the claws of a beast, waiting to grab my legs when my feet hit the floor.

"D-Daddy?" I whispered.

"I'm here, baby, don't worry. Now, I want you to do something for me. I want you to put your hand in front of your face, and I want you to stare at it."

"Why?"

"Just trust me, honey."

I had no longer been afraid, of course. My father was with me, so the monsters would stay away. I brought my hand up in the darkness and stared.

At first I saw nothing at all, but as the moments passed, I became aware that Dad was right. The darkness wasn't total. The moon, though only a quarter full and hidden behind a blanket of clouds, provided the barest hint of illumination through the curtains. The streetlamps in the distance bounced off the clouds and sent faint light my way. My hand ghosted into view. Just an outline, but it was there.

"I see it, Dad!"

I try it now. I stare and stare and stare. Time passes. I see nothing. Nothing but blackness.

"Shit," I say, alarmed at how shaky my voice is already. I lower my hands. The clink of the handcuffs is strangely comforting in the otherwise complete silence.

"Work out your surrounds," I say aloud.

I picture the room as I'd seen it before the door closed.

"Bed should be to my left."

I move left slowly, until I feel the metal edge of the cot. I reach down with my hands and run them over the cool metal sides. I find the blankets, which are sparse and rough. A sheet covers a thin mattress, and a lumpy pillow sits at the head. I fumble further and find the bolts that were used to secure the cot to the wall.

"Like a prison bed," I mutter.

It was apropos. This was a cell, right?

I straighten and turn, putting the bed to my back.

"Toilet should be to my right in the center of the wall."

I walk to what I think is the center of the room, and then I face right and walk forward. I keep my hands out in front of me and soon touch cool concrete. I hunch forward, searching.

No toilet.

I remain bent over and crab-walk to the left. A moment later I feel the toilet, which is made of metal, not porcelain. Again, like a cell. Porcelain can be broken; its pieces can be made into knives.

"Don't want anyone slitting their wrists, now, do we?"

I realize that the darkness throws off almost all of my spatial sense.

I was certain that I'd walked to the middle of the room, but I'd been off by almost three feet. My admiration for the blind is rising by the minute.

I decide to pace off my cell. I follow the front wall back until I reach the side wall to which the cot is bolted. I put my back to it and walk slowly, counting as I go. I keep each pace to what I think is a foot. I reach twelve by the time my toe contacts the far wall.

"Twelve feet. Okay."

I walk the distance between. It's five feet.

"Twelve by five. Gotcha. Bed, toilet. Blanket, pillow."

I find my way back to the bed and sit down on it. I stare out into nothing. The blackness is oppressive in its completeness. I cock an ear and hear the low *swish swish* of air being pumped into the room. There is nothing else. I lay back on the bed and stare into the blackness that leads to the ceiling.

"Jesus," I whisper, and it's almost a sob.

I'd judged Heather Hollister. It's a natural reaction. We see someone sicker or weaker and we're stronger and healthier and we assume at some unconscious level that there's an innate difference between us and them. Be it luck or karma or inner strength, we must somehow be superior, else we would be like them.

I sit now in the darkness and the silence and the *swish swish swish* and I understand. Eight years of this would destroy anyone, anywhere. The fact that she could still string words together into sentences was a sign of tremendous strength, not fundamental weakness.

"I'm sorry, Heather," I say aloud.

I have no problem speaking to myself. I've done it, off and on, since the loss of my former life. I realize it's not healthy, but it was my original truce with insanity. It's worked so far.

"We'll have whole conversations, Alexa, if I'm here long enough."

Terror shoots through me like an electric shock, strong enough to make me swoon. I'd been thinking about talking to a dead child. What about the live ones? Bonnie can't lose another mother. I reach down with my cuffed hands and touch my belly.

What's going to happen to this baby?

An image of the camera in the first room comes to mind, and I jerk my hands away from my abdomen.

What if he's got an infrared camera going in this room?

It would make sense. I resolve to hide the pregnancy for as long as I can.

*We'll have to talk silently, baby. I can't chance that he's listening in.*

The silence and the blackness are numbing. I hadn't realized how much of my sense of self is wrapped up in the visual perception of my body. You walk and see your arms swing from the corner of your eyes. You pass a window and see a shadowed reflection in the glass. You exist. In the darkness there is only thought, touch, smell. It doesn't feel like enough.

"Then make it enough." I say the words loud, but the concrete sucks them away, preserving the hush.

I decide to concentrate on why I'm here. Why did he grab me? I'm not particularly surprised that he knows who I am, but why grab me now? What purpose does that serve?

I hear a faint sound in the hallway. The lights in the room go on, and I scream in shock as the world disappears in a sheet of white. I'm blind again, blinded by light this time rather than by dark. I press the heels of my hands to my eyes but see only spots. I register the sound of the door opening, and then I feel something press against the side of my neck. A moment later an electric shock jolts me, causing me to cry out in pain and making my muscles contort. It goes on and on, and I feel my bladder let go a moment before I black out.

I wake up a few seconds later. I'm facedown on the floor. I try to say something, but only a parched moan comes out. I feel a needle in the crook of my arm and get the sense of something being forced into my veins. A great dizziness washes over me, and then I'm blind again, overwhelmed by a whirlpool of warmth and white.

I come to again facedown, naked, bound to a metal table, blindfolded. My head is clearing quickly. Whatever he used metabolizes fast.

I cringe into myself, overwhelmed with a sense of shame about my vulnerability and nakedness that is all too familiar. Though I know rape isn't his thing, all I can think of is, here I am again, that place I swore I'd never be. A man who is not my husband is looking at my body, taking in both its beauties and its flaws. I want to vomit in despair.

I ache everywhere. My eyes and throat feel raw from the pepper spray. My wrists are sore from the cuffs. The muscles in my neck are spasming from the stun-gun hit. Shooting pains run screaming to the base of my skull, promising to turn into a bad, bad headache soon enough.

"This is just a demonstration," Dali says.

He no longer sounds bored. The quality of his voice has changed in a subtle way. He doesn't sound excited so much as attentive. Whatever it is he's about to do, he assigns importance to it. It deserves his concentration.

I break out into a sweat.

"We're all meat, you see? We are creatures. Animals. We can fool ourselves, but in the end, Pavlov's dog lives inside every one of us. If you want a man to obey you, all that's required is the ability to inflict more pain on him than he can handle. It's not enough to say it. You have to prove it. Prove it enough and he'll fall into step. Appeal to his fear, not his intellect. Terror is much more reliable."

I smell something now. It's not an unpleasant scent. The odor of aftershave, faint but recognizable.

"The most important thing is to keep your promise. If you say 'don't do this' and someone does it anyway, then you have to provide the penalty. In your case, I told you to stay away. You chose to hunt for me instead. Thus you are being punished, and your punishment will serve as an example to others."

"That's crazy, Dali. Do you have any idea who I am? I was just chosen by the director of the FBI to head up a national strike team investigating serial offenders. I'm a federal agent on the president's radar. People are going to be looking for me, in force."

The bravado falls flat. I can hear the tremors of fear in my own voice, and I despise my own weakness. Later, if I escape, others will tell me in soothing voices that it wasn't my fault, but it won't matter.

"They may look, but they won't find you. The next time my name comes up, they'll remember what happened to one of their best and think twice."

He sounds calm, reasonable.

"Do you really believe that?"

"It's a universal law. A certainty of fear and pain is the best guarantee of obedience."

"You're wrong. They'll never stop. You've underestimated them."

"Initially, maybe, but an animal with a badge is still an animal. Pain and fear will always eventually supersede belief. You just have to provide it in adequate quantities and make it a certainty. The FBI will look for you, but they will not find you. They'll start thinking about what that means for you, what you're experiencing, and they'll realize the truth: It could just as easily be them."

The room is far too warm. I feel drops of sweat pooling in the curve of my lower back. The sensation of my damp skin against the metal of the table is somehow grotesque. I'm sweating at my hairline, underneath my breasts.

"Debate is never fruitful in the face of hard reality. Let's say a man speaks against you. Hit him in the face with your fist, make him eat your knuckles. Splinter his teeth and split his lips. Then ask him to repeat what he said. What do you think he'll do?"

"Tell you to fuck yourself."

"You can say what you want, but I'm going to provide you with a demonstration of my tenets regardless. You can make up your own mind about their efficacy."

"Wait," I say. He ignores me, continuing on as though I hadn't spoken. He's unhurried, patient, like a golem or an automaton.

"I'm going to whip you. It's going to hurt, particularly with all that sweat that's covering your body. You will scream and cry and beg, but I will not stop. I never stop. I don't take pleasure in doing this. I do this to show you what to expect in the future if you disobey me. Do you understand?"

The bored tone is back, which frightens me the most.

"Wait," I say again.

Something thin and leather snaps down against my upper back. The fact that I couldn't anticipate it makes it somehow much, much worse than it normally would be. There's a split second of numbness, followed by an unbearable burning pain. I start to scream but manage to bite it back.

"You should go ahead and let yourself scream," he says. "You will, anyway."

It ends in silence. I'd been trapped in a haze, a miasma of agony and flashing bright lights, like lightning captured inside a thundercloud. I had screamed, until the screams themselves became too much of an effort, as the brain shut down and all I could do was writhe.

It ends as it began, without warning. I wait for the next crack on my flesh, but it doesn't come. I continue to cringe anyway, a reflex response to the rhythm he'd set up. I realize it's over and I allow myself to cry. I hate it, but I just can't help it.

My whole body hurts. The cuts in my back and buttocks and on the backs of my legs burn as the salt from my own sweat contacts them. It's like being covered in biting ants, or having a bad sunburn slapped again and again.

The only thing I am thankful for, through my grief and shame and pain, is that he seems to be satisfied with the back of my body. He's stayed away from my belly.

"You've experienced one of the penalties for disobedience. I think you'll find that it's fairly brilliant. I'm careful not to completely debilitate you. I'll put antibiotic ointment on your deeper cuts, and you'll be very, very uncomfortable for a number of days, but there's no permanent damage. There's not even likely to be any scarring, unless you force me to do it a number of times."

I am filled with sickness at my own helpless gratitude. *Yes, good, no more scars. Thank God.*

"You have simple rules and a simple life. Follow them, and I'll leave you alone. Disobey me, and you'll find yourself back in this room. You should know that I took it easy on you this time, as this was just for the purpose of demonstration. It can get a lot worse. I can make it last twice as long, three times as long, all day if I want. I can dab you with drain cleaner. I can burn you with cigarettes."

I don't say anything, but I shiver.

"The rules are as follows. I will provide you with three meals a day. You are to eat the food you're given. You are to exercise for a minimum of thirty minutes daily. This will include push-ups, crunches, and running in place. You are to use the toilet to relieve yourself. That is all. Once a week, when I am here, I will provide you with dental floss, a toothbrush, and toothpaste. I will watch as you clean your teeth thoroughly. Try to attack me or harm yourself and the penalty will be severe. This is all I require. Do you understand?"

My mouth doesn't seem to want to work. He slaps a hand down on my back, making me scream out loud.

"Do you understand?" he asks again, calm and patient as ever.

"Yes!" I moan.

"Very good. Obey these rules and you also remain unshackled in your cell. Disobey them and you won't just be punished, you'll be chained. Now, before I tend to your wounds and take you back, I want to show you something. I'm going to lift your blindfold. Turn your head to your left and look."

He lifts up the cloth and turns my head. I blink at the light. The room is concrete and fluorescents, like everything here. I see another table about four feet away, another naked body bound to it, facedown and blindfolded. I close my eyes and open them again to dispel the blurriness. What I see freezes my heart.

"Leo," I whisper.

Leo Carnes lies on the table, trembling uncontrollably. It has to be even worse for him; he's been here the whole time, listening to what Dali did to me.

"Leo, I'm here," I say.

"Smoky? Is that you? He shot Alan! What's happening?"

"Quiet," Dali admonishes, though not angrily.

"Hang in there, Leo," I tell him. "Do what he says."

Dali replaces my blindfold and then smacks my back again, harder than the first time. I arch against my bonds but bite back the scream.

"Quiet, I said."

"You killed Alan?"

"The black agent? I don't know if he's dead or not. I shot him twice. Now, be quiet or you get another ten minutes with the whip."

This shuts me up. He proceeds to apply ointment to my back. It's painful, but I endure it. When finished, he uncuffs me from the table and undoes my other bonds.

"From this point on you'll be naked. You don't need clothes in your room. The good news is, you'll also be uncuffed. Isn't that better?"

I don't reply, and this earns me another slap. It's hard enough that I cry out. I grit my teeth and fight back my rage. "Yes," I say. "It will be better."

He maneuvers me into a sitting position.

"Stand slowly. You're going to be a little unsteady."

He's right. I ease off the table, and my knees almost buckle when I try to stand. Dali keeps me from falling.

"Walk forward as I direct you. Do you understand?"

Back to rote and bored.

"Yes."

He marches me forward. I sense a temperature change against my body and surmise that we've gone through a doorway. We go down a long hall, turn twice, then stop.

"Why didn't you drug me for the trip back to my cell?" I ask.

"Room," he corrects me. "Better if you look at it that way, trust me. You should be too weak to resist after what you've just been through. If you're not, then I want to know that too."

I'm surprised that he answered, so I push my luck one last time as I hear the door open.

"How do you see all this, Dali? What you're doing to us?"

The briefest pause, then:

"Doing to you? I'm not 'doing' anything. I'm just storing meat."

He yanks off my blindfold and pushes me forward into darkness.

PART TWO

THE MOON

# CHAPTER THIRTY-FIVE

I travel behind my eyes, inside my mind, and I speak to both the living and the dead. Matt is there, Alexa is there, my faceless, unborn child is there. Bonnie is there as well, but she is mute again and her eyes are full of sadness.

It was darkness when I closed my eyes, because it's always darkness. Three times a day a rectangle of light appears at the bottom of my door, and food is dropped inside. It's always the same: oatmeal and oranges in the morning, ham or roast beef sandwich with an apple in the afternoon, hot dogs and lettuce in the evening. A packet of vitamins also comes with each dinner. And water. Always plenty of water.

"Eat it all," he told me. "Not just because I'll punish you if you don't, but because I'm including what you need to survive. I'm giving you meats for protein, and fruits and vegetables to prevent scurvy. The vitamins are a new thing. I'm working to find a balance that doesn't cost me too much per head but prevents loss of teeth due to a lack of calcium. Milk spoils too quickly. We'll see how it goes."

I've had no further experiences in the punishment room. I long to defy him, but I can't chance it. I have a baby growing inside me, and it, along with the light behind my eyes, has become my lifeline.

Three weeks have passed. Three weeks of darkness and ennui.

There are no books, no TV, no radio. There is nothing to do but think, and eat, and exercise, and walk from one end of the cell to the other, and use the toilet, and sleep. Once I started to masturbate, simply to relieve the crushing boredom, but then I remembered that he might be watching on a camera, and I stopped myself.

Once a week, as promised, he visits to make me brush and floss my teeth. It's always the same. The lights go on without warning, blinding me. The door opens and he shocks me with the stun gun. Then he blindfolds me. When I'm able to stand again, he guides me to the pail of water he's brought with him. He hands me dental floss and I floss my teeth. He gives me a toothbrush, with toothpaste already applied, and I brush and rinse. He shocks me again, turns me face over as I spasm, removes my blindfold, and exits the cell, returning me to solitude and darkness.

The first time, he talked. He said: *Excellent, number 35.* That's what he calls me. Number 35. I file it away into the numbness I've become.

The last two times, he said nothing at all. I sat on the floor while he waited for me to finish. His patience is becoming the thing I hate the most. It is indifference, and in this place, indifference is a poison all its own.

It's only been three weeks, and I already feel myself wanting to break down. I want him to say something to me. I hate him, but I long for him to speak, or to yell, or to hit me. Anything that involves interaction with another human being, however twisted.

Is this the same loneliness that keeps battered women with their abusive spouses? Is that what it's like for those women? A stony solitude of hushes, where the silence and the lack become a living pain? If it is, I'll never judge them again, at least not in the same way.

I long for anything to acknowledge my existence. It doesn't even have to be human. I saw a movie once in which a prisoner of war made friends with a rat. I was repulsed at the time. Now I wish for my own rat.

The darkness and the silence and the solitude grind on that least protected thing: the soul.

*That's right,* I said to myself, just the other day (day? Or night?). *The soul.*

I'm done wondering. Once you turn out all the lights and the body disappears from sight and you are left alone, what is it that remains? The sense of self, the *me*, the *am that I am*.

*If that's not the soul, what is?* I don't care to hear the answer.

Madness in this place and places like it, I think, comes from too much thought. Thought is all you have. It's the one thing you can do that can't be taken away. The problem is, once you start thinking, it can be hard to stop. Like getting a tune stuck in your head, your mind can get rolling, grooving, heading down the highway, and you can watch as the sun rises and sets and the trees go by but find, when the sun sets, that the brakes have failed. You don't coast to a stop, you writhe on your cot instead and curse, or rage, or weep.

I worried in the beginning about Leo and Alan. As time moved on, and my sense of time became a floating thing, I found less and less desire to consider either.

Just three weeks, and it's already a hell on earth I could never have imagined.

I hold on to my sanity with tricks taught to me by Barnaby Wallace. His seminar, as it turns out, was a hell of a good investment.

*Fear comes from too little certainty or too much. Torture is about denying one or the other, or both. The torturer takes away your certainty through different methods. Sleep deprivation. Sensory deprivation. No clocks or windows so you can't track the time. He gives you too much certainty by promising to give you a good shot of pain and then delivering on that promise. So how do you conquer that fear?* He stopped then, a hand going absently to a scar on the side of his neck. *First thing you need to know about torture: Everyone breaks eventually. There's no foolproof method, not for anyone on this earth. Give a dedicated man enough time, and he'll crack the bravest down the middle. Period. What I can teach you is how to delay that breaking point. How to put it off in the distance. Will it work for you?* He shrugged. *Everybody's different.*

One of the methods he talked about had to do with a kind of self-hypnosis. Creating a *world behind your eyes,* he called it. He showed us a video of a Japanese man deep in meditation. Various people try to distract him, first by screaming into his ears and then, later, by smacking him in the back with boards and rods. He remains serene throughout, a half smile on his face, even when they once draw blood.

*That's an extreme example,* Wallace admitted. *This is a guy who's been sitting in the lotus position since he was four years old. But the principle is the same. It's workable.* He'd smiled a thin, crooked smile. *We like workable.*

I've turned Barnaby's lessons into a small salvation, and it is keeping me tethered to myself, in the dark.

Everything is black when I close my eyes, as now, but once they are closed, the light goes on, or the sun comes up, or the moon rises.

Right now I am in a meadow at noon. The meadow is full of flowers. They stand as tall and thick as wheat in a field and are a rich riot of rainbow colors. They are vivid and vibrant and beautiful. In the center of the meadow is a large circle of the greenest grass I've ever seen. Birdsong and wind are the dominant sounds, both low and perfect. I am overwhelmed with images that contain beauty but no sense: a silo filled with sawdust, rich in smells; apples with sugar sores; fresh cut wheat, spring's rebellion.

I sit on the grass in the meadow and I talk to my unborn child. It is neither he nor she, it is a small blur of roughly human-shaped light. I speak to it aloud, but it talks to me with its mind.

"What do I do when he knows about you?" I ask, and then laugh at my own poetry. "Time, time, to make up a rhyme. But seriously, baby, what do I do?"

*You wait, Mother. And you hope. If you want to, you can pray, but only if you want to. The faith you need here is in you and me. God needs no faith to survive. He is here now beside you, regardless of your regard.*

Baby is very theological, which I find somehow both comforting and annoying.

"God, here? Give me a break."

*He is here.*

"Reaaaaally. What kind of God are we talking about? The serious-looking dude with the big white beard? The Indian-type God with eight arms and a mysterious knowing smile? Or should we go animal? A white buffalo in the distance, maybe?"

*God doesn't have to be an embodiment, Mother. God can be an activity. God is loving a husband, raising a child. God is reading a good book or saving a life. God is pride in a job well done and forgiveness given when it's deserved. You don't have to prostrate yourself, or burn incense, or live in fear of a lightning strike. You just have to live and love and do your best in both. That's God, and that's heaven, and it's not something we have to wait until we die to find. It's here, now, in all of us.*

Baby is wise, of course, as all disembodied children of light tend to be. The words ring in the meadow air, even though they were only thought, not spoken. They are dulcet, birdsong, pure.

I take in a deep breath through my nose, smelling the flowers. I turn my head toward the sky so the always-high-noon sun can beat down on my face unencumbered, and I taste the sun-sugar on my lips. I close my eyes behind my eyes, but here there is no darkness, only light.

"Jury's still out, baby, but I have to say, I like that version of heaven better. You know the problem I always have with the heaven concept? The people who believe in it have no vested interest in leaving behind a better world. You know what I mean? I don't buy into the whole rein-carnation thing either, but at least it tells you, hey, you're coming back to this world, so it's in your interest to leave it in better shape than you found it."

Baby glows brighter, then softer.

*Belief isn't important, Mother. What you do right now is who you are.*

I smell the jasmine and I laugh. It doesn't belong in this beautiful place, that laugh. It has too much despair in it.

"So what does that make me? I escape in my head to a place that does not exist but is more real to me than reality, and I speak to a glow-ing baby/theologian that's actually just a collection of cells in my tummy. I guess that makes me nuts, huh?"

*It's keeping you sane, not making you crazy.*

I consider this possibility.

The sound of footsteps coming down the hall jolts me away from the light. My eyes fly open and I am in the blackness again.

*No, no, no, keep your eyes closed this time! That was the plan!*

*Create victories,* Barnaby Wallace had told us. *It doesn't matter if they're small. It only matters that you can feel them. Torture, imprison-ment, these are about taking things away. Find things to keep. Might be exercise. Might be small bits of disobedience. As long as you feel like you're doing something to prepare for the eventuality of escape, you'll probably stay sane.*

The footsteps approach and I squinch my eyes shut, as tightly as I can. The footsteps stop and the lights come on. Even through my eyelids, it's almost blinding. I hear the sounds of the locks being disengaged. I open my eyes a little. The light comes in, but I am not blind.

*Good! Good!*

I keep my eyes open now but feign the usual disorientation and blindness. The door opens and I look while trying to appear as if I'm seeing nothing. I see Dali for the first time. I am both elated and disappointed.

He's a small man, dressed in a baggy jacket over a T-shirt, loose blue jeans leading down to hiking boots. He's wearing a ski mask over his head, which hides his features. He approaches me with the stun gun, and I scan for any other distinguishing marks as I pretend to be blind. I see one thing just before the gun contacts the side of my neck. It's subtle, and I am uncertain. I have no time to process it fully before my body begins to spasm, and I go down.

He shocks me again, twice. Grayness soaks my vision and I really am blind.

A moment later, the prick of a needle and a white light explodes inside my head like a bomb blast. I fall into it.


I wake up as before, facedown, shackled, bound. I shiver against my will at the thought of getting whipped again. I wonder frantically what I could have done to deserve punishment?

*Watch that "deserve," Barrett. That's prisoner-think. That's victim-think. You don't deserve anything that's happening here.*

"You're probably wondering why you're here, number 35," he murmurs. "Don't worry. I didn't bring you here because of any infraction. You've been a model unit."

Unit. Number 35. Just storing meat.

"You're here because I'm going to be asking you to make a choice. I'm going to ask you to decide whom I cripple and release: you, or number 36."

"Who is number 36?"

"The other young agent I brought here after you."

My heart lurches. Leo?

"Cripple and release? I don't understand."

"You've seen what I'm talking about. Dana Hollister is an example."

Now it's my stomach that responds. It rolls dangerously.

"I don't want to make that decision." My mouth is full of phlegm and bile. I force myself to swallow it all down.

"If you don't decide, then you are the decision."

A moment of blackness, almost like unconsciousness, passes over me. The world's full of cotton.

"Why?"

"They're continuing to hunt me. I need to send another message."

"It won't work. They won't listen, don't you see? There's no reason for you to do this if it won't make a difference."

"It's going to happen. The question: Who is it going to be?"

"Why do I get to be the one who decides?"

"I flipped a coin. You won the toss."

I can't speak for a moment. My face wants to twist into a sob. I fight it back.

"Why—why am I here, in this room?"

"I'm going to bring him in, and then I will leave you two alone for five minutes. You can tell him about the choice you have to make or not. I'll leave that up to you. You are not allowed to discuss the subject of escape. When the five minutes are up, I'll come back. I'll return him to his room, and then I'll ask you for your decision. The procedure will be performed an hour later."

I feel cornered, panicked. I'm having trouble getting a full breath.

*Five minutes? An hour later?*

Worst of all: *the procedure.* Dark and clinical, an unconcerned word meant to stand for the loss of awareness of self. A scalpel word, bright and gleaming, metal fashioned from a nightmare.

"Why are you giving us the time together?"

This is the one weapon left to me, whether I get to put it to use later or not: my ability to understand him. Why is Dali Dali? Is there something giggling and drooly hidden under a mask of money and practicality? Or is it a simpler mantra: *I kill, therefore I am?*

"Because I'm not a cruel man, number 35."

It's always the cruel who feel the need to prove otherwise. I file the answer away. Depersonalization is essential for him. That's useful.

*Or maybe it's just a thought that will die in the darkness with you.*

"Enough questions. Do you understand what I've told you?"

"Yes."

"Very good. I'll bring him in shortly. He'll remain facedown on the table. I'll remove his blindfold so he can see you. I'll move you over to stand next to his table. Your feet will be shackled, and your wrists will be cuffed to his table. Do you understand?"

Time, time, I need more time. I have none.

"Yes, I understand."

He acknowledges me by leaving without another word. Gone to blind and stun and drug Leo.

What am I going to do?

Panic has turned into something more distant. There's a wall of unreality and numbness between me and the sharper edges of my terror.

What are the factors? List them.

"One," I whisper. "He means what he says. Two: I can decide if it's Leo or me. If I don't decide, then it's me."

That's it. There are no other factors.

What should I do, baby? Tell me, please. Help me.

Baby does not reply, and I can't get either the meadow or the light to appear behind my eyes right now. I search for words from Barnaby Wallace, something to fit the situation, but all I can find is fear.

Leo's face comes to me, an image that swims into bright clarity. I see him smiling, on the plane where we met years ago, a young man, an earring in one ear, fighting not to become the establishment he worked for, full of the life ahead of him. He found himself in our orbit, and he walked away wiser and darkened as a result. He was seasoned by what we revealed to him, perhaps for the better, probably for the worst.

He's here because he knows me.

I am bad for the innocent and the young. Doves light on my finger and fall off dead. Matt and Alexa paid the price for loving me. Maybe Alan has too. Will I make Leo buy me life? Will he pay for my baby?

I'm shivered from these thoughts by a susurrus of soft steps coming through the door. Dali wears hiking boots but walks like a cat. Leo will be nude. His bare feet won't ring on the concrete.

"Lie down on the table, number 36."

Leo mumbles something and, I assume, complies. It makes me wonder about the drug that Dali is using. I'd always assumed he had to carry us in here.

Chain clinkings, more mumbles. A pause, then more soft sounds against the stone, coming near me. Dali removes my blindfold. I am staring at Leo. His eyes are half lidded, his mouth open. He drools.

"I'm going to move you over to him now. Are you ready?"

"Yes."

He undoes the shackles at my ankles. He removes the straps at my waist.

"I'll undo your hands. You will come to a sitting position with me behind you. I have a stun gun in my hand. If you attempt to escape or make any motion I'm not comfortable with, I will stun you, reattach you to the table, and punish you for an hour. Do you understand, number 35?"

"Yes."

I have no time for my usual rage at his indifference. I can't take my eyes off Leo.

Dali releases my wrists. "Come to a sitting position."

I comply. It occurs to me that I'm almost oblivious to my nudity now.

He grabs the back of my neck with one hand. "Stand up."

I stand, swaying slightly. My head is light.

"Walk forward."

I walk until we come to the table where Leo lies insensate.

"Wrists forward, and together."

He cuffs my wrists and then uses a third set to attach me to an eye ring on the table.

"I'll cuff your ankles now. Try to kick me and there will be a penalty. Do you understand?"

"Yes."

*Yes and yes. Yes, I understand that you control me, that you are a monster; yes, I understand that hope dies a long, slow death here.*

He cuffs my ankles.

"Number 36 should come out of it soon. Perhaps twenty minutes. I'll be watching. You'll have your five minutes, and then I'll return."

He walks off, and I am left there, staring down at Leo. It hurts me to look at him. He's so young, too young. Was I ever that young? Yes. I was almost his age when Alexa was born. It seems like a lifetime ago.

Time passes. Leo's eyes open once, then close. They open again a few minutes later and he blinks to clear away the fog. I wish he could sleep forever, baby-faced and serene.

"I'm so sorry, Leo." I start to cry.

"Hey," he says. His eyes fill with concern. "Wh-what's happening?"

He's here but still sluggish.

"I'm not sure. He's given us five minutes together, but . . . but I don't know why."

The decision to lie comes from somewhere I can't identify. I haven't decided what I'll decide, but I do know that I want to spare him the knowledge. This uncertainty.

A sly voice creeps around inside me, cozening and impure. *You haven't decided? Are you sure about that?*

"How are you feeling?" I ask.

"Shitty. I . . ." He pauses, swallows. "I talk to myself a lot. I think I'm going a little bit crazy."

"Yeah." My voice cracks.

"Jeez. Stop crying, Smoky. We only have five minutes; don't waste it being all weepy."

I laugh, tribute to the hollow humor.

"Tell me about your girlfriend, Leo."

"Christa?" He smiles. "She's got long, soft brown hair and green eyes. Wicked combination. She laughs a lot. She thinks I'm sliced bread. She's smart." The smile fades. "I was going to ask her to marry me. I guess I'll never see her again, though." He sighs. "I was really looking forward to being married. I wanted to see what that's like." He glances up at me. "What is it like? Is it cool?"

I bite back more tears, aghast. A train of answers runs through my mind. What's it like? It's a collection of moments, constantly falling like the leaves of October, burnt-orange happiness, dark-red anger, brown for the normal. It's sharing a bed, day in and out, through tears and sex, laughs and fights. That bed becomes an island, where nakedness is more literal than actual, the place where all the biggest decisions are made, where new life is made, where new you is made.

Above all things, marriage, when it works, is not being alone.

"Yes," I say, unable to express all of these things to him. "Yes, it's cool."

He nods, cheek against the steel. "I thought so." He looks at me again. "I need to ask you something, and then I need to tell you something."

I glance at the camera in the corner. "We're not alone."

"It shouldn't matter. The first thing: If you get out of here and I end up like Dana Hollister, I want you to promise that you'll kill me. I won't lie around like that. I won't do that to my family, to Christa, or to myself."

"Don't ask me for this, Leo."

"Who else am I supposed to ask?" The desperation in his voice matches the fear in his eyes.

"Okay," I say, to soothe him. "I promise."

I am made aware of the time by the far, faint sounds of Dali coming this way. Leo hears it too. "Lean forward," he says, his voice urgent. "I don't want him to hear this. Hurry!"

I lean forward so that my ear is next to his mouth.

"It was Hollister," he whispers. "Hollister has to have tipped Dali off. Check out the servers Hollister worked with. Get"—his voice cracks—"get someone really good to look at them. I think you'll find something there."

"Stand up, number 35," Dali orders, coming into the room.

I kiss Leo's cheek and turn my lips to his ear. "I'm sorry, Leo. I'm so sorry."

*Sorry for what?* the sly voice asks.

*Sorry for what?*

They're not the last words I ever say to Leo, but almost.

# CHAPTER THIRTY-SIX

"Comes a time, baby. That's what Neil Young said. A time to live, a time to die. A time to go fucking insane."

Baby is silent. There's no light in this meadow anymore. The sun is eclipsed by the moon, shooting out light from its circular edges, bathing the world in hush-lit shadow. The trees have been stripped of leaves, and their branches twist and creak in the harsh and ever-present wind. The flowers are gone, and a dust cloud, a thousand feet high, sits on the horizon, rushing toward us in slow motion. Baby remains fuzzy and faceless, and half lit like everything else.

Leo was destroyed one week ago. I chose myself over him, though I tell myself that if I wasn't pregnant I would have taken his place. I don't know if it's true, but it keeps me from chewing through my wrists to get to the veins.

"Decide," Dali had said, then nothing else.

I had stalled with my silence. I knew what I was going to say but didn't want to say it.

"Decide in ten seconds or it's you," he urged.

"Don't make me do this," I whispered.

"Five seconds."

Then four and then three and then I spoke.

"Leo! Take him, you fuck." I started to cry, continued as he un-cuffed my wrists and then pushed me into the darkness of my cell. What was now my home.

The guilt crushed me into oblivion and has continued to obliterate me every day since. Dali never came back to tell me that it was done, but I have no doubt of it. Dali may play games, but not those kinds of games. He does what he promises where destruction is concerned.

I have dreams about Leo. I don't dream about Tommy or Bonnie or Alan or anyone else. I dream about Leo. I dream of his smile, and then I watch as it falls into slackness, as drool begins to drip from his chin, as his eyes fill with a blowing wind of nothing. I fall asleep on my back. I wake up curled into a fetal ball.

Nothing has changed about my environment. I breathe darkness. The rectangle of light appears three times a day. I eat. I expel. I exercise. I talk to my baby under the eclipse and the daytime stars, and I dream of Leo losing knowledge of himself as a person. Christa, his girl-friend, appears in these dreams sometimes. She points at me with an ac-cusatory finger and laughs like a hyena, then she gathers Leo into her arms like a baby and lopes off into a forest of dead trees. I search for my small victories, the dictate of Barnaby Wallace, but victory these days is bitter.

"When are you going to start showing, baby? And what happens when you do?"

I didn't really start looking pregnant with Alexa until I was into my fourth month. What will Dali do with a pregnant prisoner? Has he dealt with it before? I am certain that I don't want to know the answers. Dali's God is pragmatism. He'll do whatever is most cost-effective.

"Perhaps he'll let me keep you." I shiver at the thought of Dali being gone while I go into labor. Giving birth in darkness, fumbling for my child in blindness, bringing him to my breast without ever having seen his face.

"Is that why you're fuzzy, baby? Maybe I can't give you form be-cause I'm not sure you'll ever have one."

Baby stays silent. I moan in my dream, and my eyes fly open. I wake up to the black, and then I force myself to fall back asleep.

Unreality is a better world than here.

One more day passes before he appears again. The lights blind me, and he stuns and drugs me. I fall into nothing and wake up facing Dali. The table, it seems, can be upended to a vertical position. Dali regards me, wearing his ski mask and jacket and hiking boots.

"It seems you were right, after all. They keep hunting me, number 35. They're very tenacious."

I don't say anything. I'm too afraid.

"You're becoming a liability to my operation. I'm going to need to get rid of you."

"No, please," I croak. My throat has almost closed in terror.

"I'm not going to perform the procedure on you, number 35."

The relief I feel is so deep, so physical, that I almost lose control of my bladder. I'd rather die than have my baby in that state, I realize. Leo was right.

"You're going to kill me?" I ask.

"No. I'm going to release you."

Confusion. As with Heather Hollister, this is a deviation. I'm grateful for it, but it makes no sense.

"Why?"

"I'm going to take one thing to remember you by, number 35," he continues, ignoring my question. "It won't prevent you from doing what you do, but it will serve as a last example to you and others: Hunt me, and I punish."

He'd had his hands behind his back. He brings them into view now. They are gloved, and the right one holds a knife. He says nothing else. He moves to the side and cuts off the little finger of my right hand, below the first knuckle, in a single motion.

I scream instantly and do not stop. I begin to faint, no help necessary this time, and I see it again, that physical feature I had noted days ago but was unable to articulate. I realize what it is just before unconsciousness claims me again, a welcome brother.


"Someone call 911."

"What happened to her?"

"God, did you see her face?"

"Forget her face—what happened to her finger?"

The voices rise and fall, as the drugs inside me rise and fall, as the pain in my finger rises and falls, as the ocean pounds the shore on that Hawaiian beach somewhere, rise and fall, rise and fall. The permanencies of this world carry on regardless of what happens to humanity. The sun shines, the moon glows, the world turns.

I am on concrete. My mouth is so dry it feels filled with dust. I am surrounded by strangers with cell phones and worried eyes.

I find a woman who looks like my mother, and I reach my arms out to her.

"Please." It's all I can manage.

She hesitates and then comes to me and pulls me close. She's not my mother, but then again, no one is.

# CHAPTER THIRTY-SEVEN

Bonnie bursts into the hospital room. That's the only way to describe it. The door bursts open and she seems to fly across the room into my arms. She's sobbing.

"Mama-Smoky!"

Her whole body shakes. I draw her close to me, inhaling the scent of her hair as I press my lips to the top of her head.

"I'm okay, honey. I'm okay."

And I was, for what that was worth. Dali had dropped me nude on a sidewalk near Hollywood Boulevard. The woman who looked like my mother turned me over to the paramedics, and the ambulance screamed as I drifted in and out of consciousness. My finger needed surgery, but I refused general anesthesia because of my baby, despite of the doctor's assurances. The work on the bone was painful, but I took it. The doctors thought I was insane, but they couldn't budge me, and in the end, when Tommy saw that I was never going to give in, he stood with me against them.

The baby, I was assured, was still there, still alive. I hadn't been worried, not really. I had the sense of it inside me, that faint consciousness, now silent, that I'd spoken to so often. I knew all that was delusion and dream, but still, I was convinced I would have known if my baby was gone.

Strangely, the thing that's left me feeling most violated is not the loss of part of my finger or the few new scars on my back. It's that Dali shaved my head before depositing me on the sidewalk at noon.

Well, aside from Leo, of course. But I'm not ready to think about that. No, sir. That's a deep, dark ocean, waiting to suck me in and drag me down.

"I'm sorry you had to wait, baby," I whisper to Bonnie. "I wasn't ready to be seen."

She nods into my chest. She understands. Of course she does. Tommy takes a seat by the bed and stares out the window at the early April sky. He's been very, very quiet since my return. I can't seem to get a sense of him.

The FBI and the LAPD had turned the city upside down looking for me. There were no turf wars, no complaints about overtime. Everyone pitched in because every cop knows the truth: It could always be you. Dali had been right about that, even if he'd been wrong about the response.

My own team, I'm told, barely slept. They were run by a grim AD Jones, who'd had a short fuse and yelled more than he spoke.

They found nothing. I don't blame them for this, but it doesn't help my nightmares. The same thought keeps coming to me when I'm alone: If Dali hadn't let me go, I'd still be there.

In the dark.


A week after being found, I leave the hospital. It's against doctors' advice, but they're not too pushy about it. I get the idea that it's more a cover-your-ass kind of thing than actual medical concern. I was a high-profile pregnant FBI agent who'd been the victim of torture and amputation. They'd probably thought they'd hang high if something went wrong.

"You sure about this?" Tommy asks, after helping me into the car. Bonnie sits in the back, watchful and silent.

"I have to start doing something, Tommy, or I'm going to lose it. Take me home, and then take me to work."

Leo had been the final straw. I visited him yesterday. He lay on his bed, eyes staring at nothing. He was being fed by a tube. Various automated indignities dealt with his bodily functions. I met his girlfriend.

"Hi," she said to me. "I'm Christa."

I didn't know what to say, but I recognized what she needed. I opened my arms and took her in.

She let me have some time by myself with Leo. I stared down at him, crushed by numbness and self-loathing and a sense of being filthy, which I couldn't seem to get rid of. "I'm so sorry, Leo," I said. It was all I could come up with. What was I supposed to say? I'd traded him for myself and my child, and he'd never even known it. He'd probably gone to his oblivion still thinking I was a friend to be trusted. I leaned over to kiss his forehead. It was warm and dry, like living paper. "I'm going to find him and I'm going to kill him, Leo. I promise."

I walked out remembering the other promise too, the one Leo had dragged from me.

We get home and enter. It feels surreal. No, that's not right. It feels unreal. The cell is still more palpable to me than this. It renews my hatred.

"Want some coffee?" Bonnie asks, watching me. I recognize this kind of behavior from the time after my assault by Sands. She's worried that I'll fall apart right in front of her. Who knows? Maybe I will.

"That'd be wonderful, babe. I haven't had coffee in a month."

Her eyes darken a bit at this reference, and I regret it immediately. She braves a smile of assent and goes off to brew the pot. Tommy stands by a window again. Staring off at something I can't see.

I wish I could reach him. The distance isn't cold, it isn't like that. He is here. I feel his love. But there's some part of him that is in an elsewhere place.

"Tommy? Did you get the ibuprofen?"

He jolts back to the here and now, chagrined. "Sorry, yeah. I got it this morning. Be right back." He jogs up the stairs.

"Here's the coffee, Mama-Smoky," Bonnie says, bringing it to me. I accept and sip. "Heavenly," I say to her.

And it is.

Tommy reappears with a bottle of Advil. The doctors had offered me Percocet, but I declined because of the baby. I don't even like taking the ibuprofen, but the pain is just too constant and gnawing.

"How many?" he asks.

"Two."

He opens the bottle and gives me the pills. "You want water?"

"I'll drink them with the coffee."

I pop them and sip my coffee. It won't help much, but that's okay. I welcome a little bit of pain. It keeps my mind on my goal.

Killing Dali.

"You hungry?" he asks.

"No, I ate at the hospital. The old line about hospital food is kind of becoming a myth. I had a few good meals there."

He nods but says nothing. He gazes off again. The distance widens. I stand up, coffee in my hand.

"Come upstairs with me, Tommy. Help me get dressed."

"So, what's going on?" I ask him, after closing the door.

"What do you mean?"

I move into him. He takes me in his arms and hugs me close, careful of my finger. It feels good, but it also feels empty. I disengage a little, looking up at him. "I mean this. You're here, I'm not arguing that. But you're somewhere else too."

He steps away gently. He tries to avert his eyes before I can see the struggle there.

"I . . ." He frowns. "I'm not used to having trouble with my words."

I sit down on the bed, pat the space next to me. He follows my lead. I study his profile as he studies the wall.

"I'm trying to figure out how to get rid of all this anger, Smoky. I'm coming to the conclusion that the only solution is killing the man who took you away from us. That bothers me on some level, but maybe not as much as it should." He shakes his head. "I'm not Kirby. If I cross this line, it might have consequences for me. That's what's on my mind."

I reach over and take his hand. "I feel the same way. I'm just not conflicted about it."

He looks at me—really looks at me—for what seems like the first time. "Why not? How'd you get there?"

"I got there because a man came into my home a few years ago and stole my life and my face. Not long after that, another man almost killed Callie, and that same man then took Bonnie and held her hostage while he watched me cut my face for him." I grip his hand. "In spite of all that, do you know what lets me sleep at night? What gives me just a little bit of comfort?"

"No."

"That both of those men are dead. That I killed them. That's the penalty from now on, Tommy. Mess with my family and you die."

"Even if it means murder?"

"Even if."

It occurs to me that we could part ways right here. This could very well be a moral burden beyond Tommy's ability to rationalize. He's not the kind of man built to bend.

He raises my hand to his lips and kisses it. "I can live with that."

Then he does the last thing I'd ever expect. He cries. It's a soundless expression of grief, just tears pattering against my skin. It transfixes me. I feel as though I am witnessing something that shouldn't be allowed by nature, like a black sun, or a child with a knife in his hand and a grin on his face.

It ends as quickly as it began. He kisses my hand again, dries his face with two swipes of his hand, and stands up.

"What do you want to wear?"

He helps me dress when I need help. He gets my backup gun from the gun safe. He finishes by presenting me with my cell phone.

"Dali left it with you, along with your FBI ID. The techs checked it. It's clean."

"Thanks."

I look at myself in the mirror. My face crumples in dismay. "I'm ugly!"

He's standing behind me, and he cups each side of my bald head with a calloused but loving palm. He kisses the very top of my head. "You're alive. The hair will grow back. And you're never ugly." He steps away and checks his watch. "We should get moving. I'll meet you downstairs."

I'm left alone with my reflection. His words are both inadequate and more than I need. The dismay is visceral; it will always be the first thing I feel until the hair grows back, but Tommy's words will follow in my mind and bring me comfort. That and the tears he cried for me, which I know we'll never talk about again. They were a gift, something to treasure, something else to kill for.

# CHAPTER THIRTY-EIGHT

"Honey-love!"

"Boss woman!"

"Smoky!"

Only James is silent, but his gaze lingers longer than usual. His version of a welcome, I suppose.

Alan's arm is in a sling. Dali had been kind to him, just two bullets—one in the shoulder, one in the upper chest. Which leads me to wonder: kind to him, but not to me? Why? He knew Alan's wounds weren't fatal. Why tease me with the possibility?

"Not sure the chrome-dome look works for you, she-boss," Kirby says, giving me a critical eye. "Too much fish-belly white."

"Kirby," Callie chides. Surreality—Callie preventing someone from giving me a hard time.

"Relax, Callie," I say. "I'm not that fragile."

*Not while the lights are on, at least.*

"Well," Callie says.

Kirby punches Callie's arm. "She was worried about you, that's all. Big old softy, just as I suspected."

"Hit me again, and we'll see how soft I am," Callie sniffs, tossing her hair back.

Kirby grins. "That's my cue. I had to say hi and watch the entrance. I'll go check on my guys now." She stops as she's walking by me and gives me a bump with her hip. "Maybe we'll start calling you Nine-Finger Barrett, boss lady. Whatcha think?" She is out the door before I can offer a reply.

I'm left alone now with my team. Somberness sets in. Kirby is liked, but she's not one of us. Time for our true faces to come out.

"Too bad about the kid," Alan offers.

Callie sighs. "Leo was turning into a good man."

"We won't give him justice by talking about it," James says, razoring over us with an impatience that's just a little too raw. I look at him and I catch what I think is a spark of grief in his eyes. There, then gone. "Let's find the man who did this to him. You're our best and newest witness. What can you tell us about him?"

*I will tell you everything but the one thing, the thing I saw. Why? I don't know yet. It's a feeling, something whispering in my subconscious.*

"We're missing something about him, who he is," I begin. "Contradictions. The car crashes. The fingerprints. Letting Heather Hollister and me walk. If we operate on the assumption that he's pragmatism personified, then we have to assume that all of those things are purposeful, that they serve a higher aim. The other side of the argument would be that we got it all wrong to begin with."

I tell them everything I can remember about my incarceration. I leave out the specifics of the sun-drenched meadow and the theological debates with my baby.

"Again," James muses, "the sadism. Cutting your finger. It's at odds."

Alan shrugs. "Maybe not. What he does is pretty damn twisted. Maybe sadism is the altar he's praying at after all, and the money motivation is just a smoke screen, a way of hiding the truth from everyone. Even himself."

"Many of them do develop self-deception to an art form," Callie says.

Except the ones who have no shame about what they are. Nothing I saw painted Dali in that light. He knows what he is, and he's not worried about the next life.

"None of that is going to get us anywhere right now," I say. "Let's focus on what Leo told me. He thought Hollister was the one who tipped Dali off."

"Sounds like we need to have a little private chat with Hollister," Alan says.

"Leo also said that we should have a really good computer tech examine whatever server or servers Hollister used at his job. He said we might find something."

James nods, thoughtful. "Perhaps Dali made a mistake. It's almost impossible not to leave any footprints in the digital age. Maybe he knew that and knew his only option was to hide it really, really well, by enlisting the aid of those who could."

"I don't follow."

He waves me off. "Supposition. Let Callie and me get a tech on this. We'll chase the warrants. You and Alan should go and interview Douglas Hollister."

"Who died and made you boss?" Alan grouses.

"Am I wrong?"

"No, James," I say. "It's the correct division of labor. Let's get on it." My cell phone rings.

"Barrett," I answer.

"Who the hell cleared you to get back on the job?"

AD Jones.

"That would be me, I guess, sir."

"Too fucking soon, Smoky."

"Sir—"

"Get your ass up here."

I put the phone back into its holster. "I have to see the AD, Alan. I'll meet you in the lobby."

"Good luck," he calls after me.


"Jesus Christ" are AD Jones's first words when he sees me.

"Just me, sir," I joke, taking a seat in one of his leather chairs.

He rose as I came through the door. He sits down now. He regards me long enough to make me feel uncomfortable.

"Take a picture, sir. It'll last longer."

I get a sour look. "All flippant bullshit aside, Agent, what are you doing back here? I read your debrief, what there was of it. You just finished four weeks of incarceration and torture, culminating in the partial amputation of your little finger. Not to mention that you're balder than a billiard ball and pregnant to boot."

"Thanks a lot for that, sir." I'm losing my sense of humor about the hair loss.

He rubs his face with both hands. Sighs deeply. When he looks at me again, I see a man trying to get himself under control, to be reasonable. "You're on mandatory leave, Smoky."

"That won't stop me, sir."

Anger rises in his eyes. He tamps it down. "Why?"

"Because I'm not crazy now, but if I don't work on getting him, I really will be. That's the bottom-line answer."

He tries on a sympathetic face. It doesn't sit well on him; that's not how this man is built.

"I understand, Smoky. I really do. But I'm sorry. You're on paid mandatory leave until you get clearance from a shrink to return to work."

Rage sweeps over me, leaving me a little bit dazed by both its suddenness and its fury. I do my best to bite it back, but some of its fire and bile leaks into my voice.

"Can't follow that order, sir." The words sound like rock grinding against rock.

He points a finger at me and shouts, "You'll fucking follow orders or I'll have you escorted off the premises!" So much for sympathy.

"Go fuck yourself," I shout back, jumping up.

I hear myself speaking from a distance. It's me, yet it's not.

*Rein this in now, or something's going to happen here that you can't take back.*

AD Jones hits his feet as well. I'm not sure I've ever seen him this angry. It strikes me that this reaction is probably based as much on fear for me as anger at my defiance.

"Give me one good reason to keep you on the job!"

I explode inside. It's all internal. It's as though I'm in the meadow again, but this time the light is atomic. A mushroom cloud rises, and the winds erase the living.

This rage, I realize, is for Dali, not the man in front of me.

"Because, sir." My voice shakes. I grip the desk and look into his eyes. "Because he came into our world and he took two of us away and one of us is never coming back. He has to answer for that. Nothing is going to stop me from going after him."

I watch him struggle. He wants to destroy something right now, but it's not me. He slumps back down in his chair. "Fuck it and fuck you. Get out and catch him, then." He doesn't look at me. "If you screw up, you're fired."

My mouth opens in surprise. I'm angry again, rage thrums. "Fine." He doesn't seem to care.

No other response is forthcoming, so I turn and leave the office. A final glance back catches him looking after me. I'm shocked at the sadness I see in his eyes. It's as if he's already mourning my loss.

Why? Does he know something I don't?

# CHAPTER THIRTY-NINE

"Rough one?" Alan asks me as I drive. He'd offered to take the wheel, but I need the control and the speed.

"He wanted me to stay at home. Ordered it, actually."

"And?"

"I refused. He gave in."

He looks doubtful. "Just like that?"

I grip the steering wheel with my nine good fingers. The injured one throbs. "No. He said if I screw it up, I'm fired. Can you get a couple of Advil from my purse?"

He hands me two pills after a little bit of searching. He offers no wisdom but silence. We watch together as the road disappears beneath us. The sky is what California is always so ready to offer up: hopeful, blue forever, blessed by the sun.


We pull into the prison parking lot. It's about half full. A handful of people, mostly women, some pulling children along, head either to or from their cars. No one looks very happy.

"Up place," Alan observes. "Gotta love a prison."

It's true. The sky here somehow seems less blue. The sun frowns, shining not quite as bright.

"Good place for him."

"True," he agrees. "And others like him. Look, when we're done with this case, I'm out. I'm retiring."

I swivel my head in shock. "Retiring? Why?"

Alan peers at me with a mix of pity and . . . what? Disbelief? Yes. "Why? Are you serious?" He indicates his arm in the sling. "It's happened again, Smoky. I got shot. Leo got part of his brain carved away. You lost half a finger and spent time getting tortured while you're pregnant, for Christ's sake!" He shakes his head once, vigorously. "No more. Price is too high. You should think about the same."

"Quitting? No. Never."

"Why? What's so important about this job that you can't just walk away? You've done your part, sure as shit."

I twist my hands on the wheel and think about my answer. "It used to be because I know that evil exists. You understand? I'm not talking about morality or religion. I'm talking about an understanding. A certainty. There are people out there who exist—who *exist*—to hurt others. I know that. Can't unknow it. Have to do something about it."

"I follow that."

My finger is really starting to throb. I hope the ibuprofen kicks in soon. "Now? Truth? It's all I know. I'm afraid of being left alone with myself. If I don't have the job, I'll have to spend too much time with me. What'll happen then?"

"You'll heal, love your husband, love your daughter, raise your baby. Not a bad deal if you ask me."

If anyone else had been asking me these questions, probing me in this way, I'd be on the attack. Alan is different. He has seen the whole of me and remained my true friend.

"I'm hanging on by a thread here, Alan. I appreciate what you're saying, and I promise I'll give it all some thought, but right now it's going to take everything I have to finish this. Can you back me up?"

"'Til the cows come home. Let's go fuck this fucker up."

———

Hollister is a changed man, and not for the better. If his unraveling began during the interrogation at his home, it's been completed here.

Bruises decorate the right side of his face. He's missing four of his upper front teeth and four of the lower. His skin is gray and his eyes are filled with wildness and despair.

"Looking good, Hollister," I tell him. It is cruel. I can't help myself. I point at the bruises. "Gifts from a friend?"

Hate replaces the despair. "Fuck you, cow."

"Got a lover?" I press. "Let me guess, he got rid of those teeth so his cock could slide in easier, right?" Alan's hand against my arm, warning me.

I wanted to hurt Hollister, and his expression tells me I've hit home. "Fuck you!" he screams. Tears roll down his cheeks.

I grin. The cruelty is like a living thing inside me, something demonic and real. "So it's true! You're someone's property." My grin grows wider. "How's your asshole, Douglas? Got AIDS yet?"

He launches himself at me, tries to jump across the table. The restraints yank him short, like a dog on a leash. I laugh at him as Alan watches, aghast. Douglas collapses into himself, the rage burning away as fast as it had arrived. It's replaced by despair.

"Fucker won't leave me alone," he mutters, more to himself than to us. "He's too big, a monster. If I fight him off, he makes it worse."

My hatred evaporates, as his rage had. I feel tired, drained. "This is you paying for your sins, Douglas," I tell him. "You killed your own son."

To my surprise, he nods in agreement. "Yes. You're right, I think. Heather got what was coming. But Dana? And my boy? No, no, that's all on me. I got greedy."

Alan steps into the breach between us, taking advantage of the cessation of hostilities. "Douglas. I want to ask you something. If you answer honestly, it won't add anything to your sentence, but it might help make up for some of the things you've done."

He takes Hollister's silence as assent.

"Approximately five weeks ago, the man you call Dali shot me and took Agent Barrett and another agent hostage. The other agent was a computer expert, and he told Agent Barrett that he was convinced Dali had been tipped off by you."

He tries to hide it even now, but I see the truth in his eyes. It's a cunning light, a flash of self-satisfaction.

"Piece of shit," I whisper. I struggle to breathe, and I understand, at this moment, here and now, why they make you surrender your weapons before entering an interrogation room. I have no doubt that, if I had my gun, Douglas would have been dead a millisecond after I saw that light in his eyes.

He grins now. The missing teeth make it hideous. I can see his tongue.

"Did he do that to you? Cut off your hair? What else did he do?"

I recognize his cruelty. Warning bells clang in my head; the similarities between us need to end. But I'm helpless. All I can see is Leo and the choice that I made.

I lean forward, keep my voice calm, and put as much promise in my eyes as I can muster.

"You're going to die in here, Hollister. Fucked to death or shanked in the shower. You're going to die. That's a promise."

The grin fades slowly. I see uncertainty, followed by fear. I nod.

"That's right."

He rips his eyes away from mine with effort. Focuses his gaze on Alan. "All I did was send him an email. I told him that I was pretty sure you were trying to set him up." He glances at me. "I told him about *her*."

"How'd you send the email?"

"Prison library. Not supposed to have access, but there are some smart people in here. They have ways."

Alan digests this. I manage to hold my tongue. "That's good, Douglas," he says. "But the thing is, you told us you didn't have a way to contact Dali, remember?"

Douglas remains silent.

"Is there something on the servers you worked on that we need to know about?"

There it is again. The cunning light. Alan sees it too.

"Douglas?"

"I need protection. I'll trade segregation for information." He fumbles with his hands. He looks humble and frightened. "Please. I'll tell you what you want. Just get me away from him."

I want to jump up, tell him to fuck off. I want to laugh in his face and slap him. I hold myself back, waiting for Alan.

"Tell you what, Douglas," Alan says, his voice mild. "I'm going to let my experts comb those servers first. If they don't find anything, if I need your info, then I'll be back and we'll talk deals. If it turns out I don't need you"—he shrugs—"then have fun getting passed around." He leans forward. "Leo Carnes is a vegetable now because of you. Fuck off and die."

He stands up and heads toward the door. I follow, dumb.

I stop before leaving, turn.

"Why?" I ask Hollister.

He glares at me, his eyes full of tears and hate.

"Because," he says. "You ruined everything." He stands, strains against his chains, and shouts at the ceiling. The cords on his neck stand out; veins throb at his temples. "You ruined everything!" he screams.

Guards rush in as we leave.

Back to hell. I shudder a little at my own satisfaction. But only a little.


Alan sits as we drive, silent, brooding.

"Sorry about that, back there," I offer. "I'm still . . ." I sigh. "Maybe AD Jones is right and I'm not ready to come back. Anyway, I'm sorry."

He waves me off. "I understand—and that's the problem. Five years ago I might have reported you. Today? I was just as bad, and I still don't care." He sighs and falls silent.

The sky is blue again as we leave the prison behind, but invisible rain falls, trapping us, and only us, in a prison world of gray.

# CHAPTER FORTY

"We found it," James tells me.

It's mid-afternoon. Alan and I barely spoke on the hour-plus drive back to the office. What was there to say? We'd condoned the rape of a man because of our rage. We felt vindicated and soiled, all at the same time.

"That was fast," I say.

"It didn't take long. It wasn't that it was well hidden. It's that no one would have found it unless they were looking for it. It seems innocuous enough, and under most circumstances, it would be, but it did the job it was meant to do."

"Which was?"

"There were two programs. Both were installed with root access on the key servers at the ISP where Hollister worked. One was a search program. It would search email, chat rooms, instant-message logs when kept, and various other things, looking for combinations of keywords. *Kill my wife, divorce,* and *hate,* stuff like that. It was pretty sophisticated."

"Sounds cumbersome," I say. "Wouldn't you come back with thousands of results?"

"Yes, but the sophistication of the program was that it grabbed a one-line snippet of each 'conversation.' It's pretty easy to scan through and to then know what to discard and what to follow up on. Take a look."

He hands me a printed page. Each line is preceded by a date, a time stamp, a number, and, at times, an email address. "What's the number? An IP address?"

"That's right."

I read over the page and see that James is right. It's simple to separate the wheat from the chaff. The keywords are highlighted in bold type.

One excerpt from an email sent by bob4121 says: That diamond ring as a gift, just **killed my wife!**

"Good job, Bob," I murmur.

Another begins: I **hate my wife.** We are **getting divorced** and I **wish she was dead.**

I hand the page back to him. "I get the idea. What was the other program for?"

"It was a kind of digital drop. Like a mass mailer. Send a message to it, and it forwards that message to two or three hundred different free email addresses."

"Free makes it virtually impossible to trace," Alan points out.

"The first program interacts with the second. It puts together a summary and then passes it over to the digital drop. The drop program sends the summary to every email address on its list."

"What were the benefits to him of doing this?"

"Numerous. Since the programs are given root access, they have permission to access anything on any server they're placed on. This lets them perform without raising any red flags. They can get into email, server logs—anything they have the password for."

"Let me guess: Hollister provided the programs with the passwords they'd need."

"Unconfirmed, but it's the best guess. Initial installation of a program like that would have had to be done by an administrator or someone with the admin passwords to the server."

"Dali probably offered him a discount," Alan says. "When he found out that Hollister worked for an ISP, he probably said, *Put these programs on your servers and I'll cut fifty thousand off what you're supposed to pay me.*"

"Sounds risky," I say. "Wasn't he taking a chance by leaving a trail?"

"Yes and no," James explains. "They were very well written. They execute in the background and put no strain on the servers at all. They keep no logs themselves, and Hollister would do regular purges of references to the programs from the server logs. That's actually how we found them. Hollister hasn't been around to delete from the logs. Even if they were discovered—if Hollister had been hit by a car or had a heart attack—so what? They'd be dismissed as an interesting but generally unimportant exploit from a hacker. Even if they were followed up on, good luck tracing him via those hundreds of email addresses. Most of them are probably dormant, and even the ones that aren't could be set to forward to another address, which could then forward to another, ad infinitum." He shakes his head in reluctant admiration. "It's his brilliance. Keeping it simple. He had you for four weeks, for example. Can you tell us where the building was or what he looked like?"

"No."

"Same principle here. The difference is, Douglas Hollister took out some life insurance."

Excitement surges inside me. "What?"

"He modified the program, or got someone to modify it for him. It had a built-in IP logger. Here's how it worked: Dali would occasionally access the server directly so that he could modify variables that the programs used, such as adding or deleting keyword combinations or email addresses. Hollister had the program log every access to it."

"Why not just look at the server logs?" I ask. "Isn't every incoming access logged?"

"Sure. Millions of them."

"Ah."

"This was easier. It was isolated to the programs themselves, which meant the IPs logged would belong to Dali."

My eyes widen. "That's good."

"There's more. Douglas compiled a list of all the email addresses Dali was using and plugged them into a custom email program, which he then made Web-accessible. He could access the program in any Web browser and do two things with it: send an email out to those addresses, or email a list of them to himself. It's obviously how he sent the warning email to Dali from prison."

"More insurance," Alan says. "Maybe that's why Douglas got over-confident about not paying Dali off. Thought he could blackmail him."

"A miscalculation," James observes.

I frown. "Seems strange Dali wouldn't consider the possibility of something like this happening."

Callie speaks up for the first time. She's stayed quiet, though I've felt the weight of her gaze on me. "I think it goes back to what I talked about before: risk assessment. He could have weighed the possibility against the necessity and decided the risk was justified."

"He did take precautions," James continues. "We've tracked the IPs used to a series of Internet cafés, a library—he used public systems, probably paid in cash."

"Shit," Alan says.

Something stirs inside my head. A glimmering. I frown.

James looks at me closely. "What is it?"

"I don't know. I feel like what you just told me is trying to meet up with some other information about the case. I can't grasp it yet. Tell me again where he accessed the Web?"

He checks a paper. "Internet café. Internet café. Internet café. Library—"

"Stop." I feel it now, swimming toward me, growing in size and clarity. "Library. That's it."

"What's it?" Alan asks. "I'm confused."

"Earl Cooper," I say. I smile at James. "Which of these things is not like the other?"

"Library," he answers, nodding. "I get it."

"Explain it to the lesser minds, honey-love."

"Cooper talked about mental maps. We find places of comfort and security both consciously and unconsciously."

"I remember."

"Dali goes to Internet cafés because they provide anonymous access. It's a faceless location. He goes to a library for the same reason, and while it does provide the anonymous computer access, the location isn't faceless. Think about it. Libraries are personal places. They're cared for by someone, and they belong to a community. Librarians remember people. They keep an eye on the books, make sure the patrons don't mistreat them; there's a sense of ownership in a library that you're not likely to find in an Internet café."

"Not to mention the difference in the level of traffic going through it," James adds.

"Okay," Callie says slowly. "I'm starting to understand."

"Dali's careful, and while the choice of a library's not exactly what I'd call *high* risk, it is a behavioral anomaly. Remember what Earl said: Mental maps are formed both consciously and unconsciously. They exert their influence in both ways too. So why does Dali feel a connection with this library? Why does he feel unconsciously safe enough to use it?"

Alan snaps his fingers. "Because it's familiar."

"That's right. And why is it familiar?"

Callie supplies the answer this time. "Because it's in the area."

James sits down at his computer. He checks the library address and types it in. A moment later the location appears on Google Maps. "Down in the Valley," he says. "Near Reseda and Oxnard."

"Where are the property searches you guys did?" I ask.

"Here on the computer. I tabulated them by zip code. It didn't lead us anywhere. Too many of them, incomplete records, and so on."

"It's a shot in the dark, but let's try again. We can narrow the area now. Let's take the lists five miles in each direction from the library and look for anything that pops out. From what I recall, Cooper was on the money. It felt like a storage place. It had six- to eight-foot-high chain-link fencing around it."

"Lot of storage places in that area," Alan says.

"We can eliminate any franchises," James provides. "You're required to pay royalties, and you run the risk of inspections."

I nod. "That's good. So?"

"It's better than nothing," Alan agrees. "Start printing, James. We'll divvy it up and see what we see."

Five miles yields nothing. Excitement wants to die, to become discouraged, but we're used to this. Sift through the useless, nine out of ten times you find nothing but more useless. One time in ten you find a diamond. We've all found enough diamonds over the years to keep going.

We widen the diameter to ten miles. Alan grinds his heavenly grounds and brews coffee for all of us except James, who drinks green tea. He's always been that way. I've never seen him drink whiskey or Coke or take a sip of coffee. Tea and water, that's it.

When it does appear, it stands out in neon, and it makes my stomach dip. It's too simple, far too cute, and it makes me wonder again about Dali and the truth of what drives him.

*Meet Storage Solutions,* the entry says.

*I'm just storing meat.* Those were his words.

I check the distance. Just eight miles away from the library.

"I think I have it," I tell them.

I explain. Callie makes a face of disgust. "'Storing meat'? Gross."

James takes the address and types something into his computer. A page comes up with a list of facts. "It's been in business for more than twenty years. The building itself has been there longer than that, but not by much."

"He could have converted an existing structure," Alan points out. "Lot cheaper to do that in Los Angeles."

"Building permits were pulled twenty years ago," James confirms. "Doesn't say what they were for, but there were quite a few. The building was a concrete structure from the beginning." He taps a few more keys. "No income information. That's all I have. Not enough to be sure or to get a warrant, on the face of it."

"Let's go see it," I say. "I'll know if it's the place, and my testimony will get us a warrant if it is."


Space exists at a premium in Los Angeles, as with any large city. The best butts up against the worst, as all try to live in relative harmony. The address we find ourselves at sits on a large lot on a side street off Victory Boulevard. Next to the structure is a fenced-in, boarded-up gas station. A sign asks patrons to PLEASE BE PATIENT WHILE WE UPGRADE OUR FACILITIES! The sign is rain-battered and sun-faded, as though the upgrade of the gas station is long forgotten.

A half block away is Victory Boulevard, busy at all times of the day and night. Just around the corner is a bustling adult-video store, a fish-and-aquarium shop, and a haberdashery, just to name a few. Most signs are in English, some are not, but other than the gas station, every storefront seems occupied.

We've parked on a side street, and I stare at the structure from a distance. I'm standing outside the car. It's late afternoon now. The sun is still up but is lower in the sky, and a cool breeze kisses my baldness.

Is that it? Is that where it happened?

The fence looks the same, but I'm starting to understand just how little I actually got to see. Dali's brilliance, as James had said. The chain-link gate is padlocked.

"Well?" James asks.

"I can't get the angle I need to be sure."

"Then get the angle you need."

I raise an eyebrow. Sweat beads on my upper lip. I am a dichotomy of emotion. Flippantly afraid. "You mean climb over? That's breaking the law, James."

He looks away. "Leo Carnes was an agent. You're an agent. If we don't make someone pay for this, then we're all in danger. I'm going to emulate Dali's pragmatism on this one."

I look at Callie and Alan. "How do the two of you feel about this?"

"Hell is freezing over." Callie winks. "I agree with James."

"You know where I'm at," Alan says.

I examine my injured finger, flexing the hand. It hurts.

"I don't think I can climb it."

"We could cut the lock," Alan offers.

"No. What if he's there and watching the entrance? Even if he's not, what if he comes back while we're trying to get a warrant, sees that we've cut the lock, and bolts?"

"Good point. Then what?"

I use my hand as a visor, scanning the surrounding area. The gas station sits to the right. "What if we cut the lock to the gas station instead?"

We find a hardware store just a block away and buy a pair of bolt cutters. We cut the chain rather than the lock, so we can make it seem as though the fence is still buttoned up tight.

"Here goes nothing," I say. I enter the lot.

I make my way past the side of the station, parallel to the Meet Storage Solutions building, until I reach the back of the lot. I put my face close to the chain-link fence and peer at the concrete structure. I see a roll-up door that's big enough to let a car through. I turn around, putting it and the fence to my back. I crouch down, trying to get myself to the level I would have been when I was in the trunk. I stare at the sky, searching for certainty. I see nothing I could swear to recognize under oath.

*But you know this is the place. Do what's right.*

In my years as an agent, I have always prided myself on the truth that never once have I bent the law to serve my own ends. Searches have always been preceded by a warrant cleanly gotten. Arrests have always included a reading of rights, and those rights have been respected.

*What's a little lie if the plan is to kill him anyway?*

Something inside me answers, but I block it out. I walk back to the front of the lot and exit the gate.

"This is the place," I say. "This is where Dali took me."

"Goooood," Callie purrs. "Let's go get our warrant, my hubby's team, and a bunch of guns."

I'm going to voice my agreement when we hear a loud bang, as from a gunshot. Everyone reaches for their weapon.

"That came from the Meet Storage building," Alan says.

"Sounds like probable cause to me," I say. "James, cut the lock."

He doesn't hesitate—none of them does—and this, if nothing else, gives me pause. I am the leader. The shot caller. We should call it in, ask for backup. Let the guys with the big guns do the job they're trained for.

Another gunshot goes off, obliterating my doubts.

We draw our weapons.

Another gunshot.

"Jesus," Alan mutters. "What if he's executing prisoners in there?"

"Go!" I say.

James shoves the gate open and we make a beeline for the building's front door. I try the knob.

"Locked!" I whisper. I wave to the right. "Let's go around."

We head at a dead run toward the right side of the building. Sweat runs freely down my scalp. My heart hammers in my chest. My teeth chatter, and I feel cold and hot at the same time.

We get to the roll-up door. "Try it," I tell James.

He reaches down and, to our surprise, it opens without difficulty.

I recognize the space immediately. My heart does a jig.

This is where the darkness came.

"This is where he brought me," I say. "Entry into the main part of the building is through that door."

James rushes forward and tries it. Again, it opens without a problem. My finger throbs and, for a moment, I wish I could take a Percocet after all. Bells of alarm clang away in my head.

"Too easy," I tell James, putting my free hand on his back. "Let's go slow."

He frowns back at me. Nods. He takes the lead, entering. I am behind him. Callie and Alan are behind me. We head down the hallway, passing the three doors that I remember, turning right to find the stairs. We climb the stairs until we reach the top. To the right is the door that leads to the hallway my cell was in. To the left is another door.

"Left one," I whisper.

James opens it and we enter a longer hallway. Doors are on both sides. My stomach churns when I see the padlocks and hasps.

How many? Ten doors on each side? Are they all occupied?

I ignore my nausea and the yammering. We head down the hallway until it turns, and then there are only two doors, one at the end and one on the wall to the right. The doorway to the right is open. James puts a finger to his lips and inches toward it. I smell blood and death, that scent of shit and copper. James enters the room, gun trembling in his hands. I follow. The smells are stronger here.

I almost faint when I see the two tables and the two women there.

*This is it. The place where he made me choose.*

I lurch forward and vomit. Not because of the women with the fresh bullet holes in their foreheads, but because of the memories. My vision swims, and I stagger to one knee.

"You okay?" Alan whispers.

I can't respond. I point out to the hallway. We have another room to clear.

Then a sound of another gunshot, the fourth and last, louder this time. James and Callie race out the door toward the other room. I hear a door open and then I hear nothing. I force myself to ignore the flashing white lights behind my eyes. The meadow calls, maybe my baby is there waiting, but now is not the time. I walk out of the room on unsteady legs. The other door has been flung wide.

"What is it?" I call out. "Is everyone okay?"

"Come and see," Callie calls back softly. "Come and see."

I enter the room with my head and finger throbbing. It's a large room, made into an office. It's stark. The floor is uncarpeted, the walls bare and unpainted. A single file cabinet sits next to a cheap faux-wood desk. There's a computer monitor on the desk. A man is there too. His brains are splashed on the wall behind him.

"Coward," James mutters. "He must have known we were coming." He sounds frustrated. I understand. I wanted to kill Dali too.

"What about it?" Callie asks. "Do you recognize any part of him?"

I lean forward. I see an obliterated forehead above a set of surprised eyes and a slack mouth. I put him in his late forties to early fifties. His hair is in a crew cut, and it's a semi-handsome but mostly unremarkable face. All of these things fit, except for perhaps the most important thing: the thing I saw and kept to myself. I wasn't sure why I did it, before. Now I do.

"Yes," I say. "That's him. That's Dali."

It's a lie, but that's okay. I think I understand everything now.

# CHAPTER FORTY-ONE

We sit in my living room, Tommy, Kirby, and I. Bonnie is being watched by Alan and Elaina for a few days. They think it's to give me time to recover from everything that's happened. The truth is that it's to give me time to do what must be done.

"He knew you were coming because he was tracking the GPS chip in your phone," Tommy says. "The techs didn't find anything when they checked out your phone because there was nothing to find. He just locked on the signal and kept an eye out. A little reverse telemetry gave us what we need."

Kirby examines me with an unreadable gaze as she cracks her gum. "You sure about this, boss lady? I have no problem with it, but this is new territory for you." She nods a head at Tommy. "And you."

"I'm sure," I reply.

Tommy says nothing.

"Okeydokey," Kirby says, grinning. "Let's saddle up."

Eric Kellerman. That is the name of the man with the obliterated forehead. He was forty-eight years old. He was an orphan, adopted by no one but the city, put out to pasture when he was eighteen. There's not much after that but an excess of evidence.

His fingerprints matched the unknowns that were inside the body bags. Videos and photographs of the car accidents were found at the Los Angeles location, along with some poetry he'd written about how watching a car crash was better than having sex with any woman. There was a trunk containing over fifty thousand dollars in cash. Finally, in a desk drawer, held inside a plastic bag covered with his fingerprints, was the severed end of my own finger. It was all incontrovertible.

"The symphorophilia is what really clinches it," James had remarked. "The statistical probability that someone else would have that particular paraphilia at that location combined with all the other factors is next to nil. He was Dali."

The victims were the worst. Three women, all missing for a various number of years, most of them in worse shape than Heather Hollister. The husbands of these women were rounded up. Some broke quickly, some broke slow, but all of them broke. They were cowards at the core, narcissists whose biggest regret was being caught. They each had the same story, just sung to a different tune.

There were no clues to the locations of the Oregon or Nevada buildings. That's okay. Tommy, Kirby, and I found them ourselves. It took a little work, but we have them, and we'll provide an anonymous tip once we've done what we need to do.

I asked for time off, and it was given without any fuss. I think AD Jones was too relieved at my request to be suspicious. I hope. Director Rathbun wanted to do a press conference first, but he relented when I insisted I was in no shape to get in front of the cameras.

"Fine," he said. "Go home; rest. Get yourself together. But don't let the hair grow in too much before the conference. It's a great image. We'll use it to our advantage."

It wasn't all a lie. I did take a day or two to rest. Then I sent Bonnie packing and pulled in Tommy and Kirby and told them everything: what I knew, what I suspected, what I was unsure of. They were skeptical at first, until I told them about the thing I'd seen. After that, they shut up and listened.

Tommy had been the one to figure out that Dali was tracking the GPS chip in my phone. It's how Dali knew that I was closing in on the LA location. Once again, simplicity had been his brilliance. He knew the techs at the FBI would check out my belongings for bugs, so instead of installing one, he just figured out how to track what was already there.

Tommy had used his knowledge and technical contacts to reverse-engineer the GPS. This enabled us to track Dali. We counted on him taking no chances, and he didn't disappoint. Declared dead or not, he kept the tracker active, wanting to be sure that he knew where I was. Pragmatism was his higher power and, I had to admit, it had served him pretty well, until now.

He'd been busy, spending time in Nevada and then in Oregon. It was pretty simple to figure out the addresses of the other locations. He was in Nevada now, and we were getting ready to go see him. To end this.

To kill him.

I long to kill him. I want to watch the life go out of his eyes. His death will be like water pouring down a parched and dusty throat. Will it quench my thirst? I don't know. But it will keep him from coming after the people I love. That'll have to be enough.

"I'm going to give Raymond your phone," Kirby says. "He'll carry it around with him while he's watching Bonnie; that way it'll look like you're still here in LA."

"Good. Are we ready?"

"I am," Tommy says.

"The family that slays together, stays together," Kirby chirps, then giggles.

Tommy and I don't laugh.


We leave in the afternoon so we can arrive around dinnertime. The dark is better for what we're after. There isn't much talking; even Kirby keeps relatively silent. I watch California turn into the desert, feel the change of the temperature in spite of the air-conditioning. Watch as nothing turns back into the overwhelming something of Las Vegas. It appears as it always does, like some Flying Dutchman of a city. Mammon pricked his finger and let a drop of blood fall onto the sand. Up sprang Las Vegas.

There are two locations. One is the storage facility where he's kept his Nevada victims. The other is a house, titled to a name that surprised me, even as it confirmed what I suspected about Dali based on what I'd seen. The reverse GPS confirms that Dali is at home.

We rent no hotel. No paper trails, thank you very much. Besides, we won't need one. If you're going to commit murder, better to come in and leave with the night. A page from Dali's playbook of simplicity.

We do stop to eat at a diner on the outskirts of the suburb Dali's home is in. I have a cup of coffee and a slice of toast. Tommy has even less; he skips the toast. Kirby has a T-bone steak, two eggs sunny-side up, hash browns, toast, orange juice, and coffee.

"What?" she asks, noticing that I'm staring at her. "Girl's gotta eat. Who knows when we'll get a chance again?"

I'm sure she's right. She certainly has more experience at this than I do. My stomach, though, seems to contain the last bastion of my conscience. I stick to my coffee and toast.

Kirby finishes and sighs in satisfaction. "Good stuff. So—we ready to go kill someone?"


"It's the third house down," Tommy says.

We are parked on a suburban street, hidden under the nighttime shade of a rare tree. The homes are all adobe exteriors with rock and cactus front yards. Water is at a premium in Vegas.

"Small place," Kirby says. "Good cover. Never a smart idea to flash those ill-gotten gains around."

"Dali will have cameras," I say, "but not too many. No reason to feel insecure here, and, again, too much concern for security makes you stand out. This is a safe house, probably used only when Dali is in town. The primary residence will be in Los Angeles."

"How should we approach?" Tommy asks Kirby.

She grins, winks. "I'm for the direct method. I'll go knock on the door. It's not likely Dali knows who I am, right?"

"There's no guarantee of that."

She shrugs, pats the gun hidden under her light jacket. "If Dali doesn't answer, then I'll just have to pull out Big Red here and let myself in."

"Kirby," I caution. "We can't afford to draw attention to ourselves."

She rolls her eyes. "Relax, boss lady. Professional here, remember? This is a throwaway vehicle with false plates. You two pull those stocking caps over your faces, and we're golden. Trust me."

I don't trust her, I don't trust any of this, but I have no choice. Kirby is the assassin of the group. She's been killing for a long time and by all accounts is very good at it.

"Fine." I sigh. "We'll follow your lead."

"Just relax and wait to hear from me. Either I'll give you a chirp on the cell phones or you'll see me kicking the door in. Okay?" She winks one more time and exits the car.

"Crazy," Tommy mutters.

"Yeah."

We watch her saunter up to the door of the house and knock. A few moments pass. Then another few. Sweat beads on my head, annoying me.

The door opens. We can't see the occupant, but we do see Kirby reach into her jacket, push forward, and disappear into the home.

"Jesus," I breathe.

The lack of hesitation. Given who Kirby is, what she does, it's a disturbing glimpse into just how quickly a person could die.

About five minutes pass before my cell phone rings.

"I got Dali secured," Kirby says. "I left the front door unlocked, so just park in the driveway and come on in. No worries, right?" She hangs up.

I stare at the house. No turning back now.

"Well?" Tommy asks me.

"Let's go."


The home is not what I expected. I had pictured a kind of suburban gulag. No decorations on the walls, a single carton of milk in the refrigerator, freeze-dried microwavable food in the cupboard.

Instead, I find various paintings, photographs hung in tasteful frames. Most of it is good. Some of it is very good, particularly the photographs, which are a mix of subjects, from people to landscapes. The floors are honey-colored hardwood, inviting and warm. Throw rugs are tossed in tasteful and useful places. The furniture is clean and just less than new.

"Kirby?" I call out.

"In the living room."

"Is that music?" Tommy asks.

I strain an ear. "Classical. Beethoven, I believe."

We move through the entryway and sitting room and arrive in the living room. It's next to the kitchen, one broad, open space that builders are calling the "great-room concept." I don't like it. I like my rooms with walls. The living room has a nice couch, a midsize flat-screen TV, and a coffee table. Floor lamps light the space. The curtains on all the windows are drawn, and the blinds are closed on the sliding-glass door that leads into the backyard.

Dali sits in one of the kitchen chairs, cuffed at hands and feet, eyes cool.

"Hello, Mercy Lane," I say.

"Hello, number 35," she replies.

I suspected it, and then the name on the house's title confirmed it, but it still surprises me in the flesh: Dali is a woman. That thing I'd seen in my cell, the thing I'd kept to myself, had been a smooth neck, sans Adam's apple. Eric Kellerman's corpse, on the other hand, had a prominent one.

"How'd you know?" she asks me.

I don't answer right away. I take time to study the person who brought me to this shadow land, a place where murder is both accept-able and desired. She's a short woman, with a beautiful, aquiline face. She keeps her brunette hair cropped close, and it works for her. Her eyes are a shocking blue. She's wearing blue jeans and a thin pullover shirt. She looks stunning and innocuous, like a cobra with its hood down.

"That was some plan," I say. "How long have you had that escape hatch in place?"

Dali had been pragmatic in all things. This included planning for the possibility that we might someday find her. She'd decided to have a patsy, ready-made and waiting, and she'd sown the necessary seeds years ago. She put Eric Kellerman's fingerprints on the body bags. She faked the symphorophilia fetish, choosing it because it was so unique. If anyone closed in, it would be Eric Kellerman's corpse they'd find, along with his collection of car-crash memorabilia and his fingerprints.

Dali would be officially dead, and Mercy Lane would be safe for-ever. I'd considered the possibility that they were working together but had dismissed it; Dali was a solitary machine.

She shrugs. "The last piece fell in place eight or nine years ago. Eric. But I'd been laying the groundwork for a long time."

"The car accidents."

"Yes."

I vocalize what I've surmised, not so much for confirmation but because I want to show her that, yes, I figured it out, you weren't smarter than me, I win in the end. I want to wave it in front of her face and taunt her with it.

"So if we caught on to you—or someone else did—you could suicide your patsy and leave incontrovertible evidence behind to link him to the crimes: the videos and photos of the car wrecks. Too unusual, too distinct, to be any kind of coincidence. The fingerprints left on the body bags would serve as confirmation. Is that right?"

"Essentially. It was a good plan. Where did I go wrong?"

"You grabbed me."

She shakes her head. It's not assertive, just dismissive. "That's posturing, not logic. You were really no different, in terms of risk, than any other unit."

*Unit.* My finger twitches on the trigger guard at her use of the word.

"Fine. Let's just say that I'm more observant than most people. I saw something germane, and then you made the really big mistake of letting me go."

"What did you see?"

There's an edge to her voice, to the question. It's not driven by idle curiosity. She wants to know where she went wrong. Where did her pragmatism fail to serve her?

"Something. I saw something." I smile, and I know it's a cruel smile, even worse than the one I gave to Douglas Hollister.

Mercy scowls. "You're not going to tell me."

"No."

"Childish."

"But satisfying."

"So? What's the plan, then? Am I under arrest?"

"I'm afraid not."

Her face clears. "Ah, I see. You're going to kill me." She nods her approval. "That's smart. Practical."

"How'd you get Eric Kellerman to pull the trigger on himself?" I ask.

"I kidnapped Eric and a young woman almost nine years ago. I convinced him that the young woman was his illegitimate daughter. Eric was an orphan, so this had a particular significance to him. I tortured them both for years to demonstrate to Eric what I was capable of.

"A few years ago I told Eric I'd moved his 'daughter' to another facility. I gave him the choice: pull the trigger when the time came and I'd set her free, fail to do so and I'd keep her in darkness 'til she was old and gray." She shrugs. "He made his choice, as planned."

"And did you? Let her go?"

"Of course not. I killed her almost two years ago."

"Why?"

Mercy looks puzzled. The question, it seems, is a stupid one. "Eric had been suitably prepared. I had more than one hundred hours of recorded video available, on the off chance he demanded visual proof she was still alive. The woman was using up space, water, food, and electricity. I didn't need her anymore."

I feel Tommy stir next to me. He is as disturbed by this answer as I am.

"Why, Dali? Why did you do this?"

Mercy; Dali—I move back and forth between the names. She is both of them but neither.

"For the money, number 35, of course. My father had a daughter, but he raised me as a son. He taught me three basic lessons: Joy is everything that comes after survival. Survival is based on money. There is no soul; we're all just meat. He didn't only say these things to me, he proved them." She pauses. "For example, he took the woman meat of me and turned me into a man."

I frown, taking in the beautiful face. "You look pretty female to me."

"That's my cover, number 35. The mask I wear in the outside world. Would you like to see the real me?"

"Yes."

The eyes go flat. The face changes subtly, becoming more brutal. The shoulders drop, and a faint aura of menace surrounds her. "Go ahead," she says, speaking to Kirby but looking at me. Her voice has changed, lowered, deepened, becoming the voice I'd heard outside the trunk. "Go ahead and check my breasts."

"Excuse me?" Kirby asks.

"Feel my breasts."

Kirby raises an eyebrow at me. "Go ahead," I say.

"If you insist." She winks. "I prefer the men, but I've been known to like the ladies too." She reaches down without hesitation and squeezes Dali's right breast with her left hand. She frowns. "That doesn't feel right." She reaches inside Dali's shirt. I watch as her hand fumbles.

Distaste passes over her face. Her hand comes out clutching something breast-sized and rubbery. "Silicone," she says. "Nothing else."

"Do you see?" Mercy Lane rasps. "Just meat to be molded. Dad cut away my breasts when they'd finished growing. He said they'd make me weak, that it was too hard for a woman to survive in this world." She smiles. "He made me strong."

I search for pity, but even now all I see is Leo. My desire to pull the trigger has been transformed into lassitude. The injured finger throbs.

"Time to die, Mercy," I say.

She shrugs. "Meat to meat. I was going to die sooner or later. We all go back to the dirt."

I screw on the silencer and walk over so that I am facing the creature in the chair, this breastless woman with the man's voice and the faded, empty blue eyes. I raise the gun and point it at her forehead.

A last question.

"Why did you change such a successful MO? The notes telling us you existed, letting Heather go without a lobotomy, releasing me: Why'd you do those things, Mercy? They made no sense."

She cocks her head and gazes up at me. I see no fear there, no anger, no acceptance. Mercy Lane lives in the now of an animal, a human convinced that it has no soul. She has nothing to lose to death.

"I devised my business plan years ago, after a tremendous amount of analysis. I tried to consider everything, and that included my retirement. However perfect the execution, if you do the same thing too many times, you'll eventually make mistakes. Eric's involvement was a part of that plan. He wasn't just a—what did you call it? An escape hatch?"

"Yes."

"Right. Eric wasn't simply something to use in an emergency, he was the cornerstone of my retirement plan. The best way to fade into the sunset, when you've been running a criminal enterprise, is to let people think you're dead."

"We've already covered this. You're not answering my question."

She continues blithely, as if I hadn't spoken, as though I'm not holding the gun that is going to kill her.

"I needed someone to find Eric after searching for me, in order to bring my retirement plan to completion." She looks at me again, and I see an acknowledgment of some kind in her eyes. "I'd researched you, among others. You're very good at what you do, very competent.

"When Douglas Hollister violated our agreement, he provided me with the opportunity to start laying bread crumbs. You were the logical recipient, given the geographical area. Dropping Heather off at the wedding was the first step. I knew keeping her cognizant, so she could tell you what she'd been through, would motivate you more than handing her over as a vegetable."

I stare at her and my head starts to spin.

"So . . . you *wanted* us to find you?"

"On my terms, but, yes. More precisely, I wanted you to find Eric Kellerman and think it was me. That would allow me to retire un-incarcerated."

It all shivers into place. The discrepancies in the profile. The notes. Letting Heather go intact, grabbing me. These weren't accidents; they were planned, purposeful anomalies.

"Kidnapping you was key," she continues, "as I knew it would provide motivation like nothing else."

I press the silencer into Mercy's forehead, hard. My hand shakes and my heart thunders. "So all that—everything you did to me—it was just for *show*?" My voice is too loud, almost a shout.

"Quiet, boss woman," Kirby murmurs. "Don't wake the neighbors."

Mercy gazes up at me, unafraid. "It needed to be authentic."

"And Leo?" I ask, the gun trembling in my hand. "Why him?"

She shrugs. "More incentive. When I found out who he was and what he was doing, I decided to utilize him as well."

My stomach heaves, and I feel momentarily faint.

*If . . .*

I try to push the thought away, but it rolls over my resistance, inexorable and oh so ugly.

*If I hadn't used him in the undercover operation, he'd still be okay.*

I want to vomit. I am filled with self-loathing and regret and a terrible rage. I stare at Mercy, and I search for something, a reason to wait. I see nothing, nothing at all.

I take one step back and raise the gun and I quiet my mind, but my mind is a hurricane of hatred and grief and it breaks that silence. I see too many things all at once, visions of light tracers and dark moons and Leo's empty eyes.

"You deserve to die," I whisper, the gun trembling in my hand.

"No one deserves to die," Mercy says. "It just happens."

A wide wind blows through me, pushing me toward a chasm with no bottom, an ocean with no shore. My senses have sharpened to an excruciating point. I can smell gun oil and the scent of shampoo. I hear Tommy's foot shift on the floor and feel his eyes upon me like touching hands.

*Don't do this, Mother. I don't want to be born in death.*

I don't know who this voice belongs to. Is it Alexa? Is it the baby? Is it just me?

My finger tightens on the trigger, feeling the resistance that is both too much and not enough, a march toward destruction that can't be reversed once the final step is taken.

"What are you waiting for?" Mercy asks.

A phrase rolls through my mind. It sounds like a gull's cry, echoing above the wind.

*The lighthouse! Swim out too far and the light goes out forever!*

My finger moves back on the trigger, pulling it toward me.

*I want to kill you so bad. I want to look into your eyes and pull the trigger and watch as the hole opens up and your life pours out. I want to know that you died because of me, because of what you did to Leo, because no one gets to touch my family like that and live.*

I lower the weapon. Small rivulets of sweat run down my cheeks, dancing across my scars on one side. I feel as though I've run a mile and then boxed ten rounds.

*I want to kill you, but I can't.*

"You're under arrest, Mercy." My voice quavers.

She shakes her head, a gesture of pity. "You're weak."

Tommy says nothing. He places a hand on my shoulder and squeezes it once, gently. He is with me.

"What an anticlimax," Kirby murmurs.

But there's a quality to her tone that tells me maybe, somewhere down inside her, she is relieved that I did not do what she would have done so easily.

I wade back in from the big, dark deep and collapse on my shore, while the lighthouse burns and the foghorn blows.

# CHAPTER FORTY-TWO

AD Jones sits in the living room, watching me. I called; he came. Mercy Lane remains shackled and silent. Tommy is tense. Kirby is bored.

"Sir?" I venture.

I can't decipher the look he's giving me. It seems weary and angry and rage-filled and sad. There is no confusion. It's as though he's been expecting to find himself in this place. He is not surprised, but he longs for all the moments that came before.

"I'm going to do something here," he says to me, finally speaking. "Just this once." He surveys Dali/Mercy, who is unperturbed. "Because she took your finger and your hair. Mostly, because you didn't pull the trigger, which means you're still a person to me."

I swallow and nod. I'm unable to speak. My throat is choking suddenly with the force of unshed tears. Grief has replaced my desire to kill. My finger and my hair, he says out loud, but those just stand for all the other things, the things he means but has left unsaid.

"This is it, Smoky," he continues. "This is what you get in return for what you've lost. This one pass. *Just this once.* You understand me?"

My eyes tell him that I do.

"Okay," he says. "Here's what's going to happen."

It was a simple lie, the best kind. I'd gone to AD Jones with my suspicions about the identity of Dali. He'd given me permission to poke around on my own. Everything else followed on the heels of that. The reverse GPS. The trip to Vegas. The confrontation based on manufactured probable cause.

Mercy Lane will be taken into custody by the AD and flown back to Los Angeles on the jet. Kirby will fade into the background, never here. Tommy and I will drive home while the AD flies in Callie and others to oversee evidence collection.

It's a rickety story, full of holes, ready to leak, but it'll be enough. We know how to break the law. It's something you do quietly, with few witnesses, and only ever with those you trust.

"Your involvement has to be at a minimum from this point on," he says to me. "I'll handle everything else."

"Thank you, sir."

He sighs. The rage is gone; just the sadness remains. Watching him be sad is like watching rain fall against a mountain. Something solitary. He folds the sadness away after a time, back inside himself, and the rain ends. Just the mountain remains, eroded by such moments.

Mercy Lane clears her throat, attracting our attention. "Let's bargain."

AD Jones frowns at her. "What the fuck do you have to bargain with?"

"I've been weighing all the variables, and you haven't left me with any options. You're going to find evidence of the GPS tracker here, as well as other things. I could try to tell a story about kidnapping and attempted murder by the FBI, but I wouldn't be believed. The only thing left for me to control is the comfort of my incarceration and whether or not I live or die."

"It'll be hell and then you'll die," Kirby chirps. "Count on it."

Mercy ignores her. "The easiest way to lie is to not have to lie at all. If you'll concede to certain comforts and agree not to pursue the death penalty, I'll confess freely and accept whatever prison time you want to impose. Our stories will match and no one will ever be the wiser."

She's calm, reasonable, cold. AD Jones gapes. I touch his arm with a hand.

"You confess here, now, on video," I say. "It has to be bulletproof. And you go to jail forever."

She inclines her head. "Agreed."

This is Dali, this is Mercy Lane. The face of pragmatism. Survival is the only prize worth having.

"I don't know," AD Jones mutters. "We'll have to get approval from the attorney general's office first."

"We can get it," I say to him. "Tell someone who's interested that I'll owe them a favor. They want me, remember?"

He is quiet for a time. "Yeah. I guess that's true." He waves a hand, dismissing us. "Get out of here. I'll go sell your soul for you."

Tommy drives us home, as silent and inscrutable on the return as he was on the approach. I have no sense of him right now. Kirby seems untroubled but empathetic, content to keep quiet as long as the radio is on.

We pull into our driveway as the sun is coming up.

"Hop on out and turn over the keys," Kirby says, fresh-scrubbed and bright, a blond and guiltless Pontius Pilate. "I'll get rid of this vehicle and the guns and that'll be that." She winks. "What happens in Vegas, stays in Vegas right?"

Tommy sits on the edge of the bed, examining his hands. I sit next to him. His silence has become a solidity, something pervasive, like a wall of smoke or a bank of fog.

"Tommy," I venture. "Can I ask you something?"

"Sure." He continues to look at his hands. His voice sounds far away.

"Are we okay?" I ask.

His eyes focus on me now, but he seems confused, as if I just shook him awake.

"Of course we're okay. We're fine."

"Then what's wrong? You're a quiet guy, but never for this long."

He goes silent again. Watches the wall. "We almost killed a human being, Smoky," he murmurs. "We hunted her down and we were prepared to execute her, to bury her body in the desert. That deserves some thought. That deserves my *attention*. Don't get me wrong, I knew that's what we were going to do. I played my part with both eyes open. But we almost took a life, cold-bloodedly. I would have done it too. You pulled us back from the brink, but I would have done it if you hadn't. I don't want to hold that under or push it aside or ignore it in any way. I want to feel it."

I swallow my grief and my pain and my faint self-loathing.

"How does it feel?" I ask him.

He doesn't answer right away. I watch him struggle. I observe evidence of sadness and strength, a mixture of love and loss, and, above these things, endurance. Tommy, I realize, is what my dad called "a laster."

*A laster,* Dad told me, *is someone who can endure everything without losing who they are. Like this woman I read about recently. She and her family were sent to the concentration camps in World War Two. She was twenty-five, married to her childhood sweetheart, had three children. She was the only one who made it out alive. She healed and went on to find new love and have another two sons. She died surrounded by her children and her grandchildren. A laster. Your mom is one.*

*What about you?*

*Me? No. I'm not a laster.*

Dreamer though he was, Dad always judged himself honestly. I think that's one of the reasons Mom let herself love him.

"It feels bad," Tommy answers. He flexes his hands into fists, releases them. "But it'll pass."

I come into his arms, a sign of assent, but in my heart of hearts, that place where we're always alone, I am less certain.

What does that make me?

Am I a laster?


We nap through the morning. It is a fitful sleep, filled with dreams I forget the minute I jolt awake. Just one image I am allowed to keep: my mother, silent. She watches me, not judging, not sad, warning me even as she understands.

*Don't forget the lighthouse,* her eyes seem to say. *Swim out too far and you're too far out. Don't forget, honey, because that ocean is always dark and always bottomless and when you sink, you sink forever.*

I snuggle into my husband and search for whatever peace he can give me.

# CHAPTER FORTY-THREE

"What was your father's name?"

"Thomas Richard Lane. *Corporal* Thomas Richard Lane."

Here we are again, I think. Back to the center of the circle.

I am sitting across from Mercy Lane in a cold, concrete interview room. We are alone. The walls soak up all the sound, and this gives me goose bumps, reminding me of the dark and the meadow behind my eyes.

But I hide my discomfort.

"Your father was in the army?"

"He fought in Korea." She pauses, mulling something. "He was really made for it."

"For what?"

"Surviving."

I had reached out to Mercy with the offer of a standard interview, the kind I'd done for the BAU ten or more times before. She'd accepted, whether out of boredom or because she was, in the end, no different from all the rest of them, I don't know.

It's an opportunity to try to understand this person who almost turned me into a murderer. It's also a chance to get the answers to some questions. There are some loose ends. They've been gnawing on the soft parts of me at night and interrupting my sleep.

"Why was survival so important to him?"

"Because survival is the only thing that *is* important. Everything else is a bonus, not a necessity."

She's impatient with my question, even a little hostile. I consider her reaction and change gears. "Fair enough," I say, keeping my voice agreeable. "But your father seemed especially attuned to that truth. Why do you think he was able to recognize it so clearly?"

She relaxes. I've told her that her father was not just right but a visionary. This is comfortable ground for her. It doesn't matter that he hacked off her breasts and twisted her spirit. She's a cripple who thinks she can run.

"Various reasons. He grew up very poor, I know that. His mother was a prostitute and his father was a drunk who molested him. He had a younger sister and a younger brother. His mother died when he was still young, and then his father pimped out the children to keep himself in booze. It all prepared him for an understanding of the realities of life. He passed those understandings on to me."

It's a terrible story, but I find myself unmoved. I've heard of worse things happening to good men and women, people who didn't grow up to abuse their children or become serial killers.

"That must have been difficult," I allow.

She shrugs. "That's life. Eat or be eaten."

"How did they get through that?"

"Two of them didn't. The sister killed herself. The brother was murdered by a john."

"And your father?"

A glint of pride appears. "Once his brother died, he decided he'd had enough. He killed his father and buried him in the woods with the rest. Then he went into the army."

"Why do you think he chose that path? The military, I mean."

"Pragmatism. The army would house him and feed him and teach him how to kill skillfully. Also, the Korean War was happening."

"Was that a major factor?"

She nods. "My father said that war is a bloody crucible. You go in human. You come out with death in your veins. You become stronger. He'd learned the necessity for strength."

"Stronger why? Because you've lost your humanity?"

She looks into my eyes and I look behind hers. I try to see into the emptiness, but there's nothing to see.

"Are you familiar with Buddhism?" she asks me. It's a strange, abrupt question.

"Not very."

"At its essence, Buddhism is based on the idea that the spirit is the only thing that's true. Everything else that we see or feel"—she slaps her chest with her hands, indicates the hushed concrete walls that surround us—"all these material things are just illusion. Mara. According to Buddhism, as long as man believes that Mara, is what's real, rather than the soul, he's trapped. Doomed to the cycle of rebirth, life, and death, what they refer to as Samsara. Reincarnation."

I say nothing, fascinated at this story of the soul from a monster's mouth.

"But Buddha had it backward," she continues. "Don't you see? It's not Mara that's the illusion. It's the *soul*." She slams a fist down on the table. "This table is real. The pain I feel when I hit it too hard, that's real. The soul?" She shakes her head. "Just a dream. Buddhism, Christianity, they all put you to sleep." She leans forward, excited and grim. *"War wakes you up."*

I stare at her, speechless. I can't help it. She looks off, seeing something invisible to me.

"He loved it there, you know. In Korea. He told me a story one time about strangling a man in a rice paddy while the sun rose and the rain fell. *That man died with water in his eyes and rice in his ears, hearing thunder.* That's what my father said." She pauses. "All the lies are stripped away in war. All those illusions about beauty and ugliness, or goodness and badness, about any of them being important. In war, it's meat against meat, to the death. The naked truth." She sounds almost wistful. My stomach turns a little.

I gather myself and continue.

"What happened to your father?"

"He died of cancer."

"Were you sad when he died?"

"I was regretful. He was my teacher. If he'd lived longer, I would have learned more."

Nothing rises in her eyes at this. No hint of grief, no longing for the man who raised her. I try to picture him in my mind, but he is faceless, a burning man, branding his child as he'd been branded, scarring her deepest where it would never show.

It's the same story I've heard before, too many times. Monsters who were made by monsters who go on to make monsters themselves. A chain stretching both forward and back into darkness.

Sometimes the link breaks, the light abides. Too many times it does not. I think about Hawaii, about the blackness between the stars, about how there will always be more darkness than points of light.

"What did you do with the women you kidnapped once you received payment from their husbands?"

"I killed them, of course."

"And the bodies?"

"They were cut into pieces and the pieces were burned. The bone was ground to powder and everything was scattered."

I sigh inside at this. Though it wasn't entirely unexpected, I'd held out hope for reuniting at least some of the remains with their loved ones.

"How many victims did you take in total?"

She doesn't have to think to come up with the number. "Forty-seven, including the women you would have found when you raided my other facilities."

Forty-seven. It sounds like such a small number until you extrapolate it. Heather Hollister, forty-seven times. Avery and Dylan and Douglas again; all the world in a water drop.

I consider the number and something occurs to me.

"If you'd gotten up to forty-seven, why was I number 35?"

"Obfuscation. I didn't number in sequence. If someone escaped, they wouldn't be able to give an accurate count."

"Very careful of you."

She shrugs, dismissing the praise. "You can't control all the factors in life necessary to guarantee survival, but failing to control every single one you *can* is simple incompetence."

"I can see that." I consult my notes. "The next set of questions has to do with some apparent inconsistencies in what you called your retirement plan. There are some actions that don't add up, at least on the surface."

"Go ahead," she says, infinitely agreeable.

"First, broadly: How did you plan to ensure we'd find your Los

Angeles location? I get the factors you put into play—Heather, the messages, kidnapping me—but none of those in and of itself was a guarantee. I'd assume you'd want a lock."

She nods. "The plan was to continue to drop clues that would lead you to me—or Eric as me—and to do it in a believable fashion."

"Believable how?"

"By laying the groundwork for the apparency of what you call decompensation."

Decompensation means, literally, "the deterioration of a structure." In the area of profiling serial offenders, it's used to describe a pattern of devolvement. Many serial killers, even those who begin their careers as extremely organized individuals, eventually fall victim to their own underlying insanities. They start to deteriorate. To fall apart.

Words come to me:

*I flipped a coin.*

*I'm not a cruel man.*

Mercy said these things to me when I was imprisoned in her custom gulag. They contradicted her profile at the time. They might make sense now.

"Forcing me to make that choice about Leo, trying to convince me you cared about seeming cruel—those were a part of it, weren't they? They were supposed to make you look a little bit off."

She smiles, but not in pleasure or cruelty; those emotions appear absent in her. "That's correct. The messages and the deviation with Heather were a part of that framework as well. They were illogical changes to a formerly flawless methodology. My plan was to continue increasing evidence of my 'aberrant behaviors' until a huge and obvious mistake became a believable act. You'd assume I'd decompensated, and you wouldn't question the incompetence that led you right to me."

"That's also why you left some victims behind for us to find, right? To show us that, as far as you were concerned, it was just business as usual and you were unaware you'd started losing your marbles?"

She shrugs. "As I've already said."

I tap a pen on the notepad in front of me. "That's all very elegant, Mercy, but it leaves a big question unanswered: Why go through any of it at all? No one even knew you existed. Why not just walk away?"

She gives me a tolerant, almost pitying look.

"What I said earlier applies: Failing to control all the factors you can control is simple incompetence. If I 'walked away,' as you put it, I would have left uncontrolled factors behind that might have become detrimental to me. No one knew I was there then, but that could have changed in the future. Someone like yourself might have seen a pattern, become suspicious, and started looking. It's always possible I forgot something or made a mistake, however slight." She shakes her head once in the negative. "Hope is not a viable scenario. Certainty is."

I take all this in, almost as dumbfounded as I am enlightened.

What does this remind me of? Some computer phrase. Ah, right: *garbage in, garbage out.*

Mercy had locked herself into the necessity of calculating every possibility. In the end, it was that need to control all the variables that undid her. Pragmatic simplicity was defeated by an overabundance of complexity. Her brilliance became her psychosis.

Another question occurs to me now. I hesitate before asking it, not sure I really want the answer.

"Mercy, what would you have done if I'd told you to take me instead of Leo?"

"Oh, I still would have selected him. You were a necessary part of my plan. He wasn't. It wouldn't have mattered; going against my own rules for no apparent reason would have only made me seem more irrational in the end."

I have spent time dealing with my grief and rage about Leo. I've plumbed my own depths, and while I haven't found peace, I've managed to restore my equilibrium. This revelation threatens to unseat me. I feel the anger rising, and it speaks to me in tongues, hinting that it might not be so bad to kill Mercy Lane, after all. I struggle against it and manage to push it back down.

Something to deal with later, not here.

"Let's move on." It comes out a little bit hoarse. I clear my throat. "I want to discuss your methodology."

"Certainly."

I spread my hands palms up, in a gesture of query. "Why did you keep them?"

She frowns. "I don't understand. Why did I keep who?"

"The victims you kidnapped. Why keep them? We had our theory, but I want to hear what you have to say. If the motivation was money, wasn't that an unneeded expense?"

"I considered that for a long time when I was doing my initial business plan," she says, nodding. "In the end, I realized that keeping them alive was the best form of control when it came to the husbands. It has to do with what they really needed." She cocks her head at me. "Consider it. I'm sure you'll get it if you do."

It's a riddle or a test. They rarely give up everything for free. When they're locked away, mind games are the last games they have.

I think about the words she said. *What they really needed.* I turn them over in my mind, again and again, and then it comes, like a flare of light. This, I think, was the extra piece, the motivation James and I had sensed but not seen.

What was the one thing, above all others, the husbands had wanted when it came to their wives, more than money or freedom or custody?

*They wanted them dead.*

It was all about hate at the bedrock. Mercy had withheld this prize until payment, like a carrot on a stick.

I consider her with new eyes. I'd assigned a certain heavy-handedness to her methods before. Now I see she had a genuine gift for understanding all these emotions—revenge and rage and fear—for how to grow each one and make them move where she wanted.

"Very insightful."

She shrugs again. "I found out early that I had a gift for estimating behavior."

Except for your own, I think. But then, I guess that's true for all of us.

"Next question: why that particular business plan? You say your motivation was money. Keeping someone for seven years seems like a very long time to wait for a payoff."

She shakes her head once, impatient with me. "You keep saying that. The motivation wasn't money, it was survival. Money just happens to be crucial to survival in this society at this time."

"I apologize. But why that plan?"

She pauses for almost a full minute before answering. "I examined the subject of wherewithal in detail a long time ago. Unless you are very lucky and win the lottery, or inherit, or have a special talent such as an actor or musician, wealth is unlikely. The surest way is to take from those who have."

Her face is almost animated as she talks. This is a subject she feels something about, at whatever level.

"Think about it. Commerce at its core is simple. It's about finding someone with money and taking it from them. In the traditional non-criminal world, that translates into bargaining, and since force is not applied, the outcome is always uncertain. Perhaps he likes the car you're selling but his wife doesn't. Perhaps the stock market takes a downturn that was never expected and—worse—was beyond your control." She shakes her head, dismissing the idea of being a victim to these scenarios. "As I said before, you can never control every factor in life. The key to survival is to control the ones you can, and criminal enterprises satisfy that paradigm. You identify the man with the money, and you take it from him. That's the most controlled way, the most *likely way,* to acquire wealth."

I interrupt her. "Why is wealth so important? If it's all just about survival, like you say, then what's the worry about an excess? Isn't it enough to pay the grocery bill and the rent?"

"Factors, control. Better to have too much money and never need it. Abundance deals with probabilities. It increases the possibility of survival in the face of eventualities you can't predict."

It's an answer to the question, but it seems empty somehow. In spite of everything I've heard so far, I still can't *feel* Mercy. The intimacy I usually achieve, that sense of almost becoming what they are, is absent. When I try to understand her, it's as if I'm peering into a void. It's like trying to merge with nothing.

"Go on."

"So I examined all the most direct methods. Theft. Bank robbery. Selling drugs or women. They all had their pluses and minuses, but one glaring fact stood out: Most criminals end up in jail. It's almost inevitable. Rather than picking a criminal enterprise and planning how not to get caught, I decided to look at the factors that encourage that outcome and derive from there.

"I spent a lot of time listing the reasons a criminal ends up in prison. There were two I kept returning to as basic common denominators. One of them is partly an answer to your question about waiting. It's also an answer, though you haven't asked, about why I always had a plan for my retirement."

Now we're getting somewhere. This is important. I can sense it.

"What were they?"

She ponders me for a moment, as though she's trying to decide whether or not to share these insights. "The first became a kind of axiom. I even wrote it that way: *a greater or lesser inability to define and control the factors of the environment in which the crime is committed*."

It's my turn to frown. "Sorry, I don't follow."

"Let's use the thief who breaks into homes as an example. Each time he goes out to commit his crime, he's stepping into someone else's environment. It's not his. It doesn't belong to him. However much he plans, something could have changed the day before he enters the house. Perhaps the family bought a dog that morning, or the father finally gave in to his wife and signed that contract with the alarm company."

"When you took those people, you were entering into an environment that wasn't yours," I point out.

"True. But remember what I said: You can never control every factor, you simply control as many as you can. If you look at my business, there were really only two times I had to leave the environment I controlled: when I kidnapped the women, or in the rare instance when I was forced to punish husbands who refused to pay. Everything else was done if, where, when, and how I decided, within the environment I had created.

"Of all the variables in a strange environment, the one that can be the most unpredictable is the human factor. The more people there are, the less control you'll have, no matter how much you plan. In my business model, the human factor is kept very, very low. Me, the husbands, the wives. That's it. Control of the environment."

There are a hundred possible holes in Mercy's logic, but I remember what Callie said about Mercy's assessment of risk and reward, and decide she was right. Mercy had accepted that zero risk was impossible, so that wasn't the goal; the goal was the least for the most.

"What was the second factor?" I ask.

"The answer to your original question: time. Kill once in a lifetime and you're far more likely to get away with it than if you kill every year. Kill every year and your chances of getting caught are less than if you kill once a month, and so on. That encompasses going on too long, which is why I had a retirement plan envisioned before I even started.

"From another view, steal a valuable item and sell it a week later and your chances are worse than if you wait a decade. *Speed is greed*.

My father used to say that." She nods, partly to herself, caught in a memory. "My business model wasn't perfect, because perfection is impossible, but it certainly solved the time factor."

She smiles at this, and then she stretches, her bones creaking comfortably. She settles back, regarding me. She seems as she has since I came here: relaxed, patient, neither striving nor avoiding. "The thing is," she says after a moment, "I've answered your question, but I don't think you'll ever *understand* it. Not really."

It's an echo of my own earlier doubts. I want to understand, I really do. I've spent my life hunting these creatures. In the end, whatever the twists or turns involved, I've always come to that understanding, deep and intimate, of who they are. It's what's kept me sane. Shine the sun on them and they lose their power over you. Fail to drag them out of the shadows . . .

"Try me," I say.

She leans forward, intent. "All we are is our next breath, and joy is everything that comes after survival. As long as I had sufficient funds to keep a roof above my head and to eat my next meal, time wasn't important. It wasn't about acquiring wealth quickly. It was about knowing it would be there one day and not getting caught in the meantime."

The last part of that gets my attention, and I pounce on it. "Where does freedom fit with your philosophy, Mercy? If it's all about meals and a roof, what's the big deal about jail? You'll go on breathing, sleeping. You have your three hots and a cot right here."

Regret flashes in her eyes. "I was right," she says, shaking her head at my apparent obtuseness. "You'll never understand." She rubs her eyes with one hand, like a teacher with a difficult student, searching for patience. "We'll try it one more time. Listen. Are you ready?"

"Yes."

She speaks slowly, enunciating the words as if she were talking to someone a little slow on the draw. "The only thing wrong with prison happens to be the most important thing that can be wrong: *It's an environment you can't control.* A lack of control always includes the possibility of death. It's not about the freedom, it's about the *variables* and how they could affect your ability to draw that next breath."

I stare at her, and suddenly I do understand. The sun bursts out, and the shadows die, and there she is: strange, but no longer scary. I understand why she was trapped by her own brilliance. I grasp her endless need to calculate every variable and why she needs to control every factor to the point of obsession. Mercy was a new kind of monster, that's all. It had taken me a little more time.

"You're a machine," I murmur, a little bit amazed, a little bit sickened. "A machine tasked with reducing the factors that could result in nonsurvival to as close to zero as possible."

She blinks, surprised. Then she smiles, and it's the first genuine smile I've seen from her. It's almost beautiful. Maybe it just seems that way because it hints at the truth: Once upon a time, this was human.

"Yes!" she says. "That's *exactly* right."

I spend the next few hours asking about her childhood and her life, but they only serve to confirm what I already know. She is an empty box of air, a moving mannequin, three dimensions outside, two dimensions in. She has become what she preaches and what she was made: just meat, devoid of love or hatred, a machine with legs, calculating the problem of bare survival for as long as she continues to breathe.

She's lost her power over me. I will file her away with the others, in that vault inside my mind. Her folder will be crisper and newer at first, but it will fade in time.

I finish and gather my papers into my satchel. I stand up to leave but turn around before reaching the door.

"One last question."

"Go ahead," she answers, endlessly agreeable.

"Did you love your father?"

I know the answer, but I want to hear it spoken.

"Thanks to what my father taught me, I am still alive. I'll go to sleep tonight. I'll get up tomorrow. I'll eat three meals. I'll piss and shit and breathe. I'll do that the next day and the next, until the day I don't." She smiles. "I'm surviving. It's all that matters. To answer your question directly, I didn't love him, because there is no such thing as love. But I am thankful."

I walk out the door, leaving her with her perversity of peace.

# CHAPTER FORTY-FOUR

Heather Hollister sits across from me, dressed in hospital clothes. Her hair has started to come back, a light fuzz on her head. Her eyes have stopped darting, but they are hollow and deep, filled with too much thinking.

She got worse before getting better, while I was locked away. She required restraints for weeks, both actual and chemical, as she raved, and wept, and screamed. Her doctor had advised strongly against telling her about Avery's death, saying that it could drive her over an edge she'd never return from. Shielding her from the fact of Avery's death had also required keeping her from the hope of Dylan's life.

But she has begun to settle, and now, after much debate and arguing, the doctor has agreed that it's time to offer her the truth of both.

Daryl Burns waits in the hallway. He is not up to the beginning of this task. Some part of me wants to curse him for this, for his weakness, but I have long been aware that in some ways, key ways, women have a strength greater than men. When it comes to family, especially to our children, we are able to do and stand almost anything.

I met a woman once who'd come very close to being the sixth victim of a serial killer who targeted escorts. He would set a date, and then he'd show up and torture them with cigarettes before killing them with a butcher knife. She was an Asian woman, and her husband had killed himself after losing all of their money gambling. He left her and their six-month-old son with nothing, and they were poor already. She was finding it impossible to make ends meet and was a month away from eviction when she decided to start selling herself.

I remember her with such clarity because she was such a proud woman. Not arrogant but dignified. She had a sense of herself, of her own hopes and of what was right and wrong. Selling her body was something that degraded her in the deepest ways, so I broke my own rules and I asked her why.

"I'd live in a box on the street and eat dog food before doing this, if it were just me," she'd said. "But I have my *son,* you see? He'll have a good home and good clothes and go to school and his children will prosper. Yes." She'd smiled at me, a heartbreaking mix of serenity and sadness. "God will forgive me if my son lives a better life. It's enough."

Her husband had solved his poverty and his shame by jumping from a building. The woman remained, suffering, and her son was healthy and never hungry.

"She shaved your head too?" Heather asks, startling me.

I had told her about Dali as Mercy Lane.

"Yes. She did."

She sighs, looks away. Her eyes crawl back to mine again. "Did you . . ." She hesitates, dreading the question but fascinated nonetheless. "Did you see the darkness?"

I shiver. My mouth goes dry. "Yes."

She closes her eyes once, then opens them, a gesture of shared pain, and in this instant I understand the binding power behind support groups. Heather Hollister understands what I've been through. She *knows.* No one else does, not really. We are all alone, in the deep-down places, but sometimes others are alone with us.

I take a single deep breath and attempt to empty my mind. This will be a terrible, terrible moment, but it will also be a moment of hope. Will the mix of the two make the other more powerful, or will they lessen each other?

"Heather, I need to tell you some things. One of those things is very, very bad. One of them is very, very good."

She regards me with her hollowed eyes. "Will it make a difference which one you tell me first?"

"No. The terrible thing is going to be terrible, period."

She squints at me. "It's about my sons, isn't it?"

I gape, pulled up short. "Yes," I manage to reply.

She nods. "I thought so. One of them is dead, and one of them is alive." Her gaze is intense. "That's it, right?"

I swallow, fascinated, terrified. *How does she know?* "Yes."

She stares away from me toward the window, listless.

"I think I could spend the rest of my life just sitting by an open window with a view of the outside and the sun. When I was in that *room,* the only place I could see sunlight was inside myself. I used to close my eyes in the dark and 'call forth the light.'" She smiles crookedly. "That was a saying from my dad. I was scared of my closet when I was five. I was sure there was a monster in there. Who knows? Maybe there was. Dad didn't pooh-pooh the idea. He treated it very seriously. *All you have to do, honey,* he told me, *if the monster comes out, is call forth the light. There's not a monster that's been made that can stand up to real light.*" She turns her eyes back to me. "It's a nice idea, don't you think?"

"And a true one."

She half-frowns, semi-shrugs. "Maybe. Regardless, when I was in that hellhole I remembered what he said. I'd close my eyes and call forth the light. I'd be on the beach with my sons. Avery and Dylan. They never got older, and they always loved me, and we never stopped laughing." She pauses. "There were cloudy days, of course. Sometimes the sun turned dark, or the rain fell. Sometimes I'd find myself on the beach at night, and the ocean would be gripped in a storm, with waves a hundred feet high. I'd stand on the sand and gape up at the dark water, always opening my eyes just before it crashed down on me." She shifts, sighs. "Sometimes there were creatures on the beach. Vampires would come crawling out of the water, rotting and hungry and covered in seaweed. They always had Douglas's face. But on the sunny days, it was just crystal-clear water as far as the eye could see, white sand, blue sky, bright sun, and my boys." She stares down at her hands, blinking away tears. "They kept me alive. I don't mean physically. They kept the most basic part of me alive. A seed of myself, that's how I'd think of it. No matter how bad it got, I told myself I could hide away that seed, so if I ever got out, if I somehow survived, I could regrow the me that used to be." She clenches her hands into fists, flips them over, watches them uncurl and gazes at her palms. "My sons did that for me."

She falls silent now and watches the sun falling through the window. I wait, letting her ruminate, sensitive to the otherness she's feeling. The moment passes, and she turns back to me.

"Which boy died?"

"Avery."

She closes her eyes tight, and a flash of sorrow rushes across her face, there and gone.

"Avery, the oldest. I had a C-section, and they pulled him out first, and he cried like no one's business. Dylan was always the quieter boy. Not more thoughtful, just less aggressive. Avery loved music. He'd dance to my CDs, bobbing up and down on the carpet in his diaper." Her body trembles, her eyes still closed. "Avery Edward Hollister. One day, not too long before I was taken, I had both boys with me. We'd just come home from the store, and I was distracted for a minute. Avery slipped away, and the next thing I knew, I heard the neighbor screaming for help. I dropped the groceries and picked up Dylan and ran over there." She shakes her head in fond disbelief. "Avery had gone into the yard next door. The dog there was unfriendly and was trying to make a meal of him. The neighbor woman was struggling to hold the dog back, while Avery, completely unaware, was yanking up flowers from her garden by the roots. I ran to get him and he just grinned when he saw me, one of those big, beautiful baby grins. He held up the flowers and said 'Mama!'" She falls silent. "I guess he'd seen those flowers earlier and had been planning all along to pick them for me when we got home."

She pitches forward in her chair at the last part of this eulogy, bending at the waist, wailing without words. I come forward and take her in my arms, and we are alone together.

Heather's grief—at least this incarnation of it—passes. She pulls away from me, and I return to my chair as she returns her gaze to the window and the sun.

I've seen this before, I think, feeling a shudder of déjà vu. Another prisoner freed who couldn't keep her eyes from the light.

"Where's Dylan?" she asks me, her voice quiet, still sorrowful.

"He's here. But I need you to listen to me now, Heather. This is really important. If you want Dylan, you need to hear what I'm telling you."

She frowns, her eyes piercing. "What do you mean, 'if I want Dylan'?"

Here it is, the telling point, the place where I learn whether Heather's light has gone out for good or if she'll find her way back to shore. If ever there was an impetus, this will be it.

"Dylan is being cared for by social services, Heather. They're concerned about your state of mind. They're not sure you can take care of him."

The frown deepens, then smooths out. "I see," she says. "They're afraid I'm too crazy to be a good mother right now, is that it?"

Why soften the blow?

"Essentially, yes."

Rage spasms across her face. "But I'm his mother!" There's a crazy edge to her voice.

I lean forward, trying to reach her with my words, with my own intensity. "I want you to have this, Heather. Hell, I need you to have it. I think Dylan belongs with you, period, and I think you can pull it together enough to make that happen. But if you can't, and you don't—and they'll be watching—then he's going to be taken away from you. At least for a little while, and there's nothing I'll be able to do about it."

She glances at the sun, back at me, clenching and unclenching her fists. "Do you?" she asks haltingly.

"Do I what?"

She grabs my hands in hers, surprising me. "Do you think I can take care of him?"

I look right into her eyes and tell her the last of it. "His dad killed his brother. I don't think anyone else *can* take care of him, after something like that."

Her mouth opens, closes. "Douglas did that? He killed my Avery?"

"Yes."

The rage mutates into something harder and more enduring. Mother anger. "Scum," she hisses. She drops my hands, stands up, paces around the room, shaking her head. "Jesus!" I watch her pass through the desire to kill, the need for revenge, the despair at what she's lost. She stops, and she turns to me, and I see the light I was looking for. Bleak but strong. "Help me," she pleads. "Please, please help me."

"Yes," I tell her. "Of course I will."

Something lifts inside me now that I know her hope will survive against her despair, and I look to the window myself, searching for the sun. My four-fingered hand finds my belly and cradles it and the burgeoning life within. For all its horror, life is filled with so much wonder sometimes, such beautiful irony. I am happy I've chosen life over death, whatever that means, wherever it takes me, whomever I lose. Life is monstrous, but life is beautiful.

"Let's go see your son," I tell her.

She smiles, and for a moment she is the sun.

# EPILOGUE

# CHAPTER FORTY-FIVE

I sit in the chair in Leo's room, watching his chest rise and fall. It is evening, the door is closed, and we are alone.

Another week has passed. Much has happened. Law enforcement raided the other locations. Another five women were freed. Some were thankful, but many will never recover. Mercy Lane stole something fundamental from them, some certainty about the worth of the way the world turns. Too many years in the dark.

Heather Hollister is making a comeback. She held her son and she has no intention of ever letting him go again. Social services seems as happy about this as I am. Her light grows stronger day by day.

I run a four-fingered hand over my head. I trail it down my face, feeling the scars left by others.

Who am I? Am I a result of what I decide or what's been done to me?

I think both, perhaps.

Life rolls on. Sometimes I dream that I did shoot Mercy. I see the play of headlights on the sand, hear the *chunk chunk* sound of shovels against the dirt. Bonnie knows something happened but seems content to let it go, as though she can sense when she shouldn't ask some questions. Baby is just a baby again, not a fetal Buddha dispensing wisdom from a mind-lit meadow behind my eyes.

Life rolls on. I return to work tomorrow. Alan has remained mute, and I don't know if he's really serious about retiring or not. I'll have to wait and see. The promised press conference is scheduled, and I find myself ambivalent about it.

Life rolls on. Months from now a child will be born to a nine-and-a-half-fingered mother. He'll have killers for parents, an ancient thirteen-year-old for a sister, and a collection of mildly crippled aunts and uncles going blind from peering into the darkness. What does that bode for the child? Good or ill? I have no answer to this question.

I've thought about Mercy a lot in relation to my wondering about the soul. Mercy Lane was taught that she was just meat, but it takes more than cutting off her breasts to make a woman a man. What drives a runner, puking, to the finish line? What makes you love a child you haven't laid eyes on yet? What makes you saw the breasts off your own daughter?

When I close my eyes and remember Matt and Alexa and Mom and Dad, when that overwhelming surge of sadness and love and joy and grief runs through me, is that just a chemical reaction? Do cells feel love? Or is something far, far more beautiful involved?

I don't have all the answers, but I do know this: I have looked into the eyes of Mercy Lane, and I have looked into the eyes of my husband, and I found something very different behind them both.

It's this certainty that's brought me here now. If we're all just meat, if I really believed that, I'd feel no onus to keep my promise to Leo.

The machines hum and whisper. His chest rises and falls.

I've agonized about Leo and the choice I made. I've asked myself the hard questions, and I've wept and doubted. I've examined myself without filters, in the brightest internal light. It's a process that's humbled me, that's given me answers but little peace.

I know now that if I hadn't been pregnant, I would have chosen to give myself over to Mercy. I would have been willing to let my mind die so that Leo could stay Leo. I became a hunter of monsters because I want others to live. I'm driven by a duty to protect them, and I've been compelled by that instinct since I was very young. I don't know where it came from—God, the soul, genetics—but I am certain of its existence. Mercy's puzzle asked me to choose between Leo and myself, but in reality I only ever chose between him and my child.

Knowing this has calmed me, but it doesn't help with the guilt. Neither does the truth that it would have been Leo, whatever I decided. I am here, and he is there; it's a scale that will never be balanced.

I stand up and walk over to Leo's bedside. I reach out a hand to touch his forehead. It's dry and warm. The body lives.

"I'm so sorry, Leo," I whisper.

It doesn't matter that I would have taken his place under different circumstances. It doesn't matter that Mercy was just playing a game. I chose, thinking a choice was needed. There is a world where he died so my child could live. I lean forward and I kiss his cheek. The machines hum lowly. One tear falls. "Thank you."

Then I keep my promise and I send him gently into the darkness, hoping the stories are all true, that, for the good souls, the dark turns into light.

## ABOUT THE AUTHOR

CODY MCFADYEN is the internationally bestselling author of *Shadow Man, The Face of Death,* and *The Darker Side. The Face of Death* was #5 on Amazon .com's Best Mystery/Thriller Books of 2007 list. McFadyen lives in Colorado.

www.codymcfadyen.com

## ABOUT THE TYPE

This book was set in Sabon, a typeface designed by the well-known German typographer Jan Tschichold (1902–74). Sabon's design is based upon the original letter forms of Claude Garamond and was created specifically to be used for three sources: foundry type for hand composition, Linotype, and Monotype. Tschichold named his typeface for the famous Frankfurt typefounder Jacques Sabon, who died in 1580.